Fatal Gift

Fatal Gift

H. MICHAEL FRASE

Carroll & Graf Publishers, Inc.
New York

First edition 1996

Carroll & Graf Publishers, Inc.
260 Fifth Avenue
New York, NY 10001

ISBN 0-7867-0351-2

Library of Congress Cataloging-in-Publication Data is available.

Manufactured in the United States of America.

for Anita—

A long winter's promise of spring,
no matter how warm and bright,
pales beside the radiance
and beauty of the true spring . . .
when it finally arrives.

My sincerest thanks . . .

to Bill A. for being tenacious;
to Lisa S. for telling me what I didn't want to hear;
to Terry P. for making the late nights at the keyboard possible;
to Sgt. Bill W. ("Bubba") for the procedures & detail;
to Brian & Carol for the occasional shelter;
to Todd S. & Holly L. for being friends;
to Dusky N. & Charlie H. for help when I needed it most;
to Gary & Glenda S. for the waterway;
to Chris K. for the Iguana;
to Chuck, Micki, Sybil, & Casey for always making me proud;
to Shelbey F. for simply being;
to BRF and RAF for cramming seven of us in a travel trailer—
and traveling;
and to Anita . . . for always being the spring.

Fatal Gift

ONE

As Kasey Riteman leaned painfully over the tiny porcelain sink, chipped and stained from decades of neglect by an endless stream of urban nomads, it was all she could do to keep from throwing up.

It wasn't the yellowed bowl, or the moldy smell of forgotten laundry in an unseen corner of the bathroom that had her stomach dancing to some silent demonic dirge.

It was the tequila.

Her mouth felt dry as sand, and the red and brown eyes that stared sluggishly back from the dingy mirror were barely recognizable.

She rested her forehead against the cool glass for an hour, or a second—the brain refused to acknowledge any difference—and then took a long, depressing, second look.

Someone she thought she once knew stared back in disgust.

The sight was no less agonizing despite the familiarity—perhaps even magnified by the awareness that the sad eyes staring back belonged to someone she knew well but seldom liked anymore.

She quietly bounced her forehead against the mirror as she cursed silently under her breath: "Perfect, Kasey. Just perfect. Your mama'd be proud of you this time."

She closed her eyes and tried to fend off the dizziness that was clutching at her brain when a sudden and emphatic outburst of deep nasal snoring—like an unexpected clap of thunder—shattered the stillness. She turned her eyes reluctantly toward its origin.

The bedroom that adjoined the small bath was almost completely dark, the blinds over its one little window pulled tight—the last of the light trying to pass through the heavy faded curtains held in place by the addition of cheap wooden clothespins spaced every few inches.

The only illumination to strike either room crept through a tear in the black plastic that was stapled across the small window above the toilet. The beam of pure white light that slipped past heralded a glorious spring day being played out somewhere in another world, beyond the cracked Sheetrock and peeling wallpaper, but in these two dingy rooms—stinking of dirt and sweat and sex—it was the most solemn and dreary of winters.

As she squinted toward the bed, she did not recognize the shape of the face that was half hidden between the wrinkled cotton sheets and the lifeless, sagging feather pillow that partially covered it.

Quietly, she crept closer to the body and knelt beside the mattress, almost losing her balance as she crouched down—steadying herself against the wall to prevent accidentally awakening someone, or something, she would rather leave sleeping.

A closer look confirmed that her gut feeling had been correct—it was the jerk from the bar last night who wouldn't take no for an answer. When she had consented escaped her completely. Kasey consoled herself that perhaps she hadn't actually *spoken* the word "yes."

She had been right not to wake him.

Maybe, with luck, she could collect her things and get out without having to deal with him while she was sober—or mostly sober. Her head and stomach were not quite certain as to the degree of sobriety. When she stood too suddenly, she had to squeeze her eyelids tightly together to prevent her throbbing brain from shoving her eyeballs out of their sockets. The nausea returned.

Partly to avoid detection and partly because standing again promised to be too painful, Kasey crawled around on the matted shag carpet as stealthily as she could, feeling for her things among the clutter. First she found her jeans. Then her shirt. But she had to dig through a mound of *his* clothing to locate her bra. She shuddered and tried to block the graphic images that seemed to form involuntarily. Her panties were nowhere to be found, but this, now, seemed of little consequence.

When another eruption of erratic snoring rocked the room, she decided she would be satisfied if she could just locate her favorite pair of boots and get away from the strange apartment as soon as possible.

Despite a frustrating search in the poor light of the cramped little bedroom, the boots refused to show themselves. She had even reached into the abyss under the bed as far as she dared, until some childhood bogeyman warned her not to venture any farther into its domain lest she be sucked in never to be seen again. She wanted the boots, dammit, almost as much as she wanted to be anywhere other than in this room.

Almost, but not quite.

With what clothes she had found in hand, she turned and crawled the few feet to the bedroom door, cursing under her breath at having lost her boots.

When she stood finally, her skull tried to explode. Dizziness overcame her and she was certain she was going to pass out. She fell noisily against the wall and had to grab the doorknob for support. She felt certain that the racket had been at least that of a wrecking ball ripping its way through the structure. Her eyes went immediately back to him. The grim outline of his half-nude, half-illuminated form could be seen only a few feet away, but his only response to the clamor was an exaggerated snort.

She released a long and grateful sigh.

After a few deep breaths—her brain having assured her that it could provide a measure of stability for at least the next few moments—she tried the knob.

It turned with a slight squeak, but compared with the racket of moments before, was imperceptible.

Kasey eased the door open only a fraction of an inch, afraid the outer room, filled with the brilliance of morning, would come racing into the bedroom like a river through a ruptured dam, awakening the nightmare she had almost managed to escape.

Like the others, however, this room, too, was nearly devoid of light, its heavy opaque curtains pinned shut.

The thought of having spent the night in this morbid apartment sent goose bumps racing across her nude body, like whitecaps on a sea of flesh.

The door closed behind her with barely a sound, and she quickly moved away from it toward the faint silhouette of a couch on the wall opposite. Her head hammered with each step.

As she sank in the center cushion and began stuffing her right leg into her jeans, her left foot brushed across something on the floor.

She reached down and found her left boot—yes!—the right one must surely be close by, she prayed. She ran her hand along the carpet and felt something sticking out from under the tasseled fringe that adorned the lower front edge of the couch: it was the other half of the whole week's take-home pay that she was relieved would be going with her after all; she had made up her mind in the horrid bedroom that she was willing to exchange the boots for freedom.

With her jeans pulled up and zipped, Kasey quickly shoved an arm into each sleeve of her denim shirt. She buttoned only the bottom two of its six buttons, and stuffed her bra into her back jeans pocket, concealed by the shirttail that was left hanging out.

She checked her other pockets.

"Damn!" she mouthed in disgusted anger—no car keys. She knelt in front of the couch and swept her hands back and forth across the carpet.

Nothing.

"Damn, damn, damn!" she groaned again, her Louisiana accent—still with her after a decade in Tennessee—adding color to her disgust. With boots in hand, she moved to the front door.

Kasey could not remember having seen a more brilliant morning than the one that greeted her pounding brain and out-of-focus eyes as the front door yielded to her pull.

The light almost knocked her down, as if it were something with weight and substance—something physical, like the wind or the sea.

Everything went white in a flash and then totally black as her irises instantly constricted and her eyelids slammed shut protectively. Only a latent reddish image of the rectangular doorway remained behind her closed lids.

It took nearly a full minute for her eyes to accept the challenge and begin to form shapes the brain could recognize. She pulled the old wooden door behind her, unconcerned whether she had locked it or not. She was positive no one wanted *in* the apartment she had just left.

Using the outside wall for support, she eased past a row of identical doors toward the first pavement she saw.

"Be there! *Pleeeease,* baby, be there!" she prayed in an anxious mumble as she walked with slowly increasing stability toward the parking lot. "Please don't let me have lost my mind as well as my taste in men."

Kasey chuckled out loud as she listened to the words of her petition, grateful that her sense of humor was still intact. Remorse and self-recrimination could come later, she vowed, but for now, the priority was transportation.

Like a loyal and noble steed from a John Ford western, her trusty mount waited patiently—if less gloriously than in a Hollywood epic—for her return. The right front wheel was perched precariously on a curb and the right rear wheel was pressed tightly against the rough concrete, its sidewall badly abraded by this most recent of numerous insults.

She immediately checked the ignition—the keys were hanging as she had left them. She looked skyward and said a silent but sincere "thank you."

Kasey then quickly examined the diminutive car and saw no new dents. Somehow she had driven to this place—where *was* this place? she wondered—without the use of a brain, but also without having added to the police department's list of as-yet-unsolved hit and runs.

A second heavenly "thank you," this time spoken aloud.

Although her car had seen worse nights, she was still irritated with herself for having done such a poor job of hitting the parking space—for having driven at all when she should have gone home with Brenda or one of the other girls. She refused to consider her reason for having obviously, finally, said yes to the snoring creature.

Faithful still—despite a decade of shabby treatment by its only owner—the faded blue and silver CRX cranked without complaint and started on the first try. She patted the dash gratefully, as she had done many times before, certain her genuine affection for the old Honda was the only reason it had agreed to see her home one more time, though she knew a change of oil and some new wiper blades would be appreciated far more.

Within three minutes of leaving the unfamiliar apartment complex, Kasey had found a recognizable landmark amid the hilly suburbs of Nashville and had made the turns necessary to take her to Murfreesboro Road, and then, to her own apartment.

As the tires sang rhythmically on the asphalt, and the warm April air racing through the open windows began to breathe life back into her haggard body, she swore never to drink tequila again as long as she lived.

Not if she lived to be a hundred—a thousand!

Not until the South rose again!

She considered the soundness of her solemn and heartfelt resolution as the pavement dividers ticked monotonously beneath her wheels. Not unless she gave her keys to one of the other girls beforehand she amended—ever so slightly.

She shoved a well-worn tape of Chris Isaak's *Heart Shaped World* into the cassette slot of her radio, and cranked up "Wicked Game" loud enough for its soulful sounds to be heard over the wind and the tires and the angry little inner voice that had begun its overdue sermon.

Kasey always listened to Chris Isaak loud when she wanted to forget.

❖

As the Honda wheeled unerringly into its own parking space, Kasey practically leaped from the car, taking the keys this time, but not taking the time to lock the door behind her. Sam would be waiting, and he would be upset with her for not having come home all night, especially after she had promised him—and herself—that she was going to do better this year.

As Kasey rounded the top of the stairs that led to her third-floor apartment, she could see his eyes staring at her through the opening in the livingroom curtains.

She quickly located the deadbolt key on the small ring of keys in her hand and eased the door open.

TWO

He was lost in the mesmerizing image of her long flaxen hair sweeping across his chest, like a field of golden summer wheat in a soft Kansas breeze. Or perhaps, he reconsidered, it was more like a river of silk, glistening in pastel hues of honey and amber beneath a warm afternoon sun.

The sight of it never stopped spawning new fantasies in his mind, and though many years had passed since his boyhood on the mean streets of Chicago, he always felt a little like that boy again when he was with her. Perhaps that was why he would come to Nashville to see her whenever he could steal a day. Maybe he would take her back with him this time: he liked owning beautiful things.

The thought amused and pleased him. Few things in his complex life did anymore.

Suddenly, he dug his nails into the bed and a deep breath locked in his throat; his body arched upward and his head pressed deeply into the pillow. Then, as quickly, every muscle in his firm, stocky frame gave up at once and he melted into the sheets—it was the second time in as many hours. She was amazing, he reminded himself when his brain was once again able to form cohesive thoughts.

She raised her head quickly, tossing her long golden mane over her shoulders, and smiled up at him. "You like that, don't you?"

The question was as ludicrous as asking a fish if it liked water. His strong, thick fingers—capable of brutal savagery, swept across her cheek and traced the outline of her full and glistening lips. "There is little, if anything, you do which I do not like, though I must confess, that is perhaps my favorite."

It's every man's favorite, she noted silently, while smiling warmly at him.

His rich Italian accent, the result of intentional cultural segregation by his family, had not softened in nearly six decades of living in America's Midwest. The man still referred to Chicago's west side as home—his parents had originally settled there when they fled the turbulence of prewar Sicily in 1933—though he now had addresses in the Lake Point Tower, where his twelve room penthouse overlooked Lake Michigan, as well as a twenty-room mansion in a picturesque academic community north of the city.

Wanting more for their children than their life in the Italian slums had promised, it was important to the humble shoemaker and his wife that their children have a secure home, a home to live in, a home to grow in—a home in America. And so, fifty-nine years ago, Mario Antonio Giacano became the firstborn of Augusta and Prietta Giacano—new immigrants in the "Land of Opportunity." In the years that followed his father's death, Mario Giacano had allowed those three words to become his driving motivation, and had risen, through scheming and savagery, to the position of undisputed head of the most powerful crime family in the Midwest. By 1985, with ten million a week in profits from gambling, whores, extortion, and drugs, the Giacano empire had reached a plateau. Mario Giacano decided it was time to "grow" the business by expanding his territory and his opportunities. The old turf no longer paid the bills as well as it had in the past. This was the nineties—time for new thinking and new opportunities. His mind turned to the floating gambling palaces that littered the Mississippi River and the Gulf Coast.

He wanted his share.

"Would you bring me something to drink?" he asked. "I am afraid you have robbed me of all of my strength."

"Like Samson and Delilah?" she teased.

His eyes smiled but he did not speak.

"I'll be just a moment. Would a mimosa be all right?"

The prominent chin moved slowly up and down. He tucked his large, short arms behind his head and waited for her to stand: for him, looking at her was almost as good as being inside her, and certainly less tiring.

She slid to the end of the bed on her stomach and lowered her knees to the thick wool carpet. She remained there, pressed against the sheets, teasing him with her sky-blue eyes, knowing he was waiting.

She grabbed a double handful of the down comforter that had slipped to the floor and covered herself modestly with it as she stood.

He folded his arms across his chest, his hard brown eyes—framed by countless lines that cut through the dark skin like cracks in old leather—simultaneously ordered and begged her to reveal herself.

As he was about to speak, she let the comforter fall.

His breath deepened in reflex: she was surely the most desirable expression of woman he had known in his life. Since his virginity fell to the advances of an "older woman" of seventeen in the backseat of a Packard V-12, there had been many women, far too numerous to be counted or even remembered. They had spanned the gamut in looks, color, and age—but she was the unforgettable one: that one rare alloying of physical perfection and sensuality from which all sexual dreams—and fantasies—are spawned.

She stood proudly, but not vainly, in complete silence. When she was sure the image would be fixed in his mind until the next time he could arrange a visit, she disappeared toward the kitchen.

He closed his eyes and decided that he would take her with him. He knew she would not refuse; he was not the kind of person you refused.

When she returned with his drink, she was wearing his silk shirt, buttoned only at the bottom. As she sat on the edge of the bed and handed him one of the long-stemmed pewter goblets, the shirt opened slightly, partially revealing her left breast, its pale-pink nipple taut and erect.

She gave it no apparent notice, though it had taken years of practice to make such a carefully planned erotic gesture appear innocent and un-rehearsed.

"What shall we drink to?" she asked with a warm smile.

"To Packards," he responded with a coy smile, his eyes fixed on the nipple, his memory lost in the backseat of his first automobile.

"To Packards?" she questioned.

He tapped his goblet against hers with a sharp "tink" and took a generous swallow. The orange juice was tart, the champagne cold and aerated.

"Maybe I'll show you someday," he grinned. "I'm afraid it is a thought which would not translate well into mere words."

"To Packards, then," she toasted, though she hadn't the slightest idea to what she was drinking.

Donna Stanton touched the remote control on the bedside table and raised the volume on the small Bose stereo several notches. A song that she remembered as one of his favorites had just begun playing on the classical FM station.

He smiled and set his drink on the table beside the credit-card-size remote. "You forget nothing," he stated admiringly.

"I know some of the things you like, but I don't know everything yet. You must tell me anything you wish me to remember. How else can I let you know how much you mean to me?"

She leaned across his chest again and kissed his lips. Then she stood and set her drink on the table beside his. She undid the one button and laid his handmade shirt across the chair to her left. "Would you like to join me in the whirlpool?" she asked, knowing neither he nor any other man could refuse such an offer.

He held out his right hand and she filled it with hers. He began at her feet and slowly made the inspiring journey upward with his eyes until they met hers again. "Shortly, my sweet. There is an important matter I must attend to first. Will you excuse me for a few minutes while I conduct a little necessary business? I, too, must make a living."

He kissed the back of her hand and then squeezed it gently.

"Of course. I'll be waiting," she answered, and left for the master bath with her drink in hand.

Mario Giacano sat on the edge of the bed and checked the diamond dial on the Rolex President he was still wearing—it was time to make the call.

He set his goblet on the table and then carefully punched the seven digits from memory.

It was answered on the second ring.

"Yes" came the deep, rich voice from the other end. The call had been prearranged and the need for pleasantries between the men had long since passed.

They would not have been exchanged anyway.

The disagreeable relationship was now into its fourth year.

"How did your meeting go with our new group of friends?" Giacano asked. "I trust all of them have chosen wisely, and decided, like the others, that it is far better to join with us, than to oppose us."

No emotion of any kind was displayed in his words—it was impossible to tell whether he was agitated or curious. To him, there was no place in business for emotion, and this was big business.

"There has been a slight problem. I'm afraid two from our list will not go along unless they get larger shares."

"Did you explain their options clearly?"

"Explain their options!? Jesus Christ, Mr. Giacano, I didn't exactly come out and tell them you were going to have them killed if they didn't go along with us, if that's what you mean." The other man knew when Giacano's name passed his lips that he had broken a fundamental rule, the first rule that had been established between them. He closed his eyes and waited.

Mario Giacano took a short, impatient sip from his drink and put it quickly back on the bedside table. By accident, the base of the goblet came to rest on the edge of the wafer-thin stereo remote, depressing the slightly raised Power button. The room fell silent as the stereo switched off.

He barely noticed the absence of sound at first as he considered a fitting reply to the man's last words. He took a deep breath and exhaled slowly. "I see that you are not only inept but stupid as well." The voice was frigid. "Two failings of character for which I have little patience—or use. Perhaps I have erred in choosing you. Do not think for a second I will hesitate to terminate our relationship if I feel it might prove to be unproductive or compromising to my position."

Giacano decided to let the full weight of the word "terminate" sink in before speaking further. He heard only silence from the other end: the respectful silence that comes from having your life pass before your eyes.

The other man thought to speak in his own defense, but reconsidered. He didn't have the words in any case.

Giacano, content that he had made his point, laid the receiver across his bare thigh and reached again for his drink.

It was then that he noticed it: a faint, repetitive squealing sound strangely out of place in the silence of the bedroom.

He leaned closer to the table.

Of all the sacred rules of life and business, there was only one that could not be broken. He counted betrayal as the blackest of sins, the act from which there could never be absolution. He returned the phone to his mouth. "Something has come up. I'll call you later. Be there."

Giacano did not place the receiver back in its base, but instead, held down the switch-hook with his right index finger, as if placing another call. The faint squealing instantly stopped. He let up on the button and pressed the receiver tightly against his bare thigh to muffle the dial tone. As he feared, the squealing returned. "Goddammit!" he mouthed in silent rage. "Goddammit to hell you bitch!"

He closed his eyes and tightened his jaws to the brink of pain—a part of his heart was breaking which he thought had died forty years earlier. For almost a minute he remained in this state, far longer than he had suffered when, at nineteen, he had killed his first man with his bare hands.

He left the phone off the hook and prayed that he might still be wrong.

It took only a minute to locate the tiny microcassette recorder, its sleek gold body held tightly to the bottom of the bedside table with Velcro, an auto-record switch cleverly and expertly wired into the phone line, activated whenever the receiver was lifted.

His immediate impulse was to rip it from the table and stuff it down the throat of the woman in the other room, but he remembered having been in this same room on at least four previous occasions: on how many had he made the same call? "Goddammit!" he swore again—two to be certain. Perhaps three.

He left the tape in the unit to avoid alerting her to its discovery and then dressed quickly, careful to leave nothing of his in the room.

❖

As he stood in the bathroom doorway and studied her lovely form submerged beneath the clear, hot water of the huge whirlpool tub, he loathed her for her disloyalty.

Whatever her reasons, they were irrelevant now, though he needed to know them, to hear them from her own sweet lips as much as he wanted to hold her beautiful head below the water until she had paid in full for her betrayal.

His voice almost broke in anger as he spoke: "I am sorry, my love, but I'm afraid I must leave you now."

The words, spoken softly, were offered with as much warmth and regret as he could summon.

"Oh, not so soon," she pouted, startled from a dreamy half-sleep. She sat upright in the middle of the black marble tub, facing him squarely. Water ran off her skin and dripped from her breasts. "I was counting on having lunch with you, as usual." She stuck out her bottom lip as a four-year-old might when told that her birthday party was coming to an end. If he could resist both her nude body and pitiful expression, then the reason for his sudden departure must be unavoidable.

"Will you be here for the rest of the day?" he asked. "I am meeting someone important and would like him to meet you as well."

She leaned across the edge of the tub and reached out a long, slender arm. "I'm always available for you, Mario, whenever you want me."

He squeezed her hand and stared for the last time into the bluest eyes he had ever seen.

His bodyguards, outside her front door where he had left them almost three hours before, joined him in the elevator. As the gleaming brass doors closed and the car began its descent from the penthouse, he slammed his right fist violently against one of the polished surfaces, leaving a dent where the side of his hand had made contact. Even the massive hulks on each side of him were respectful of the power that remained in the older man's arms. Though eight and ten inches taller, and each more than sixty pounds heavier, neither would have willingly traded places with the brass door at the moment.

During the brief ride to the underground garage, he forced his mind to set aside the anger and pain in his heart and concentrate on the business at hand.

There was much to do, and very little time in which to have it done.

❖

"Oh, Sam, sweetheart, I'm so sorry," Kasey pleaded as soon as the door shut behind her. "You're really mad at me this time, aren't you?"

Of course he was mad—mad as hell! What'd she think, that he *liked* being left alone all night while she did whatever it was humans did when they weren't at home taking care of their pets like they were supposed to? He turned his head away and pretended not to care that she had returned.

Kasey knelt in front of the couch where Sam-I-Am, Sam for short—a sleek black spoiled seven-year-old Burmese cat—had spent the previous night. She kissed him on the nose and softly played with the tip of his ear while she whispered a litany of apologies and promises into it.

Forgiveness was not going to be as easy as she had hoped, it appeared. This made the second, no the third time this month, she noted with a trace of shame, that she had left him all night to guard the place and fend for himself.

This time it was going to cost her, and not just a half-bowl of Fancy Feast. That might placate some minor peccadillo, but this called for a serious peace offering. Perhaps the chicken strips she had brought home from work on Friday, or better still, the nine-ounce can of chunk white albacore tuna in spring water that she had been saving for her own lunch.

Yep, the tuna, she decided.

Sam remained stubborn and alone in the livingroom until the can opener had almost finished making its whirring noises before bolting from the couch and rounding the corner into the kitchen.

The phone began to ring.

"Hello," Kasey answered.

She finished filling Sam's bowl as she cradled the portable phone between her chin and her shoulder.

"Ms. Riteman?"

She didn't recognize the man's voice.

"Yes, this is Kasey Riteman."

"I'll come straight to the point, Ms. Riteman. My name is Mr. Polson with Consolidated Collection. I'm calling in regard to your past-due account with Walter L. Magnason, DDS."

Oh, hell, why in the world had she answered the phone before getting a cup of coffee and a shower? It was way too early in the day to be dealing with bill collectors. She pictured the guy from the bar as she listened to Polson speak.

"I sent Dr. Magnason twenty bucks only a week or two ago," she stated in her defense.

"Actually, Ms. Riteman, the last payment his office received from you—I believe it was twenty dollars—was forty-one days ago. Your account has since been turned over to us for collection."

Kasey's headache returned and she grumbled out loud for not having allowed the answering machine to get the call. She was tired of bill collectors, but could never seem to get rid of them. As soon as one was paid off, another would take his place, like crabgrass. It had been like this for almost five years. "Oh, that's ridiculous, Mr. Polson! Dr. Magnason knows I'll pay him, I always pay him. I've never stuck him for a dime in the five years I've been going to him. Hell, it's not my fault I had to have a root canal and a damned crown in January!"

"That may be the case, Ms. Riteman, but it's certainly not ours, either. According to his records, the last balance you had with his office took over fourteen months to clear."

The man's voice was almost electronically flat and lifeless.

"That can't be right. Fourteen months?"

"I'm afraid it is correct, Ms. Riteman. That's why your account was placed with us. For your information, your present balance is $529.50. When can we expect a certified check or money order for the full amount?"

"The full amount? It might as well be five thousand dollars as five hundred. I don't have that kind of money, Mr. Polson. I'm barely able to put gas in my car for work as it is."

"A certified check, Ms. Riteman; when can we expect it?"

"You don't hear a word I'm saying, do you? I don't have it at this time."

Polson heard nothing he had not heard a thousand times; he continued without missing a beat—Polson the machine. "Then, it appears, Ms. Riteman, we will have no alternative but to collect our money in a court of law."

"Oh, that's just great. I need the threat of a lawsuit right now. It just about makes my life perfect." She took a long breath. "Let me ask you something: if I can't pay Dr. Magnason's bill as it stands now, *how the hell do you expect me to pay it with a ton of legal fees added to it!?*"

She thought about throwing the phone across the room but knew she would only have to replace it.

"I'm sure you'll find a way, Ms. Riteman. Your type always does when push comes to shove."

"My type!" He had her complete attention now.

She started to speak but Polson pressed on undaunted. "Since that appears to be your final word, Ms. Riteman, you'll receive a letter from our attorney in seven to ten days. Thank you for your time."

"That's not my final word, you pencil-necked little accountant wanna-be! You and Consolidated Collection can—"

Before she could finish the tirade she wanted so desperately to deliver, the other end went "click."

Then an obnoxious dial tone filled her ear.

Kasey jabbed the Off button hard enough to break her nail.

"AAAHHH!" she screamed in overwhelming frustration. "I'm getting sick of this!"

Sam studied his mistress for a moment to determine whether he should prepare to avoid flying objects and then returned to his chunk white albacore tuna in spring water.

❖

With a few extra unplanned hours suddenly on her hands, Donna Stanton luxuriated in her bath, taking the time to shave her legs especially close, though having been shaved less than eighteen hours prior, were still as smooth as porcelain. Legs could never be too smooth, she felt.

It was like being too rich or too beautiful.

She sat at the vanity and ran a brush through her long, wavy hair, adding just a touch of blow dryer to lend some body. She was blessed with enviable hair—she had been told repeatedly since she was a child—the kind of hair that looked as good soaking wet as it did dry and styled.

She had patted her skin dry with a thick cotton towel when she stepped from the tub, and though there was a sumptuous muslin robe hanging on the back of the bathroom door, she had remained nude, a feeling she preferred to even the finest lingerie.

Donna Stanton casually strolled toward the kitchen in search of a refill for her mimosa.

As she entered the hall that lay just outside the master bedroom, a feeling came over her, like a sense that someone was watching her.

She spun around but saw and heard nothing.

Then she realized what it was—she *heard* nothing.

What had happened to the music?

With her empty goblet still in hand, she dropped across the bed and reached for the remote control. It was when she saw his goblet resting across the upper right edge of the remote that she connected with the strange feeling that was nagging at her: he had turned off the stereo.

But why?

It hadn't been turned up loud enough to have interfered with his call. Was it some other reason then?

She tried to—wanted to—let it pass, but the oddity of the simple act controlled her thoughts.

Concerned, she lifted the phone from its base and buried the receiver in the pillow beside her to silence its tone. The most frightening sound she had ever heard became the horrifying price of her curiosity—had he heard the same faint squealing? Even if he had, could he have understood its origin?

At first the thought seemed preposterous, but then she remembered who she was dealing with. Mistakes or misjudgments were paid for in blood.

She leaned off the bed and moved her head closer to the base of the side table: the sound—intensified by the open space beneath the bed—almost screamed in her ears. She felt sick to her stomach.

For what seemed a lifetime, Donna remained frozen and shaking in the middle of the wrinkled satin sheets. Now she understood Mario's sudden and urgent need to leave. She also knew who he wanted her to meet this afternoon—not by name, of course, but by occupation, by intent.

She looked at the small green digital display on the front of the bedroom VCR. It was exactly three minutes past noon: if she was to save her own life, every precious second counted.

❖

Kasey washed down four Advil with a glass of lukewarm tap water while Sam retired—his belly delightfully full of peace offering and the previous night forgotten—to the spot in the livingroom carpet where the sun created a small, warm, oddly shaped patch.

With her domestic relationship stabilized, it was time to get cleaned up and run a few errands before heading to the restaurant.

She removed the blouse from last night and tossed it into the wicker hamper by the sink in the bathroom of her four-room apartment. The bra, retrieved from her blue jeans back pocket, was added to the small pile of laundry. The jeans followed. All would be washed in the morning, Wednesday at the latest. Though her place was small and not in the finest part of town, Kasey had not been raised to be untidy, and prided herself on having a clean and presentable home at all times. Someday, she vowed, when she had made it to the big time, she would have a maid, perhaps even a cook. Until then, she enjoyed things that were neat and orderly, even if they were only remnants or second-handers. "Class, like cream, will always rise to the top," her father had often said. For a fleeting moment she missed him terribly. It was a familiar feeling.

The shower rained down in her face and splashed across her skin, washing away the smell and memory of last night's "error in judgment." As the hot water and soap-covered washcloth slowly painted the curves of her body, her fingers brushed across the two small, circular scars on the side of her left breast, each a quarter inch round and less than an inch apart, their tissue now cold and lifeless. An image of that horrid night flashed across her mind like lightning from hell. Her stomach knotted and she pulled her hand away. The image and the feelings would pass—as they had many times before, she reminded herself—and forced her mind to think of more pleasant things.

Kasey stayed in the shower until the water began to run cold. As she dried herself, her pink image filled the narrow mirror on the hall closet door opposite the bathroom. Overall, she was generally pleased with her figure, no longer regretful that she had not become the sleek and slender model from the glamour magazines of her youth. Somewhere along the way, she had come to terms with the reality that she had been given an ordinary body with ordinary proportions.

It was just that there were those irritating places where extra pounds would have too willingly come to stay if not for her faithful—if somewhat reluctant—devotion to jogging and Kathy Smith tapes.

Each morning—except "bad mornings," like this one—she would leave her third-floor apartment before seven A.M.—after having suffered through one of her six workout videos; the one that seemed appropriate for the mood of the particular morning—and not return until she had covered five grueling miles at a steady, even impressive, pace.

It helped keep the pleasant, all-too-average curves from becoming all-too-bountiful.

In truth, there was little about her figure or features that should have yielded complaint, and no man had ever voiced a syllable of dissatisfaction. Some had even told her that she was beautiful at times when their words had not been born in the heat of lovemaking. Though Kasey often felt she had not learned enough in her seven years since becoming an "adult," she *did* know not to trust anything spoken in the presence of an erection.

❖

After a trip to Wal-Mart to gather the items that had accumulated on her refrigerator scratch pad during the previous week, followed by a stop at Kroger for bread, milk, coffee, and another can of tuna, Kasey headed back home to prepare for work.

The uniform at the restaurant—even for shift leaders, to which Kasey had recently been promoted—was black pants and a clean white oxford blouse with bold red stripes. Kasey ironed and starched five uniform shirts each Sunday morning and meticulously pressed as many pairs of loose-fitting black cotton slacks. This way, she didn't have to touch an iron during the week, a chore she detested. Washing would be done as it collected in the hamper, but the iron would be plugged in only once a week; her "someday maid" must be willing to iron.

Though Kasey tried hard not to think about her boss as she finished putting on her makeup, he was again becoming increasingly difficult to ignore. Even more so than when she had started at the restaurant nearly eighteen months ago. After Cal's comment on Friday, she knew today could be a very long shift.

As she tried to fill her mind with more pleasant thoughts, the situation she had escaped from a few hours before, accompanied by the vexatious Mr. Polson of Consolidated Collection, took Cal's place like a nightmare in stereo. She squeezed her eyes tightly together and dropped her head to her chest.

Cal had better keep his hands to himself today, she vowed.

THREE

Donna Stanton turned through the pages of the journal with great care, reading each handwritten entry and glancing nervously at the clock by the bed: she could spare a few more minutes, she consoled herself, confident that her self-imposed time table had not yet expired. After all, none of her clients even knew about her sister or the home in Belle Meade the two women shared.

Donna had carefully planned it that way, primarily to shelter Laurie from a life the older of the sisters—actually, half-sisters—would not have understood or approved of, but also to give herself a place of sanctuary whenever the emotional strain grew too great. But, despite the planning, Donna did not, could not, have anticipated the catastrophic error that had turned her well-choreographed life upside down.

When she reached the last page, she tore it from the spine, adding it to the pages that had already been pulled from the book.

There were now four in all.

She then took the clear plastic sleeve with its twenty pockets, each containing a sixty-minute microcassette. She matched the date that had been neatly written on each label with the dates from the four torn pages. She slipped three cassettes from their pockets and added them to the paper stack. A fourth tape—the squeaky one which had spawned the last two hours of fear, and which now prompted the unexpected but imperative exodus—was tossed in with the trio of identical tapes.

She wrapped the written pages tightly around the miniature tapes and fastened the precious bundle with a single brown rubber band. She opened her sterling silver cigarette case and dumped the Dunhill Menthol 100's onto the bed—the little package took their place as if the case had been cast for that singular purpose.

With the gleaming top secure once more, she returned it to her open purse. Something felt wrong with that location. Donna decided on the waistband of her white jogging pants instead, in front where the huge sweatshirt gathered the most and where she could easily feel its presence.

She was satisfied with her work.

The last item to be packed was her jewelry. It had taken her nearly five years to accumulate the impressive array of treasures that almost filled the cherry-wood box, and she wasn't about to leave it behind. It would provide considerable cash anywhere in the world if her other money ran out, though she was certain she had enough saved to avoid that unpleasantry for many years.

Donna zipped the suitcase and gave the bedroom one last look.

❖

For the second time in as many hours Mario Antonio Giacano dialed the same local number and waited for it to ring. He was standing, his patience long since gone, at a pay phone opposite gate C-24 in the American Airlines Terminal of Nashville International. Preliminary boarding of Flight 1198 to Chicago had been announced but he had business left to do before he took his seat. He had opted to send his private jet on to Chicago without him. He wanted to be seen leaving Music City as early in the day as possible.

The phone was answered in mid ring. "Yes, sir."

"I won't even waste my time asking if you knew that the woman, the one *you* introduced me to, was taping our conversations, because I know that you are neither that brave nor that stupid. I want to know just one thing from you: is there any chance, I repeat, any chance at all, she's working for the Feds?"

The other man knew that something had gone wrong this morning but he had not been prepared for the words he had just heard.

His first impulse was to ask Giacano if he was certain.

It took only a split second to reconsider.

"None," he stated defensively. "I had her background thoroughly checked all the way back to grammar school, for Christ's sake! There's no way I would have allowed her anywhere near you if there had been even the slightest possibility she was working for someone else. I don't know what she has in mind, but I'm positive she's acting on her own."

"For whatever reason it was done, it is enough that I have discovered it. I only wish that I could be the one to deal with her in person. That deed, my incompetent associate, now falls on your shoulders. I must have three full hours to get to a public place in Chicago. By then, I want to hear from you that you have put our little bird in a cage."

"Three hours?" The man's ulcer knotted his stomach like a boatswain's lanyard.

"One more thing."

"Sir . . ."

"I want those tapes."

"The tapes. Of course. You'll have them."

"Don't tell me that they're lost or destroyed. I will do that myself. Clear?"

"Perfectly."

"You will be notified when I land. Have good news for me."

"I will, I swear, and I'm sorry for this morn—"

An unsympathetic dial tone abruptly ended his petition.

❖

"Yoo, hoo," Maggie Ketchum waved from her front lawn as she spotted Donna Stanton scurrying down the driveway toward her car. Mrs. Ketchum was working in one of her flower beds as usual, trying to earn Yard of the Month honors for the third time in a row. It had not been done in Davidson County in years.

The elderly woman—with the latest bit of gossip and a glass of sweet tea for anyone who stopped by—thought it odd that the prettier of the two sisters didn't return her greeting. She echoed the welcome with added volume and then watched silently as her neighbor tossed a lone bag into the trunk of her Cadillac and backed quickly out of her driveway.

"Must be in a terrible hurry," Maggie Ketchum said to herself, always willing to give everyone the benefit of the doubt. "Probably going on vacation." She returned to her begonias. "How nice for her."

Though generally more than willing to spend a moment or two with her friendly but nosy neighbor, today Donna Stanton's mind was not on social niceties. In fact, she had not even seen the woman who still knelt less than fifty feet from where the Cadillac had been parked: Florida, and the wide choice of Caribbean islands that lay to the south, held her attention.

She sped north on Belle Meade Road for a half mile to Harding Place, then east for three miles to the closest interstate heading south. As she neared the on-ramp, she let out a loud, spontaneous laugh—a nervous release from the fear and anxiety that had gripped her since realizing she'd been discovered.

When the sign indicating I-65S passed her right window, she knew that the freedom she was desperately seeking lay only moments away. Her pulse quickened and she felt herself shake as if she were standing naked in the snow.

With her little-girl mind lost in the rich, cocoa-colored sands of Barbados, Donna Stanton never gave a second thought to the new black pickup that slipped effortlessly in behind her on the expressway and remained exactly three cars in back of her at all times.

❖

Donna Stanton stood at the teller's window, the requisite two pieces of identification accompanying her check; she needed some quick spending money, though she did not wish to carry more than would easily fit in her small purse. She could transfer the balance of her funds to her new account—wherever that was to be.

The sour-faced woman across the green marble counter—Tammy Akers according to the wood-grained plastic nameplate which bore the standard "Next Window Please" on the other side—stared at the tiny picture on the Tennessee driver's license and then back at the woman for the third time in ten seconds. The hair was a little darker in the photo, but otherwise she appeared to be the same Angela Marie Jackson as on the license. The teller took the check and quickly pecked Ms. Jackson's account number into her terminal. She secretly doubted there was anything approaching the desired ten thousand dollars in the account but kept the thought to herself. When she discovered that the check could have gone through ten times with her own annual pretax income left over as change, it did not improve her disposition, nor her disagreeable expression. Akers could not know that this account was only one of many such accounts Donna Stanton held in other names across Tennessee.

As directed, and without speaking a word, Tammy Akers counted out precisely one hundred crisp hundred-dollar bills and then had the head teller at her right verify the count. Content that the amount was correct, she squared the bills as quickly and neatly as a seasoned Vegas croupier might square a deck of cards and then slid the orderly bundle across the marble top with a forced smile that lasted only long enough for her customer to acknowledge it.

Donna Stanton gathered the money, the license, and the Mastercard bearing the name Angela Jackson and put them hastily in her purse, shoving the bills to the bottom of the handbag. She returned the sunglasses to her face.

The attractive blonde, now ten thousand dollars richer, stood in the doorway of the bank in Columbia, Tennessee, forty glorious miles farther from her problem and forty miles closer to freedom. A grin parted her lips and her eyes smiled beneath the nearly black lenses. The ten grand would last her for several weeks even on the run, she decided, and there would be ample time to formulate a long-range plan and establish a budget once she got settled.

She lifted the door handle on the gleaming white Seville and slipped lightly into the red leather seat.

A ten inch stiletto was at her throat the moment the door closed; its edge stung against her skin and she could feel a trickle of blood on her neck where her warm flesh met the hard steel. Her eyes darted to the rearview mirror but she could only see the side of her assailant's head. It was completely shaved and there was part of a tattoo visible above the right ear: it appeared to be some kind of animal's foot, with wide green scales and hideous long claws dripping blood. She almost wet herself and her heart felt as if it would burst the walls of her chest.

"Didn't your mommy ever tell you to lock your car door so the bogey-man wouldn't get you?" the man's voice taunted quietly in her ear. The breath was a thick, sickening confusion of cigarettes, coffee, and cheap bourbon.

She almost vomited.

"Now be a good little girl and follow the pretty black truck. I know you're smart enough not to do anything that would get you hurt. Right? I'm not the kind of person you want to piss off, especially on our first date." The faceless man ran his wet tongue slowly along the back of her ear while increasing pressure on the blade.

She shook her head cooperatively, careful not to move her neck.

Though she had not thought it possible, he moved his lips even closer to her ear, lowering his voice to a faint, mocking whisper: "Perfect. We're all going to get along just splendidly. And we were led to believe you might be a real bitch about altering your travel plans and coming with us."

Donna's eyes filled with water as the ignition key brought the Cadillac's engine to life.

Within ten minutes, the two vehicles were east and north of Columbia, moving steadily toward the rural farmlands that lay ahead.

The three had only one stop to make before their final destination.

FOUR

Mario Giacano dropped a quarter into a pay phone and punched the same number he had already called twice that day. He wanted no record of the calls, not even from one of his cellular phones. Again, there was no cordiality wasted when the other man answered. "I'm at O'Hare," he said without expression. "I trust you have good news for me concerning our little problem?"

There was no mistake this time. The other man was only too aware that his earlier faux pas had put him in imminent danger of becoming part of a parking lot or building foundation. It was not a feeling a man in his position—or any man for that matter—cherished.

He hoped that his quick response would restore Giacano's confidence in him. "I sent for the cleaners as soon as I learned of the spill," he responded, being as euphemistic as possible, just like he'd seen on TV. "They have collected the item and should have the stain removed before midnight. It was my understanding that you did not wish to see the item again, and the cleaners were made aware of that as well." He hesitated, but only for a second: "I am sorry for any problem I may have caused you."

Problem? Giacano thought. *I cause problems. An insignificant little bug like you can only cause irritation.* "Just be certain that I am never troubled by this matter again. Do I need to speak further?"

"No. These are my two best men. I would guarantee their work with my life."

"Oh, but you have, my friend," Giacano said flatly. "You have, indeed."

The burly Italian walked briskly through the maze of passageways and escalators that makes up Chicago's largest airport, eager to put the morning and the problem behind him.

Before he piled into the waiting limousine, his twin shadows only a step behind, Giacano stared back toward the south for a single moment—to Nashville and the incredible woman who had once brought him so much pleasure. He cursed again in mumbled tones and barked impatiently for his driver to take him to Garibaldi's.

For the next three or four days—aware that forensic science was often not able to pinpoint time of death more closely than within twenty-four hours either way—it would be important that as many people as possible saw him in Chicago.

❖

Kasey parked her car in her regular space between the large brown Dumpster and the waist-high wall that bordered the rear and right side of the restaurant. Though it was a tiny spot, her diminutive CRX fit with ease. Besides, it was only five or six steps from the rear entrance to the kitchen, a fact that came in handy whenever it rained.

When she first entered the parking lot, Kasey had noticed that it was nearly empty. She preferred a good crowd: tips were larger, the time passed more quickly and, though it meant more work for all the staff, also had the indirect but certain benefit of keeping Cal away from her.

She drew a deep breath, pulled her five-dollar faux Ray-Bans from her eyes and stepped into the relative darkness of the kitchen.

"Hi ya, Kasey" came the greeting from Desmondo, the lead cook on the evening shift.

"Hi, Mondo," she returned pleasantly.

Kasey liked the Argentinean cook and often talked at length with him when their shifts overlapped and nights were slow. Mondo, as she called him, had painted vivid images of his homeland, a land of wide sandy beaches and lush tropical vegetation, where the people were easygoing and openly friendly to strangers. Kasey had decided to visit Argentina when she made her fortune.

"Where's Cal tonight, Mondo?" she asked as she put an arm around his waist and sniffed the heavily seasoned sauce he was stirring with a long wooden spoon. He put the bowl of the spoon under her nose, earning a wide smile from her for his culinary efforts.

"On the floor, I guess. He hasn't been back here since I came on at three."

"Maybe he's sick today," she wished out loud.

"No, sorry, he's here. I saw him flitting around the floor, you know, showing off for the new girl he's breaking in." Desmondo made an exaggerated mock walk in the style of their boss, the wooden spoon held high in his right hand and the left resting on his hip, elbow stuck out fully to the side. Kasey had to cover her mouth to keep from laughing too loudly.

Desmondo returned to his sauce and made a face over his shoulder at Kasey. He had no more use for Cal than she did, and it angered him that she had to put up with his crap. Everyone knew it was happening, but no one wanted to be the first to speak out or tell the home office. Cal knew he was well thought of in Cincinnati—corporate headquarters for the Leonard's Steak House chain—and it would be their word against his. Kasey was a big girl, they decided when they talked about it among themselves. She could—and would—take care of herself they were sure.

Kasey patted Mondo on the back and headed for her locker.

❖

Cal Hardt spotted a patron at the bar whom he recognized as one of Nashville's legal elite. He quickly handed the towel he had been carrying to the new waitress. "Just keep working," he said, making a throw-away gesture with his left hand: she held no more interest for him at the moment.

He slipped in between the lawyer and his attractive female companion, placing a hand on the shoulder of each. "Mr. Sevier, it's certainly a pleasure to have you visit us again. And your lovely guest, is she also one of Nashville's top corporate attorneys?" He turned his gaze to the well-dressed woman of twenty-something to his left. She blushed; she didn't know Cal Hardt.

Sevier considered Hardt little more than a nuisance with an ingratiating personality, but he was enough lawyer to keep his thoughts well hidden and turn the man's worst traits to his advantage. "Not yet, Cal, but soon, perhaps. She's in her last year of law at Vanderbilt. I'm entertaining the idea of inviting her into the firm. She's got a four-oh average."

"No fooling. Well, congratulations, Miss—"

"Masterson. Tina Masterson," she offered.

Cal kissed the back of her hand. Sevier rolled his eyes but quickly returned to his corporate face. Tina smiled warmly, Sevier's tantalizing words still in her ears.

"Allow me to buy you and Mr. Sevier a congratulatory drink. It's not often that we have such power and beauty at the same time in our humble establishment." He snapped his fingers at the bartender, though only three or four feet away. "Champagne for my guests, Todd. Make it my special reserve."

Todd Christopher knew Hardt had no "special reserve," but he liked his job and had seen his boss pull this hackneyed stunt at least a dozen times. He nodded politely, reaching for one of the six identical bottles of Brut chilling in the small refrigerator behind the bar. He was careful to keep the bottle of only average-grade champagne concealed from the attorneys.

"If there's anything I can do to make your visit a more pleasant experience"—he alternated his smile between the two faces only inches away—"don't hesitate to ask for me."

Well, you could always commit suicide, Sevier thought behind his warm smile.

"You're too kind," Tina said, embarrassed by the unexpected attention.

Cal squeezed Sevier's shoulder and gave him a quick, furtive, "you lucky bastard" look, then dashed away, as if some urgent matter depended upon his personal touch alone.

Todd quickly filled two slender goblets and then turned his attention back to the Braves game on ESPN playing quietly at the far end of the bar.

Cal glanced at his watch as he crossed the dining room and ran the employee schedule quickly through his mind.

It produced a smirk.

❖

Kasey closed her locker and turned around. Cal's best smile greeted her surprised expression. He was less than a foot away, hands folded almost schoolboy-like behind his back.

"Good afternoon, Kasey," he said warmly. "On time as usual, I see."

Of course I'm on time, you jerk, she thought. *I've been on time every day for eighteen months.* "Good afternoon, Mr. Hardt," she said, eyeing the space between him and the shelves, hoping she could slip by without having to brush against him. No such luck. She stayed by her locker. "Is there something I can do for you?"

"Not really. It's just that the high point of my day is always when *you* arrive. You're such a welcome relief from the other pathetic cretins I have to put up with around here, the one oasis in a vast desert of incompetence." He widened his grin.

Kasey wanted to spit in his eye—he was such an obvious boor with the charm of a toad. Every time she considered slapping his stupid, grinning face, she remembered her $400 rent, her $100 utilities, her $75 gasoline bill, and her desire to continue eating regularly. She forced a return smile. "I'm no different than anyone on the staff, Mr. Hardt. You've got a lot of talented people working for you. It's hardly fair or kind to call them cretins."

"Talented—perhaps a few, but none with your looks, poise, and polish." His tone had softened. Kasey's muscles tensed.

"Really, Mr. Hardt. I thought we agreed a year ago that you and I would keep our relationship on a strictly professional basis, both working for the good of the restaurant." She attempted to squeeze past him. "Excuse me, please," she mumbled.

Hardt extended his arm to the shelf a foot to his right, blocking her path. She stopped cold and turned toward him, her back to the shelf. He moved his face a few inches from hers, until they were almost nose to nose. "Oh, yeah, we did, but that was more than a year ago. Things change, you know. Life's dynamic, Kasey, you've got to learn to go with the flow."

Sure, she thought, *things change. Your nineteen-year-old live-in bimbo got enough sense to move the hell out, and now you're after my butt again.* "Well, they haven't with me, Mr. Hardt," she answered as defiantly as she dared, the involuntary image of weasel Polson from Consolidated Collection adding to her rapidly mounting frustration. "I'm still just an employee and you're still just my boss. There's nothing else to it and there never will be. I believe that should be clear enough, since I don't believe I stutter"— she cut her eyes left to right and then brought them squarely back to his— "and I know you're close enough to hear me."

When she saw the vacant expression on his face, she knew she might as well have been talking to the wall.

Hardt took a thoughtful breath. "That's crazy, Kasey, when we could share so much more. You could be the assistant manager in a couple of months, perhaps even a few weeks. Think of what you could do with all the extra money, the things you could buy, the places you could go. You might even get back to your beloved New Orleans again. In any case, it would sure beat the hell out of waiting tables and groveling for tips paycheck to paycheck. I know you want more out of life than that." He touched her lips with his fingertip. "Tell me I'm wrong."

Kasey closed her eyes and slowly formed her words. "I'd love to have more money, who wouldn't, but any promotion I get is going to come as a result of my being a good employee"—she took his wrist firmly and pulled his hand away from her face—"and not because I'm fucking the boss."

"Ooh," he groaned theatrically. "I love the way you say 'fuck.' "

Kasey gave a shove with her shoulder and pushed past Hardt, toward the kitchen. In the distance, Mondo raised a large cleaver and slammed it noisily into a heavy cutting board, cleanly relieving a chicken of one of its legs. He hadn't heard exactly what Hardt had been saying to Kasey, but he could tell that she wasn't pleased with it. The rest of the kitchen staff kept their eyes on their tasks; some pretending not to hear, others simply knowing there was little they could do.

"For the love of Pete, Mr. Hardt," she glared turning back as she entered the main kitchen area, "give it a rest. Just let me just do the job you hired me to do. I'm a damn good waitress." She shoved her ballpoint angrily into the slot in her order pad, like a soldier returning his saber to its sheath, and then turned toward the dining room.

Hardt kept the stupid grin pasted across his face until she had vanished, completely impervious to her words or her displeasure.

As Kasey disappeared onto the main floor of the restaurant, his mind returned to the new girl—what's her name.

❖

Brenda Poole arrived at five, an hour after Kasey. She was Kasey's best friend, not just at the restaurant, but also in the world outside of work. It was she who had convinced Kasey that the man who wouldn't take no for an answer on Sunday night might not be so bad after all. With more than sixteen hours having passed since they parted company the night before, Brenda was eager to know if she'd been right. And to hear the details.

She would normally have called first thing in the morning, but second and fourth Mondays from eight A.M. to four P.M., as well as first and third Saturday from ten to six, were the only days she was allowed to spend with her son, Alex. He lived in Kentucky, forty miles to the north, with their father. After she had held her job at the restaurant for a full year, she planned to petition the court for equal visitation rights. Perhaps even joint custody, she fantasized, though she secretly doubted that would ever be granted. His family was too rich and too well placed in Kentucky, and she was just a waitress, a defiant moment of indiscretion on his part a few years back. Still, it remained a dream and a goal of hers, a dream Kasey encouraged and helped Brenda cling to. Kasey had even worked out a budget for Brenda to live on, and had helped her find a decent car that made it to work and back every day. Without Kasey's support and friendship, there had been times when Brenda was certain she would not have made it.

Brenda spotted Kasey as she was delivering an order to the kitchen. She grabbed her arm and dragged her into the employee restroom. "All right, don't lie to me, Kasey, how was he? He was awful just like you thought, wasn't he?" Kasey opened her mouth to answer, but Brenda cut her off: "Oh, my God! He wasn't awful, he was incredible, wasn't he? I knew it, I just knew it. The gorgeous hunks are always worthless as tits on a bull, and the ones that look like five miles of bad road are always great when you get to know them, right! Am I right? He *was* terrific, wasn't he?"

Brenda seldom took a breath between words, but Kasey was familiar with that. She knew that her friend would run down eventually and then it would be her turn to speak.

She seized her chance. "He had thick black plastic stapled over every window," Kasey said with a sick look on her face, reluctantly recalling the apartment that seemed a thousand miles away and a hundred years ago.

"Yuck! Plastic. You're lying to me, Kasey. That's gross as shit. Tell me you're lying to me."

"Plastic," she mouthed silently, and held her thumb and index finger a quarter of an inch apart.

"Yuck!" Brenda moaned again.

"Yeah, but I figure that was actually a blessing in disguise from the smell of the place. Thank God I was too drunk to see what a cesspool he lived in," she chuckled. "To tell you the truth, I don't even remember leaving you guys last night. I don't remember a thing until sunrise this morning." Kasey sat on the closed toilet lid and leaned against the wall, resting her right elbow on the tank cover.

Brenda let out a deep sigh. "Well, I warned you not to go home with him, but you never do listen to anyone, especially me. It serves you right." Brenda looked in the mirror at her eye makeup, making a slight adjustment to one eyebrow with a moistened fingertip. Kasey only grinned in silence; she knew it was probably Brenda who had argued in favor of the man until Kasey relented.

At five three, Brenda was more than four inches shorter than her friend, but heavier by eight or ten pounds. All things considered, though, she was a pleasant looking woman of thirty-seven, with a welcoming smile and a dare-devil personality who would do almost anything on a bet. "I still can't believe it—so he was as bad as he looked, huh." Brenda leaned against the wall opposite the sink. "That's purely pitiful, sugar. You should have known better."

"Oh, well, I guess it could have been worse." Kasey felt a slight shudder run through her.

Brenda's eyebrows raised: "I don't see how it could have been worse." She realized at once that she wasn't helping things. "I mean . . . well . . . what could be worse than black plastic?" she quickly offered in a stammer, shrugging her shoulders naively.

"He could have been awake when I left."

Now Brenda shuddered. "Oh, you're right. *That* would have been worse."

They both began to laugh, hoping their voices weren't carrying beyond the door.

Before the friends could regain their composure, there was a sharp knock followed by Cal's standard, "Anyone working tonight?"

Kasey indicated quickly that she would go out first, and for Brenda to follow in a few seconds, before Hardt had a chance to corner her. It was planned with a minimum of gestures and no words: both women had known Hardt for what seemed a lifetime.

Kasey pretended to be drying her hands as she scooted past Hardt. She made no eye contact and didn't speak. Before Hardt could make one of his remarks, Brenda practically burst through the bathroom door. She, too, was wiping her hands rapidly with a paper towel.

"Can't be too clean in the food industry, Mr. Hardt," she smiled, not letting him notice that she was drying the same extended middle finger the whole time.

She and Kasey wrinkled their noses at each other in silent ridicule when they made it to the relative asylum of the main dining room.

❖

By six, dinner was already in full swing. Weekday customers tended to eat earlier and spend less time in the restaurant than weekend customers. Table turnover was quicker, too, but with a generally lighter crowd, Kasey felt the work pace balanced out. The thing she missed most about not working Saturdays was the tip money. People didn't generally tip as well Sunday through Thursday as they did on Friday and Saturday, a combination of the clientele drinking more on the weekends and being more concerned about impressing their friends, business associates, or dates. Having gotten Saturdays off after fifteen months, she wasn't about to go back to full weekends, even if it did mean a hundred bucks less a month.

Kasey had just gone to the back to check on table 12's order when Hardt grabbed her arm and pulled her into the small pantry at the side of the kitchen, next to the employee locker room. The sudden move caught her completely by surprise.

"Jesus, Mr. Hardt, you scared me. Is something wrong?" Her first thought was that she had overlooked something on the floor, though she couldn't imagine what it could be as she tore through the last hour in her mind.

"The only thing *wrong* is that you're still playing hard to get, when I know you want me as bad as I want you. Let's just cut through all the crap and get down to business. I need to start training a new assistant manager with Shirley leaving for Boston in July, and I've made up my mind that it's going to be you." He put his hands on her buttocks and pulled her hips tightly against his. "Now, I think it's about time you showed me just how grateful you are." He moved his mouth toward hers, his tongue running slowly across his upper teeth.

Her right hand pushed against his chest. The next sequence of events, whether survival instinct or feminine indignation, occurred without Kasey having to add conscious thought to them: her right knee came up between Cal's legs with such ferocity that it actually appeared to lift his whole body several inches off the floor; in a parallel move with her left hand, she slammed him squarely in the jaw with the closest weapon she could reach—a large can of Green Giant Blue Lake Cut Green Beans. The combination of blows was effective. Cal dropped to his knees like a clumsy toddler and then fell forward, at first against Kasey's rigid thighs, and then to the linoleum floor. The only sounds coming from his bleeding mouth were unintelligible gurgles.

Kasey slammed the beans on the shelf and stepped victoriously over Cal's twisted form.

Desmondo, Brenda, and the rest of the kitchen staff had witnessed the last of the confrontation from across the kitchen and gave her a round of silent applause as Kasey ripped her name tag from her starched blouse and dropped it defiantly in the caesar salad on her way out.

FIVE

The wind was warm at seven in the evening, but the familiar smell of a recent rain hung heavily in the air. This April had already seen more rain than last year's and there was still a full week left in the month. Kasey glanced at the winter-like sky and wished she had replaced her wiper blades. She made a mental note and then just as quickly it was forgotten. The blades had been on the car for three years.

The tepid air felt good in her hair and the miles sped by. She looked at the little green clock in her Honda radio and noted that she had been driving for over an hour, heading south, away from Cal Hardt—away from herself.

She started to cry but held it back, just as she had each time before. She thought about playing one of her soulful tapes, of screaming out loud, but sat quietly and thoughtfully behind the wheel and drove south instead.

A sign announcing Columbia, Tennessee, loomed ahead on her right and she took the next exit: Sharp Road. She had no intention of going into the town. She wanted a less-traveled route away from people.

Perhaps, a road that had not been traveled in days—weeks.

Whenever a Y or intersection presented itself, Kasey would simply take the more rural path. It became almost a game as she sat behind the wheel and watched the sun setting in her rear window.

Gradually, the highways became secondary roads, and then farm roads—still paved, but only wide enough for one and a half cars.

Or one John Deere.

She hadn't noticed that the right rear tire she had scraped against the curb last night was getting softer by the mile.

At a hard left turn, something felt wrong in the back of the car, something that had not been there before. She glanced in her side mirror, trying to see if she had gotten onto a soft shoulder. It appeared not, but the uncertain footing of her trusty old friend continued. Kasey had the unsettling feeling it wasn't going to improve on its own.

"Hell's bells," she grumbled.

Certain the problem was definitely not going away, it was time to investigate.

Kasey looked for a place to stop safely, but the road had narrowed after the last turn to barely one lane in width, with steeply sloping shoulders and trees and shrubs growing right to the edge of the grading.

She slowed, having decided to risk stopping on the pavement when, just before a sharp curve to the right, she spotted a narrow dirt driveway entering from the passenger side. She cut the wheel sharply right and pulled completely off the blacktop, staying centered in the small dirt path.

Annoyed at having had her contemplative mood interrupted by something as mundane as a flat, Kasey grumbled her way out of the car and studied the tires on the driver's side: both appeared perfect. She moved reluctantly around the back of the car and inspected the other two tires: the front was also nice, plump and full of air, but the right rear looked like a piece of dark chocolate that had been left on a hot stove.

She knelt by the ailing tire and brushed her hand across what tread was visible—if there was a nail in the tire, it must be in the section that was against the ground. She didn't know why it mattered really; it had gone flat for some damned reason and "why" didn't make much difference at the moment. It wasn't as if finding the elusive cause was going to miraculously reinflate the tire. The bastard was flat, and she was stuck in . . . well . . . God surely knew, though she didn't have a clue.

Kasey folded her arms and rested her butt against the rear fender.

"Damn, damn, damn," she complained, followed by a blaring and definitive, "This is just perfect!" that could have been heard a quarter mile away—had there been anyone around to hear it.

She walked the short distance back to the pavement and stood squarely in the center of the one-lane road. It was dusk and the sun was dying rapidly. There wasn't a car in sight, but then, she didn't recall having seen a car for the last twenty minutes, on or off the road.

She looked behind her, to the east: a full moon had risen above the line of tall oaks, but, just as to the west, there was not a living soul to be seen.

"I can't believe this!" she shouted, in case her anger hadn't been fully appreciated the first time.

Kasey walked past the wounded car and up the small dirt drive in hopes of spotting the house: there *was* a mailbox, though old and dilapidated, at the edge of the paved road. *That must mean people live at the end of this drive,* she thought hopefully.

She could see for nearly half a mile up a slowly rising hill to the silhouette of trees at the top of it.

No house.

She shook her head in disgust and began unbuttoning her clean blouse: if there was no one around to help her change her tire, then there surely would be no one around to watch her change her clothes. She laid her dress slacks and striped shirt neatly in the hatchback compartment behind the front seats and grabbed a pair of plum colored sweat pants with matching top.

❖

Three of the four lug nuts came off easily, but the fourth acted as if it were welded to the rim, and refused to turn in spite of her most persuasive pulling, pushing, and kicking on the wrench. Kasey positioned the long, curved arm of the wrench at twelve o'clock and braced herself with her right foot against the fender well, her butt on the ground by the back quarter panel. The flaccid rubber wiggled slightly under her efforts as she put her full strength into the pull.

Still, the last nut refused to budge.

As her impatience grew, she added a final, powerful jerk. All four uppermost knuckles on her left hand immediately lost most of their skin as the inadequate wrench slipped off the nut; her hand went flying past the sharp wheel rim, its edge coarse and gnarled by numerous encounters with curbs.

For a moment, Kasey thought she had ripped off the back of her hand, and hesitated to look until the initial wave of pain passed. She was thankful to find the damage minor, though this discovery didn't quell her mounting anger.

She stood with the wrench clutched in her right hand and seriously considered slamming it through the back window—every four-letter word she had ever heard came to mind, though she uttered not a one.

Instead, she dropped the wrench noisily by the small scissors jack that was shoved under the center of the car and opened the passenger door.

In the glove box she found a clean white rag she used for wiping the glass and mirrors. She sat in the seat and wrapped the rag carefully around the battered knuckles. It stung as it touched the four watery, red, almost dime-size abrasions and a tear streaked down her cheek.

"Dammit," she moaned softly. "This just isn't fair."

She glanced at the clock: the light would be gone soon.

❖

Kasey had been walking for nearly ten minutes when she reached the top of the small hill she hoped represented the end of the drive. It didn't; the drive continued over a second, even steeper hill that could be seen yet another quarter mile away.

She stopped at the first crest and looked back toward her crippled car. Dusk had now settled fully and she could no longer make out its form in the blue-gray half-light.

To her left, something rustled in the dense brush. She gave an involuntary yelp and jumped to the center of the old dirt drive, as far from either side as possible.

Kasey stared hard at the source of the sound, ready to dart in either direction if some unearthly creature came out of the brush with the intention of having her for dinner. A fat red squirrel scurried up a pine tree thirty feet from her and froze—about eye level with the human—and stared back, ready to bolt in either direction if the monster in the center of the road suddenly made a threatening move toward it.

Kasey placed her hands over her heart and let out a deep, relieved sigh. Beneath her palms, she could feel it pounding like a kettle drum.

Although the sun had been down for nearly fifteen minutes, the moon that seemed to fill the steadily darkening heavens was bright, lending a fluorescent glow to the April sky. Thick gray clouds began to clutter the upper atmosphere, like ice flows in a slowly moving river, occasionally blocking out the moon and momentarily plunging everything into an eerie and malevolent darkness. Kasey knew she needed to find help—she didn't cherish the thought of spending the night in a disabled car on a dirt road in the middle of nowhere, Tennessee.

❖

After several more minutes of brisk walking, slowing to a crawl each time the moon disappeared behind a cloud, Kasey found herself near the end of the drive. Not far ahead, at the crest of the second hill, was the outline of a house. In the side yard, the form of a car could also be seen. No lights were visible within the structure. Still, Kasey proceeded cautiously for the last two hundred yards, certain a family would be resting comfortably on the livingroom couch after a hard day in the fields and a pleasant dinner together.

Dinner—what a wonderful thought.

Kasey realized that she had not eaten since before noon, over eight hours ago. At once, her stomach felt completely empty, and she had to stop for a second to fight off a sudden spell of dizziness.

Somewhere, deep in the quiet recesses of her brain, the tequila headache began to awaken, adding to the misery of the moment.

She stood in the road, bent forward, hands on her thighs, and breathed deeply several times, hoping to lose the sick, disoriented feeling that was sweeping over her. Mercifully, in a few seconds it subsided, and she continued the remaining forty yards to the house and hopefully, at last, the help she sought.

It was when she stopped at the edge of the yard that had once been that

Kasey realized the inviting rural home was nothing more than an abandoned, half-collapsed rotting shell.

It had once been the clapboard and tar paper residence of a sharecropper and his family of six, though she had no way of knowing such things nor what had become of her would-be rescuers; it was enough that they were gone.

In the side yard, a bullet-riddled 1963 Ford Fairlane lay decomposing in the weeds: it had been a favorite target of every boy in the county with a new BB gun or .22 rifle for over a decade.

Everywhere there were beer cans, cheap whiskey bottles, cigarette butts, and old, used condoms—dried and shriveled like dead worms on a hot summer sidewalk.

When the hopelessness of her situation became clear, Kasey sank to the ground and laid her forehead on arms that were folded in despair across her knees.

The tears came freely, running off her chin to become small brown shapeless balls in the soil between her feet. She had no idea what to do now—now that she knew there was no one to help her.

Now that she was completely on her own.

Her parents, dead almost ten years, filled her frightened mind with rich, well-remembered imagery. They, too, had left her to make it on her own.

The tears increased and came from silent, lonely places within her that she seldom visited any more.

❖

It was the sound of a woman's voice that first pulled Kasey from her sorrowful retreat, reawakening her senses to the world around her, forcing the secret doors to close once again.

Kasey looked up and listened attentively, not certain that she had actually heard it. She turned her head side to side—like a puppy might do—trying to home in on the faint words that had managed to filter through the grief and despair and had dragged her back to reality.

Nothing. Silence.

It must have been the wind.

No, there it was again! She surely heard it that time.

From somewhere behind her a woman was talking, or crying—Kasey wasn't sure. What she *was* sure of though, was that she was no longer alone.

Yes! Her heart soared.

She jumped to her feet and moved in the direction of the voice. She could hear it clearly now, coming from beyond where the old dirt drive ended—out of sight, over the crest of the hill.

She started to call out when she heard a man's voice: It stopped her cold. He was yelling and his words, though also indistinct, sounded angry. Kasey covered her mouth with her fingertips and took a few more steps toward the couple. Thick weeds blocked her way.

In the unearthly lunar light, she studied the scene: the road had come to an end; the old shack and car sat in the remnants of the only clearing she could make out, lying to the right of the road; on either side of the drive, thick woods framed the narrow strip of yellow Tennessee earth. Almost as if the road had been meant to continue south—many years before—the trees directly ahead of her had been cleared and only tall, dense grass now grew where towering oaks and pines had once flourished.

Kasey looked for a path through the weeds, past the house and the rusting Ford, between the dense woods that framed the scruffy hill.

No easy route existed.

She looked behind her, north, toward where her CRX should be. She could not see beyond the first hill, but she knew it still sat lame and waiting.

She also knew there was no help in that direction.

Kasey dropped to the dirt drive and drew the laces on her Reeboks tight, double-tying each knot. She pulled her white cotton socks over the cuffs of her sweat pants as high as they would go, sealing off any easy access to her skin from ground level.

When she stood again, she tucked her sweat shirt into the band of her sweat pants and pulled the ends of her sleeves over her hands and held the cuffs in her hidden fists. She wanted no more flesh than necessary exposed to the ticks, fleas, and chiggers she knew were everywhere in the tall grasses, waiting patiently for any warm-blooded animal to pass.

She refused to even consider whether there might be snakes in the thicket. She was certain she remembered seeing on the Discovery channel that most snakes sleep at night. The comforting thought, correct or not, gave her the courage to continue.

When she heard the woman's voice again, Kasey drew in a long breath and forced the tall grass before her apart with her arms.

❖

Donna Stanton knelt between two apple trees in the abandoned orchard that lay a few hundred yards to the south of the sharecropper's shack, at the base of a small hill. The knees of her white jogging suit were soaked from the damp ground; her lower back ached painfully from having been in the humiliating position for what seemed an hour.

Despite the discomfort, she never took her eyes from the man who had driven her to this scary place, and who now stood over her speaking angrily.

She knew that the moment she told him what he wanted to know, she was dead. She had no illusions about Giacano's anger or wrath. Her only hope was to stick to her story and pray that this man had been told not to harm her until he could retrieve the tapes.

She also prayed that she would be given an opportunity to explain to Mario about the recordings; she was certain that if she could look into his eyes, she could make him understand her motives and forgive her. The man turned around and walked a few steps away from her, and then turned back, just as he had done a dozen times already.

He seemed like a caged animal pacing the fence line.

Under his breath he mumbled a string of unintelligible sounds and then spoke clearly, softly. "All right, Ms. Stanton—may I call you Donna?—perhaps we got off on the wrong foot, you and me." His voice had lowered, his tone now much less tense. "I've got a job to do, that's all. I don't wanna hurt anyone. If you help me do my job, then we can both go home. It's as simple as that. My boss just wants the tapes you made, and as soon as you give 'em to me, you're free to go. He wants nothing else from you—no harm, if that's what's bothering you—not after all you've shared. Am I making myself clear, darlin'?"

He dropped to one knee a few feet in front of her and stared squarely into her eyes.

She stared back, unblinking.

In the weird gray light of the full moon, he looked almost like a ghost. His nearly black eyes completed the mien and sent a chill through her.

"I know you don't believe me," she pleaded, "but I don't have them with me."

It was not a lie: when she had first been ordered from his truck, moments after it came to a stop near the two trees where she now knelt, she had seized the opportunity to pull the cigarette case from her waistband and toss it into the tall grass at the edge of the orchard clearing. In the moment it took him to switch the headlights to parking lamps and close his door, he had missed it all.

"I was afraid when I realized Mario had found out I was taping his calls. I didn't know what to do, so I ran. You know what kind of man he is. You can understand my fear, can't you?" She lowered her head and started to cry. "I left the tapes, all of the tapes, hidden in my apartment. I swear."

It was the first time Donna had actually mentioned a location for the tapes. She hoped she had held out long enough to make the soulful confession believable.

❖

Kasey plodded her way clumsily through the tall undergrowth, thick and lush from years of uncontrolled growth. Twice she had fallen, losing her footing when the moon disappeared behind one of the thick clouds that seemed more numerous with each passing minute.

Each time she fell, she had remained still for a moment, straining to hear what was being said between the unseen couple, certain it was some kind of lover's disagreement, but never able to decipher any words.

Afraid that she would frighten them—perhaps anger the obviously troubled man to the point where he would be unwilling to help her— Kasey crept cautiously forward, staying low and well concealed.

As she began to part another stand of weeds, she encountered the strands of a barbed-wire fence. She knelt at once, near a post, and peered through the tall grass that rose nearly a foot above the fence on her side. On the other side of the fence, the orchard had been recently cut, leaving the grass only a few inches tall.

Kasey was surprised to find herself now less than thirty feet from the couple.

"Let me get this straight," the man stated in his thick Alabama drawl. "You mean to tell me that after all the trouble you went through to make 'em, you didn't take the damned things with you when you left town? You just grabbed that one suitcase full of clothes and got the hell out? Is that what you're tryin' to tell me, Donna?"

"Yes, that's *exactly* what I'm telling you. Go back there and look for yourself. I left everything in my apartment."

The soft blue eyes did not betray her terror.

The man lowered his head a bit and shook it side to side.

"Well, that ain't exactly true, is it?" he grinned, pulling a couple of the most recognizable pieces of her jewelry from his jeans pocket. "You also took the time to fill a box with these pretty little doodads, and then stopped along the way to grab a shit-potful of cash, remember?" He cocked his head sarcastically, chin elevated. "I guess you weren't planning on coming back any time soon, huh, Donna?"

Donna Stanton eyed the once treasured items and emotionally distanced herself from them with surprisingly little regret. If they would help secure her freedom, they had more than served their purpose.

"Listen, there's more than enough in my jewelry box to buy you anything you could ever want," she quickly offered. "You can have it all—it's yours."

"I know it's mine," he grinned. "I'm the one with it, ain't I?" He shoved the baubles deep inside his pocket again and then stood and stepped back. He shook his head as if he were confused, waiting for a long moment before speaking further. "I don't know, Donna, I gotta think about this. I'd like to believe you, but I was ordered not to come back without the boss's stuff. You could be lying to me, and I wouldn't like that at all. I hate people lying to me."

"I'm not lying, I swear to God! What you're looking for is back at my apartment, not here. Take me there and I'll get everything for you. Then you can give them to Mario in person. You'll be the hero and no one but you and I will ever know about the jewelry you've got. That way you make out on both ends." She stared at him, watching every move. It had been her best delivery.

The man continued to shake his head and began to mumble to himself again. He needed a cigarette. When he turned his back to find the lighter and Camels he had laid in the grass, Donna instinctively looked toward the place where she had thrown the tapes.

The last things she expected to see were the bewildered eyes of another woman staring back from the tall grass at the edge of the orchard.

❖

Mario Giacano had not spoken for nearly thirty minutes. The other three men in the back of the Lincoln limousine sensed the tension emanating from their boss and none wished to be the first to break the icy silence. They knew he did not appreciate efforts to elevate his mood when he was sullen or angry.

Finally, as he turned his attention from the ceaseless flow of evening traffic just beyond his window glass, Giacano spoke. "Have any trouble getting us a table?" he asked the eldest of the other men.

Michael Filippo had no idea what was troubling his employer and friend, but had been with him long enough to know he would learn what it was when Giacano chose to confide in him. "Of course not, Mario. Mama G sounded pleased you were going to pay her a call this evening. She said to tell you it's been far too long since you visited and that she would have your usual table ready."

Filippo smiled warmly. His attempt at pleasantry had failed.

Giacano nodded silently and without expression and returned his dull gaze to the stream of cars on his left. Her incredible nude body, standing at the foot of her bed, began to construct itself from the scattered palette of broken reflections in the tinted glass until the image, only inches away, seemed as real to him as a painting. A hard brown hand moved involuntarily up to caress it. It became, instead, a tight, defiant fist.

Giacano closed his eyes and leaned his head against the leather seat.

Michael Filippo touched his friend's knee reassuringly and then tapped two Advil from a small plastic bottle he had taken from his coat pocket. One of the bodyguards quickly filled a crystal glass with chilled Evian and handed it to Filippo.

Giacano took the glass and made a simple gesture with his right index finger. The other shadow rapped on the divider glass, motioning for the driver to pick up the pace.

The limo eased into the express lane as a late April rain began to soak the city and the Parkway deliquesced into a warm, gray ooze.

❖

Kasey remained frozen on the unkempt side of the fence, scarcely ten yards from the woman who now stared mute and disbelievingly in her direction.

Although she had sought out this couple for help, now—as if in the clutch of some primal protective grip—Kasey found herself pulled involuntarily to the ground. Lying as motionless as a statue, Kasey was certain the woman could no longer see her, though she could still make out the woman's face and most of her form through a small opening at the base of the thick weeds.

The woman continued to stare toward the fence for a few more seconds and then turned her face back to the man. To Kasey's surprise, she gave him no indication whatsoever that they were no longer alone.

With his cigarette lit, the man dropped the well-worn Zippo lighter back into the scruffy grass by his feet, its boldly emblazoned black-and-red Harley emblem still visible in the yellow light of the truck's parking lamps. He sucked in a deep lungful of blue-gray smoke and blew it out slowly through his nose. He was still mumbling to himself as he turned around and faced Donna again: "Where in your apartment, Donna?" he asked gently, then more firmly: "Where exactly?"

"Taped to the bottom of the sink bowl in my bathroom," she answered hurriedly, her heart beginning to race fully again.

"You see, I gotta know exactly. I can't show up empty-handed, you know. I'm not having the old man in my shit because you did something dumb like lie to me."

"I haven't lied!" Donna pleaded. "I swear I'll get them for you if you'll just take me back to my apartment." She watched carefully for some reaction, some sign that he believed her.

Though only hours ago it had been the last place Donna Stanton had planned to revisit, she looked forward to seeing her apartment again. Tucked cleverly away, in two well-concealed, yet easily accessible hiding places, were a matched pair of .32-caliber derringers. She had no doubt she could reach one of them and put a hollow-point slug in this scumbag's brain before he knew what hit him. Why in hell hadn't she tucked either of the palm-size pistols in her waistband as well when she left?

Kasey tried to follow the broken conversation as best she could but still had no idea what was going on between the couple. *Why was she kneeling?* Kasey wondered. *What had they been fighting about?* The man did seem calmer now, no longer angry. Perhaps now would be the right time to announce herself and ask for help; she was tired of laying in the damp grass and the image of blood-hungry ticks crawling over every square inch of her skin was becoming harder to suppress by the second.

She thought about what she would say and then imagined herself emerging from the weeds with her babbling tale of a flat tire. *Why hadn't the woman mentioned seeing her at the fence?*

After more careful consideration, the time did not seem right.

"Damn! Damn!" she moaned.

Perhaps in a few minutes, after they had kissed and made up. *What a complete jerk he is to make her kneel there while he bitches at her*, Kasey thought. "Tell him to take a swim in the bayou, girl. I sure as hell would," she whispered angrily.

Ready to be on her way, Kasey tried to identify their car. All she could see at first were the parking lamps and the right front amber side light. It took her a minute to recognize the muted shape as that of a truck. With the full light of the April moon on its black surface, its dark form barely revealed itself against the dull green grass and trees that filled the orchard. She decided that it was a new Dodge Ram "dooley," just like the one Mondo talked of owning someday; he kept a brochure picture of a bright red one, with four-wheel drive, taped to the outside of his locker and patted it like a centerfold whenever he passed it.

"Well, at the very least I can get a ride back to town," she muttered to herself. Things were beginning to look up. "Now, if they'll only finish their little spat so I can get on with the rest of my life, I'll be eternally grateful." Kasey thought about Sam and knew he would be angry if she didn't come home on time two nights in a row.

She moved aside a few long blades of grass that had been blocking her view of the man and wondered how much longer the whole thing was going to take.

The man stepped closer to Donna Stanton and knelt on the grass directly in front of her, less than three feet away, his back squarely to the fence: it was the first time since they left the truck that he had gotten this close. Convinced she could easily read any man's mind and mood, Donna understood the danger in this man, despite his acceptable appearance and Southern mannerisms.

Slammer, the man with the knife who had been waiting in her backseat, was just plain bad, as bad as they get—Donna had known it in her gut. An evil aura surrounded him. She had been grateful to leave his company intact and unhurt, and despite still being held captive, would certainly choose her present captor over Slammer any day. As ludicrous as it seemed, she was actually grateful it was *this* man across from her, and not the one with the prehistoric reptile tattooed on his skull and back.

"Let me ask you something, Donna," he spoke. "You wanna be on your way, right, to go wherever it is you were going?" He raised his eyebrows awaiting a response.

"Oh, yes, please," she begged, the tears returning to her eyes. "Please let me go."

"I might just do that," he smiled, "but only on two conditions." His left hand touched her right breast lightly, his right hand still held the last of the unfiltered Camel.

"What?" she asked quickly, though she had little doubt as to at least one condition of her release.

"First, you gotta swear on your life that the boss's stuff is in your apartment, under the sink just like you said, and that you'll get it for me as soon as we get there. No games, you understand, darlin'?"

"I understand. Everything is there, I swear. Just like I said," she whimpered. She waited for the other condition, wondering how he would word it.

The man nodded approvingly, as if completely satisfied with her sincerity, and then took a long drag of his cigarette. He blew the smoke intentionally away from her.

"Second, you gotta fuck me, just like you did all those rich bastards. I've had a lot of pussy in my life but I've never been with a real first class act like you before. It ought to be a hoot."

Donna Stanton had known that sex would be the second condition. No man had ever passed up the chance to have sex with her, not even her uncle when she was barely thirteen. She knew she could put up with it one more time. She would close her eyes and imagine the one boy she had truly loved many years ago, with his kind words and gentle touch—as she always did. In a few minutes it would be over. "It will be a lot of fun for both of us," she said, digging deeply inside herself for strength. "What would you like me to do?" she smiled.

Though Kasey could only make out some of the words spoken softly between the couple, she had seen the man touch the woman's breast and had seen her smile in response. "Oh, I don't believe this!" she moaned between clenched teeth. "I don't believe I'm going to have to wait for these two lovebirds to have sex before I can get them to help me with my damned car."

She squeezed her eyes shut and laid her forehead against a clenched fist, shaking her head back and forth as she did. "Just perfect. What else can possibly go wrong today?"

If there was another living soul within ten miles, she swore, she wouldn't be sitting in the weeds hoping like hell that snakes really do sleep at night.

"I want to look at your body," the man said without hesitation. "Real slow, like you're on stage." He indicated for her to rise.

Donna Stanton took a silent breath and stood slowly, painfully, as the blood rushed back to her calves and feet.

The man noticed and found it amusing. He flipped his cigarette away.

With her head clear again, Donna slipped off her sneakers. After taking another deep breath, she grabbed the bottom of her sweatshirt with both hands and pulled it over her head in a single move.

"Slowly!" he barked. "Go slower. Don't cheat me, Donna, we've got a deal. If I'm gonna take you back to your place in a little while and never see you again, I want this to last."

Donna let the sweatshirt drop to the grass behind her and stood tall and erect without further movement. Her large round breasts pressed tightly against the delicate white lace of the French bra, filling both cups. It was apparent to her that the man had never had a woman of her beauty before by the tilt of his head and the boyish smile that lit his eyes. She let the bra remain while she slid her jogging pants slowly down her long legs.

Beneath the thick sweat pants, a pair of white silk briefs rose high on her well defined hips. The sweat pants were drawn slowly, teasingly, up across her thighs, stomach, and breasts, and then dropped beside the shirt.

"Jesus, Donna, you're some kind of good-looking woman, I'll tell you that for sure. No wonder you got all those diamonds and shit. Hell, I'd have given you my last buck, too!"

He laughed at his own joke and then motioned for her to turn around slowly.

Kasey watched as the other woman undressed. She moved almost unconsciously toward the part in the grass in order to gain a less restricted view. Every voyeuristic feeling she had ever suppressed swept over her like a cold prairie wind. She looked instinctively to either side to be sure she was not being watched as she spied on the couple.

She marveled momentarily at the seemingly ridiculous act, then returned her gaze to the small illuminated spot between the trees.

In the golden glow of the truck's parking lamps, the woman was truly beautiful—slim and tall, Kasey noted with a trace of envy—but the man remained lost in the penumbra of the amber light, his back to her as it had been for the twenty minutes she'd been there. Earlier, when he reached for his cigarettes, Kasey could have seen his face, but at that moment, her attention was fully on the woman who was staring back at her.

As the man stared silently at her incredible body, like a child mesmerized by a porcelain figure turning slowly on a music box, Donna Stanton's eyes searched the bushes frantically for the face she'd seen moments earlier.

Kasey read the gesture as an attempt to communicate with her and rose slightly from her prone position—the man's back to her—to meet the other woman's eyes again.

"Help me," Donna mouthed as boldly as she dared, praying the man was more interested in her body than her face. "Please."

Help you? Help you how? Jesus Christ, Kasey thought incredulously, *there is no help. I came to you for help!* "What?" Kasey mouthed, parting the grass as much as she could without exposing herself. "What do you want?"

"Take the rest of it off," the deep male voice commanded, and though the words were spoken softly, they pierced the silence, forcing Donna's eyes to focus on him again. "And do it real slow, remember."

Again, Donna put her mind on her task: satisfying this son-of-a-bitch and then getting the hell away from here.

She turned her thoughts from the stranger at the fence. There would be better opportunities to escape or get help when she reached Nashville, but to do either, she first had to survive. She closed her eyes for a second and tried to picture the boy from long ago. *It will be over soon,* she kept telling herself.

With sensual movements polished to perfection by years of practice, Donna slid both straps of her bra from her shoulders and took its center clasp between her fingers in the same gesture. She slipped the small metal hook out of its delicate satin loop and withdrew the bra with her right hand, sweeping the left arm across both breasts as the lace moved slowly from their bounty.

The man grew visibly restless, rocking impatiently back and forth as he watched. When she lowered both hands to her sides, she heard him swear under his breath.

The silk French-cut briefs were slid half-way down the long legs before they dropped the remaining few feet on their own. She pushed them to the side with her toes, never taking her eyes from him.

The nervous rocking stopped and he appeared to have fixed his stare at her natural blond pubic hair. After a long moment, the man motioned for her to turn again. "God, you're beautiful, you know it?" he said with a muted whistle.

"Thank you," she answered insincerely, doing as she was told.

"I gotta have a cigarette," he announced quickly. "Sit, but don't touch none of your clothes."

Before she could respond, he disappeared around the side of the truck, scooping up his lighter and empty cigarette pack as he passed them. He tossed the crumpled pack inside the pickup through the open driver's window.

At the side of the truck—near the back glass—the man unsnapped a corner of the black rubberized tonneau that covered the bed. He withdrew a long canvas bag and headed back toward the woman.

Donna Stanton took a quick, deep breath, locking it in her lungs.

The man gently laid the bag in the spot where his lighter had been and unzipped it fully.

Donna put her hands to her mouth and watched intensely. After a few seconds of digging around inside, he withdrew an unopened carton of Camels.

Kasey started breathing again at the same instant Donna Stanton let out a short, relieved gasp.

The man looked at the nude woman sitting a few feet away and shook his head. "It ain't nothing but a carton of smokes, Donna. Jesus, you'd'a thought I had a damned rattlesnake in here." He withdrew one pack, dropped the carton in the bag, and walked to where she was sitting. "Hell, if I was gonna hurt you, Donna, I'd have done it by now, wouldn't I? You're too damn beautiful for any man to put a mark on, and that includes me. So relax. We're going to have a good time, you and me. Hell, I'll get me a cigarette later," he laughed. "Right now, I'm in the mood for love."

Kasey watched as he unbuttoned his brightly colored western shirt and threw it toward the canvas bag. He then pulled his undershirt over his head. The boots, socks, and Levi's were tossed beside the western shirt. He had been wearing no underwear.

The man now stood nude in front of Donna Stanton, and Kasey found herself unable to look away. It was as if a spell had been cast over her.

Her heart raced as she inched ever closer to the fence.

The man gently took the woman's hair and pulled her head toward his waiting penis. As she worked her magic, he arched his back and thrust his face toward the heavens, breathing in slowly through his nostrils. After a minute or two, he pulled quickly away from her mouth. He dropped to his knees in front of her and pushed her indifferently onto the small mound of her clothes that lay behind her. He grabbed her firmly behind each knee and jerked her pelvis toward him, forcing her thighs apart as widely as he could.

She grimaced as the tendons in her groin felt like they were going to rip, struggling to keep a seductive look.

Clumsily, hurriedly, he mounted her, pressing his body against her breasts and crushing the wind out of her. He thrust several times, missing her vagina. Almost angrily he leaned up on one hand and forced his penis inside her with the other.

In less than a minute of sporadic grunting and jerking he had climaxed, collapsing his full weight against her, his chin buried painfully in the crook of her neck.

Kasey suddenly felt unbelievably sorry for the other woman, a person she knew nothing about, but a sister in spirit just the same. Though the woman had apparently agreed to have sex, Kasey was certain she had not done so out of passion or desire. Whether this man was a boyfriend of the woman's or a man she had just met, he was certainly no prize catch.

Kasey thought about Cal Hardt, and the man from the bar she had been with the night before, and sank back into a seated position behind her grassy wall, angry and disgusted.

Maybe now, she thought, *I can finally get the jerk to help me. I hope he'll still have the strength left to loosen one lousy lug nut.*

As she thought about the best way to announce her presence, she quietly swatted a mosquito that had landed on her cheek, amazed that more hadn't found her in the brush.

Just give me two minutes of your time and I'll be on my way, she grumbled silently. *Whatever it is the two of you are fighting about, it's no concern of mine. I have too many problems in my own life to be worrying about your squabbles.*

She turned her eyes back toward the fence to see if Don Juan had resurrected yet.

To her surprise, the man was on his feet, standing over the naked woman, her legs still outstretched and spread. She was half sitting, resting on her elbows, looking up into his eyes. "Was it okay?" she asked humbly, though she would have much preferred to slit his throat.

He smiled curtly, and bent to pick a single blade of grass from her tangled hair. He grabbed his undershirt and wiped himself, dropping it between her legs for her to use.

Donna continued to force a pleasant smile, as if to assure him that he was one of the finest lovers she had ever enjoyed.

The man turned without speaking a word and walked to his clothes, dropping to one knee by the open bag. He retrieved the pack of cigarettes he had removed from the carton earlier and slit the end with his thumbnail. He lit the cigarette he shoved between his lips with the old Zippo, flipping it open and producing a flame in a single, swift move, just like he had learned in reform school as a kid.

Donna Stanton could no longer bear to watch the creature and rose to her knees, turning her back to him, careful to conceal her feelings. She dug through the crumpled clothes in front of her and found her sweatshirt. As a tear streaked down her cheek, she pulled it over her head and down across her bare breasts.

She prayed it would all be over soon.

In a macabre answer to her silent petition, it was merciful that she wasn't aware that the man held a 12-gauge sawed-off shotgun less than a foot behind the beautiful head with its long golden curls.

The blast from the huge slug made a hole the diameter of a half-dollar in the crown of her skull, passed through the center of the brain destroying a massive amount of tissue and gaining size and momentum in the process, and exited as large as a softball between the beautiful sky-blue eyes.

The back blast from the entry hole covered the man's bare chest and face with blood, brain fragments, and strands of silken hair.

He spat the particles from his mouth and blinked several times to clear his vision.

A large drop of wine-colored blood dripped from the end of his nose.

"Whoa, shit!" he exclaimed out loud, surprised at the amount of debris that had struck him. "I guess I got too fuckin' close that time!"

Kasey urinated on herself as the brilliant white-hot fireball appeared to engulf the woman's head.

She wanted to scream in terror but nothing came out; something instinctively told her that the slightest sound from her direction would simply mean *two* assassinations instead of the one she had just witnessed. Panic swept over her.

She lowered quietly onto her stomach and pressed herself into the wet thatch, digging at the matted grasses with her fingernails, desperately trying to pull herself even closer to the ground—beneath the ground—trying to make herself invisible to the man with the gun.

As she lay there in frozen horror, the image of the woman's face literally exploding played before Kasey's eyes, repeating itself mercilessly in vivid detail, growing more brutal and horrific with each replay.

Her mind begged for it to stop, but the thundering blast that began to echo in her ears triggered a whole new wave of imagery: in relentlessly slow motion, huge splashes of blood and bits of flesh and bone flying in every direction.

She began to vomit but pressed her hand so tightly over her mouth that her bottom teeth dug into her lips. She felt no pain from it.

Like a rabbit riveted to the ground by the gaze of a hungry wolf, Kasey lay there silently, unable to move, unable to think. Pure survival-response from countless centuries of evolution was in control. Every dark emotion she had ever felt coursed through her spine like molten lava through a cane field, reducing her to a quivering mass of loss and despair.

She wished the man would simply pull the trigger a second time, and put an end to the agony of waiting for it to come.

The man reached beside Donna's lifeless body and used his undershirt to wipe the specks and droplets from his face, arms, and chest. Long scarlet streaks were left in their place, lending an unholy, sacrificial look to his tan skin. He took a bottle of vodka from the bag and soaked the cloth. It removed the last traces of red from his body, but left the undershirt a sickening pink.

He looked at the human debris at his feet that had, only seconds before, been a vibrant woman. Her twisted form lay slumped across the small mound of sneakers and sweat pants, the blond hair now a confusing weave of gold and crimson.

He kicked her right heel with his foot.

There was no movement, not even the reflex response that sometimes remains in a body for a few moments after death.

He reached down, pulled the delicate white panties from beneath her hips, and rubbed them slowly against his cheek. "I'll say this, lady, you were certainly the best looking bitch I've ever seen. Too bad you pissed off the wrong guy."

When Kasey heard his voice again, and realized that he was still beside the woman's body, she slowly raised her head and turned it toward the small part in the weeds. It was more than a foot to her right. It was impossible to see anything from where she lay, and she wasn't going to risk making the slightest sound.

She laid her cheek against the damp grass and prayed to God for him to leave.

After he placed the sawed-off shotgun back in the canvas bag, the man dressed—not in a hurry like someone who had just committed a heinous crime, but with the ease and leisurely manner of a Saturday morning stroll.

He stuffed the blood-soaked rag of a shirt in the bag as well and pulled out a folding shovel and short handled rake. In less than fifteen minutes, he had dug a grave deep and long enough to conceal the corpse.

With the hole complete, he took the shovel and rolled the body toward it—it made a half turn to the left and dropped into the pit facing upward.

The only part of Donna's body that wasn't nude was the upper torso—the sweatshirt she had pulled on still covered her chest and most of her abdomen.

The man realized that the thick sweatshirt posed a minor obstacle in properly disposing of the body. He pulled a folding knife from his back jeans pocket, knelt at the edge of the grave, and sliced the sweatshirt from collar to waistband, tossing each half to its rightful side and exposing the incredible body that he had used just twenty minutes earlier.

With his full weight on the blade of the shovel, he crushed the rib cage, opening the chest and abdomen. That way, as the body began to decompose over the coming days and weeks, there wouldn't be a noticeable depression left in the ground: his cell mate at Brushy Mountain Prison had tutored him on the finer points of concealing a body.

The man was now grateful he had paid such close attention.

Kasey lifted her head when she heard what sounded like digging. She prayed the sound would conceal any noise she made.

She produced another small break in the weeds, below the bottom strand of barbed wire, and watched as the man dumped the woman's body into the shallow grave and then brutally crushed her remains. She became dizzy at the sight of him jumping up and down on the shovel, and felt as if she were going to pass out. Some inner strength kept her conscious and her eyes fixed on the morbid scene being played out thirty feet from her.

When the last of the soil was packed hard, and the grassy sod that had been scalped set carefully back in place to make the grave look like every other patch of grass in the orchard, there still remained a sizable mound of dark, rich earth.

He cursed aloud and then filled his shovel.

Kasey almost wet herself again when the man began walking toward her exact position. *Surely he wasn't going to dump it on the other side of the fence!*

Oh, God, of course he was! she suddenly realized. *He had to remove every clue that he'd ever been there.* And when he did, he'd find her and kill her as surely as he had the other woman. Perhaps with even less hesitation or mercy.

She nearly bit through her lip as she tried to decide what to do. There were only seconds left before he would spot her.

Think, Kasey!

She tensed her muscles to stand and run back up the hill but they simply wouldn't respond to the brain's confusing commands.

Kasey turned her eyes quickly toward the part in the grass to see how much time she had left to act—to her horror, he was now less than twenty feet away.

She buried her face in the grass and waited for the worst, her body still refusing to move.

Without willing it, Kasey was filled with a sensation she had gone her entire life without having felt; a feeling only those in similar circumstances ever knew. She wanted to live!

She knew she had faced the possibility of death before—the flash of unexpected headlights around a corner when she had made a risky pass on a two-lane highway, or in that instant when the decision was made to go for the light instead of stopping—but these were milliseconds of possible tragedy, diluted in their intensity by the focused necessity to accelerate or steer or hit the brakes. All had passed in a flash with little reality attached and rarely more than an acrid aftertaste, hardly worse than opting for jalapeños on an otherwise plain turkey sub. There was nothing hypothetical about this moment, or this hellish man.

The end of her life, her hopes, her *existence* was at hand and still his steps grew closer.

The desire to live became far more than simply *not* dying, far more than seeing another sunrise or laughing with friends. It became a need to continue existing, to have the time she had been promised—every single, insignificant, wasted-in-front-of-the-boob-tube minute of it.

She was sure the thumping of her heart was as loud to him as his boots crashing against the earth were to her.

Ten feet now.

Oh, sweet Jesus, holy Jesus, her mind screamed. *Please let me live!*

All at once something struck her on the top of the head and then it felt as if it were raining dirt: everywhere around her clods of cold, brown earth fell. Her mind and heart shrieked but her teeth and lips remained locked.

When the shower stopped, she heard the man's footsteps moving away from her. Her eyes went to the window she had created—the man had apparently, mercifully, stopped shy of the fence and had thrown the shovelful of earth from that position.

Kasey thought her heart would explode.

Tears of relief poured from her eyes, worsening her already cloudy vision.

After six similar trips, the mound had disappeared.

Each time the particles struck Kasey's body, she shook as if an electrical charge had been applied to her; the experience felt like hell—not the earthly equivalent she had experienced many times before, but the biblical place, the place where sinners were damned to spend eternity in torment.

For a moment, Kasey wondered if she had actually died and been sentenced by God to languish forevermore with the sight of the woman dying in her eyes, and the blast of the shotgun in her ears.

No hell in the Old Testament had ever been painted more vividly.

When he had raked the area carefully, and had policed it with the aid of the flashlight he had brought, he returned all items to the canvas bag and zipped it tightly shut. He walked to the back of the truck and tossed it into the bed, snapping the tonneau back in place.

Kasey watched intensely; the thought of him finally leaving made her light-headed.

The man opened the door of the cab and stuck a cigarette between his lips for the fourth time in twenty minutes. He lit it with a single flick of the lighter. The interior light of the truck burned like a searchlight in the dark orchard, painting the right side of his face and body. It made him look like half a person, the other half lost in the blackness of the night.

Kasey stared at the profile but her eyes were too blurred to see it clearly. She wiped them with the backs of her index fingers but the tears and sweat refused to yield to her damp hands: her actions only served to create a thick, salty paste that mixed with her makeup and burned her eyes even more.

Suddenly, he flipped on the headlights, spilling a brilliant river of white across the grassy plain between the rows of trees, and stood on the running board, his eyes following the twin beams of light.

Kasey, too, turned her eyes to the area where the man had worked so diligently for the last forty minutes. Nothing. There was not a visible trace that the other woman had ever been there or that her murder had ever taken place! The sight was more offensive than her body lying motionless on the grass.

It seemed now as though none of it had been real, and for one insane moment, she tried to convince herself that it had all been a hallucination, nothing more. Her eyes continued to scan the small patch of grass between the trees.

Nothing.

Satisfied with his work, he cranked the engine, pulled the transmission into gear, and mashed the throttle of the massive engine, spinning the truck in a noisy half-circle until it faced away from the grave.

A scream that could no longer be contained erupted from Kasey as the unexpected noise filled the orchard. It was drowned out by the throaty roar of the truck's dual exhausts.

She clamped her hands across her mouth and locked her gaze on the driver's door: when it remained closed, she was able to breathe once again.

The man moved the shifter into a higher gear and made a long, lazy arc to the south before heading east, away from Kasey and into the blackness broken only by his headlamps.

As the rear of the truck came into view, she was able to read the license, centered in a heavy chrome bumper between twin pairs of huge Goodyear tires.

The tag was a Tennessee vanity plate, its seven capital letters—navy blue against a glowing white field—spelling out the single, vile word: "JOEYBOY."

SIX

Kasey lay in the grass until the truck's silhouette disappeared over the eastern horizon. She searched frantically through her makeshift "window" in the grass for any sign of movement remaining in the clearing beyond the old wire fence.

When she was sure that she was the only person remaining within sight or hearing, she forced herself to stand. The aching muscles, tensed beyond endurance for nearly an hour, quivered uncontrollably and then collapsed, sending her to the ground in an exhausted heap.

Through sheer will and the determination to get away from this evil place, Kasey tried again, pulling herself up by the top strand of barbed wire, placing her hands carefully between the sharp, twisted points that were spaced every few inches. The legs still shook and her heart hurt like a strained muscle; she felt like there was a fist in her throat; her lips throbbed as if she'd been struck in the mouth.

Kasey stared for a moment at the eerily peaceful area between the first two apple trees: it looked like every other spot in the orchard.

If she didn't ache in every fiber of her body, and didn't stink of dirt, sweat, and urine, she might still have convinced herself that it had all been a horrifying dream.

As the leg muscles slowly awakened, she moved away from the fence. She forced herself to run, to retrace her steps back up the hill toward the sharecropper's house, and ultimately, to the car she had left—when was it, a hundred, no, a thousand years before.

Twice along the route she fell: the first time, when her sneakers slid in the wet grass where the weeds bordered the old dirt road; and the second, when the muscles of her legs quit, sending her face first into the gravel and dust of the drive.

If her body had been able to register any more hurt, it would have been a murderous fall, with painful lacerations to both palms and the left side of her face, but, in her state of mind, no damage registered.

Finally, mercifully, she reached the familiar shape of her crippled CRX.

For the first time after more than ten minutes of hard running, Kasey stopped to catch her breath. Then, from the core of her soul, the feelings erupted; all the pain, all the fear, all the horror. She was practically thrown to her knees beside the driver's door, vomiting uncontrollably until nothing remained but an acidic burning.

As she knelt on all fours in the dirt beside the car, coughing, crying, begging for it all to end, she heard a sound that fused her body into a frozen mass: the unmistakable throaty roar of a truck's exhaust—*his* truck—a sound her brain would never allow her to forget. "Oh, God!" she cried aloud, crawling for the brush at the side of the road. "Oh, Jesus! God, please help me!"

Kasey dragged her tortured body from the roadside and took cover amid the pine trees and scruffy bushes that lined the narrow drive and road.

From its low rumbling sound, the truck appeared to be moving slowly—deliberately—as if searching for something.

Or someone.

Having just run the full length of the long driveway, Kasey was certain the sound could not be coming from behind her. She snaked along the ground, staying eight or ten feet off the side of the road—well hidden by the foliage—and made her way the short distance to a spot where the driveway intersected the paved road. From there, in the moonlight that spilled through the clouds, she could see no more than fifty feet in either direction: to the west, the part of the road she had driven two hours before; and to the east, the point where a bend seemed to swallow the pavement.

Though her head turned repeatedly east and west, there was still no sign of Joeyboy or the truck.

And yet, the sound grew louder, coming closer.

Kasey buried her face in a thick mat of pine needles and tried to fight back the mounting fear. She knew she had to think, to act, to do whatever was necessary to stay alive.

She again looked to the left.

Nothing.

She jerked her head back to the right just in time to see the hideous black silhouette of the truck easing around the curve, its lights off, navigating by what little moonlight remained.

Though she was already pressed against the ground, Kasey instinctively lowered her head.

As the truck passed her concealed position—on a slight rise between the trunks of two towering pines—Kasey found herself at eye level with the driver, less than ten feet away. As he rolled slowly by, going no more than five or six miles per hour, Joeyboy inhaled deeply on an ever-present

Camel, painting his profile in satanic hues of red and amber as the coal of the cigarette flared brightly.

Kasey knew the next crucial moment would mean life or death for her: if her car was seen, it would not take long for Joeyboy to locate its driver. She wasn't sure she had the strength left to run.

As he passed the drive, a flash of moonlight reflecting off the rear hatch of the CRX momentarily caught Joeyboy's eye. By the time he turned toward it, it was gone, an apparent apparition. He took another drag of his cigarette and put his eyes and thoughts back on the road.

Kasey noisily exhaled the breath she had locked in her throat.

Then there was something new, something she had not heard until the truck had passed. She swung her head back to the right—in the path of the Dodge pickup came another vehicle, its headlights also off.

The second vehicle, in no more apparent hurry than the truck, had deeply tinted windows, making it impossible for Kasey to see even a profile of the driver. She recognized the car as one of her favorite late model Jaguars. Except for the unusual wheel treatment—gleaming, gold-toned wire wheels—the car was also entirely black.

She froze again as the Jaguar neared the dirt drive, but it too passed from view without incident.

She dropped her head to the pine needles and wept.

❖

Kasey placed the lug wrench on the stubborn, damnable fourth bolt—the son-of-a-bitch that had turned her life inside out—and set its arm at nine o'clock. She opened the back hatch and grabbed the heavy lid for support. With one determined leap, driven by a reawakened desire to celebrate another birthday, she brought her full weight down on the handle.

The nut broke loose.

It didn't matter that she also lost her footing and slammed her butt into the drive in the process.

In retrospect, it would be seen as the high point in a long and horror-filled evening.

She wasted no time exchanging the donut spare for the flat tire, pitching wheel, tools, and jack helter-skelter into the hatch area behind the front seats.

She backed to the pavement and then accelerated rapidly to the east, in the opposite direction of Joeyboy and his mysterious associate.

Only when she was around the curve did she turn on her own headlights. Wherever the road led, one fact was irrefutable and of paramount importance to her at the moment: it lead away from them.

❖

Within a half-mile, Kasey came to the top of the hill that formed the southeastern end of the orchard.

At the apex of the hill, in a slight turn to the west, another driveway intersected the main road, the only one she had passed since beginning her flight.

For some reason, she slowed and then stopped.

To her right lay a gate with an old plywood sign hanging lopsided over it. The words read: "SWEET WATER FARMS" in peeling black letters with a faded painting of a red apple on each end.

When a thunderbolt discharged overhead, as if some colossal strobe light had just been fired, she could clearly make out the neatly arranged rows of trees, and the old barbed-wire fence that ran around their northern perimeter—the fence that had inadvertently saved her life.

As quickly as the flash vanished, so did the scene before her, leaving the orchard as black as coal tar. She felt nauseated again as her mind changed the flash of lightening into the blast of a shotgun muzzle.

❖

Kasey drove without regard for time or distance, racing down any road or highway that led *away* from the orchard, looking for one which she hoped might, eventually, return her to Nashville. She found herself on roads with names like Berlin Verona and Wade Brown, Ownby and Wiles Lane.

She was lost.

Finally, at a deserted four-way stop, where she sat peering through the windshield into the blackness of night for what felt like an hour, a sign pointing to US-31A North silently announced itself.

She recognized the highway as the same one which ran through downtown Nashville as 8th Avenue.

❖

Within fifty minutes, she pulled into her usual space in the Bradbury Arms Apartments and switched off the ignition. Her body wanted to collapse right there but her mind needed the safety of four walls and a locked door.

When she limped up the last flight of stairs that led to #3381—her apartment—she missed her footing on the middle step, sending her crashing to her knees and face.

Angry, scared, and aching in every muscle and joint, she lay there sobbing, searching for the will to go on, the strength to make the last few feet. She had given so much for *so* long that there seemed to be nothing left to draw from. Right now, this moment, she no longer cared if she died. At least it would be at her own home, on familiar ground, and not in some godforsaken tick-infested field where no one would find her body.

When the woman's lips, pleading silently for help, begging for someone to save her, flashed before her eyes again, Kasey tapped her last reserves and stood.

With the door closed and the deadbolt locked securely behind her, she fell across the livingroom couch, facedown; one arm hanging to the floor; her face buried in the crack where the cushions met the back.

Sam curled up in the small of her back and drifted to sleep, grateful and content that his only friend had finally returned.

❖

Garibaldi's Restaurant had two qualities that were of particular interest to Mario Giacano at the moment: authentic Italian cuisine—something he missed whenever he spent time in the South—and a large late night crowd who would hopefully remember his presence in Chicago as Donna Stanton was paying for her sin.

Every Monday evening, beginning at seven, Garibaldi's Fine Italian Restaurant featured all-you-can-eat lasagna, one of Mrs. Garibaldi's specialties. Mr. Garibaldi had passed away eight years earlier, and there was seldom a seat left vacant by the neighborhood families who saved Mondays to dine out at their favorite restaurant or by the college kids who would drive halfway across the city to stuff themselves for less than ten bucks. It was often the one large meal they could afford in a week, something Mrs. Garibaldi—Mama G, as she was known to most—was only too happy to provide the students who reminded her of her own son, Leo. His name, along with the names of fifty-eight thousand others, was etched on a black marble wall in Washington, D.C., in the shadow of the Lincoln Memorial. He would have been forty-four this summer, and so, for the last twenty-five years, Mondays had been lasagna night, in honor of Leo's favorite dish. At first, the special meal was just for the immediate family and a few close friends, but soon it became a popular tradition.

Despite the crowd, made even heavier than normal by the warm, clear spring night and brilliant full moon, a tall-backed wooden booth in the far left corner remained empty. At the two neighboring tables, three of the four chairs were also vacant.

No one bothered to ask if the six unclaimed chairs might be borrowed; no one ventured toward the empty booth.

If asked, the staff made it clear that the booth, as well as the unoccupied chairs, were not to be taken. Most customers quickly determined that the unpleasant-looking men seated near the booth had not come there to eat—their faces were blank, but their mean eyes missed nothing.

The other guests would simply gather a little tighter around their respective tables—making room for five or six in spaces normally seating four—while Mama G found more chairs and distributed them without hesitation and without complaint.

The man who held the mortgage on her small business was on his way, and his regular booth would be ready for him as she had promised. It didn't offend her; Giacano had acquired the paper on her restaurant from the bank a number of years earlier, indicating simply that he wished to have a place where he could get good food in a quiet, undisturbed atmosphere. Mama G liked her landlord. He had never asked her to make the first dollar's payment to him in nearly a decade, despite having only eaten at her place—his place—on rare occasions. Mama G was of the personal opinion that *Mr.* Giacano probably owned a number of restaurants throughout Chicago, and thought him to be a wonderfully kind and generous man, perhaps even a philanthropist (she believed that was the correct word) who simply didn't want to be disturbed while he ate. She welcomed him warmly whenever he called. If she lost a handful of paying customers for a few hours once or twice a year, it was an insignificant price to pay for his splendid generosity.

Besides, Mr. Giacano's party always paid their tab in full. In cash.

Even though Mama G had never presented a bill—never would have done so—one of the men at the front tables would always leave more than enough money to cover the food and wine that had been consumed, including a large tip.

Though given only an hour's notice, Mama G had heated for Mr. Giacano and his guests a pan of her special sausage and pepper lasagna, the pan she had made earlier for her own family.

Whenever a customer had been rude enough to voice an unfavorable opinion about her esteemed landlord, or comment rudely when some mention of his alleged criminal activities appeared on television or in the *Sun Times*, Mama G would simply, and unceremoniously, invite the guest to eat elsewhere in Chicago. For the rest of his life.

Those who recognized Giacano understood the rules whenever his party was in the restaurant. A few, the more timid of heart, would leave whenever they noticed the corner booth being held in reserve by thick-bodied men with no necks. But for most people, the food was simply too good to care who they dined with. Warm, heavily buttered garlic bread was consumed by the loaf, lasagna was devoured by the pan, and Chianti flowed like water from an open hydrant on a hot July day.

After all, those who did remain reasoned, a gangster was not unlike a snake: if you left it alone, all would be well; if you disturbed it, there was little likelihood of escaping without a bite.

❖

Giacano stared across the table at Michael Filippo, his top lieutenant and the man responsible for enforcing the laws of the extensive Giacano empire.

Filippo, a short, irritable man of nearly sixty, hadn't uttered a word in almost twenty minutes, taking in everything his boss had to say about the situation that had developed unexpectedly in Nashville. It upset Filippo that anyone, especially the woman his boss had become so enamored of, would commit an act of treason, and he knew there could only be one outcome.

Giacano knew how Filippo thought, that only a word needed to exchange between them, but something drove him to tell the whole story to the only man he completely trusted. There would be no mention of the pain, the disappointment in the plans that had died. Filippo could tell from the anger in his boss's tired eyes as he spoke. He was Giacano's best friend at age ten, a title he still carried with honor more than five decades later.

Filippo only needed instruction on what he wanted done about the other members of the "cast" in Nashville. The woman's fate had been sealed. Giacano would not have spared her had she been his sister.

When Giacano stopped speaking, his throat was dry. He looked at his glass and it was automatically filled by the wide, silent man standing to his left, one of six bodyguards inside the restaurant. Outside, there were a half-dozen more, all outfitted with concealed Kevlar body armor and armed with Glock .45 automatics, watching the front, sides, and back of the building.

The President ate dinner with less security, but then, the President's death would have had less impact on business in the Midwest.

"So, what do you think, my friend?" Giacano asked.

"It's a touchy situation, Mario, any way you look at it. We've got to get our hands on those tapes, there's no compromise there. If the Feds get them first, we'll have one hell of a time working it all out. It ain't like the old days. That fucking broad they got running the show now don't play games."

Giacano knew all of this, of course, but enjoyed hearing the opinion of his closest associate; or perhaps, he hoped that talking about it might relieve the pain he was feeling.

It had not helped.

He sipped his wine. "You have a plan, Michael?"

"We've got a man well placed in Nashville who can monitor the situation moment to moment, and in the unlikely event the tapes surface other than in his possession, he will see that they never reach the Feds."

"Do I know this man?" Giacano asked.

"You've never met him, he's a recent acquisition. A greedy but capable man who would love to do another favor for us."

"Another favor?"

"A couple of months back, he took care of that state legislator who tried to run his own action without including us. You remember, Fordyce—from Memphis."

Giacano nodded.

"Very clean, if you'll recall. Not a question about it being anything other than an accident. He would love to help us again."

"What does he want?" Giacano asked, emptying his glass of wine. It was filled before his hand moved to his fork.

"An early retirement. Wants to sit on a boat and deep-sea fish for the rest of his life. Says he's tired of serving the public interest; wants to serve his own interests from now on."

Filippo began to eat his meal before it lost all of its warmth. He hated cold lasagna.

"Retirement?"

"From Nashville Metro. He's a cop."

"I like dirty cops," Giacano intoned. "They're so . . . so trustworthy." He let the word roll slowly off his tongue. The old man smiled for the first time since mid-morning. He folded his hands, resting his elbows on the table. "You tell our 'trustworthy' cop, that when he hands me the tapes in person, I'll buy him a yacht from which to fish."

"How about the others?" Filippo inquired, assuming nothing.

Giacano stared at the flame of the candle in front of him. "Let's just watch them for the time being—but closely. As long as the tapes don't surface in the wrong hands, we can still proceed, and some of them will still be of use to us. After all, Michael, let's not forget our plan. It's taken us four years to get this far, dealing with Bible-thumpers and honest politicians all the way, and I'll be damned if I'm going to just walk away from one of the sweetest deals I've seen in half my life because of some whore." He reached across the table and held his palm over the candle, moving it slowly side to side, his eyes fixed on the dancing flame. After a moment of silence he made a tight fist and touched it to his lips. "Just keep a close eye on things for now, Michael."

He turned his head toward the front of the restaurant, looking at but not actually seeing the many faces that were laughing and talking and devouring Mama G's lasagna: Donna's ice-blue eyes stared hauntingly back at him from every table, now mocking him for not seeing through her before; ridiculing him for having grown soft and careless in his old age.

He rolled his eyelids slowly shut and tried again to remind himself that soon she would no longer exist.

It helped little.

SEVEN

A dull clang echoed deep within Kasey's brain, summoning her to come out of hiding and greet the new day that had been born while she slept. The tip of one finger—pressed lightly against the carpet where it, along with the rest of the hand to which it was attached, had remained motionless for the last eight hours—twitched slightly at the subliminal wake-up call. The movement was barely visible even to Sam, who ordinarily let little escape his emerald gaze. If not for the shallow breathing that raised and lowered the filthy purple sweatshirt every few seconds, Kasey could have convincingly passed for dead.

The twitching finger grew still again and the little bell in the brain fell silent for the moment.

It was almost ten A.M.

By noon, her brain had once again grown restless, and chose to opt for a more direct approach: Kasey's stomach started to growl from lack of food—it had been twenty hours since she'd eaten—and began its long, and normally effective, plea demanding attention.

As before, the right hand tried to awaken—for only a moment—but the rest of the body continued to show little interest in joining it. Her position had not changed perceptibly since she collapsed into the thickly padded cushions almost a half-day earlier.

By two P.M., the bell in her subconscious tolled with a vengeance, having decided that the body it governed had slept long enough for the present. Since none of the more subtle tactics had worked thus far, it decided to try pain, recalling the most recent of its many stored agonies: the blast of the sawed-off shotgun exploded in Kasey's ears while the angelic face of the helpless woman burst into bloody, splintered fragments before her eyes: the grisly scene was played out in "wide-screen color and stereo," humbling the most graphically grotesque of Hollywood horror scenes.

Kasey bolted to her feet as if she'd been kicked, her eyes still half-shut, trying desperately to accept the bluish-white light of midday that poured through the open blinds; the mind begging for some point of reference;

the heart pleading to know whether the imagery was real again or just another horrid nightmare.

"Holy shit!" she blurted out painfully as she crashed into a wall and dropped to the carpet.

Her eyes wide as silver dollars, Kasey looked quickly around, still disoriented, and slowly began to realize that she was in her own home. She sat breathing short stabs of breath through swollen lips. Her tongue felt like it had been stepped on.

Sam moved cautiously toward Kasey and sniffed with great initial interest at her filthy clothes. It took him only a moment to realize that he would be happier in the chair by the coffee table: the new smells were not interesting after all—they were just plain awful.

Kasey rubbed her eyes with the palms of her hands, intending to brush the sleep and stringy hair from her face. The moment the battered palms met the bruised and abraded cheeks, she thought she would come out of her skin; a sharp pain burned where she had touched her left eyebrow, and her eyes began to water.

She looked toward the bathroom.

It was time to assess the damage and begin repairs.

❖

Kasey threw her stinking dirt-, sweat-, and urine-soaked clothes into the washer and dumped in the Tide. She studied the water, with its blue and white bubbles beginning to form on one side, and decided to add more powder. A lot more.

She set the dial to "heavy duty" and then stood naked in front of the full-length mirror on the hall closet door to have a look. With her long auburn hair pulled back and clipped, the body that was fully revealed looked like it had been thrown from a speeding train: the bridge of her nose was scraped from brow to tip; both eyes were swollen and the left one had a laceration running diagonally through the brow; her chin was scuffed, creating two dime-size abrasions about a quarter-inch apart; and her left cheek had a nasty-looking array of scratches that ran from its high point below the eye to her chin line just below the ear.

Everywhere, purple and black blotches were beginning to surface, ringed in unnatural shades of yellow. But, despite a face that ached every time she moved one of its many muscles, and ribs that felt like they'd been kicked by a mule, it was the palms of her hands that hurt the most: each had a series of cuts from fingertips to wrists. She vaguely remembered falling forward on the gravel road when her legs had given out, but the collision itself remained lost in a maze of confused images. Apparently, her hands had managed to prevent more serious facial damage, but had paid the price for their heroism.

Donna's exploding face began to form slowly in front of her, in thin air, like a three-dimensional hologram. She blinked it quickly away, but knew it would not be the last time she would have to banish the ghastly visage.

Kasey could not remember another time in her life when she had felt as helpless and out of control as she did now, a hellish moment that appeared to possess no end to its rationing of pain. She sank to the closed toilet lid and rested an arm and her forehead against the cool sink. Hot water ran noisily in the tub. "Sam," she called softly, her voice about to break.

The faithful pet appeared almost as if by magic.

"There you are, old boy." Kasey lifted Sam and held him against her bare chest, rubbing his face gently as she spoke. "We've got a hell of a problem, you and I. No job. Bill collectors. And now . . ."

Kasey found that she could not even speak of it. She just let her words taper off as if the thought had vanished.

It had not.

Each time an image of the event would try to surface, she would struggle to banish it to a hiding place in her memory. Sam looked up at her as if to ask why she had stopped talking. He liked her to talk to him. He did not understand the sudden silence and grew bored when the rubbing stopped. He vanished as quickly as he had appeared.

Kasey tried not to cry, but the tears slipped easily past closed lids. No matter how tightly she pressed them together, the liquid pain managed to escape.

She lowered herself into the hot, still water.

Twice over the next hour, as the water began to cool around her body, she added more hot, working the knob skillfully with the toes of her right foot: it required less effort than sitting up and using her throbbing hands.

❖

No longer smelling of death, Kasey's mind slowly began to relax a bit, allowing the body to follow its lead. A wave of hunger burned in her belly, and reminded her that, despite all that had happened, the mysterious process of healing—physically *and* emotionally—had already begun.

Carefully, respectful of her sore hands, she dug through the pantry shelves, setting item after item on the counter, in search of something that struck her fancy. She had no idea what it might be, but she knew she'd recognize it when she saw it.

Sam loved this part—it had to do with food.

As Kasey sat curled up on the couch, munching graham crackers filled with crunchy peanut butter and gooey marshmallow cream and trying to decide how to tell the police about last night, the one phone in the apartment began to ring.

The sudden shattering of peaceful silence made her jump.

The sound was coming from the bedroom at the end of the short hall; she had left the portable phone on the bed when she left for work the day before and hadn't given it a thought since.

It's funny, she considered, *how insignificant some previously essential things become when you are suddenly served an ultimate dose of reality.*

She popped a cracker into her mouth and strolled slowly, painfully, toward the annoying noise. She answered it on the seventh ring with a hesitant and soft, "Hello."

"Kasey?" came the impatient voice from the other end.

It was Cal, the last person she wanted to hear from.

Her desire to submit to him had not grown with the events of the last twenty-one hours. "What do you want, Cal?"

"Hey, I'm glad I caught you. I've been calling since yesterday afternoon. Why didn't you answer your phone?"

She gave no response and offered no explanation for her absence.

Cal waited until it was obvious that he was going to have to do this without her help. "Well, anyway, I just wanted to apologize for being a little forward with you at work yesterday. It was . . . well"—he chose his words carefully—". . . insensitive of me."

Kasey could tell the apology was difficult and unnatural for him. If not for last night, it would have been quite enjoyable.

"Insensitive?" she grumbled disbelievingly, amazed by his choice of words.

He let it pass.

"You are coming in today . . . so we can . . . well . . . so we can talk about this, aren't you?" Kasey heard him swallow hard. She wished the can of green beans had been a sledgehammer.

Indignation began to swell deep within her.

"I don't know, Cal. I hadn't thought much about work to tell you the truth. I've had a lot on my mind." She knew she could not wait on customers with her face as scratched as it was and her hands hurting as they did, regardless of how much he wanted her to come in, or how badly she could use the money.

"You sound funny, Kasey. Is everything all right?"

All right? Other than having witnessed another woman get raped and brutally murdered, and having laid in the weeds half the night covered in piss and mosquitoes? You mean, is everything all right other than that, *you arrogant ass?*

She swallowed hard, forcing the lump of anger back down her throat. "No, Cal, everything is *not* all right."

With that one simple statement, her battered mind erased the line of reality between Cal and Joeyboy. "As a matter of fact, Mr. Hardt, my attorney has advised me not to speak with you until your own attorney, and the attorney for Leonard's, have each prepared a formal response on the matter of our forthcoming sexual harassment lawsuit and are ready to talk settlement, or better still, ready to go to *trial!*"

The rapid flow of thoughts was barely formed into coherent sentences when they sprang from her mouth. She had no attorney, didn't even know one personally. She did know, however, despite the lack of forethought, that her words would have a profound effect on Leonard's corporate darling, Mr. Calvin S.—for Scumbag!—Hardt.

She waited.

Dead silence.

Kasey wandered back down the hall toward the livingroom, the phone pressed lightly against her ear.

"Attorney? Sexual harassment? Trial? You've got to be kidding me, Riteman!"

Kasey didn't utter another sound, knowing instinctively that the first person who spoke lost.

Now, he waited.

An interminable moment passed at his end as Cal saw his twelve-year career vaporizing before his eyes. He could picture *Hard Copy* storming into the restaurant—his restaurant—during the Saturday evening dinner rush, with their damn cameras and lights blazing like cannons. The image made his forehead break out in little beads of sweat. He started to shout, but forced himself to remain calm. None of the other girls had ever reacted this way. Jesus Christ!, his enraged brain shrieked, what a damn bitch!

Cal took a controlled breath: "I'll tell you what, Kasey, I can see that you're upset. You could probably do with a little rest. Why not take tomorrow . . . uh . . . I mean, the rest of the week off? I'll tell the bookkeeper you're on sick leave. I'll personally approve the time off—with pay, and a full share of the tip pool, of course," he quickly added. "When you get in next Monday, after a restful week, we'll talk a bit, just you and I. How does that sound?"

He could not comprehend a woman reacting this way. What he wanted to do was strangle her, not negotiate with her.

His pathetic, cheapskate bargaining and feigned humility was not at all what Kasey wanted to hear.

Now she was mad.

"Do you think you can buy your way out of a multi-million dollar sexual harassment lawsuit with a few measly dollars of my own damned money!?"

She wanted nothing more to do with this man today.

"I'll tell you what, Calvin"—he hated being called Calvin—"I suggest you call your attorney *and* the home office. Tell them you've been a bad boy, because I'm sure as hell gonna tell them!"

Her voice reached a crescendo with her final angry words.

She stabbed the Off button with her index finger as hard as she could, hoping to underscore the unbelievable contempt she felt.

She threw the phone at the couch and dropped into its cushions. Sam darted behind the chair by the window, staring back at her with guarded attention.

"Not bad, huh, boy? How'd you like the part about the lawyer and the million bucks? Nice touches, don't you think? You could hear ole Cal quaking in his boots." She grinned broadly, feeling like she had just slain a dragon; dressed only in frayed gym shorts and a cut-off undershirt which barely hung below her breasts, the battered body added a touch of battlefield authenticity to the illusion. "I bet that burns the roux at the home office, huh?"

The last thought was only half spoken, and tapered off to a whisper.

For a moment, just a brief moment, she thought about what she would do with a million dollars. The image dissolved before she allowed it to take shape; it wasn't in the cards for her to be rich. Of life's many uncertainties, that one fact seemed etched in stone.

Kasey leaned back, folded her sore legs across each other, yoga style, and stuffed a throw pillow between her thighs. "What a total putz he is," she muttered.

She turned on the TV, but its mindless afternoon drone brought on an instant headache. She silenced it and stared motionlessly at the light slipping past the closed miniblinds.

Sam curled into a tight little ball on the chair and drifted back to sleep, indifferent to the phone which continued to ring unanswered.

Kasey knew it was not Cal who had her tied in knots. The woman's silent plea for help deafened her to every other sound in the apartment.

❖

The gleaming sedan was parked with its rear bumper just beyond the corrugated tin door that had been swung down, sealing it inside the old metal building. There had been barely enough room for it in the shed, but when a long, rusted work table was moved toward one wall, it squeezed in. It could not be seen from the outside. For that matter, the old building itself—abandoned and forgotten for nearly two decades—was barely visible, even by air. The dirt road leading to it was overgrown from lack of traffic, and the trees near the building—not pruned since the deep budget cuts of the late seventies—had created a scruffy canopy over its round tin roof. It stood more than a mile from the closest paved road and hadn't been used officially since the CSX Railroad discontinued use of its nearby spur in early 1980. Before that, it existed to cut rails to length and provide welding repair on box and flat cars.

Today, it was a chop shop for stolen cars; its latest victim: Donna Stanton's pearl white Cadillac Seville.

"What does he want us to do with the chassis when we're done stripping it?" Slammer asked the other man as he wiped the sweat from his tattooed skull with a dingy towel.

It had been less than four hours since work had begun in earnest by the pair, and already the car had yielded a generous cache of marketable goods: AM/FM radio with cassette, CD changer, leather seats, four perfect doors with electric locks and windows, cellular phone, radar detector, electric fuel pump, magnesium alloy wheels with new Michelin radials, and the highly prized fuel-injected Northstar engine with its automatic four-speed overdrive transmission. The money would be good, and it was theirs alone to enjoy, a perk for a job well done.

The car parts did not, however, represent full payment for the neat and efficient way in which they had disposed of Stanton, and, when combined with the money she had withdrawn from her bank, as well as her wealth of fine jewelry, had made for a very profitable venture, indeed. Better still, no one knew of the cash or jewelry but the two of them.

"Just make certain there are no damn serial numbers left on the frame or underbody before we move it, not even the hidden ones. You know where they are. Cut 'em all out with the torch. When we're done, we're supposed to dump what's left in the Tennessee River. I figure we'll drop it just south of Paris Landing. If they ever do find it, they'll never be able to identify it as hers." Joeyboy stopped working and slumped into one of the leather bucket seats that had come from the Cadillac. Slammer took the other one, following Joeyboy's lead to stop working for a while.

"Hey, man, you haven't told me what you did with the bitch. How'd you do her?" He stared with prurient interest at his buddy.

"How do you think, butthead?" Joeyboy looked incredulously at his grinning companion, and raised his eyebrows twice in rapid succession with a twisted smile.

"Oh, shit, man! How close'd you get?" Slammer leaned forward, excited by the thought.

"I don't know . . . maybe a foot . . . less." Joeyboy pretended not to know, but was proud of the fact that he'd practically been able to put the shotgun in Stanton's ear without having been heard or seen.

It had not been the first time and he was sure it would not be the last. He enjoyed his work.

"Oh, shit, man, that's bad! That's really bad!" Slammer stomped his heavy boots on the concrete floor. "She see it coming?"

"Hell, no. Had her back to me. I told her I was taking her home."

"Oh, shit, man! You're absolutely the fucking best." Slammer leaned back in his seat, taking a moment to savor the grisly scene his mind was painting. A demented look swept across his face and his smile vanished. "You get some first?"

"What do you think, fool? Like, I'm gonna pass up a sweet piece of ass like that, right? What are you, touched in the head or something?" He slid a Camel between his lips and flicked his old Zippo, producing a broad yellow flame.

"Goddammit, man, I knew it! You said you were just gonna pop her and plant her. Why the hell didn't you let me fuck her while she was here? She was such a fine bitch, man, finest I've ever seen." Slammer was visibly angered at having missed the opportunity to have sex with such a beautiful and refined woman.

"Right, Mister Brains, and spook her for good before she told me where the tapes were stashed. That would've been real cool, fool. I guess that's why the old man put me in charge of this deal, huh, Lizard-Head?"

"Yeah, well what if the bitch lied to you, man?"

"Not a chance in hell. She was scared out of her wits and, besides, I got her to trust me. Bitches never lie when they trust you. That's why you can fuck 'em over so easy. I know where she hid the tapes all right, I'll bet your life on it." Joeyboy grinned and blew smoke directly in the face of his friend.

Slammer sat defiantly without batting an eye and then smiled broadly. He would get over it; the two had been through a lot together, and there would be other opportunities. Still, the thought of having missed out on Donna Stanton would trouble him for most of the day.

He changed the subject. "How'd everything go? Anybody get nosy?"

"Naw, man. Just the lovely little lady and myself. It was almost romantic, moonlight and all that shit." He winked at his buddy, knowing it would piss him off. "Besides, we were too far off the road to be seen even if a car had come by. In fact, I didn't see another car until . . . I got all the way . . . to . . ." Joeyboy hesitated as an image, as faint as an unfamiliar form standing across a fog-shrouded lake, tried to push its way to the front of his mind.

"What, man?" Slammer asked, unwrapping a piece of Juicy Fruit gum.

"It's nothing, just . . ."

"Just *what?*"

"I don't know, something I saw, I think."

"You think? When?"

"When I was leaving the orchard, about a half-mile or so from the old gate, you know, back toward Columbia." The apparition remained indistinct, unable to convince the brain to work its image enhancement and bring it into conscious focus.

"Well, what the fuck was it, man? A person? You think someone might have seen you leaving the place?" The thought of this unsettled Slammer, even more than the thought of having missed his chance with the woman.

"It wasn't nothing. Relax. I mean, I didn't *see* anything, you know, see it with my eyes, and no one saw me. It was just a funny feeling I got when I was leaving."

"Maybe you were just scared. You know, having a case of the willies or some shit like that," Slammer chided.

"Fuck you, asshole. I ain't scared of shit and you know it. Ain't had the willies since I was three." Joeyboy rose.

He spoke the truth, for Slammer had never met a less fearful soul in his life, even among the hard-cases and nut-cases of the many prisons in which he'd been a guest for much of his adult and adolescent life. When it came to fear, Joeyboy's response was always the same: action, and action usually meant that the person responsible for that unwanted feeling was soon granted an early release from the struggles of life.

"Let's finish this thing. I'm ready to hit the club and down some brews. This is way too much like a real job to suit me," Joeyboy barked, flicking his cigarette toward his friend's face.

Slammer, having hung around Joeyboy for years, anticipated the move and blocked the oncoming butt with a hand. The glowing red coal created a shower of sparks as it glanced off the leather-tough skin.

He stood beside his buddy as Joeyboy bent over the right fender, working to remove the brake booster and master cylinder. "Okay, smart guy, so where'd she hide the sons-a-bitches?"

❖

Kasey studied the keypad of the portable phone. She had been looking at it for nearly an hour without having pressed a single button. She knew she had to tell the police—*wanted* to tell the police—but each time she listened to her own rendition of the events leading up to her being in the weeds by the barbed-wire fence at the exact moment of the woman's murder, it sounded more and more ludicrous.

The last thing she wanted was for the events of last night to invade her life any more than they had already.

She felt truly sorry for the woman, but had no desire to be implicated in her death. In her own mind, the crazy story that began with Cal's sexual advances—which he would deny—and ended with a stuck lug nut that she strangely couldn't loosen until *after* innocently witnessing a murder, wouldn't sound convincing to a first year law student, to say nothing of the experienced D.A. of Davidson County.

She tapped the side of the cordless phone with a broken fingernail and tried to make up her mind.

When the phone suddenly rang in her hand, Kasey almost pitched it in the air.

Sam looked up from his spot a few feet away—atop a crocheted afghan—and decided, finally, that his mistress had lost her mind. He turned his back on the insanity and tried to get some well-needed rest.

Kasey watched the dial lights flicker with each ring and finally answered it.

"Hello."

"Kasey?" It was Brenda Poole.

"Hi, Brenda." Despite hearing from her friend for the first time in the toughest twenty-four hours of her life, Kasey did not feel talkative. She had thought of calling Brenda a dozen times since awakening, but each time she had reached for the phone, the memories of the previous night left her mouth dry and unable to form the words that would adequately convey the horror—to anyone, even her best friend, a person with whom she had been able to share everything before now. The image of the woman dying, only moments after silently petitioning Kasey for help, left Kasey feeling responsible for her death. She could have and should have done more than just lie there like a scared rabbit, protecting her own life at the expense of the stranger's. The constant admonition was almost deafening in her mind's ear.

"Are you okay, Kasey?" Brenda's voice rang with concern.

Kasey began to cry. She took a slow, deep breath, careful not to be heard on the other end. "Yeah, I'm fine, Brenda. Just stressed out, that's all. I just got off the phone with Cal." For the moment at least, a partial truth was better than a lie.

Or the whole truth.

"What a son-of-a-bitch that bastard Cal is. I still can't believe you decked him with that can, though. None of us can. Oh, my God, Kasey! It's all over the restaurant. Hell, even the valet guys were talking about it by the end of the night." Brenda was on one of her rolls. Kasey placed the phone against her chest and let her talkative friend ramble for a while.

"Brenda," she interrupted.

Brenda stopped in mid sentence. "What?"

"I've got a hell of a headache. Do you mind if we talk in the morning?"

"Aren't you coming in tonight?" she asked, surprised by Kasey's last words.

"Cal offered me a couple of days off and I'm going to take them, kind of just lie around for a while. Maybe go shopping. I don't think I could face him at the moment." A lie; Kasey could take anything Cal—most men—had to give and return it with interest when she wanted to, and Brenda knew it, but it was good enough to buy her a little time before an extended conversation with her friend would be required.

"That's probably a good idea, Kase. You want me to go shopping with you?"

Kasey wanted company even less than she wanted conversation. She thought about her damaged face and knew that she couldn't go anywhere for several days yet, not without having to explain that, no, she was not the victim of domestic abuse or a motorcycle accident. It didn't matter, though. She was in no mood to venture anywhere beyond the safety of her own walls. "No, thanks. I might not even go."

"You sure? I can be there in fifteen minutes if you change your mind."

"I'm sure. I just want to be alone for a while. Thanks, though."

"No prob. Listen, if you need any money, anything, you'll call me—right?"

Kasey grinned at her friend's loyalty and generosity. Brenda had even less money than she did, but would have gladly given up her last cent for the asking.

"Right. I'll talk to you later."

"You know where I'll be."

"Yep. Thanks."

Kasey switched off the phone and set it on the arm of the couch. Having talked with her closest friend, even for the short time they had spoken, was enough to convince her that now wasn't the time to call the police. She would fall apart under the questioning and the scrutiny. The dead woman, whoever she was, wasn't going anywhere, and she could just as easily give them Joeyboy's name tomorrow, or the day after tomorrow, as today.

The lame rationalization didn't sit well with Kasey. She knew she was lying to herself; what kept her from the police was the mounting fear in her heart, the fear that he would come for her.

She reached for Sam and pulled him into her lap. They stayed curled together on the couch until long after the open blinds went dark, and the only light to enter the livingroom crept down the hall from the bedside lamp.

❖

By Wednesday morning, Kasey felt a little more like her old self, despite the tenderness in both palms and the very sore spot just above her left eye. She had fallen asleep on the couch Tuesday night, Sam cradled in her arms, and had slept until Brenda's call at seven A.M. She had managed to get off the phone without having to actually answer any of Brenda's ceaseless questions about her mental state, and without having to agree to meet her at the mall.

No sooner had she hung up the phone than a restlessness overcame her, almost propelling her from her self-imposed lethargy. She knew that if she kept busy, she wouldn't have to think about Monday night. She had things to do, could find things to do; she would tell anyone who asked about her strange array of injuries that she was a clumsy jogger. Screw 'em. Kasey now needed to escape the prison in which she had taken refuge almost as badly as she had needed its security thirty-two hours before. Her mind wandered and she found it hard to focus her thoughts. Always, images from hell tried to force their way through to her conscious mind. It made her weary just keeping them in check. She called Brenda back and asked her to meet her at the food court at the mall. Brenda was ecstatic.

Over a large slice of meat-lovers pizza and a Dr Pepper from Sbarro Pizzeria, after explaining to her friend that she had fallen while jogging to release her pent-up anger (gratefully, Brenda bought the explanation without question), Kasey related the conversation she'd had with Cal on Tuesday afternoon, and Brenda suddenly understood why he had remained sequestered in his office all during her shift. The exchange of stories about their repugnant boss brought tears of laughter from both women, the first laughter Kasey had enjoyed in days. It felt heavenly.

Brenda had been delighted to report that the absence of Cal's ever-watchful eye had been a pleasant change at the restaurant, even after only one day, and delivered a collective "thank you" from the rest of the staff.

After superficially exploring the wonderfully agreeable thought of actually suing Calvin S. Hardt for sexual harassment—a conversation that had engendered a second bout of laughter—the two continued to talk about nothing in particular, as only good friends can. In the almost three hours that passed before they parted company, not one syllable was mentioned by Kasey about the events of Monday night.

As soon as she left the mall, Kasey stopped by Crest Honda on Murfreesboro Road to purchase a new center emblem for her right rear hubcap—she was certain she'd lost it in her haste to change the flat Monday night—but almost balked when the man behind the counter told her it was going to run her twelve dollars.

She held the small disk in her hands. "Twelve bucks!? For that little bitty thing!?" she complained. Her ire did not help to lower the price of the emblem, but when it was installed in the parking lot, bringing all four wheels back to their original appearance, she was glad she'd spent the money. The old girl had been good to her over the years, the least she deserved was a set of matching shoes.

The wiper blades would still have to wait.

Finally, Kasey reluctantly headed back home, almost afraid to be alone with herself. She knew the images would come as soon as she stopped filling her hours with trivial chores and simpleminded activities.

Though normally hating ironing, today it seemed soothing and easy. Her beleaguered mind appreciated the break. The Oprah Winfrey show droned softly in the background as Kasey moved the steam iron mindlessly across a pair of indigo-colored jeans, pressing the same spot four or five times.

For the moment, Monday seemed like a lifetime ago. She had almost convinced herself that she could keep the bad images at bay by sheer willpower alone. In time, it would become second nature, as it had after her parents' death.

Kasey suddenly found herself hungry again, a phenomenon that didn't upset Sam in the least. As she walked toward the couch, a grilled ham-and-cheese in hand and Sam at her heels, Channel 9 suddenly flashed a photograph of a beautiful woman on the screen with the lone word: MISSING, written beneath it.

Kasey froze, and stared in disbelief at the picture.

It was *her.*

In a heartbeat, it all came back, as if it had just happened moments before. Kasey sat slowly, setting the small plate on the carpet at her feet. She never took her eyes off the screen as she dug for the remote control that she had tucked between the couch cushions and quickly raised the volume enough to be heard. Her stomach twitched nervously and her heart thumped.

The photo of the woman, no longer occupying the full screen, now rested over the left shoulder of the news reporter, Brandie Mueller, as she spoke:

"Donna Louise Stanton, 33, of Nashville, was reported missing early this morning by her half-sister, Laurie Ann Latham, also of Nashville. The two shared a home in Belle Meade, where they had lived for the past three years.

"Ms. Latham alerted Metro police when her sister had not phoned after suddenly disappearing from their home Monday afternoon, something Ms. Latham insists is entirely out of character for her sister.

"Metro police have refused to speculate whether foul play is suspected, and are just beginning a preliminary investigation into the matter, according to Metro Detective Lieutenant, Pete Vanover . . ."

The photo of Stanton's face changed to a full-length picture of her in a stunning low-cut evening gown standing between two men, one wearing a western-style tuxedo and the other in a more conventional tux. Kasey recognized both men.

". . . Viewers may recall seeing Ms. Stanton in a previous Channel 9 report, when she attended Governor Buddy Williams' inaugural ball in the company of country music superstar, Rocky McCall. The two were reportedly engaged at that time, but later separated amid a barrage of media publicity. McCall, on tour with his band in Scotland, could not be reached for comment.

"According to an unnamed source, after the breakup, Ms. Stanton spent much of her time with other celebrities and executives from the country music world, as well as numerous politicians and influential businessmen from across the state.

"More on Donna Stanton's sudden, and seemingly inexplicable, disappearance on our ten o'clock report.

"As always, stay tuned to Channel 9 for all the news from around the Metroplex—and around the globe.

"This is Brandie Mueller reporting live from the Channel 9 studios."

Kasey pressed the Mute button and fell back against the couch. She now knew why the woman had seemed so familiar to her in the orchard: on at least two occasions while she was on duty, Donna Stanton had eaten at the restaurant. Once, Kasey recalled, with a record producer known for dating all the beautiful women in Nashville, and the other time, with a man she had not seen in the restaurant before or since.

Kasey recalled the photograph she had just seen of Donna Stanton, beautiful, stylish, proud—*alive.* She remembered the woman from the orchard, the same woman, humiliated, afraid, begging to be taken home. It made her sick to her stomach and she dashed to the bathroom, her mouth and eyes watering.

When she returned, Sam was steadily at work on the ham-and-cheese sandwich, concluding it must have been left there for him. Kasey collected the plate and the remains of the crust and tossed them into the sink; her appetite had vanished and Sam didn't need to eat the whole thing, despite his certain disagreement had he been asked. She phoned Brenda. Wednesday was the only day of the week Brenda didn't work.

"Hello," her friend answered before the first ring had finished.

"Brenda, you been watching Oprah?"

"That's a dumb question. Don't tell me you've been watching. You never watch shows like that. Did you see what that fool on there was wearing. I'm a woman and I wouldn't . . ."

"Brenda!" Kasey interrupted.

"What?"

"Did you see that thing on the missing woman?"

"You mean the Stanton woman, the one who ran around with all those country music stars?"

"Yes, *that* one," Kasey quipped. Sometimes her friend was a little slow.

"What about her?" Brenda asked, trying to listen to Kasey and her talk show at the same time.

"Did you recognize her? From the restaurant. I mean, have you seen her there before?"

Brenda hesitated for a moment. Then: "Oh, yeah! I knew I had seen her somewhere. That's creepy, her being in our place and now missing." Suddenly, the TV was of little interest. "You think maybe somebody abducted her? One of those rich guys she was always seeing? Maybe one of 'em got pissed off at her for leaving him or something. Maybe it was Rocky McCall, you think? You know she was engaged to him a couple of years back. I'll bet that he's only pretending to be out of the country . . . or . . . maybe she ran off with him and they're living—"

"Brenda!" Kasey never ceased to be amazed at the endless directions her friend's mind could take. But despite Brenda's vivid imagination, she would be shocked, speechless for once in her life, if she knew the actual truth.

"What?" Brenda responded almost with a snap, having no idea why Kasey had interrupted her.

"I just wanted to know if you knew the guy she came in with about a month ago. A scary-looking guy about fifty or sixty. Angry eyes. They sat near the bar I think, but I'm not certain."

Brenda thought again for a moment. "Nope. Don't remember seeing him. Might have been off that day. I only remember her being in the bar with that producer guy from RCA or some other big record label, but that guy was nowhere near fifty, I don't think. Why the interest in her, Kase?"

"Oh, it's nothing. I just thought you might remember that other guy, that's all." For a reason that was not even consciously clear to her, Kasey hoped Brenda might know who the man with angry eyes had been. It didn't matter, Kasey decided: the connection was probably just in her head.

Brenda persisted: "You think the old guy had something to do with her disappearance, don't you?" Brenda was on the edge of her chair. She even went so far as to mute the television. "You gonna call the cops and tell them what you know?"

"Jesus, Brenda, I don't know anything. It was just a question. You've got to turn those soaps off and get back to the real world, girl." As soon as she said the words, Kasey realized how ludicrous they sounded coming from her; what had happened in her own world in the last few days had surpassed anything she'd seen on daytime television.

"They are the real world to me, Kasey, don't you understand? Nothing exciting ever happens to people like you and me. I'll bet you a buck that right now Donna Stanwick is sitting on a beach in the Bahamas soaking up rays while her poor sister worries her head off."

"Stanton."

"What?"

"Her name was Stanton, not Stanwick."

"Whatever."

Kasey shook her head. "Get back to Oprah. I'll talk to you later, okay?"

"Later," replied Brenda, and switched off the phone.

❖

Joeyboy and Slammer finished for the day and locked the old tin shop behind them. Their Harleys, one a few years old and the other new and still gleaming from its first wax job, were waiting at the rear of the shed where they had been parked since mid morning. Slammer quickly strad-dled the older of the two and it fired without hesitation. He nailed the throttle and roared off down the gravel road, attempting to cover Joeyboy in a shower of dust and loose rocks kicked up by his fat rear tire. The intended victim of this never-ending game of one-upsmanship leaned hard to the left and twisted his own throttle at the same time, narrowly missing the hail of stone missiles, each intended to knock a little of the new from his bike.

Despite the mandatory helmet law in Tennessee, both men rode with nothing on their heads but a pair of mirrored Oakley Blades—the helmet law was seen as a violation of their inalienable right to ride free. They were seldom stopped, however, as their normal routes rarely took them through areas that were well patrolled. Side by side they blazed down the black ribbons of back road that led to the topless bar that served as their second home.

❖

As Slammer stuffed a badly wrinkled dollar bill into the G-string of the latest dancer to take the stage, rubbing his free hand suggestively along the back and side of her thigh and then up across her buttocks, Joeyboy poured down the last of his second beer. He would finish a dozen more before leaving with his stripper du jour around two A.M. It was the same ritual practically every night: drink beer, smoke a little dope, and party with the nude dancers.

Today, there would be the slightest deviation from the normal routine; it would take Joeyboy away from his entertainment for only a minute.

He squinted in the bad light of the dark bar and tried to see the face of his watch. The colorful plastic gels taped over the spotlights that illuminated the stage provided less than ideal reading light—they were intended for another purpose altogether. Few of the patrons spent time reading anything other than beer bottle labels.

Joeyboy maneuvered his wrist until the hands of the dial caught the light: it was approaching six P.M. straight up.

He stood and walked to the only pay phone in the small building, around the corner from the bar, between the restrooms. As he reached the phone, he saw that it was already in use. The man was unknown to him, though it wouldn't have mattered to Joeyboy if he had been a longtime acquaintance. He read his watch again more quickly this time: the lights at this end of the room were not as heavily filtered as the lights painting the stage.

He had less than a minute.

"Hey, what the fuck you think you're doing!?" came the outraged response from the man on the phone as Joeyboy snatched it from his hand and shoved it into its cradle. The man had been looking the other away, leaning against the wall, and turned quickly, ready and willing to underscore his surprise and displeasure with a fist.

"I'm using the phone, asshole. You have a problem with that?" Joeyboy made no move toward the stranger, didn't so much as raise a finger. He simply stood beside the phone, arms relaxed at his side, chewing animatedly on a wooden toothpick.

The other man, both fists tightly knotted, took one brief moment to look into the face of his opponent; it was long enough. In that scant second, the self-preserving decision to reconsider his actions was made. It was not as much a conscious choice of the mind as a decision made by the soul in defense of the life it had been entrusted to preserve. Something in the blond man's quiet, relaxed face told the stranger that allowing his fist to find its mark would be a mistake. A serious mistake. Just below the surface, amid the subtle lines, the sun-baked skin, and the almost platinum hair, death lurked—unadulterated, conscienceless death.

"Uh . . . no . . . sorry, man. It's all yours." The words were mumbled almost apologetically as he withdrew. Joeyboy turned his back defiantly, not noticing or caring that the other man hastily left the bar.

The phone rang almost immediately.

"*Iiiiiiit's Johnny,*" Joeyboy answered sarcastically.

"They weren't there, goddammit!" the other man spat excitedly.

"You look under the sink in the master bath, in back like I told you?" Joeyboy hated the man on the other end and didn't give a damn about his precious tapes. He'd been paid in full for getting rid of the Stanton woman—the tapes were the other man's problem entirely as far as he was concerned.

"Of course I looked under the sink, you dumb fuck! The only thing under there was a goddamn gun stuffed between a couple of the towels!"

Joeyboy grinned, quite pleased he'd decided not to take the woman back to her place to get the tapes. Once again, fate had smiled on the life he had no doubt was charmed: death always eluded him as surely as it relentlessly found others. "Well, that's a real bitch, man. Sorry, but that's where the whore told me they'd be." He studied the wall art, his mind more on a hastily scribbled poem he had not seen there before than on the irritating voice in his ear.

"Yeah? Well, she lied, you stupid shit! The old man's going ballistic to get the goddamn things. He's been on my case for two days straight, and now you hand me *this* crap! You are a seriously dumb shit, you know it, Joey? You should have *never* capped the woman before I had the goddamn tapes in my hands. I *want* those tapes and I want them now!"

Joeyboy, hearing only what he wanted to hear of the tedious conversation, laughed out loud when he'd finished reading the lascivious limerick. He was ready to get back to the dancer he'd been working on for the last hour: Lacey, Laura—something starting with an L.

He tossed the toothpick aside and lit a fresh Camel, blowing the smoke noisily into the mouthpiece. "Well, in that case, Mr. smart-guy detective, I suggest you find 'em yourself. That's the first thing they teach you little bastards in detective school, isn't it? To detect things? So go detect, dickhead. I'm busy."

He jammed the phone into its cradle and reread the poem, committing it to short-term memory. Slammer would get a hoot out of it.

So would what's-her-name.

EIGHT

The six P.M. news story of Donna Louise Stanton's disappearance was considerably more detailed than the teaser report had been. Kasey sat on the livingroom floor studying the screen, the morning paper scattered at her feet. There had been no mention of the story in the *Banner*, the missing person's report having been filed by Laurie Latham after the presses had run, and though Kasey had suspected as much, she couldn't resist buying one at the Mapco Express below her apartment complex and scanning its pages. Just in case.

Kasey had found herself pacing the floor for the last hour, nervously awaiting the evening newscast. At least a dozen times since four o'clock, she had flipped through the channels, hoping to catch the story on one of the other local channels. She had learned nothing more.

Frustrated and impatient, she had waited. As soon as Brandie Mueller, news anchor for Channel 9, appeared on-camera with the photo of Donna Stanton over her shoulder again, Kasey ran the volume up another few notches:

"Earlier today, Channel 9 News reported to you on the mysterious disappearance of Donna Louise Stanton, the socialite from Nashville who was once engaged to country music superstar, Rocky McCall.

"Since that first report, Channel 9 has spoken with one of Stanton's neighbors, Mrs. Maggie Ketchum, who stated that Stanton appeared to be upset as she drove away from her home on Monday afternoon last. She has not been seen or heard from since.

"We have a report from Deb Jensen, taped earlier today at the Ketchum home in Belle Meade:

Jensen: "Mrs. Ketchum, what can you tell us about the strange and sudden disappearance of Donna Louise Stanton?"

Ketchum: "Well, it did seem a bit odd to me, her just driving off without so much as a howdy. She's usually the friendliest young lady, and always so polite. Why I remember—"

Jensen: "Did Ms. Stanton appear to be in an unusual hurry?"

Ketchum: "You know, I'd say she did at that. Just pitched her bags in the trunk of that big white Cadillac of hers, and off she went. Not the least bit of a 'hello' even when I—"

Jensen: *"Mrs. Ketchum, did your neighbor appear upset or distraught to you?"*

Ketchum: *"Well, I don't know that I'd say upset exactly, now that I've had some time to think about it. She was more like . . . in another world. Kind of distant, like her mind was elsewhere, but I wouldn't exactly say distraught. Usually, she would take the time to stop and admire my flowers. I've won Yard of the Month twice in—"*

Jensen: *"Do you have any idea why Ms. Stanton might have been in such a hurry to leave?"*

Ketchum: *"She was always coming and going, like a movie star. The Bahamas, Mexico. I think she even went to Italy once. I guess maybe she was just running late, her mind on wherever it was she was going. I've always wanted to go to—"*

Jensen: *"Thank you, Mrs. Ketchum." Then turning back to camera: "I see Detective Pete Vanover coming out of the Stanton house, now. I'll see if we can get a word with him."*

Jensen and cameraman move quickly toward Vanover's car: "Excuse me, Detective—Deb Jensen with Channel 9 News. Can you shed any light on Ms. Stanton's strange disappearance?"

Vanover: *"At this point, Ms. Jensen, I can't say that we're talking about a 'disappearance' here, at least not in the accepted sense of the word. It could well be nothing more than a simple case of Ms. Stanton having taken an unscheduled vacation, and not bothering to inform her sister."*

Jensen: *"So, you don't expect to find foul play of any kind involved in her disappearance?"*

Vanover: *"You keep using the word, disappearance, not I, and no, I don't. Her sister and I have made a cursory inspection. At least one suitcase is gone that we know of. A number of clothing items appear to have been taken as well, along with some personal things."*

Jensen: *"Personal things?"*

Vanover: *"You know, toothbrush, hair dryer. Also, according to the sister—"*

"Laurie Latham, the woman who filed the missing person's report?"

Vanover: *"That's correct. According to Ms. Latham, her sister also took some of her jewelry and her camera. Sounds to me like the lady just wanted to get away for a while."*

Jensen: *"Are we to assume then that the Nashville Metro Police are going to remove Ms. Stanton's name from the missing person's list?"*

Vanover: "Unless, and until, further information warrants otherwise, that is correct."

Jensen: "Thank you, Detective Vanover."

Jensen to camera: "Well, there you have it. What began as the sudden and inexplicable disappearance of one of Nashville's more celebrated faces, now appears to be nothing more than a simple case of getting away from it all.

"This is Deb Jensen, Channel 9 News."

"Getting away from it all! Christ, you mindless bimbo, you don't have a damned clue what's going on!" Kasey—now at full attention in front of the television—roared angrily at the reporter, as if the added volume of her words would somehow propel them through the picture tube, down the wires and airwaves leading to the station, and magically end up in Jensen's earpiece. "Dead is one hell of a way to get away from it all!"

She mashed the Off button and threw the remote control at the couch.

Kasey grabbed the first pen her fingers touched—from a Garfield coffee mug holding a variety of pens, pencils, and assorted paraphernalia on the kitchen counter—and scribbled down the detective's name. She had made up her mind.

Kasey flipped impatiently through the blue pages of the phone book and finally found what she believed to be the correct department: Davidson County Metropolitan Government, Metro Police, Detective Division, Homicide. She marveled at how well-hidden it was amid the endless montage of offices and departments, and was glad she hadn't needed to locate it while a homicidal maniac hammered at her bedroom door.

She jotted the phone number down on a piece of scrap paper, scribbled the words "homicide division" beside it, and took a deep breath.

It was time they learned the horrible truth about Donna Stanton.

And about Joeyboy.

As she pressed the seventh and final number she had written, an icy thought suddenly struck her. She quickly depressed the switch hook, canceling the call.

"Oh, Lord, that was close," she mumbled to Sam, realizing that, in her haste to inform the police of Stanton's assassination, she had almost inadvertently given them her full name, address, and phone number in the process. "Not a good plan, not a good plan at all," she scolded herself aloud, remembering that Nashville—all of Davidson County for that matter—used the Enhanced 911 System, providing each police and fire dispatcher and operator with all of the caller's relevant information even before the phone was picked up at the other end. If she was going to keep herself out of the inevitable circus of courtrooms, lawyers, police, and reporters that would irrevocably be spawned by the sensational news of Donna Stanton's grisly murder, she could not give her own name, or use her own phone. An image of Joeyboy wiping the blood and brain bits from his face, with less emotion than another man might wipe spaghetti sauce from his chin, suddenly formed on the wall before her. She blinked it away.

She cradled Sam against her chest with one arm while the phone dangled, silently, at the end of her free arm. She had to rethink her actions more carefully.

Kasey tried to remove the emotion from the events, and allow herself to think logically, weighing her own interests against the other woman's—someone who could never suffer any more of life's indignities. Donna Stanton would be no less dead, and Joeyboy no less guilty, whether she became involved or not. It would certainly be a great deal easier for her to make the call anonymously and then simply back away from the ensuing maelstrom, than to give her name and become hopelessly entangled, possibly implicated in the killing. Or worse still, the thought suddenly struck her with full impact, targeted by the killer. She knew that Joeyboy, as well as the men who had probably hired him, would not just sit around idly while she waited to go to trial to testify to what she had witnessed. She had to fight to keep more horrid images from forming. She was less successful than she would have wished. Perhaps if she just made the call, did what she knew she must do eventually, the images would stop.

Kasey laid Sam on the livingroom chair and dug around in the bottom of her purse. With a pair of quarters, the scrap of paper with name and number on it, and her keys in hand, she locked her door and darted across her apartment complex to the Mapco Express at the corner of Murfreesboro Road and Glengarry, the same convenience store where she had purchased the newspaper earlier in the day.

The pay phones at the Mapco Express were located on the front side of the store, to the left of the wide glass entrance, beside a neat double row of white propane tanks that were greedily consumed during spring and summer by weekend chefs with secret sauces and aprons that read, Kiss the Cook or Bar-B-Que Naked. Kasey was forced to wait several minutes to use the one phone that worked at the moment. The one beside it—the only other pay phone within sight—had a broken cord and no handset.

She folded her arms and leaned against the wall, bouncing her butt lightly, and impatiently, against the brick. She glared as three kids with skateboards made a call to a young girl during which each had to take his turn saying hello and detailing their plans for the day. She gave the last one a stern look hoping to speed things along. It worked, and their call quickly ended, though the boy with whom she had made full eye contact proudly and enthusiastically shot her the bird as he skated off across the parking lot with his buddies.

Her heart thudded beneath her shirt.

"Homicide. Lieutenant Vanover speaking" came the rich, authoritative voice as Detective Vanover picked up on the first ring.

Without speaking a word, Kasey immediately slammed the phone back into its cradle. She had not expected the man she was trying to reach to actually answer the phone. As silly as it seemed, she had counted on the time that usually exists between speaking with a receptionist and waiting for the other party to pick up to collect her thoughts.

She felt foolish, but consoled herself that when she called back, Vanover would have no way of knowing it had been she who had so rudely hung up.

She would give it a few minutes and try again.

Kasey waited. Waited, and practiced her speech. The plan was to blurt out the important details of Donna Stanton's murder and burial spot and then get the hell off the phone without a further word.

Silently, she mouthed the mock conversation.

Even in the indirect light of early evening, with a soft, temperate breeze blowing from the south, sweat poured down her back and between her breasts as if she were standing in the middle of an asphalt parking lot at noon in the middle of July; her palms perspired and she had to wipe them against her jeans. The salty moisture irritated the scratches that had not yet healed.

Kasey leaned her forehead against the chrome of the phone's wide square body and forced herself to be calm.

Just keep breathing slowly and deeply, she reminded herself. *Just like jogging.*

"You gonna use that thing, or make love to it?"

Kasey almost let out a scream and turned immediately toward the man's voice. "What?" she asked in a startled whisper, shaken by his unexpected appearance.

The man realized that he had frightened her and chose a less sarcastic approach. "I need to use the phone," he said with a slight pointing gesture. "How long you gonna be?"

Kasey backed quickly away, stepping off the walkway into the parking lot, and motioned for him to go ahead.

"Thanks," the man said, fishing for change and silently marveling at the woman's odd behavior. He was off in less than a minute, having been given directions to a nearby construction site by the party on the other end. Kasey watched him get into a dusty red truck and drive away.

Finally, with enough time having lapsed to comfortably distance herself from the caller who had hung up on the police, she dropped in her remaining quarter. She fumbled with the wrinkled scrap of paper and dialed the wrong number when she reversed the last two digits. With nervous, shaking fingers, she depressed the switch hook, redeposited the quarter which had thankfully dropped into the return slot, and then slowly entered the seven numbers again, making no mistake this time. Her heart stopped as the bell rang annoyingly in her ear.

"Detective Division, Sergeant Stark speaking."

"Lieutenant Vanover, please." She found herself trying to disguise her voice, as if Vanover would have known who she was merely by its sound. She grinned.

"Who wants him?" The words were abrupt but businesslike.

Kasey froze. *Jesus!* she thought. *Why does he need to know that? Wasn't he raised with any manners at all?* She hesitated. "Mary Jones," she blurted out before realizing how ludicrous it sounded.

"All right, Ms. Jones, I'll see if I can locate him."

Kasey knew the cop hadn't bought the name.

Detective Sergeant Brad Stark looked across the desk at his partner, and immediate superior, Detective Lieutenant Peter "Pete" Vanover, a tall, handsome man of thirty-nine, with sandy-brown hair and bright gray eyes. As the top graduate in his academy class fifteen years earlier, Vanover had made rank faster than his forty-three-year-old partner. Stark silently resented that fact, but understood that Vanover was a better detective, probably the best on the force, with a nearly photographic memory and a keen nose for things that simply didn't smell right. The men got along better than most.

Stark set the receiver in its base. "Call for you on line two, Pete. 'Mary Jones,' according to her, but that ain't her real name." He rested his elbows on the desk and yawned a bored yawn as Vanover signed a report he had been working on.

Vanover looked up, amused. "Mary Jones, huh? That's real original." He grinned and crushed his Marlboro in a glass ashtray that had no room for another butt. "She sound pretty?"

Stark shrugged his shoulders. "She sounds like a dame to me."

Vanover cleared his throat and pressed the blinking yellow button. "Ms. Jones, this is Lieutenant Vanover. How can I be of assistance?"

Kasey drew in a deep breath and began the half-memorized string of thoughts she prayed wouldn't be interrupted before she got them all out: "I just saw you on the six o'clock news, being interviewed by that reporter from Channel 9. You know, about Donna Stanton's disappearance. I've got some information about her I think you need to know."

A bead of sweat trickled down Kasey's chest. She hesitated only long enough to grab another breath. "She's not on vacation . . . she's . . ." Kasey almost couldn't get the words to come out; she squeezed her eyes shut and rocked back and forth at the end of the steel phone cord, the handset gripped tightly in both hands. "She's not on vacation," she repeated slowly, "she's . . . she's been murdered!"

The words almost burned as they slipped passed her lips. A tear ran down her cheek. The fireball engulfed the beautiful blond head and thunder rang in her ears. She felt nauseated.

Vanover kept the receiver tight against his ear while he turned the mouthpiece straight up. "Trace this!" he mouthed impatiently to Stark, who immediately put Vanover's demand into motion: it would be accomplished as soon as one call across the building could be placed. There was no mechanism for tracing calls in the Detective Division.

Stark dialed the number; he nodded to let his partner know it was underway.

"Ms. Jones, Mary, was it?" he asked, buying a few needed seconds.

"What?" Kasey mumbled, her mind's eye picturing the horrible night as if it were just now happening. The spoken words "she's been murdered" had evoked frightening and powerful emotions.

She turned rapidly when she felt Joeyboy standing behind her. It was only the wind moving a piece of paper slowly across the parking lot.

"I asked you if your name was Mary. That's what you told my partner, isn't it?" He looked across at Stark who gave him the signal to stretch it out: it wasn't the slowness of the electronic process, the digital data sent with each call placed could be attained in milliseconds; it was the bureaucracy of getting a trace initiated that required time. All traces had to originate at the switchboard where the incoming routing took place, and that was all the way across the expansive municipal building from the detectives' location.

"Yes, that's right," Kasey muttered. "Mary Jones." Her ears seemed to ring and she again had the feeling that someone was standing behind her. She spun around a second time; the only eyes she met were in her mind.

"Ms. Jones, that's quite a piece of news you've just dropped on my desk. I wonder if I could persuade you to come to Headquarters and tell me everything you know about Donna Stanton. I'm interested in learning how you came about this startling bit of information, if it is indeed true." He looked impatiently at Stark. The other detective scribbled quickly on a bright yellow Post-it Note, shoved it across to Vanover, and then grinned broadly, the satisfaction evident in his expression.

"How about it, Ms. Jones, would you be agreeable to meeting with me, since you alone seem to be privy to information we need to authenticate?"

Vanover pressed. He read the words Stark had written. *"Get a car there—now!"* he mouthed silently to the other detective.

Again, Stark placed the call.

Kasey—hearing little other than Donna's pleading words echoing endlessly in her ears—breathed deeply again and wiped the sweat from her forehead. "I can't . . . I have to go. Maybe I'll call you later." She wanted to hang up, but the phone remained locked in her hand.

What else did she want to say? Why hadn't she hung up? she wondered. All she had to do was set the phone down and walk away.

Her feet refused to move.

"No, Ms. Jones—Mary. Please don't hang up. I need you to talk with me for a moment. You obviously have something important to say and I'd like to hear what it is." Pete Vanover tried to sound as nonthreatening as he could, a friend simply extending a comforting hand to another friend.

"I can't. I'm sorry, but I can't come in. I have to go now," she rambled.

"At least stay at the Mapco Express and I'll meet you there."

Kasey froze.

Oh, God! she thought.

She remembered: of course, the enhanced 911 system! That's why she'd used a different phone in the first place. But it all seemed too quick, too real, too threatening when the detective mentioned her location by name. She realized the bastard had been playing her for more time while he probably had a car dispatched to her location.

It was time to run.

Without the slightest regard for Bell South's property, Kasey practically hurled the receiver at its cradle—wildly missing its slot—and bolted back across Glengarry toward her apartment.

Halfway across the street, at full stride, she found herself directly in the path of a dark blue Toyota which had slowed for a turn onto Murfreesboro. The driver, startled by the sudden appearance of a woman squarely in his lane, buried the brakes, producing screeching tires and thick rubber smoke. He had not reacted soon enough: the far right tip of his front bumper hit Kasey's right leg, sending her spiraling like a fallen figure skater onto a scruffy patch of grass at the road's shoulder. She narrowly missed a thick concrete light pole as she struck the ground beside it with a punishing thud.

By the time the driver was able to stop his aging Celica—a few feet ahead of the point of impact—and leap from his car to see if he had killed the crazy woman who had materialized out of thin air, she was nowhere to be seen.

Even with the painful limp from a shin that was beginning to throb, Kasey had made it to her third-floor sanctuary in less than two minutes.

She almost tore the curtains down snatching them closed; the miniblinds were quickly twirled shut, the deadbolt thrown.

She turned Sam's fat chair by the door around to face the window and dropped into it, massaging her leg with both hands and peering out toward the intersection below through the tiniest of cracks.

She knew they would be coming for her.

❖

Vanover and Stark climbed into their unmarked car and sped off in the direction of Murfreesboro Road and Glengarry. The short drive would take less than ten minutes, even in Friday traffic. Neither man spoke as they hurried toward the location that had been identified by their call-tracing system, a system which, though more sophisticated, was not unlike the one employed by most Caller-ID boxes found in many private homes.

In the parking lot of the Mapco Express, the closest patrol car that had been available for dispatch came to an abrupt stop, its front wheels almost touching the narrow walk bordering the pay phones. Both officers jumped out and began to search the area. Their target: a Caucasian woman, mid- to late twenties, probably alone, anywhere in the immediate vicinity of the store—the description had been Vanover's best guess, based on her voice, mannerisms, and his years of experience.

While one of the patrolmen took a look inside, questioning both the clerk and the only customer—a young man whose full attention was consumed by a video game—his partner whistled for the three kids on skateboards who were just crossing Glengarry in the direction of the store. He indicated for them to join him. The boys had not found their fourth running mate at home as they had hoped and had decided to try calling the young girl again from the phone they had used earlier.

"Hi, guys," Patrolman Meadows called out when they had crossed the street and most of the parking lot. "Got a minute?"

Meadows was a hulk of a man, handsome with almost coal-black eyes and skin; he stood a quarter of an inch over six four and weighed two thirty; he carried little body fat. Even after a decade in the South, a touch of his Brooklyn accent still remained. Despite an unusually pleasant disposition, the impression he gave was of someone it was best to obey.

The eldest of the group, David, a seventh grader at Antioch Middle School, was the first to speak—as usual. "So, what's up?" he asked, sounding his coolest while still being respectful. After getting a good look at the huge man who had called for them, David decided to extend his complete cooperation.

"You guys been hanging around the area this morning?"

The boys immediately looked startled and none volunteered an answer.

"It's okay, none of you has done anything wrong. We're just trying to find someone—an adult."

Meadows folded his arms and tried to appear casual. He knew kids wouldn't rat on a peer as quickly as they would a grown-up. They all took turns staring at the gun on his right hip.

"I don't know, maybe. We've been over at the mall mostly. They've got the best blacktop and really cool slopes." The other two skaters nodded in agreement. They lived for large, smooth surfaces and long, rolling hills.

"About five or ten minutes ago, were you guys around here by chance?" Meadow's partner joined them in the middle of the parking lot, near the gas pumps, and signaled with a head shake that he had found no one fitting the description either inside or around back. "See that the pay phones aren't touched until the lab boys get here, will you, Eddie?" Meadows asked, and turned his attention back to the trio of skaters. His look silently repeated his question.

"Yeah, we were here then, I guess. After that, we went to see if our friend Charlie was at home. He lives over there." David pointed toward the neighborhood east of the store.

"Great. Do you guys remember seeing a white woman, probably about twenty-five or thirty, using the pay phone over there?" He removed his sunglasses and looked seriously at all three, one at a time, indicating that they should consider it carefully before they made up any story.

The boys whispered among themselves for a moment. Again, David was the spokesman: "I don't know. We saw this woman, she was white like you said, but she was, you know, pretty—"

"Yeah, and a great body," added Brian, the youngest of the group, feeling it necessary to let the other boys know that he had noticed something as important and mature as a woman's body.

The boys grinned in unison.

David continued: "Like I was saying, she was pretty, a real babe, but I don't think she could have been *that* old."

The others nodded their agreement.

Patrolman Meadows—well into his thirties himself—chuckled inside but appeared to remain serious. He remembered feeling that way once. "That's fine, guys. Did you see where she went?"

Again, they looked at each other before speaking. "Nope. She was still on the phone when we headed for Charlie's," David reported. "She looked upset, or mad, like something was bothering her."

"Can you describe her for me, son?" Meadows asked, pulling a small pad and pencil from his shirt pocket.

"I guess she was like this tall." David held his hand several inches above Brian's head.

Meadows studied the measurement and then jotted five five to five seven in his pad.

"She had brownish-red hair—"

"It was auburn," interrupted Mark, the one normally silent around adults. "I know 'cause my mom has the same color hair this week, and she told my dad it was auburn."

David nodded his head, conceding that, upon further consideration, it could indeed have been auburn. He continued: "It was kinda long, like about here." He touched just above his left elbow with his right hand as it hung by his side. "And kinda curly."

"It was more wavy than curly," added Mark. "Like my sister Kate's." The women in his family were into hair.

Meadows was impressed with the accuracy of the boy's description. "And you have no idea which way she went?"

They all shook their heads.

David suddenly remembered: "Oh, yeah," he blurted out. "When we were on the phone, she just walked up. No car or nothing."

The officer looked straight at the oldest boy. "Any idea at all where she came from?"

David pointed his right index finger at the large apartment complex across the street. "I think from over there."

Meadows returned his Ray-Bans to his eyes and stared across Glengarry toward a group of two- and three-story apartment buildings tucked attractively behind a short, well-trimmed hedgerow and six-foot black wrought-iron fence.

When he saw the unmarked car arrive, Meadows rightly assumed it was the detective responsible for his partner and him being dispatched to the store. "You guys wait over there." He pointed to the front of the store where the row of newsstands stood. "Another policeman may want to ask you a few more questions."

Meadows laid his note pad on the roof of Vanover's car and the detective copied the information the officer had just taken. While he didn't say so, Vanover was not surprised that he had guessed correctly when estimating the woman's general description.

He thanked Meadows and strolled toward the three skaters while Stark called for the lab boys to dust the phone for prints. Since the unidentified female caller had indicated that a capital crime had been committed, and that she possessed knowledge of that crime, trying to retrieve her fingerprints was standard procedure.

Though he told neither the patrolmen at the scene nor his partner the reason for his conclusion, Pete Vanover had been certain the anonymous caller was not a crank.

Now his task was to add a name to the description and the voice.

❖

Kasey was able to see most of the convenience store parking lot from her livingroom window, despite being three buildings away (the arrangement of the first two structures in the complex was such that a gap produced by them fell perfectly along a line between the store and her top floor unit). The only other apartment in her building with such a view lay on the floor directly beneath her. The rise of the hill on which the complex had been constructed prevented the store from being seen from the first-floor end unit.

She had watched in horror as the tallest of the three boys she'd seen earlier pointed his damned finger in the exact direction of her apartment. Her heart had skipped a second beat when the huge uniformed cop donned his dark glasses and stared along the line the boy indicated. She would have sworn that the officer had actually made eye contact with her as she sat crouched behind the pulled curtains and tightly closed mini-blinds.

Such a feat was impossible, of course, her mind had insisted logically.

Her heart had insisted otherwise, and at this tumultuous time in her life, held far greater authority in dictating her feelings.

When the unmarked car arrived, Kasey recognized the camel sport coat she had seen during the TV interview earlier in the day, and though the detective who wore it was too far away to make out his face with certainty, she knew in her gut that it was Vanover, and that he was there to find her.

Kasey's mouth went dry. She turned out the livingroom light and checked the deadbolt on the front door—locked. She hadn't remembered actually turning it earlier. Although not quite seven P.M., with twilight still more than an hour away, the room was nearly dark with the heavily lined curtains closed.

Sam filled her lap as soon as she sat on the couch and tucked her legs beneath her. She rubbed her throbbing knee and Sam's head with opposite hands, alternating every few minutes. They would not move from that spot for the next four hours, though she would jump nervously every time someone knocked on any door within the range of her hearing.

At eleven o'clock, her eyes too heavy to hold open any longer, Kasey decided that they would not be coming for her on this night.

Perhaps tomorrow, but that seemed an eternity away.

She made up her mind not to contact the police again. She hated courtrooms and lawyers, and she certainly wasn't going to end up the target of Joeyboy's wrath.

If they wanted to know the truth about Donna Stanton, they were going to have to learn it without her help.

NINE

Laurie Ann Latham was surprised to hear from the nice-looking detective again so soon; he had been to her home only a few hours earlier, and had left quite convinced—and convincing—that her sister had suffered nothing more alarming than an unexpected yearning to take an unscheduled holiday. It seemed strange to her, therefore, and a bit worrisome, that he should ask to have another look at her room, "more thoroughly this time," he had stated on the phone in his car.

But then, Laurie was a worrier.

Wishing desperately to locate her often exasperating sister, and not wanting to appear uncooperative in any way—after all, it was she who had alerted the police in the first place—she had told the polite Detective Vanover that he and his partner should feel free to come right over. She would put on another pot of coffee.

And worry.

"I'm sorry to impose again on such short notice, Ms. Latham," Vanover offered apologetically, hoping that nothing more need be said before they were allowed to begin their work. From the distraught look on Laurie Latham's face as she stood holding the front door with one hand and leaning against the jamb with the opposite shoulder, blocking the entrance, he could see that he would have to continue. "We've received some new information which leads us to believe that your sister might have had a reason for leaving other than pleasure." He had put it as kindly as possible, given what he'd just been told by the anonymous caller. He had no idea what he would find upon further investigation, but he knew there would be something out of place if he only looked hard enough. There always was.

The detective's words had not allayed her fears, had actually served to heighten them, but they had been enough to gain admission. "It's no imposition," Laurie assured them as she pushed the door away from her and stepped back. The two men instinctively wiped their spotless shoes on the small hemp mat just outside the double cut-glass doors of the exquisite stucco home. She put her hand to her mouth: "You've heard something dreadful, haven't you." The words were stated more than asked, a disquieting look sweeping across her face.

"I'm sure it's nothing, Ms. Latham," Vanover assured her. It was a standard detective lie. Stark studied the pattern of the marble entrance floor, not wishing to meet the woman's eyes.

"What is it?" she insisted fearing the worst, suddenly more than just annoyed by her sister's most recent prank. She slumped onto a thinly padded antique settee which sat along the north wall of the foyer.

Laurie Latham, unlike her younger half-sister, was never one to say "the hell with it." She was a perfectionist who marched to a rigid, self-imposed routine, and who took everything that occurred in her life personally. Even her sister's sudden disappearance was taken as much as an inconvenience as it was a potential tragedy. It was impossible for Laurie to fathom any motive that would send one running off to God-knows-where without having filed the appropriate plan beforehand.

In the brief time he'd had to speak with Latham, Vanover had concluded she was the exact opposite of her sister. "It was probably just a crank call. Some crackpot phoned Headquarters and said she believed your sister might have left town under duress. We get this kind of thing every time someone is reported missing on the tube, especially someone famous. Every celeb-wannabe within a hundred miles tries to get in on the action surrounding the case. All the same, we'd like to look around, with your permission, of course, and see if we can find anything that might support that claim. It's just routine, ma'am."

Vanover was ready to get on with it; he'd had enough polite hand-holding for a lifetime; he wasn't a minister, he was a cop. What he'd rather have told the rich snob was that her sister had been reported murdered, and he and his partner were there to find a possible motive for it, so stay the hell out of their way while they did their jobs. But diplomacy was one of the talents responsible for his rapid advancement, and it made more sense, under the circumstances, to stick with what had always worked. Vanover the social worker; the title fit like an itchy sweater.

"Do you think—"

"I don't think a thing at this point, Ms. Latham, I'm only here to check things out. I assure you, the moment we have anything to report, you'll be the first to know." Vanover's look indicated that he was through explaining for the moment.

Laurie, sensing that there was either nothing more to tell, or that nothing more would be told to her, acquiesced. "Would you gentlemen care for some more coffee?" She had started a pot when they called. It was, after all, the polite thing to do when company arrived.

Though the two men had already consumed enough coffee since six

A.M. to keep a cadaver awake, Vanover knew that Ms. Latham would be annoyingly under foot without something to keep her mind off their work. "That would be great. I take mine black, remember."

She nodded with an exaggerated smile. "And you, Detective."

Vanover looked at his partner who could still taste the cup he had just finished in the car on the way over. He gave him a wink to accept.

"You have cream?" Stark asked with a plastic smile.

"I've got Half 'n' Half. Would that be all right?" she asked, standing again.

Would Half 'n' Half be all right, Stark mimicked sarcastically in his mind, still smiling broadly. He hated rich women with nothing to do.

When she had turned toward the kitchen, he silently poked a stiff finger in his partner's lower back.

The search began anew in Donna Stanton's bedroom.

❖

Jordan Taylor strolled casually around the first floor of the CJC, a fresh cup of coffee in one hand, paperwork in the other. As usual, the office was a vortex of hurried activity and fragmented phone calls filled with frustrated profanity and colorful street slang. Any isolated part of any call—and most entire conversations for that matter—would have been utterly incomprehensible to the average citizen. Taylor, on the other hand, had learned by the time he'd crossed the floor from the coffee machine to his corner office, that two of his men were investigating the death of a drug dealer in one of the seedier sections of Nashville; another two were trying to get the FBI to share information concerning a string of Friday afternoon bank robberies in Davidson County; and yet another pair were leaving for the scene of a drive-by shooting in which an innocent woman had been struck in the cheek by a bullet through her automobile window.

It was, all things considered, a rather quiet Friday evening in the Tennessee capital.

As Taylor reached his office, he noticed the two desks nearest his door empty. "Hey, Chuck," he called out to the nearest detective. "Where are Pete and Re-Pete?" It had been Jordan Taylor who had named Peter Wayne Vanover, Pete, and Brad Stark, his shadow of a partner, Re-Pete.

As chief of detectives, assistant to the metro chief of police, and ranking officer in the department, Taylor had nicknamed all of his men.

Charles "Chuck" Feeney, the only New England transplant on the force, and the brunt of endless Damn Yankee jokes because of a Boston accent as thick as clam chowder, looked up from his keyboard; he was trying to finish his report on a gun store shooting earlier in the day. "Got a call from some dame claiming she knew the Stanton woman was dead, Chief. He and Brad ran out like somebody had set their tails on fire."

Jordan Taylor nodded an amused thank-you and disappeared into his office. After making a quick call to dispatch, he grabbed his coat and was gone.

❖

Donna Stanton's bedroom was down a long hall, to the right off the foyer, on the southeast end of the home. It had two massive ornate windows that faced south to Belle Meade Road, and a set of matching French doors on the adjacent wall facing east. The French doors led out to a huge redwood deck with an oversize redwood hot tub at one end, and expensive teak furniture filling most of the remaining deck. The area was enclosed in a tall privacy fence, allowing Donna to use the Jacuzzi or sunbathe in the nude.

Laurie, whose slightly smaller room was on the opposite end of the home, had never joined her sister is such foolishness—and never would have—despite having been invited on more than one occasion.

In the private heart she shared with no one, though, as she would drift off to sleep alone in her big bed, she often fantasized about being that free. Such things were just not proper, however, and a lady was judged by how she conducted herself at all times, even when there was no one else to see.

But then, most of her sister's lifestyle wasn't proper, to Laurie's way of thinking.

Though sharing the same mother, Rebecca, the siblings were, and had always been, as different as their fathers: Laurie's had been a major in the Air Force, decorated twice during the Korean conflict, later becoming a pilot for American Airlines, and then a charter pilot. He had died in a mysterious crash over the Gulf of Mexico in October 1960, leaving his wife financially secure and his only child fatherless. Donna's had been a gambler, a man with no use for clocks or schedules, and no desire to do anything that looked or smelled like work. Laurie's mother had met and married him in the depths of her grief over the loss of her first husband. She had known the marriage was a mistake from the moment they left the altar, but tried valiantly to make a success of it. By the time Donna's father had walked out, Rebecca had an infant daughter to care for as well as her five-year-old, and only one-fourth of her original money with which to do it. Had she not hidden it carefully, he would have assuredly taken the balance as well.

For eighteen years, the three women kept to themselves, living modestly in a middle-class home in rural Davidson County, the girls attending the local public schools. Neither of the girls had been permitted to date through high school; something which never seemed to bother the shy, studious Laurie, but which had a profound effect on her younger sister. Donna had been the rebel, a consummate nonconformist. On the day she graduated from high school, she ran away with a boy she had been secretly dating for three years. Over the next ten years, the only time she saw her sister again was at Rebecca's funeral, the day before Thanksgiving 1991.

At first, Laurie hated and resented Donna for not having been there when their mother was diagnosed with cancer. Even more so for not having been there when she died. But true to form, the more personable and headstrong of the pair easily won her sister's forgiveness, moving in with her and helping her settle their mother's estate, an estate that had been divided equally between them despite Donna's decade of absence. Laurie always sensed in her heart that their mother had a special place in hers for the unruly Donna, and though the thought bothered her at times, it was to Rebecca's credit that Laurie never felt the balance of love as inequitable; it was just . . . different.

Within two years of the funeral, Donna had miraculously snowballed the money they had been left into nearly three times its original amount, paying more than a half-million dollars in cash for the home they shared in Belle Meade, and getting the stagnantly conservative Laurie out of her four-door Buick sedan and into a metallic red Eldorado Touring Coupe— also paid for in cash.

When asked by Laurie how she had managed to work such a feat of financial wizardry, Donna had just smiled and placed her index finger to her pursed lips, assuring her that she didn't want to know. Laurie never asked again; it reminded her of the time she had asked Donna how she'd passed all her final exams without ever having cracked a book.

Despite their steadily increasing affluence, Laurie continued working as the office manager of a small legal firm that dealt exclusively with environmental issues and maintained a quiet social life, while Donna quietly managed their money and ran at full gallop in the celebrity derby. With her high-school husband gone before her twenty-first birthday, and no desire to ever marry again, Donna had seen all men—the rich ones, at least—as fair game.

In her mind, there was only one commandment when it came to men: there were no rules.

❖

"What have you got there?" Taylor asked, eyeing the small book through which Vanover was busily flipping pages. Vanover had not heard his boss enter the bedroom, wasn't even aware he had come to the house.

"Son of a bitch, Chief!" he exclaimed, startled by the familiar deep voice over his shoulder.

Taylor grinned. He liked arriving unannounced. "Looks like a diary. Latham say you could read it?"

"She told Stark and me we could look anywhere in the sister's bedroom and bathroom for information that might help locate her. That means she doesn't have to tell us we can read it once we find it." Vanover was right, of course, and Taylor wasn't surprised his best detective had gotten the necessary permission to do a search. It was simply too much vital evidence having been excluded by judges overly liberal in their interpretation of Fourth Amendment rights that led Taylor to double check. He nodded his approval.

"Is that all you've found so far?" He tried to read over Vanover's shoulder.

"Yeah. Everything else looks normal. Not even so much as a joint or a trace of coke in the rich broad's bedroom, just a closet full of designer clothes and a drawer full of expensive lingerie. Take a look. Very nice, the kind of stuff my wife would kill for." He pointed to the wide drawer in an antique chest of drawers beside the walk-in closet.

"Yeah, but that'd be like putting leather seats in a Pacer," Stark teased, unable to pass up such a wonderful opportunity to stick it to his partner. As with most of the detectives in the division, the two swapped jabs all day long, whenever the other was foolish or inattentive enough to permit an opening.

"Fuck you. My wife looks great for having four kids. If you don't believe it, just ask her."

Jordan Taylor shook his head and then cast a quick glance at the closed drawer; for the briefest of moments he imagined what the contents must be like. He turned his attention to the diary in Vanover's hands. "I'll leave the panty sniffing to you, Pete. My heart couldn't take the strain. Where'd you find that?"

"Brad found it under the mattress, stuffed in deep, almost to the center. Seems like a number of pages have been torn out."

"Let me have a look at that, will you, Pete?"

Vanover was reluctant to hand over the ornately decorated leather-bound book before he'd finished reading it, but knew his boss well enough to understand that the simplest request from him during an investigation, no matter how politely veiled, was to be taken as a direct order. "Sure. Wait until you read what's in it. You better sit down, Chief. Your heart, you know." He raised his eyebrows dramatically while Stark, standing nearby, nodded in silent agreement.

Taylor only grinned. "What the hell could she write in her little book that I need to sit down for?" He scanned the first page, dated December 19, 1991. Before he had finished the twenty or so lines of neatly handwritten text, he had, without consciously thinking about it, dropped into the large stuffed chair near the bed. "Mother of God!" he exclaimed under his breath, and then looked up at the two other detectives.

They stood silently in front of him, no trace of humor on either face.

Jordan Taylor quickly read the following page, then another, and another. By the time he had gotten to March 1992, he was shaking his head in disbelief. "This can't be real. It's got to be a fantasy life she's writing about here. You see who she's mentioned in just the first few pages of this thing, the first three months of what . . ."—he looked at the last entry date—"a five-year diary?"

Stark dangled a small clear plastic sleeve in front of Taylor's face. It was slotted to hold exactly twenty audio microcassettes. Four slots were empty. "Found this, too, beside the diary. They all appear to be sequentially dated and seem to parallel the pages of that book. Of course, that's just a quick assessment given what little time we've had. But, based on what we've seen so far, I'd say the four missing tapes have been intentionally culled from the batch. Their dates likely encompass the dates of the missing pages."

He handed his boss a small Sony tape player, the kind each detective in the department was issued and used for on-site crime-scene description and electronic note-taking, and then extended the sleeve of tapes toward him. "Take your pick, Cap'n," Stark smiled. "They're all winners."

Jordan Taylor took the black metal device with its dull silver buttons, inserted the tape he had picked at random A side up, and instinctively mashed the Play button. He had carried the same unit for years.

After only thirty seconds of the first covert conversation, he pressed STOP. "You know who that is, the one without the accent?" Not waiting for a response from either man, he answered his own question: "It's Bill Monroe! Probably the next governor of the state, for Christ's sake, if you believe the press. How do you suppose she got him on tape like that, and who's the guy he's doing business with?"

Taylor stood and stared directly into Vanover's eyes. "What the hell was this woman up to, Pete?" His voice dropped to a whisper: "And who in God's name is she working for?"

TEN

Joeyboy switched off his bike as it neared the mouth of the old dirt driveway and allowed the normally thunderous Harley to roll to a quiet stop. He parked only a few feet off the blacktop, but knew traffic was too light on this stretch of road to fear for the safety of his machine. He lowered the side stand and stepped from the bike, sliding his mirror-tint "blades" in the pocket of his jeans jacket as he did. Mottled patches of sun and shadows created by the canopy of trees danced tirelessly in the dust, answering the voice of the wind as it gently weaved its way through the branches.

In the distance, far to the west, thick, black clouds had begun to gather with a low rumble, warning of yet another April rain. He studied them for a moment, showing detached acknowledgment more than interest or concern. His thoughts were elsewhere.

For three days now, he had not been able to get the distant, unsettling image out of his mind, nor had he been able to clarify it to the point of recognition.

It was the uncertainty more than anything else that returned him now to this spot, the uncertainty that he had actually been alone when he took Stanton's life. It was not a feeling that he liked; a feeling as close to fear as any he could recall.

Joeyboy walked slowly down the middle of the narrow drive, occasionally glancing to either side. He had no idea what he hoped to find, if anything, yet he was certain he would know it if he saw it. When he stopped, more than a hundred yards up the road from his bike, he gazed silently toward the unseen orchard he knew lay directly ahead, though still more than a half-mile distant. He lit a cigarette and inhaled deeply, blowing the exhaled cloud of smoke skyward. He returned the pack to his jacket pocket and turned back toward the blacktop.

Convinced and pleased that he had seen nothing Monday night, he picked up his return pace a bit, sending a flattened beer can scurrying across the road with a quick stab of his riding boot as he walked. As it rolled to a stop at the edge of the drive, something about it seemed unusual, odd, as though it possessed the appearance of a flattened aluminum can but none of the character. He nonetheless found himself moving toward the spot where it had come to rest.

He knelt by the narrow, sunken shoulder of the drive and picked up the small, pewter-colored disk. It was flat, with what appeared to be dried glue or tape on one side and a curious, slightly raised emblem cast into the other. As he rolled it around slowly between his thumb and forefinger, he realized that he'd seen the design many times. The disk was not a squashed Budwiser or Coke can, but the centerpiece of a hubcap. More specifically, the center of a Honda wheel cover, an item that he knew had been left in the dirt road since Monday morning's rain.

Suddenly, the fragment of image that had remained so stubbornly hidden in his mind burst forth like the clown in a child's jack-in-the-box: what he'd seen Monday night had not been a fabrication of his active imagination, but a reflection of the full moon off a car's window glass or chrome. He knew it as surely as Donna Stanton was dead.

Without minimizing the task that lay before him, he at least now had a starting point, something tangible with which to begin his search for the mysterious Honda. "Charmed," he smiled as he stood again. "Definitely charmed."

He flipped the disk like a large coin, watching it turn repeatedly in the air. "Heads . . . you die fast; tails . . . I take my sweet time," he grinned sadistically as it fell toward his outstretched palm.

He reached his bike and straddled the black leather seat, glancing for the first time at the emblem he had caught in mid-air a few steps back. He smiled maliciously. "Tails it is."

❖

Jordan Taylor popped the microcassette tape from the recorder and handed the unit back to Stark. He motioned for the detective to give him the sleeve of tapes, while still holding on to the diary. Stark obliged. Taylor stuffed the tape he had just played a small portion of into its original compartment and rose to leave.

"Hey, don't run off with those, Chief. I haven't finished with either the diary or the tapes," Vanover stated quickly. "Hell, I barely got started when you popped in." He reached out a hand, fully expecting his boss to give him back the evidence he had collected.

Taylor stopped in the door opening and looked back, slowly, deliberately. "I'll hold on to these for the moment if you don't mind, Pete."

"I sure as hell do mind. Since when have you started violating the chain of evidence, Chief?" It was obvious to the other men that Vanover was not pleased with his boss's unexpected intervention. He stepped toward Taylor. "What the hell are you planning to do with them?" His look grew cold. "You removing me from the case?"

"Case? What case? There's not even a missing person's report currently under investigation on this woman. You deep-six'd it this morning, remember?"

"That was before I got the call from the dame telling me she had knowledge of Stanton's murder."

"Not just missing, now it's murdered, huh? My, how things have changed." His sarcasm wasn't missed.

"I didn't make this shit up, that's what the woman said."

"What's her name, Pete?"

"I don't know. Yet."

"What'd she say happened to Stanton?"

"Only that she'd been murdered."

"How?"

"She didn't say."

"Did you ask?"

"No, I—"

"All right then, where'd she say we could find the body?"

Vanover looked away. "She didn't," he replied in a whisper

"Where?" Taylor taunted, pretending not to hear.

"She didn't say, all right. She hung up before I could learn anything more," Vanover responded loudly.

"Jesus, Pete, you're gonna make a case for homicide based on one anonymous call? It's not like this is the first prank call you've ever taken." Taylor looked skeptically at his friend of fifteen years. "Don't we have enough dead bodies already without inventing more?"

"It wasn't a crank call."

"Really. And what are you basing that statement on—a hunch?"

"Sure, why not? You've done it."

"We've all done it, Pete, but hunches are usually as thin as paper, thinner. We don't have time for this."

Vanover glanced at the diary in Taylor's hand. "What about the stuff in there? The tapes? They're a hell of a lot more to go on than hunches. What are you going to do about them?"

"What am I going to do with information that was obtained through an illegal wiretap, by a woman who probably would have never given her consent for the search of her bedroom which yielded that information?" He hesitated. "Nothing. Not a damned thing. I'm going to sit on it until I can speak with Donna Stanton—in person."

"What if the caller's right and she is dead?" Stark questioned.

"Listen, I don't need both of you cowboys on my back, Stark, one's bad enough." He took a breath, looking back to Vanover. "If we find out that your caller was right, though I doubt we'll ever hear from her again, I'll decide what to do then."

Vanover and Stark looked at each other for a moment and then quietly stepped past the chief. While neither was happy with their captain's decision, both recognized his authority to act as he had.

❖

Other than a moment's hesitation, Laurie Latham offered no objection when Jordan Taylor asked to borrow the diary and tapes—indefinitely. His assurance that they could possibly contain a clue to the whereabouts of, or at least a possible reason for the disappearance of, her sister, was more than enough to gain her consent. Laurie was sure her sister wouldn't mind, when Donna was made to understand how upset and worried she'd been at her leaving without so much as a word.

Jordan left shortly after Vanover and Stark, staying only long enough to talk briefly with Laurie about her sister's lifestyle and habits. Most of what he'd learned had not surprised him—especially in light of the glimpse he'd gotten into her diary—but it had come as a surprise to him that she kept an apartment (police records listed only the Belle Meade address) in the Magnolia Towers on West End Avenue, Nashville's premier high-rise, and that she often stayed there for days at a time, though never before without calling Laurie at least once a day. Although Laurie had never been to the apartment, Donna had told her that it was on the top floor.

That it was the penthouse had not surprised Taylor.

❖

Harry Winston's love-hate relationship with golf was based entirely upon one simple fundamental: if he was playing golf with Bill Monroe, he hated the game—with anyone else, he loved it. It was, therefore, turning out to be a miserable Friday morning, the last four and a half hours having been spent listening to poorly told lewd jokes and graphically descriptive tales of extramarital philandering from the man who was undoubtedly going to be the state's next governor. Winston had come to the conclusion that Monroe would likely sweep the election in November, and once having acknowledged that, decided it would be in his best interests to form a friendship with the future most powerful man in the state. Part of the dating ritual, in political and business relationships everywhere, included letting the person you needed to do business with beat you repeatedly and often at golf, but only if the loss could be cleverly disguised behind what was a valiant effort by a competent but unfortunately less skilled opponent. The better the losing effort, the better the business relationship. Winston was a master at choreographed defeat, and his immense construction business was hugely profitable, in large part, because of it.

On this particular Friday, however, Harry Winston was not trying to lose, quite the contrary. He disliked Monroe, *despised* Monroe, and in spite of his realization that the majority of victories had to be Monroe's, wanted badly to beat him just once.

For no specific reason—Monroe's game was not off and his own had certainly not been spectacular—Winston found himself, for the first time, one stroke up on his vulgar opponent by the time they reached the eighteenth green. Monroe had only a three-foot putt left for par, and the tie. Winston knew that if he didn't beat him outright, he'd choke in a sudden death match. He had the last two times.

It was that annoying cackle of Monroe's which always followed a victory that he was dreading the most.

❖

The blond man pulled off his sunglasses and delivered the small, shiny emblem to the black linoleum parts counter with an annoying slap. Two men conversing casually over a terminal that was linked to the central office computer ended their conversation and glared silently across the counter.

"I'll catch you later, Rock," the man in the mechanic's uniform stated flatly. He strolled back through the door behind the counter and disappeared into the shop.

"Can I help you?" the other man asked, with a thick drawl and obvious indifference. The clean white shirt said his name was Rocky, though he looked more like a Beevis to Joeyboy.

"What's this fit?" Joeyboy asked impatiently. He slid the disk toward Beevis.

"A Honda," the man said with a slight chuckle.

Joeyboy responded by narrowing his eyes. His lips grew tight.

Rocky's desire to be of true assistance heightened exponentially. He took the emblem and studied it closely for a few seconds: "Looks like a CRX or Civic wheel center. Need to know which?"

Joeyboy nodded once.

"And the year?"

There was no response.

Rocky vanished between a pair of tall, steel, free-standing shelves, each filled to overflowing with water pumps, radiator hoses, brightly colored taillamp assemblies, and a seemingly endless variety of other repair items: all genuine Honda. He returned in less than a minute with several boxes of similar-looking parts. "Give me a second. I'm pretty sure it's one of these." He grabbed four different emblems and set them on the counter near the original. "Yep, just like I thought, this one here—CRX. See, perfect match." He held a new center alongside the one Joeyboy had brought and smiled broadly.

"The year . . . ?"

"Oh, yeah, I forgot." The man pecked the part number on the keyboard with a single finger and took a hard look at the screen. "Nineteen eighty-four or eighty-five. They changed styles slightly after that. How many will you be needing?" The smile was now disgusting.

"One," Joeyboy smirked as he slid the original disk across the counter and held it momentarily in front of Beevis' face. "Just one."

❖

Though a lifelong Georgia resident, Harry Winston did much of his business with, and in, the State of Tennessee—usually between twelve and fifteen million dollars per year—through the commercial construction company he began in 1954 and still owned and operated at sixty-three. A former major in the Unites States Marine Corps, with Purple Hearts from his tours in both Korea and Vietnam, Harry Winston neither needed, nor wanted, anyone else to run his business.

The work consisted mostly of highway improvements and bridge repair, with an occasional state building renovation here and there. Though the governor didn't have the power to prevent anyone from getting, or keeping, state business—legally, at least—Winston knew the onerous process of securing that lucrative work was made infinitely easier when one had friends at the top.

For the last two terms, he had rigorously courted the incumbent governor, Wayne "Buddy" Williams, and consequently enjoyed a good working relationship with him and his chief administrative assistant, Warren Slade. The years of losing to them on the golf course had paid handsome dividends. But the winds of change had started to blow in the capital, and after months of slanderous campaigning by both parties, the conventional wisdom now favored the previous underdog, Bill Monroe. It was a delicate balance, juggling his association with the two men, but he had managed to do it successfully for the last nine months. If he didn't have to see either of them too often—or at the same function, for God's sake—he could maintain that balance until November.

Monroe stood carefully poised over the ball, snapping his head first left, then straight down again. Each new sighting brought with it an infinitesimal adjustment of the spiked alligator shoes on the impeccably kept green. The ritualistic dance, fully understood and appreciated only by another fairway warrior, continued for nearly a full minute—until he was certain.

Winston stood ten or twelve feet away, to the back of his opponent, praying under his breath for a minor miracle. Just this once he would like to beat the boorish bastard, even if it cost him a million dollars in business. At this moment, this exact moment, he resolved, it would be worth every cent of it.

The bodyguard was the first to spot the reporters.

"Hey, boss—" The man with a single thick eyebrow spanning both eyes spoke out the corner of his mouth, while simultaneously placing himself directly between Monroe and the approaching intruders. Standing six three and weighing just over two fifty, with a weight lifter's body crying to be freed from the tightly stretched primary blue polo shirt that imprisoned it, he posed a formidable obstacle to anyone who might think to approach his employer.

Anyone except Brandie Mueller.

When armed with a video camera and microphone, Brandie Mueller shook off her mortal coil and became invincible. Bullets didn't bother her, fires didn't faze her, and this hulk placing himself between her and the story she was determined to get was nothing more than an annoying little boy filled with steroids.

Monroe looked up from his ball and beyond his bodyguard's broad shoulder. "What the hell does that bitch want now?" he groaned under his breath. "It's okay, Andy," he ordered, producing his best campaign smile as the bodyguard moved a few feet to the side, and he and Mueller made eye contact. Though he didn't care for the woman, he respected power, and Mueller, in her own way, had power.

"Ah, Brandie, so good to see you again. How can I possibly be of assistance to you on this glorious spring morning? Surely you haven't come all the way from our fair capital just to see me beat poor Harry Winston again." He extended his right hand.

Brandie walked past the hulk, without so much as a hint of acknowledgment, and straight up to Monroe without taking his hand. She switched on the wireless mike she had been carrying in her left hand.

Tim Arnold, the Channel 9 cameraman most often sent to accompany the flamboyant and daring Mueller whenever she went to cover a story in the field, promptly flicked on his camera-mounted light. He did so, not because it was dark enough to require supplemental lighting on the bright April morning, but because he disliked Monroe and hoped a 250w quartz-halogen lamp squarely in his face would irritate him. He liked running camera. And he liked Brandie's style.

Monroe blinked for a split second when the light bounced off the backs of his unsuspecting retinas, but recovered rapidly and returned to his best campaign face.

He looked directly at Brandie and smiled broadly. Brandie was ready.

"I'm on a private golf course outside Chattanooga with Tennessee gubernatorial candidate, Bill Monroe. Mr. Monroe, do you know Donna Louise Stanton of Nashville?" Mueller never hesitated as she shoved the microphone squarely in Monroe's face.

"Stanton . . . Stanton . . . let me think." Monroe's sphincter tightened. "Why, yes, I believe I met the woman once last fall while campaigning in your lovely city. She works for an ad agency or something in Nashville, if I'm not mistaken." His well-practiced smile never failed him.

"Not exactly, Mr. Monroe. Were you aware that her sister reported her missing yesterday, and that the police now believe her disappearance may have been under mysterious, perhaps even sinister, circumstances?"

Again, the mike was stuck in his face.

Monroe didn't like the way the unscheduled and unrehearsed interview was heading. He looked at Brandie Mueller and tried to appear in charge while also trying to decide how to end the damned taping without giving her any unnecessary information or appearing to be hiding anything. "You don't say, Brandie. Tell me, what does Ms. Stanton's disappearance have to do with me, if you don't mind me asking?" He was sure no link between the two could easily be uncovered, at least not without his learning of it first and having the opportunity to prepare an adequate and credible explanation.

Brandie was only fishing, he was certain.

He cocked his head defiantly and awaited her response.

"Not at all, Mr. Monroe. According to our sources, it seems that your name was mentioned rather prominently in the personal diary she kept, accompanied by several descriptions of highly explicit sexual encounters with her."

"That's ridiculous. As I told you before, I only met the woman once—"

"And you were seen entering her penthouse on no fewer than five different occasions according to the doorman at the Magnolia Towers. On at least three of those occasions, you were again seen leaving her apartment between six and seven A.M. Do you deny these allegations, Mr. Monroe?" Mueller was a rock, and the mike was again in his face.

Bill Monroe swallowed hard and shot Andy a quick glance, but it carried a direct order with it. Andy's massive size gave no hint of his speed—he moved like a striking rattler. In simultaneous actions, he snatched the outstretched microphone from Brandie Mueller's hand while forcing Tim Arnold's camera lens to record nothing but the freshly cut grass at his feet. It had taken less than a second.

He then threw the microphone into the sand trap bordering the green and held out his hand for the videotape in the Betacam. Though there were any number of indignities and tribulations Tim Arnold was willing to endure in pursuit of a story, dying was not on the list. He ejected the tape and handed it to the man who towered nearly a foot above him and who, at the moment, seemed larger than his car.

Brandie prayed for some Kryptonite—or a .44 Magnum—but neither materialized.

With the dual threats of audio and video recording adequately removed for the moment, Monroe leaned toward a startled Brandie Mueller, putting his mouth close against her cheek. "I have nothing further to say at this time," he whispered, his hot, angry breath filling her ear. "Do you understand exactly what I'm telling you, Ms. Mueller? Now get the fuck out of my face and back to Nashville, or I'll have Andy drag you there by your black roots." He gritted his teeth. She could hear the enamel grinding against itself. "And be damned careful how you report this story, you cunt, or you'll have far more than your pathetic little job to worry about. You have no idea who you're dealing with."

The plastic smile was gone.

More likely than not, Brandie's vote as well.

Mueller and Arnold turned quietly away, Tim stopping only to retrieve the fifteen-hundred-dollar microphone from the sand. Neither looked back as they retraced their steps to the Jeep.

Andy stayed close behind, following them all the way to the parking lot at the clubhouse. If it were up to him, the annoying pair would be leaving in an ambulance, instead of a Channel 9 news cruiser. Despite the necessity of his boss's constant exposure to reporters, especially at this late date in a heated campaign, he had no tolerance for the media.

None of the other three men—Harry Winston and the two caddies—had made a sound during the entire incident. None spoke, as well, as Monroe resumed his stance over the ball.

He took a short stab of a swing, displaying nearly perfect form.

For a fleeting moment the ball appeared to travel dead straight, directly toward the hole, but at the last instant swerved right, rimming the cup and darting at an acute angle to the left. It coasted to an anemic stop, a few feet beyond, like a car that had run out of gas. Monroe's head dropped silently to his chest.

A single, definitive expletive was the only sound the other three heard.

It was all Harry Winston could do not to cackle out loud. The muscles in his face felt as if they were going to break. "Too bad, Bill. I guess they screwed up your concentration a bit" was the most he could offer in consolation without losing it altogether.

It had become, he decided after all, a perfectly splendid Friday morning. God, he loved this game!

Bill Monroe looked up with a slight twist of his head and glared angrily at the figures moving swiftly across the lawn toward the clubhouse parking lot.

He knew he had tracks to cover, and that it would take all of his considerable wealth and power to do it at this unexpected and unwanted hour.

❖

Kasey parked the faded blue Honda in her regular space by the Dumpster and switched off the key. She had dreaded this day for the last five, but knew her present financial position didn't allow the luxury of such esoteric notions as sticking to one's guns in the face of certain dismissal. By Friday morning, having spent a particularly miserable Thursday alternately waiting for the cops to knock on her door and fighting off images from the orchard, Kasey had decided to go in to work. Besides keeping her busy, and hopefully, her mind off Donna Stanton, she could use the tips. Fridays were normally her best night.

She wondered how she would endure Cal's inevitable mocking about their day in court, since he would have figured out by now that she had initiated no sexual harassment lawsuit.

Even if a lawyer had agreed to represent her for free, and had further agreed to pay all expenses in anticipation of a fat settlement, she assumed she'd have been summarily discharged from Leonard's the moment the home office received the first phone call or letter. With anywhere from one to five years between filing a suit and appearance in court, poverty loomed as a painfully real possibility. Lofty ideals were wonderful concepts, she had concluded by the middle of her paid week off, but so were the more mundane ones: like eating regularly and keeping her car filled with gas. She would tell Cal firmly that he had better watch his step or her lawyer was going to make his life darker than midnight under an iron skillet. For now, she was willing to give him another opportunity to treat her with the respect she deserved as a good and loyal employee.

"Hey, Kasey," Desmondo hailed warmly as she paused in the doorway to the kitchen, shaking the rain from her umbrella before she closed it. He dropped what he was doing and came to give her a welcome back hug.

"Hi, Mondo." The greeting was flat.

"I've got some good news for you, my friend." He hugged her like a long-lost sister and then pulled away with a smile in his eyes.

"Great, Mondo, I could use some good news for a change. Most of it lately has really sucked." She hung her umbrella and windbreaker in her bottom locker and clicked the door shut. He followed like a puppy. She couldn't help grinning. "Make my day and tell me Hardt's been run over by a train. Not a big one, maybe just four or five locomotives and a few hundred cars carrying rocks." She produced a sour, half-sincere expression as she gave the combination lock a quick spin.

He smiled even broader. "No train, but it's almost as good."

"What?" she asked.

"Hardt's on vacation until the fifth of May. That's good news, no?" His thick Hispanic accent made him sound like Ricky Ricardo.

"You're kidding me, Mondo," she said excitedly, grabbing both of the cook's hands.

He shook his head excitedly, still sporting the huge smile. "Alicia told all of us this morning. Said that he'd been under a lot of stress lately and needed some time off." He frowned a mock scowl at Kasey. "You have something to do with this sudden attack of ulcers, my friend?"

Kasey knew Alicia, the bookkeeper, always had the inside scoop on everything that happened at the restaurant, and if she said Cal had not had a good week, the threat of legal action must have produced its intended effect. Kasey smiled back at Mondo. "You never know."

Maybe things are going to be okay, after all, she thought.

She kissed Mondo affectionately on the cheek and left to see what the crowd looked like in the main dining area. She wished Brenda hadn't worked the early shift today; she could use her company this evening.

❖

Todd Ryan, Leonard's head bartender for the last three years, gladly poured Kasey another club soda and added a twist of lime. He secretly admired the waitress he thought had the best body and was the friendliest among the staff, but was too bashful to say anything to her about his feelings. He was content to have her sit at the bar and make idle conversation with him as she waited for her shift to end. The harmless drink was her third in the past hour.

Since the last of the dinner crowd had left a little after nine, the restaurant had been as quiet as a library. Even the usual late-dinner stragglers and regular bar patrons were conspicuously absent. Kasey imagined it must have been the result of the heavy rain that had been falling all day.

Despite the low tips, she was grateful for an easy shift.

She squinted at the clock on the far wall of the bar: 9:58—just over two hours to go; it seemed like an eternity amid the boredom Kasey felt when work was this slow. Outside, the rain tapped rhythmically on the metal roof and ran noisily down its corrugated surface, filling the drains and creating small rivers that coursed continuously through the empty parking lot. The streetlamps looked like fat, indistinct stars in an India ink sky. Kasey felt alone, like a child feels alone at times, and fought off the images that tried to steal her sanity.

She stirred her club soda with a plastic bar straw and stared blankly at a spot on the wall, somewhere far beyond the television, half listening to the lackluster drone of the ever-present automobile commercials that always preceded the ten o'clock news.

Suddenly, despite her efforts, Donna Stanton's pleading eyes bore through her from across the bar, abruptly shaking her from a lethargic daydream that had almost lulled her to sleep.

She bolted upright, sending her glass across the slick black Formica, over the back edge of the bar, and onto the floor at Todd's heels. With his back to her, he had no chance of catching it before it shattered into a thousand glistening shards.

"You know" came the controlled response as he turned toward his only customer at the bar, "if you didn't like the drink . . . you could have just said so." It was a typical bartender response to a broken glass.

"I'm so sorry, Todd," she offered genuinely, shrugging her shoulders animatedly as she spoke. "It was an accident, I swear. I'll clean it up." She rose from her stool.

"That's all right," he stated reassuringly, indicating for her to remain seated. "It's not the first glass ever broken in here. Hell, it's not the first glass today. I'll get it. You want me to fix you another?"

She shook her head.

"You sure?"

"Yeah."

Kasey slid the remote control across the bar and turned up the volume a few clicks as Brandie Mueller opened the late news:

"The case of Donna Louise Stanton's disappearance grows more complex and intriguing with each passing day.

"As you may recall on Wednesday, Stanton's half-sister, Laurie Ann Latham, filed a missing person's report on Stanton. She cited, quote: 'odd behavior, and concern for her safety' as her reason for filing the report.

"Since that occurred Wednesday afternoon, Channel 9 has learned that an anonymous female caller phoned Nashville Metro Police and stated that she had knowledge of Donna Stanton's death, specifically her murder. Stanton has yet to be found.

"Following that anonymous lead, Detective Lieutenant Pete Vanover returned to the home Stanton shared with Latham and, upon more thorough investigation, discovered a personal diary kept by Stanton, as well as a sleeve of microcassette tapes, similar to these. (Mueller held up a plastic sheet with twenty small audio cassettes inserted into the pockets.) This is the type of audio tape used in miniature recording devices. (Mueller then held up the tiniest of pocket recorders, no larger than a half pack of cigarettes.)

"According to our sources, that diary appeared to be missing several of its pages, apparently ripped out in an attempt to conceal their contents. The sleeve of tapes, presumed full, and sequentially dated, was missing four cassettes.

"Channel 9 has further learned that the pages and tapes that remain depict numerous conversations with well-known personalities in entertainment, business, and politics, including Republican gubernatorial candidate, William "Bill" Monroe of Chattanooga.

"Exactly what candidate Monroe's connection to Ms. Stanton was, or is, has not yet been revealed, but an exclusive Channel 9 interview with the doorman at Stanton's downtown penthouse apartment indicated that Ms. Stanton had a steady stream of male callers, including candidate Monroe.

"No one from the Monroe camp was available for comment, though a formal statement is being prepared jointly by his attorney and press secretary.

"Candidate Monroe declined our offer to appear on-camera.

"When Jordan Taylor, Chief of Detectives for Nashville Metro, was questioned by this reporter about Monroe's purported involvement with Donna Stanton, he stated only that he could neither confirm nor deny any such connection.

"When asked to show the missing woman's diary to the media, Taylor refused. When asked to play the missing woman's tapes for the media, Taylor refused. He also refused to answer any specific questions relating to the content of the diary or the tapes.

"When Stanton's sister learned of the anonymous call, she phoned Channel 9 to inform us that she was posting a twenty-five-thousand dollar cash reward for any information that will lead authorities to her sister.

"If the anonymous caller who phoned the police on Friday evening would like to tell someone her story, she may reach me through Channel

9 at any time, day or night. If desired, her anonymity will be guaranteed.

"Channel 9 will keep its viewers informed as more information in this bizarre case becomes available."

Kasey's heart pounded and her mouth hung open, astonished at the words she had just heard. She had not blinked in nearly two minutes and her eyes felt as if they were filled with sand. She squeezed them tightly shut and covered her face with both hands, her labored breath hot against her palms. Everything again seemed wild, insane, as it had exactly ninety-six hours earlier.

"You okay?" Todd asked considerately, noticing her change in demeanor.

"Oh . . . yeah . . . just tired, I guess, Todd." Kasey took a deep breath and smiled at him. "Well, I'd better get back to work."

She turned slowly in the bar chair and stepped to the dark wooden floor. The image of the woman's face exploding returned for the thousandth time, and though its ferocity had weakened, the constant exposure to the pain and horror of its memory still tore at her soul.

Kasey's mind raced between her feelings for the stranger as a helpless victim of an unspeakable atrocity and her fear of being known as the lone eyewitness to Joeyboy's crime. Whatever Stanton had done, for whatever reason she had done it, it had not warranted such brutality—it had not warranted Joeyboy being the last human touch she had felt, the last face she had seen before her short and troubled life had ended in an apple orchard off a nameless Tennessee back road. Adding her own name to the list of those who had died at the hands of Joeyboy and the nameless men who had sent him was not going to bring Donna back.

The remaining two hours passed as slowly as if the hands of the clock had been painted on its face.

❖

By the time Brandie Mueller had spoken her last words, Jordan Taylor was standing by the wet bar in his den, anticipating the call that would inevitably come. He poured himself a double bourbon and slid the phone toward him—he didn't have to wait long for it to ring.

"Taylor?" came the inhospitable voice from the other end.

"Yes, sir," he responded dryly, his voice low. Taylor detested Warren Slade, Governor Williams' chief administrative assistant and scalp hunter, but at the same time he was acutely aware of the mighty axe Slade wielded with complete indifference.

"What the fuck is going on over there? Sounds like you've got a leak that would sink a battle ship." He was referring to Headquarters.

"Seems so, sir." It was easier to agree. His head hurt and he'd been in the damned rain all day. The last thing he needed at this hour was to begin an argument that he couldn't possibly win. Nobody won arguments with Slade.

The CAA grunted his displeasure. "Governor Williams' office, eight A.M. sharp," he grumbled. It was intended neither as a request nor a polite invitation, but rather a commandment from on high. "Have Vanover with you. Brandie Mueller will be there as well, along with Chief Harvey." He hesitated, as if he were unsure of what he would say next. Taylor was not fooled by the obvious attempt to appear impromptu— Slade was never unprepared for any call or meeting; he always knew exactly what he was going to say and do, and he always knew beforehand how the other party would respond. "Oh, and one more thing, Taylor, be sure to bring along Stanton's diary and tapes, will you."

"I wonder what in the world gave me the idea our little meeting was going to be centered around them?" he asked sharply with as much sarcasm as he could muster; it was wasted on Slade, who didn't give a damn what anyone thought about him as long as they did exactly what he wanted, how he wanted, when he wanted.

Taylor jabbed the Off button and downed his drink in one long swallow.

ELEVEN

The dancer walked slowly down the narrow hall, carefully balancing two cups of coffee that she now wished she hadn't filled quite so full. She was nude except for a pair of floppy cotton socks that insulated her bare feet from the cold hardwood floors of her apartment.

When she reached the bedroom door, she eased it open with her right foot. Other than a couple of drops that struck the floor—those she quickly mopped up with her sock—the coffee remained in the cups.

"I brought you some coffee, baby. You want me to set it on the bedside table?" The dancer watched as her best customer stirred beneath the covers. She stood patiently beside the bed, sipping from one cup, waiting for the disposition of the other to be decided.

Joeyboy raised his upper body onto his forearms and looked to the side. He scratched his head with his left hand, like a dog trying to shake a flea, and then used it to comb the hair from his eyes. "What?" he asked, not yet awake.

"You want your coffee now, or you want me to set it on the table for you?" She needed to do something with it because she was getting cold standing there naked.

"No, give it to me." He rolled over and stuffed a pillow behind his upper back. She handed him the one with three sugars and no cream.

Lela sat on the edge of the bed and covered her legs with the comforter. "Who's Donna?" she asked when he had put the cup to his lips.

"What?" he asked, staring over his cup.

"Who's Donna? You kept talking in your sleep to someone named Donna. I was just curious who she was, that's all." She held her cup with both hands, letting the warmth flow through her palms. She was far more curious about Donna than jealous of her. She knew he had other women, just as she had other customers.

Joeyboy lowered the cup and rested it on the headboard shelf behind him. "What exactly did I say while I was doing all this jabbering in my sleep?" He reached across the bed and stroked her thigh.

"I don't know, just stuff. I didn't listen."

"Really. How come I don't believe you?" His eyes frightened her all of a sudden.

"I don't know, baby. I wouldn't lie to you. I was kinda tired myself. I only heard you mention the name Donna, that's all."

"Come on now, surely you can remember something else I said. I'd like to know what I was talking about while I was sleeping, and, since I was asleep, you're the only one who can tell me that, right? That's not so much to ask, is it?" He continued to stroke the thigh gently.

"I think there was something about some tapes this Donna woman had of yours. You kept telling her you had to have 'em. Did this Donna chick borrow some tapes from you and not return them? I hate it when I lend one of the girls at the club a cassette of mine and she keeps it too long or gets it stuck in her radio and it gets all tangled and ruined. Doesn't that just piss you off?"

While Lela rambled, Joeyboy realized he had a problem, a problem that he couldn't solve at the moment, no matter how much he'd like to. The bartender at the club had seen him leave with the dancer. To make matters worse, the guy across the hall had seen them entering her apartment just after two this morning. He'd have to wait for a better opportunity, though he knew he had to act soon: even a brainless stripper like the woman sitting beside him would eventually tie what he'd said in his sleep to the missing woman who seemed to be all over the damned television lately.

He took her cup and pulled her to him, kissing her fully. "Yeah, that pisses me off, too, baby. Listen, I've got to go in a minute, got a lot of shit to do today. You going in at six as usual?"

"Uh huh. You coming in tonight?"

"Sure, I can't wait to see you again." He kissed her a second time, long and hard, pulling her bare breasts against him. It was important that she remember him affectionately.

"Wow, baby, I like you like this."

"Then you're gonna love what I've got for you later."

"You've got something for me? That's sweet. Are you gonna tell me what it is, or is it a surprise?"

"Oh, it's a surprise, but not just any old surprise. I've got something special in store for you."

❖

Jordan Taylor stood at a wide casement window on the second floor of the Andrew Jackson State Office Building, watching Charlotte Avenue come slowly to life. At 7:45 A.M. on Saturday morning, most of the city was still asleep.

By the huge fountain in the plaza to the south of the Capitol, a large group of grade-school children from St. Dominic Academy (he decided from the small sea of crisply pressed blue and white uniforms), was assembling for their first look at the home of state government. He sipped a cup of lukewarm McDonald's coffee—black, no sugar—and waited for Vanover to arrive. This was supposed to be his day off, a day he had intended to spend with his daughter, Amber.

"Mornin', Chief. We the first here?" Vanover asked in a tone that was way too chipper for Saturday morning.

Taylor nodded affirmatively.

Vanover handed his boss a small paper bag from Krispy Kreme and dropped into the first chair he saw. He opened his own sack.

Taylor moved close to the side of the chair where his friend sat munching on a raspberry glaze. Vanover didn't look up as he spoke. "You know, Chief, that Slade can be a real pain in the—"

"Goddammit, Pete! How the hell did Channel 9 get all that stuff about Stanton?" His voice was low, but it was obvious he was not a happy man.

Vanover looked up and quickly licked the icing from his right thumb and index finger. "Don't bark at me! I didn't talk to anyone. You know what a nosy bitch Mueller is."

"Well, if not you, then who in Sam Hell—"

"Good morning, gentlemen," Slade interrupted cheerfully from across the wide room. "I believe you two know Chief Harvey."

"Morning, sir," Vanover blurted out, quickly dropping the sack beside his chair as he stood and lowering his coffee inconspicuously to his side, like a student caught writing on the bathroom walls.

"Morning, Leonard," Taylor added. "You're looking well. How's Betty?"

The chief of police crossed the room and took Taylor's hand. "You know wives, Jordan, they're all a pain in the ass at times. Sorry about Gloria."

"It was just a question of time."

Harvey nodded as the men shook hands.

As Vanover stood by the window hurriedly finishing his coffee, his back to the room, Taylor and Harvey made small talk. The two men had known each other for over a decade, and though Taylor thought Chief Harvey to be little more than a yes-man of Governor Williams at this point in his career, he still considered him an honest cop, something Slade would have changed to suit his particular needs had he been able.

"I see we're all here," Governor Wayne "Buddy" Williams stated in his rich, theatrical voice as he entered. He was followed into the room by Brandie Mueller; the pair had been in his adjoining office since seven-fifteen, discussing the story she had reported the previous night. "Thanks for coming in on your day off, all of you. Have a seat, please." He made a broad, sweeping gesture with his hand and then took the large leather chair behind the wide burled-wood desk.

Slade took a position at his left, hands crossed behind him like a sentry.

The others quickly found the chair nearest to each and sat, all trying to appear relaxed, all filled with anticipation.

"I'll get right to the point. I imagine none of us missed Ms. Mueller's little ditty on the ten o'clock news last night. Quite interesting, don't you all agree?" He took turns staring into each pair of eyes, beginning with Taylor on his right. All managed to maintain a steady return gaze, though each silently wished he could have been somewhere, anywhere, other than here.

Mueller, on the opposite side of the room from Taylor, spoke first: "Governor Williams, as I have already told you, that story was correctly and accurately reported, based upon the information I received from an anonymous source—"

"Ah, yes," Taylor immediately snapped at her anticipated choice of words, "the infamous anonymous source—without a face or a name, the invisible authority behind every sleazy news story and trashy tabloid cover of the past half-century. Why not cut the crap, Ms. Mueller, and just tell me who in my department leaked the information on Stanton's diary so I can personally cut the bastard's balls off." His eyes went to Vanover, seated between them.

"I told you I don't have a clue who gave out that information, Chief. When I heard the story, I thought you were the one who had talked to the media," Vanover stated flatly.

"Me! Why on earth would I do that, Pete?" Taylor asked incredulously.

"Well, you're the one who left with the diary and tapes," Vanover said. "Who else should I have thought?"

"Pipe down, you two," Buddy Williams interrupted impatiently, like a father arriving at the dinner table. "I don't give a fat rat's ass who told the news. That's *not* why we're here this morning. If you've got a problem with security down at Headquarters, and it appears you have, then my suggestion is that you plug it! For now, all I want is the information contained in Stanton's diary and tapes." He leaned back in his chair, arms folded, as if awaiting a bedtime story.

Taylor looked at the small, well-wrapped bundle he had laid on the floor by his chair. His angry eyes went to Governor Williams'. "I can't let you have them, sir, they're not mine to give. Besides, they're part of an ongoing investigation. Why not just ask Mueller what you want to know. She seems to know as much as we do."

Williams looked to Chief Harvey for intervention.

Harvey spoke softly: "Jordan, to the best of my knowledge there is no active investigation in progress at the moment, and, as I far as I can see, no reason to initiate one. The missing person's report was withdrawn by the sister who filed it, and, from what I've read, there is every reason to conclude that Donna Stanton left town under her own power and of her own volition, despite Latham's reward. I trust you'll agree with me on that." Harvey raised his eyebrows slightly, awaiting Taylor's response.

"That may be technically correct, Chief, but it doesn't paint the entire picture. What about the call from the woman at the Mapco Express on Wednesday evening stating that Donna Stanton was murdered, and not away on some impromptu vacation?"

Vanover was puzzled by Taylor's exact repetition of his own argument in Stanton's bedroom.

"What's her name? How'd she say she died? Where'd she say the body was?" Harvey asked in rapid succession, knowing each question would have the same response.

Taylor now knew how Pete Vanover must have felt, and he could do no more than offer the same feeble answers he had received. "We don't have that information at this time, but—"

"But, nothing!" Buddy Williams snarled, losing what little patience he possessed under the circumstances: he could feel the fire blazing beneath his opponent's feet, smell the piquant smoke as it carried away Monroe's chances for victory. All the fuel and kindling necessary for that most desirable of all funeral pyres lay in the pages and tapes at Taylor's feet. "All you've got is an anonymous crank call and your detective's intuition, while we, on the other hand, have Latham's written permission to obtain, and study, both the diary and the tapes, and to release to the media"—he cut his eyes to Brandie Mueller, who pretended not to notice—"anything we find contained therein that might assist this office in effecting her sister's safe return."

Slade produced a folded document from his suit coat and fanned it triumphantly in front of his chest.

Taylor sank back in his chair and crossed his arms. "And I suppose in the process of looking for pertinent clues as to the whereabouts of Donna Stanton, you might just accidentally stumble across a morsel or two of information concerning a certain political rival—let me hazard a guess, from the Chattanooga area?—which would be of immeasurable value in guaranteeing your hold on the keys to the executive washroom for another four years." Taylor leaned to his right and stared hard at Brandie Mueller. "And, I don't imagine you would be adverse to reporting such a story, now would you, Ms. Mueller? It sounds right up your alley."

"News is where you find it, Chief Taylor. Just like evidence," she grinned defiantly.

"Come now, children, let's behave," Williams said, the impending victory evident in his superior tone. "You can duke it out on the playground during recess if you like. I don't have the time for your petty differences." He turned his attention to Mueller. "Are you sure there's nothing you haven't told me, Brandie?" She shook her head. "And you have no intention of helping Taylor with his leak, do you?" Williams knew the answer.

She continued to shake her head slowly.

"Fine. Well, that's that. You can go, Brandie. I'll have that package at your feet, Chief Taylor, if you would be so kind." Williams extended his right hand palm up while Slade stood silently by, savoring the moment.

❖

Kasey woke from a restless night of half-sleep with a splitting headache. She had gotten to bed around one and had nodded right off, though the images soon came, as usual, and the darkness became a mosaic of painful screams, bursting flesh, spattered blood, and terror. Each night it was the same, and each morning the headache was there: a piercing, thumping reminder that she had not done a thing to save the stranger she could now call by name: Donna Stanton.

She stumbled to the bathroom and poured the last three caplets from a recently full bottle of Advil. Sam stared up at her from the top of the hamper, a puzzled look in his emerald eyes. He didn't understand the change in morning ritual that had occurred a few days ago: he was supposed to be fed as soon as she awoke and she was supposed to go jogging afterward. Couldn't these humans remember anything?

Kasey fell back across the sheets and pulled a pillow over her head.

When she awoke for good two hours later, at a quarter past nine, a dull, felt-covered mallet hammered against her brain anytime she made a sudden turn of the head.

She knew the pain too well: it was not so different from an old tequila hurt. It would cease its pounding in an hour or two, three at most, and remain in blessed hibernation until the next bottle of Cuervo Gold, or the next dream spent lying in the tall grass by the rusting barbed-wire fence, watching Donna Stanton die over and over and over again.

Her life had become an endless stream of guilt and pain, interwoven and inseparable. She knew she had to do something.

But what? How?

Each time she considered the police, she remembered the Wednesday evening spent shivering on the couch, waiting for them to come for her.

She saw herself hopelessly ensnared, becoming a suspect or an accessory in the woman's death; she had seen it happen on television and had read about it in paperbacks. More than that, she had seen her own father, a man who had never been anything but good and fair, painted as irresponsible and reckless, a danger to everyone on the road. She had sat in the courtroom and said nothing while attorneys described him as a man whose personal financial goals were of greater importance to him than the safety of other drivers. It had broken her heart.

And, for a long time, her spirit.

If that were not enough, there was Joeyboy.

She could still feel his malignant presence as he walked toward the fence, shovel in hand. She did not want him stalking her as she waited the agonizing weeks and months between grand jury and final verdict.

Even with the best of intentions, the police couldn't protect her every minute. Eventually, as she slept in her own bed, or stopped at a traffic light, or shopped for groceries at the market, he would ease up beside her and snuff out her life. He would take it as effortlessly as he had taken Donna Stanton's—with even less hesitation.

People like Joeyboy felt nothing akin to regret. Something in their DNA had gotten corrupted at conception and the gene responsible for love had been replaced by a second hate gene. She knew this was so, even if medical science would disagree with her.

Throughout the morning, as with each morning since Monday night, Kasey tried to placate the tormenting dichotomies of fear and duty. The exhausting struggle was tearing her apart.

The phone rang, propelling her back into the moment and out of the morose, dank dungeon of hopelessness. "Hello," she said, trying to sound cheerful. She headed for the kitchen.

"Hey, Kase. How 'bout lunch and a little shopping?" Brenda sounded unusually alert for ten in the morning.

"What's with you?"

"Not much . . . except I just got my income tax back and I'm gonna buy the town. Hang with me, honey, and I might just buy you a 'happy' as well. God knows you could use one." Kasey couldn't help grinning.

"Where we gonna eat?" Kasey asked. She eyed the cold toast she'd forgotten to remove from the toaster two hours earlier and wrinkled her nose.

"Where do you want to eat?"

"Someplace cheap. I've only got about ten bucks I can spare."

"Wrong! You don't need any money. I already told you I'm the one with money today. You paid for my lunch a bunch of times when I was broke—which was usually."

"I didn't mind."

"Hell, I know that, that's why we're going shopping after we eat. How does The Iguana sound?" Brenda asked. "They've got killer fajitas. I've always wanted to eat there."

"The Iguana sounds great, but it's kinda high. I was thinking more like Pizza Hut."

"Yuk! We eat there all the time. Save that for when we're broke again. It'll come soon enough!"

The women laughed together.

"Get your butt in gear, I'll pick you up. You've got one hour." Brenda clicked off without waiting for a response.

Kasey laughed again and scooped Sam up in her arms. "Guess what, fella. I'm going shopping. I haven't been shopping for something you or I didn't need in God knows how long. Maybe I'll persuade Aunt Brenda to buy my little man a new toy mouse."

She set him on the kitchen counter, filled his food bowl, and headed for the shower.

❖

Jordan Taylor stopped at the foot of the wide granite steps facing Charlotte Street, beneath the imposing facade of the state office building, a dozen feet or so ahead of Pete Vanover. He had not spoken a word to the other detective since they had left the governor's office, and he was still furious at the way things had gone.

As Vanover neared him, Taylor turned and spoke. "Dammit, Pete, I want to know how Channel 9 got hold of that information. If you and I didn't leak it, then it must have been your brain-dead partner." His tone was level, but his demeanor was strictly business.

"I thought about that for a few minutes up there and I don't think so, Chief. Why would he do it?"

"You tell me, Pete. And, if not Stark, then who?"

Vanover lit a cigarette, slowly exhaling a thick gray cloud of smoke. A strong, warm westerly wind carried it quickly away over his shoulder, toward the river. The sky had cleared and there was summer in the air. "It could have been any one of a dozen people—more. Brad and I talked about what we had found with most of the other guys on the floor. Jesus, it was dynamite, you gotta admit that." His words sounded more like a personal defense than an explanation. "But I sure as hell wouldn't speak to the media, and I don't believe Brad would, either. We both hate Mueller. We must have a little bird on the floor." He stood erect and deliberate, awaiting Taylor's response.

"That really ticks me off, Pete, and I'm going to find out who that little birdie is before something crucial to a criminal investigation ends up in the wrong ear. And when I do, I'm gonna make him wish he'd never heard my name." He turned around sharply and disappeared toward his car.

Vanover crushed out his cigarette on the stone steps and headed for the vehicle where Stark was waiting.

❖

Brenda played with the coasters while her friend studied the menu. Kasey had eaten at The Iguana a few times but had never been treated to lunch there. The occasion called for a more careful consideration of the culinary offerings than if she were operating under the constraints of her own meager budget. Her friend had told her to have anything she wanted: she decided on chips and salsa, a full order of spicy shrimp fajitas, and a Pete's Wicked Summer Brew.

The beer and appetizers came immediately.

"So how much did you get back, dammit?" Kasey asked finally, since her friend had not yet volunteered the information and they had been together for nearly an hour.

"Five hundred eighty-nine dollars and sixty-seven cents," she leaned across and whispered secretively, as if she had personally stolen the money from the IRS's vault under cover of night.

"All right," Kasey yipped, "it's definitely shoppin' time!" They clinked their bottles together noisily and triumphantly, causing more than one head to turn in their direction. They began to giggle like schoolgirls, their hands cupped over their mouths.

Though she was genuinely happy for Brenda, Kasey hadn't seen six hundred dollars for nonessentials since her first, and only, year in college. To her shame, Kasey felt a twinge of envy: two weeks ago, she'd had to pay the IRS seventy-eight more bucks.

Brenda fidgeted in her chair for a moment, apparently wanting to ask a burning question, but not knowing exactly how to begin.

"What?" Kasey asked, sensing her friend's anxiety.

It was all the encouragement Brenda needed; she'd waited as long as she could stand. "Well, are you going to tell me about the big lawsuit or not? The rumor floating around Leonard's is that you're actually suing Hardt for sexual harassment. I thought you were just kidding when you joked about it Wednesday, but Alicia's telling everyone it's for real."

Kasey nearly spit out her beer. She had forgotten about her heated conversation with Hardt and the threat that ended the call. She took another sip of her beer. "I was just angry the other night. You know what a butt he can be."

"You're such a liar, girl!" Brenda said knowingly, certain she had the inside track. "I don't care what your lawyer told you to say, you know you can tell me." Brenda leaned toward Kasey, to make certain she wouldn't miss a syllable. "Is that where you were Thursday? Who's your lawyer?"

"Honest to God, Brenda, I don't have a lawyer, and I'm not planning on suing Hardt."

"I would! What the hell's stopping you? It's time someone put that loser in his place."

"That's easy to say, but there's a lot more to it than just making one phone call and suddenly being handed instant justice. It would cost me thousands to even begin, and besides, I don't feel like going through all the hassle of the court and the cameras and all that stuff."

"Do you know how much money you could get if you won a suit against him and Leonard's?"

"No, Brenda, how much?" Kasey wanted to change the subject.

Brenda started to blurt out an amount but hesitated for a moment. "Well, I'm not sure, but I know it'd be more than you or I have ever seen—or ever *will* see. Don't tell me you couldn't use the money."

"Jesus, Brenda! Of course I could use the damned money. The only one who knows that better than you, is me. I'm just not going to get up in front of a bunch of lawyers and judges and tell my side of the story, only to have them attack my character and call me a liar and a whore and God knows what else and say it was all my fault that Hardt grabbed my tits. Screw that."

"But it happened, Kasey. Mondo and I will back you up, you know that. You can't let that bastard just get away with it. He's such a zero!"

"Then he'll get what's coming to him—somehow, I don't know how. It all works out in the end. Karma is like that. Besides, I've seen how lawyers can butcher a good person's character in court, and I'm not going to put myself through it just so I can put a big check in the bank, even if I did have the money to hire a lawyer—which I don't. Now, can we change the subject? Please."

"You're not suing Hardt?"

"No."

"Well, I would."

"Brenda!"

"Okay, okay." Brenda knew it was no use to say anything else. "Sorry, Kasey. I didn't mean to make you mad or anything."

"I'm not mad." Kasey put her hand on top of her friend's. "I just have this tremendous hatred and fear of courtrooms. You'd had to have been where I've been to understand it."

Brenda suddenly understood. "Your dad, huh?"

Kasey nodded as a tear began to form.

The fajitas came. The waiter's timing could not have been better.

❖

The Federal Express van pulled to a stop in front of the huge iron gate, its squeaky brakes announcing its impending arrival for the last fifty feet. A pair of men, looking not unlike a matched set of professional wrestlers, stood businesslike behind the bars, on the mansion side of the architectural impasse. Neither appeared to be the type who engaged strangers in clever repartee, so the driver quickly and silently made his delivery of the Overnight package, received an unintelligible signature hastily scratched—from the one who could sign his name, he silently decided—and went about his route. He had four stops left before he could break for lunch.

The man who had accepted the package carried it into the small stone guardhouse by the gate and carefully cut through its wrapping. He had been trained—to an adequate extent, at least—in bomb detection and disarming, and as such, bore the unenviable responsibility of opening all packages and letters and assuring they were benign before sending them on to the main house. This one contained a single videotape. It was taken apart, examined internally, and reassembled for use before allowing the boss to receive it.

Giacano lay by the pool, fully reclined on one of the numerous chaise longues, a girl of eighteen or nineteen rubbing suntan lotion on his rich, brown skin. She wore only a thong, her firm, youthful breasts showing not a trace of tan line. Giacano preferred the well-defined triangle of white skin created by a thong.

The girl did not complain, of course, not only because she was familiar with the stories of those who had failed to please Mario Giacano, but more selfishly because she had nothing to do all day but bask in the sun, be fed and pampered like a child of Pharaoh, dress in the finest clothes money could buy, and travel the city in luxurious limousines.

She would, of course, have to join him in bed, but then this, too, was not entirely disagreeable. The old man had a certain flair, a power, about him that even young girls found attractive.

Michael Filippo walked quickly across the manicured grounds of the backyard toward the pool, followed by one of the men from inside the house who was carrying a portable video player and monitor. Filippo had already viewed the tape, and knew his boss would be quite interested in its contents.

"You'll want to see this, Mario," he announced as he got within easy hearing range.

Giacano rolled over lazily and put on a pair of prescription sunglasses with a deep blue tint. When he noticed Filippo's slight head gesture, while still twenty feet away, Giacano snapped his fingers once and the young woman retreated to the main house. She would, of course, stay close at hand in case he desired her company again; she didn't want to know what he was about to discuss with his top lieutenant—she disliked and feared the man, and made it a point to stay as far away from him as she could without it being obvious.

"What is it, my friend? You have some good news for me?"

Giacano rose and Filippo helped him with his robe. The bodyguard set the player-monitor on the bar, beneath a wide red-and-white striped awning, and plugged it into the outlet near the blender. When he was sure it was working properly, he returned to his post.

"This came a few minutes ago," Filippo smiled. "It's from our cop in Nashville. I think you'll find it interesting enough."

When his boss had situated himself on one of the bar stools and had swapped his tinted glasses for clear ones, Filippo pressed Play. Brandie Mueller's story suggesting a connection between Donna Stanton and gubernatorial candidate Bill Monroe had been taped from the previous night's broadcast. Giacano watched the tape twice with intense interest. After the second viewing, Giacano put his sunglasses back on and walked behind the bar, pouring himself a tall gin and tonic while he thought. He offered Michael Filippo a drink, but it was politely declined.

As Giacano made his way back around the bar, tapping its gleaming marble surface rhythmically with the fingertips of his free hand, an evil smile formed on the dark, lined face. Filippo had seen it many times before. "It looks like the pretty little whore may have inadvertently done us a service after all. It's a shame I can't thank her in person, huh, Michael?"

The men grinned knowingly at each other as Giacano raised his glass in a mock toast to the image of Donna Stanton frozen on the screen.

"Then, you wish to exploit this . . . fortuitous accident . . . to the fullest?" Filippo asked hesitantly. He knew it would be a delicate operation requiring everything their friend in Nashville Metro had to give. Perhaps more.

Giacano raised his hand in the air to summon his playmate. She came scurrying at once. "Oh, yes, my friend," he said, "I do, indeed."

❖

As they sat at a small booth for two near the large front window facing the street, the television playing at the bar could just be heard above the din of the lunch crowd. It was noon and *The Psychic Friends Network* was just beginning on one of the cable channels; the small screen was over Brenda's left shoulder, directly in Kasey's line of sight. She found herself picking at what was left of her ribs and watching the show with inexplicable interest. Half of what Brenda said to her passed right by. Brenda didn't seem to care, but had Kasey been aware of the one-sided conversation, she probably would have chuckled at how normal it all sounded: Brenda running on about whatever entered her mind while Kasey studied the surroundings, or the men, or the last thing that had been in her mind before Brenda began.

It was a familiar picture of the two of them; and so her friend rambled contentedly while Kasey became lost in the half-heard words of Dionne Warwick and her "special psychic guests."

Every so often, as if to appear involved in her friend's chatter, Kasey would nod or wrinkle her nose, perhaps sipping on her beer or taking a bite of her fajitas. It was all Brenda needed to continue for another five minutes undaunted and unsupported by conversation from the other side of the table.

Then all at once it came to her. A sudden flash of brilliance filled her mind: here was the one chance in the world for her to help Donna Stanton, to get the hellish nightmares to stop once and for all, and to do it without becoming a target or a suspect herself.

Kasey could see the wonderful plan unfold before her mind's eye, as clearly as if she were watching a movie about it happening to someone else. "Yes!" she squealed, the thought of at last being able to provide some measure of justice for the brutal killing she had witnessed. It all seemed so simple now, and yet, the most complex and risky thing she had ever done.

The hell with the risk—anything would be better than spending another tormented week like the one she'd just finished. She reminded herself that Donna Stanton's week had been far worse.

She would do it.

Brenda had stopped in mid-sentence when Kasey squealed, and continued to stare at her incredulously. She couldn't imagine what she'd said to elicit such an enthusiastic response.

Kasey took a long drink from her bottle, trying to reign in her emotions before they caused her to blurt out something she could ill afford to share. Her mind raced. "Do you mind dropping me at the library later?"

❖

The dancer climbed slowly, mindlessly, up the dusty gray concrete stairs toward her car—the rusting red coupe that waited obediently in its slot for her return had once been a BMW 320i, but eleven Michigan winters had reduced it to little more than a rolling wreck. It was parked in the first vacant space she had been able to find when she'd arrived late for work at five after six. The all-night garage just off 7th Avenue was only a block from the club and, when she had $4.75 that didn't need to go for food or gas, her favorite place to park. With the first two floors being reserved for those who could afford a monthly pass, Lela had ended up on the fourth floor, two spaces from the stairwell. At two-fifteen Sunday morning, hers was one of only three cars remaining on this level.

Joeyboy watched silently from behind the thick, structural pillar that formed the corner of the garage closest to 7th Avenue. From the top floor, he had been able to observe her all the way from the front door of the club to where she had entered the garage at street level. It would take her less than a minute to reach his position now. He moved quickly into the shadowed recess near the stairs.

With luck, he could have her neck snapped and her body over the side in less than ten seconds.

Suddenly, Joeyboy heard the unexpected rumble of a car's exhaust as a vehicle ascended one of the ribbed ramps that lead from floor to floor. From its faint, muffled sound, he judged it to be on the ground floor; second floor at most. He listened more closely. "Goddammit!" he cursed; it continued to climb. He knew it was most likely one of Nashville's Finest, making a patrol of the garage. He put his ear to the steel door beside him and heard the sluggish, hollow footsteps generated by a single pair of tired leather soles on the concrete treads.

He knew it was going to be close. Real close.

As Lela reached the last flight of stairs, her weary legs began to complain. She'd been dancing for more than eight hours, and between her required stage performances every fifth song, and an unusually busy evening of table dances, had managed to sit down for less than twenty minutes all night. Though she'd scarcely had time to miss her best customer, she had been excited to hear from him when he called at nine o'clock to apologize for not being able to make it. He reminded her of the surprise he'd promised and told her he'd see her later. The anticipation added a little spirit to her sluggish step.

Through the narrow triangular opening between levels, Joeyboy could see the headlights of the vehicle as they reflected off the support columns on the floor below him. He touched the .45 Colt automatic in his belt—well hidden beneath a heavy oxford shirttail that had been left out—and reassured himself that he had chambered a round after installing a fresh clip. Although it would be as loud as a Fourth of July cannon in the hollow garage, and heard by every ear within two city blocks, he had made up his mind to kill the cops if the car stopped anywhere near his position. With Lela on the stairs, and a furtive exit through the garage now impossible, the cop had left him little choice.

He heard the footsteps stop on the other side of the steel door.

The car began the last turn that would put it on the fourth-floor ramp.

At the top floor landing, Lela had to switch her heavy makeup and costume bag to her left hand so she could operate the knob with her right. The door resisted her initial efforts to open, but finally yielded. She was exhausted. As she used her hip to keep the door ajar long enough for her to pull the large Guess bag through the narrow opening, her throat suddenly imploded in an unnatural fusion of bones, blood, tissue, and nerves as Joeyboy crushed it like a handful of soft clay. The pain came from beyond imagination and then vanished in an instant as the brain quit receiving signals from a spinal cord that was no longer attached.

The handle of the bag became locked in a death grip that would have taken a surgeon to release.

Joeyboy supported her body beneath the chin and dragged the woman's lifeless form into the shadows, like a reptile slithering into its lair with a meal in its fanged embrace. He eased the .45 from his belt, wrapping his gun arm around the woman's waist for added support. The car made the ninety-degree turn and its headlights momentarily painted one of the adjoining walls that formed the stairwell. Although the place he had chosen could only be illuminated by lights coming from a vehicle descending the garage—not ascending—Joeyboy nevertheless inched himself and his prey deeper into the recess, until his back pressed fully against the structure walls.

He cocked the hammer of the automatic with his thumb, raising the matte-finish barrel until it was pointing directly at the officer's head less than twenty feet away. The driver—the only man in the car—kept his attention fixed on the old, faded BMW he had seen many times, his eyes staying with the spotlight he had directed into the car. The barrel remained locked on the man's head as the car crept slowly away from the stairs.

When the officer passed Lela's car without stopping, and continued to the far end of the top level, toward the remaining two cars on the floor, Joeyboy took the few seconds he knew he had and eased the body over the railing, into the alley beside the garage. It struck the pavement fifty feet below with a sickening thud, followed instantly by the innocuous thump of the bag landing nearby. Before the sound had finished echoing through the vacant first floor, Joeyboy had pulled the stairwell door behind him and had disappeared from view.

"Charmed," he grinned broadly as he descended three steps at a time. "Can't be nothing else."

TWELVE

Sam lounged on the bed and watched through half-opened eyes as his mistress rehearsed the answers to her carefully prepared list of probable questions. It was the tenth time she had gone through the list, making corrections for credibility whenever she felt they were warranted. Sam loved it when she paid attention to him, even if he was nothing more than a mock audience at the moment.

Attention was attention.

Kasey—dressed in nothing but a white cotton bra, matching panties, and a pair of cream-colored two-inch heels—used the full-length mirror on the inside of her closet door to study her body language. She knew a lie could be spotted as quickly by her mien and physical attitude as by her words. She had earned an honorary degree in body language, both hers and others (her classrooms had been the bars and clubs of New Orleans, Knoxville, and Nashville), and had often called upon that hard-earned knowledge when screening a potential mate from the lying, cheating masses. Though she had too often opted for the more temporal gratification of weekend love—longer affairs were complex and painful—she nonetheless considered herself an expert on lying.

Soon she would have to test those skills and knowledge to their limit. As she flawlessly delivered one of the more blatant lies she would be required to tell, she was certain Sam gave a disapproving look. "Don't look at me that way, Sam. I know what I'm doing."

Sam didn't move a molecule at her words; he might as well have been stuffed.

"I know what I'm doing, dammit! Don't you understand, this can solve all our problems in one fell swoop: we direct the police to Donna's body, we put that worthless scum Joeyboy where he belongs, *and,*" she emphasized the word, "we do both without having to talk to one single lawyer and without getting ourselves killed."

Sam remained resolutely still, his steely eyes seeing straight through her.

"What, dammit? I hate it when you look at me like that." Kasey plopped on the bed beside him. "Oh, all right . . . we get paid pretty well, too. There's nothing wrong with that, is there? It's not like we're extorting money from her. She offered the damned reward, didn't she? We'd be crazy to just walk away from it, it's like a gift from God, don't you see?"

She cradled Sam tightly in her arms. She hoped that by explaining her motives to him, perhaps she would be able to understand them herself. "I can't just let that bastard go free, not after what he did to Donna. She didn't deserve to die in that field, not that way, not after she did everything he asked. He's got to rot in jail." She rocked gently as she spoke, the tears forming at the corners of her eyes. "But if I tell the police what I saw, he'll come for me, just like he came for her. We'd never be able to run far enough. I don't know much about that son-of-a-bitch, but I know that he'll never stop until I'm dead, not if he knew I saw what he did."

Kasey forced an image of the horrible night back behind its secret door in her mind, refusing to let it out, to have any energy. She was becoming quite proficient at blocking the images and denying her feelings.

Even more now than when her parents had been killed.

"And even if Joeyboy is caught right away by the police, and the judge doesn't allow bail, how about the people who sent him after Donna in the first place, the person in the black Jaguar. They might even be the Mafia or something I don't know, I'm just scared, Sam, that's all." The tears fell freely now. "I've got to help Donna now, since I didn't do anything to help her when she asked. What's wrong with a little help for me, too? He didn't just kill her that night, Sam, he killed a part of me as well. You see that, don't you, fella?"

Kasey reached for a photo of her parents that she kept in a small silver frame on her dresser: it showed her father holding her mother in his arms, as though he were carrying her across the threshold on their wedding day; it was taken by Kasey at their twentieth anniversary party, the week before they were killed. She stared at her father's broad smile and bright eyes, the two things she remembered most about him. "It's too bad you never knew my dad, Sam. He had a saying for everything. Right now, you know what he'd tell me? He'd say: 'Pumpkin, the swamp belongs to the 'gators. If you plan to go in there, and you ain't a 'gator, you'd better be prepared to be lunch.' He'd also tell me he expected me to do what was right, regardless. Well, I'm not prepared to be anybody's lunch, boy, especially not that bastard Joeyboy. We can't play the game by their rules and expect to win. This is the only way we can help Donna and not end up in a world of shit ourselves."

She returned the photo to the dresser. "Trust me on this one."

Kasey kissed Sam on the top of the head and laid him on the bed again, in the warm spot he had made for himself earlier. "It's simple, really," she stated resolutely, wiping the tears away with the heels of her hands and standing defiantly in front of the mirror again. "No grand jury, no damned lawyers, no link to the crime, and nobody coming after me. Just one lie, one harmless little lie: the police get what they want, Channel 9 gets what they want, we get what we want, and best of all—Joeyboy gets what he deserves."

She sniffled once loudly and ran a hand down the front of her only good outfit as she held it against her body in front of the mirror. "Not a bad end to an otherwise crummy deal, I'd say." She looked straight at the cat. "Should I wear cream shoes with this suit or would the mocha ones be better?"

❖

Brandie Mueller picked up the line in her office on the fifth ring; she had been in the news room, adjacent to her office, viewing some footage shot earlier in the day. She pulled a pearl earring from her right lobe as she cradled the phone between her shoulder and head, still scribbling comments on a videotape label in her hand.

"Mueller." She wasted no time on formality.

"Want to know what happened to Donna Stanton?" Kasey's question was equally short and to the point.

She had Brandie's full attention, not so much by her words, but by the tone in her voice. Brandie could feel in her gut that the woman on the other end was not another crank. "Who is this? You have a name?" she asked, reaching to the far side of her desk for the odd-looking device she had left there earlier.

Kasey stuck to her own agenda, ignoring the question. "Are you interested?" She was not worried about being traced this time: the call was being placed at a pay phone on the opposite side of town from her apartment, at an abandoned service station. It commanded a clear view of the road for a mile in both directions, preventing a surprise appearance by the police. She had parked her car on the other side of a tall wooden fence, less than fifty feet away, and had slipped through an opening in the boards that would not easily accommodate the average man's body. There was no immediate access to her car other than through this slit in the fence, since the residential street on which it sat ran parallel to the back of the service station lot, and the closest adjoining road was nearly a mile south of her position. It had been carefully scouted yesterday—Saturday—and had been deemed ideal. The handset had even been wrapped in a paper towel to prevent fingerprints. The experience at the Mapco Express prompted the elaborate precautions she now took.

"Perhaps. Do *you* know what happened to her?"

"I do."

"And how did you come by this information?" Brandie sat at her desk and stuck a dime-size suction cup to the back of the receiver. It had already been done twenty times since Friday night. The small audio tape began to turn, recording the conversation.

"You'll learn all that in due time. Are you interested in the truth, or just a story?" Kasey's palm began to sweat. She changed hands.

"Why can't they be one and the same."

"Because most reporters are only interested in sensationalizing things. If I tell you what happened to Donna Stanton, you have to promise me that you'll not attack her character just to gain a larger audience."

Brandie Mueller was suddenly intrigued by this most recent caller. She was the only one who had shown any interest in the missing woman other than for the reward. "I promise," she said in her sincerest voice, and then added quickly, "You haven't asked me about the reward. That is why you're calling, isn't it?"

"I don't care about the money. If the information I have earns me the reward, so be it. I only want to sleep again without the nightmares."

Brandie was perplexed now; this was definitely a first. "What nightmares, Ms. . . ."

Kasey's end remained silent as she felt a strange queasiness overcoming her. It suddenly felt wrong going to the media instead of directly to the police with her information. She knew, however, that she ran the risk of losing any reward if she did contact the police again. She had to stick with her plan—it was the only way everybody won.

"Ma'am, you still there?" Brandie asked impatiently.

Kasey took a deep breath and looked hard in both directions. Nothing coming but an old faded green truck from the left. It passed without incident. "I'm still here."

"So, what did happen to Donna Stanton?"

Kasey squeezed her eyes tightly shut as she spoke: "She was brutally murdered and then buried in a shallow grave less than an hour's drive from her home." The words cut as they raced across her lips. She had to hurry to get them out in a cohesive sentence.

Brandie Mueller's heart skipped. An exclusive—the two magical words that made every reporter sit up like a trained poodle. She instinctively grabbed the recorder and checked that the cassette was still turning. It was, with at least twenty minutes of tape left. "How do you know that? Are you the woman who called the police on Wednesday?"

Kasey wasn't surprised that Mueller had quickly put two and two together. "Yes," she answered softly.

Mueller stood beside her desk. "When can we meet?"

Kasey knew she had come to the point of no return. She took time to consider her words: "I'll meet you at the station at six-thirty tonight, after the news. I'll be in the lobby."

"Will you tell me your name?" Mueller asked, pen in hand. "Or at least something I can call you."

Again Kasey hesitated for a long moment before speaking. Up to now, everything could be forgotten, treated as if it had never happened. She would remain forever anonymous, a nameless, faceless voice on the phone. As soon as she uttered the next two words, she was committed— irrevocably. There could never be any going back.

She looked at the switch hook on the phone and rested a finger against it. As she began to press, she saw Donna Stanton's scared blue eyes pleading with her for help. She felt her knees buckling under her. She had done nothing but lie in the grass and shake, just like she was shaking. The image was far more compelling than any thought of money. She knew it was time to do something. "Kasey," she whispered, the word barely audible. She took a long, deep breath and thrust her face toward the heavens. "Kasey Riteman. I'll meet you at six-thirty." With that, she pressed the switch hook and ended the call.

She looked at her watch: it was nearly two.

Kasey quietly placed the receiver in its base and walked slowly toward the hole in the fence. With her name now in the hands of the most watched television personality in the area, the security measures seemed comical. By the time she had slid down the small grassy slope to her car sitting patiently at its base, she was laughing out loud. She put her arms on the steering wheel and rested her chin against them, staring through the windshield at the city that lay ahead. "You're right, Daddy," she whispered. "It is the right thing to do."

The thought did little to quell the anxiety that was building within her like a winter storm.

❖

Slammer went to the door of the trailer as soon as he heard the bike approaching. He was sure he recognized the familiar sound as that of his roommate's Harley, but the nervous man never took anything for granted. Joeyboy's familiar blond locks and mirrored Oakley Blades confirmed that he'd been right. He laid the gun he had grabbed back on the crate that served as a coffee table and sank into his previous position on the tattered couch. The Braves were playing Cleveland and had a one-run lead in the eighth. He poured down a generous mouthful of the cold Miller.

"What's up, man?" Joeyboy asked as he tossed his shades on the crowded kitchen counter. He headed for the refrigerator.

"Already grabbed you one," Slammer said, holding a second beer at arm's length. "Heard you coming and figured you'd be thirsty."

Joeyboy flopped onto the couch beside his buddy. "Thanks."

Slammer tried to watch the television as the man beside him played with a small round disk of some kind. Finally, his curiosity got the best of him. "What's this?" he asked, grabbing it in midair during one of the coin tosses.

"That's a world of shit," Joeyboy answered pensively.

"Looks like something off a Honda. Ain't this a Honda emblem here?" He turned the odd-shaped H toward Joeyboy.

"It's off a CRX to be exact. Good guess, Lizard-Head." Joeyboy killed half his beer.

"So why's this thing so bad-ass? Looks pretty harmless to me."

"I found that little fucker in the road near the spot I dumped the Stanton bitch. I think it got left there the night I capped her."

The Braves scored another run off a single from David Justice, and Slammer shook his fist triumphantly at the screen. "Hell, it could have been there for weeks or even years, man. What makes you think it was left there that night?"

"It didn't have any rain spots on it."

Slammer looked puzzled.

"It rained last Monday morning, remember. Anything on that dirt road before then would have had those dusty rain spots all over it. This thing was clean as a pin. That means it got left there after Monday morning's rain."

"Yeah, so?" Slammer was barely interested enough to maintain a conversation.

"You're such a dumb fuck, you know it? If someone was on that dirt road that night, they would have seen me leaving. They would have also seen our good buddy following behind me."

"Oh, shit." The other man suddenly grasped the delicacy of the situation. "He ain't gonna like hearing this worth a damn."

"He's not gonna hear it. I'm going to take care of this little matter myself. In a week, we'll have our money from Stanton's jewelry. We need to keep the peace until then. When I find the car, and you can bet your ass I will find it, it'll be an easy matter to deal with whoever was driving it that night."

"Yeah, and how the hell are you gonna find just the right car?"

"Don't know, but it'll happen. I'm lucky like that." Joeyboy finished his beer and stood. "Oh, yeah, remember that chick, Lela, I've been shacked up with the last couple of days?"

Lizard-Head nodded that he did. He had wanted the attractive dancer for himself, but she had expressed an unnatural fear of reptiles.

Joeyboy knew Slammer had admired the woman. "Well, she's not gonna be at the club for a while, like . . . say . . . oh, the rest of her life. Sorry, man. Better luck next time." He let out a loud, hysterical laugh as he grabbed another beer.

❖

Kasey stood in front of the ATM, studying her account balance on the small white slip of paper—the ribbon needed changing, as usual, the imprinting was difficult to read. She looked at her checkbook balance and confirmed that the light gray numbers on the receipt were most likely $65.70.

She thought for a moment and then pressed the buttons necessary to withdraw exactly fifty dollars. She would have liked to have taken sixty with her, but that would have left less than six bucks in the account, not enough to cover the checking fee that would be taken out on Tuesday.

She cursed. checking fees and banks in general, withdrew the two twenties and one ten—all crisp, new, and flat—and dropped the crumpled receipt in the trash.

As she reached for the car door, she caught her reflection in the side glass. She nodded approvingly. The off-white Christian Dior suit (actually, an above-average copy of a Dior original) still looked fashionable after nearly five years of occasional wear. It was the best suit she owned, and the only one in her limited wardrobe she felt was suitable for her crucial first meeting with Brandie Mueller. She looked successful and confident, but not pretentious. It would be okay if Brandie Mueller was dressed a touch better, it would put her at ease.

Kasey knew she had to pass this initial test without the slightest mistake on her part. The logical questions had been compiled, the answers rehearsed, though it was more an exercise in preparation than a necessity: the pictures of Stanton's last moments on earth had been so well burned into her mind that she could have described them accurately a millennium from now.

Everything she could think of had been done.

She parked her car in the far corner of the visitor's parking lot, hidden from view by a new Dodge Caravan.

In less than a minute, she had crossed the parking lot and had stopped just outside the lobby doors of the most powerful television station in the state, taking a moment to straighten the split in her skirt and brush off the front of her suit jacket. Though she'd driven past Channel 9 a thousand times since coming to Nashville, this would be the first time she had stepped inside.

"May I help you?" came the efficient voice of the receptionist, an attractive woman in her late twenties with flawless diction and a warm smile. An almost invisible clear tube with a tiny silver tip followed the contour of her left cheek and stopped at the corner of her mouth; the earpiece of the hands-free headset was hidden beneath her perfect hair.

Kasey stepped in front of her desk and silently marveled at the vast array of buttons on the phone system in front of her, some blinking rapidly, others more slowly, and some with lights solidly burning; green ones, red ones, yellow ones. Kasey had no doubt the woman knew every button on the console: she had that kind of air about her.

"I'm here to see Brandie Mueller. She's expecting me when she finishes the news." Kasey glanced at the clock above the receptionist's desk: five fifty-seven. The closing shot from round one of the NBA playoffs filled the 35-inch high-resolution monitor to her right. The highly rated sporting event—and more importantly to Channel 9, the newscast that followed it—would reach the homes of more than a million viewers Kasey had discovered during Saturday's research. The thought both frightened and electrified her.

"Are you Ms. Riteman?" the woman asked.

"That's correct," Kasey responded, a little uneasy at first that her name had apparently been passed around the station so quickly.

"Ms. Mueller wanted me to ask you if you arrived while she was on the air to please not leave."

"I'll stay," Kasey responded agreeably, uncertain what to do next.

"Wonderful. If you'll just have a seat over there"—she motioned toward three overstuffed leather couches forming a tight setting at the opposite side of the lobby—"Ms. Mueller should be with you in exactly thirty minutes. Would you care for a cup of coffee or a soft drink?"

"No thanks," Kasey smiled, and quickly took a seat at the end of the couch closest to her. There were two men in expensive-looking suits to her right, on the couch directly opposite the television, and each smiled pleasantly as Kasey sat. She found them both attractive, and for a pleasant moment, allowed herself to forget the reason she had come.

All around her, the station was buzzing with activity, creating a surprisingly loud din, far louder than a lobby of this caliber would have been in a law firm or doctor's office. It was fascinating to her, and she felt her pulse quickening.

At exactly fifteen seconds before six, everything changed. The halls at either side of the lobby grew empty and the building fell silent, as if the entire station were a single entity and someone had just unplugged it.

For an anxious moment before the news began, Kasey held her breath, certain Brandie Mueller would lead with the story of a strange woman who had phoned earlier in the day to report that Donna Stanton had been viciously murdered and then buried in an undisclosed location.

Kasey locked her teeth together as the reporter began to speak. Brandie Mueller spoke in graphic terms of a multi-car accident on I-40 near Dickson that had claimed the life of some big dog in the recording industry—she hadn't paid attention to the name. And while she knew that her moment in the spotlight was close at hand—it was almost guaranteed it if she were successful, convincing—she was grateful that it had not yet arrived.

She might be ready tomorrow or the next day, but not tonight. Her body trembled enough that she was sure the men to her right could see it.

As she half watched the rest of the opening segment—her mind lost in the dual between right and greed, a slender, balding man in a wrinkled shirt and an ugly knit tie stuck his head out from the hall to her far right and addressed the two handsome men by name. They joined him and the trio withdrew down the hall.

Kasey was sorry to see them leave, but now that she was alone in the eerily quiet lobby, she leaned back casually against the fat leather cushions.

"It's always like that at news time," the receptionist said. "One minute, chaos, the next, silence. Hang around long enough and you get used to it. You find yourself looking forward to the rare quiet moments."

Kasey nodded at the explanation and thought of similar times at the restaurant. She smiled broadly at the receptionist: "That offer for coffee still stand?"

❖

Kasey had finished her half cup of coffee and was standing near the center of the front desk, carrying on light conversation with the receptionist whenever the switchboard didn't command her attention. Immediately after the large Simplex clock on the lobby wall indicated six-thirty, the door to studio A swung open, and eight or ten of the crew and talent spilled out into the hall.

It reminded her of class ending in high school.

All but one headed for the back of the building where the break rooms and editing suites were located; Brandie Mueller turned in the direction of the lobby and walked directly toward Kasey, never hesitating in her stride, never taking her eyes from her.

Kasey made a quick and covert assessment: Mueller was tall, far taller than she had imagined from only seeing her on television, perhaps five ten or five eleven, and thinner, too. To make things even worse, she was also prettier in person, if that were possible.

Brandie offered her right hand warmly and introduced herself, despite being one of the most recognizable faces in a town ripe with celebrity faces.

Kasey returned the handshake, and then, at Brandie's direction, followed her down the same hall where the pair of good-looking men had vanished earlier.

"I hope you have time to grab a bite to eat, Ms. Riteman. I've been working on one story or another all day and haven't had a chance to eat anything since a bowl of Special-K at five-fifteen this morning. I'm starved." She stopped at the opening to her office and looked directly at Kasey.

"Sure, that'd be fine. I'm a little hungry myself." It was a lie. Since her call to Mueller at two, Kasey had only been apprehensive. Perhaps, she hoped, a little food would settle her nerves. "Where did you have in mind?"

Brandie Mueller grabbed the matching jacket to her exquisite gray cashmere and wool Giorgio Armani suit from the back of the chair near the door. She indicated with an extended arm that they should head toward the rear of the building. They walked side by side this time. "I thought the Stock-Yard on 2nd Avenue would be a nice place to talk, if that's okay with you. It's quiet and the food's hard to beat." They made the corner at the lobby.

"Fine," Kasey answered. "I love the Stock-Yard." She recalled having eaten at the fashionable restaurant only once before, when she and Fred were still married and he was trying to impress a couple of prospective investors. She knew her measly fifty dollars would not go far, and it certainly wouldn't buy dinner for both of them.

There was already a problem in her perfect plan and they hadn't even left the damned television station yet.

She cursed the ex-husband who had left her credit in total ruin when they separated, and she cursed the six drunks at table 34 for having stiffed her on what should have been a thirty-dollar tip at work Friday night. She wished she had now taken her last fifteen bucks out of the bank, even if it meant being overdrawn when the checking fee came out. Screw the bank.

As Kasey and Brandie weaved their way through the intricate ground floor hallways of Channel 9's studios, Kasey suddenly had another flash of anxiety. What if Brandie wanted her to drive?

She knew her faithful but ragged old Honda would not impress the flamboyant reporter, and would immediately make it appear that the reward was all she was after. Kasey decided she would tell Brandie she'd been dropped off by a friend who was going to return for her later—her own car was in the body shop because someone had bumped into her; it seemed credible enough in a tight pinch.

"Mind riding with me?" Mueller asked as they passed the first of six video editing suites. "I'm afraid I don't make a very good passenger."

"I don't mind," Kasey offered without hesitation.

The quick response produced a knowing grin on Mueller's face.

As prepared as Kasey was in her mind for the meeting she had initiated, she had no idea of the wealth of information available to a person in Brandie Mueller's position. In the four short hours she'd had to work with since first hearing Kasey's name (her primary contacts including banks, credit bureaus, the Tennessee Department of Motor Vehicles, the Metro Police, as well as other state and local agencies), the reporter had been able to find out a great deal about the woman walking beside her: Kasey René Riteman, social security number 416-83-1515, was currently twenty-eight, soon to be twenty-nine; married to Fred Daniels in 1990; divorced in 1991; lived in a one-bedroom flat in the Bradbury Arms Apartments; worked as a waitress most of the time—since October '94 for the Leonard's Steak House at Belcourt Avenue and 21st; drove a 1985 Honda CRX that had no liens against it; had no credit cards of any kind since her divorce; was current on her federal income taxes; had no loans; held no college degree; had applied for credit to buy a new Mustang a year ago but had been turned down because of poor credit history while married; averaged $916 a month in checking account deposits; had no savings account; and as of four P.M. today, had $65.70 in a noninterest-bearing checking account.

Brandie Mueller loved the power of the press.

Everyone's life was right there, simply for the asking.

This story would cost the station no more than three to five grand she had decided after getting off the phone with her last contact of the afternoon, and Kasey René Riteman of the Bradbury Arms Apartments would be grateful for the more than generous offer. It would, of course, be well below market value if the information proved authentic, and, in any case, an inconsequential sum to the mammoth Clarion Broadcasting Group, parent of Channel 9 and seven other stations in the Southeast.

The women reached the back door of the station, next to the canteen, and only a few steps from Mueller's private covered parking space.

Kasey looked quickly past Mueller and saw a gleaming white Mercedes SL 320 convertible.

Paid for, she was certain.

She pulled in a slow, silent breath and prayed that she wasn't about to make the biggest mistake of her life. She had made it through the initial call to Mueller.

Now, if she could just make it through dinner.

THIRTEEN

Bill Monroe stood over the phone in his office at home, nervously twirling a pencil between his fingers. He had been trying to reach the number scribbled on the blotter for forty minutes, to no avail. He used the eraser to punch Redial again. Again it rang incessantly without being answered. "Son of a bitch!" he seethed through clenched teeth.

After pouring himself a drink and lighting another cigarette, Monroe tried the number once more. As he was about to hang up on the fourth ring, it was answered.

"Jesus Christ!" he shouted. "Where the hell have you been? I've been calling for nearly an hour."

"Oh, well, excuse the hell out of me, Willie (Monroe detested the name). If I had known you were gonna call, I'd have sat by the phone bakin' a fuckin' cake." The man didn't give a damn about Bill Monroe. Liked his money, though, and didn't mind letting him know it.

In fact, he had done so often.

He set his briefcase on the floor and dropped his tired body into the swivel chair behind his desk.

"Don't give me any shit, Fieldman, you little—"

"Little *what?*" the man interrupted firmly but without raising his voice. "I certainly hope you weren't about to call me a name, Willie. I wouldn't want to have to get ill with you after all we've been through together. You know how I hate to lose my temper."

Monroe realized, despite his loss of patience at not having gotten through to the other man when he wanted, that getting on his bad side would not be smart. He quickly reconsidered his approach. "You're right. I'm sorry, Fieldman. It's just that I have a problem that requires your special touch. I've had no luck with any of my other sources. They all think things are just too hot to touch for the moment. Bunch of worthless bastards." He took a breath. "I need your help."

The other man had seen the Nashville news. His only surprise was at the length of time it had taken Monroe to call him. "I'd say you do, Willie, but it won't be easy to fix this mess of yours, in that respect, your other sources were accurate. If you'd like to discuss the few options available to you, after I've had a little more time to consider them fully, I suggest you meet me at the Cracker Barrel at the Monteagle exit, just before you get to the town on I-24. It's only about an hour from your office in Chattanooga. I'll be there at eight o'clock tomorrow night. And Willie, I won't wait long."

"You won't have to, I promise. I'm sorry about—"

The line became an intensely disinterested dial tone in mid-apology.

"Asshole," Monroe muttered.

❖

"Just a glass of Chardonnay, please," Kasey ordered, hoping it was the least expensive wine on the list. The waiter was unimpressed by her choice, though he was impressed by the generous cleavage that was clearly visible between Kasey's lapels from his standing viewpoint. He had become, as had most of his fellow waiters, a master of the furtive glance, always careful not to stare long enough to offend the clientele.

"And for you, Ms. Mueller?" Brandie was a regular at the restaurant where Nashville's elite often dined. It was not uncommon to see any number of country music celebrities in the place, partly because of the serene atmosphere, mostly because of the excellent food.

"What entree are you featuring tonight, Robert?" she asked.

"The Filet Oscar, with crabmeat and asparagus spears and a sauce Béarnaise. I would suggest the seven ounce, medium-rare."

"Sounds wonderful, that's probably what I'll have, and in that case, bring me an '89 Jordan Cabernet. It should go well, don't you think, Robert?" The waiter nodded approvingly. Brandie handed him the menu without looking at it. "Would you bring us an order of Buddy's Famous Mushrooms. We'll order dinner later."

"Very fine, Ms. Mueller. I'll be close at hand if you need anything." With that, he left for the bar.

Kasey felt as if she had just observed the Michelangelo of the dinner crowd.

Brandie Mueller unbuttoned her jacket and nestled herself comfortably against one side of the booth, directly opposite her dinner companion.

During the brief ride from the station, the women had talked casually, chatting about a variety of subjects, but not a word had been mentioned about Donna Louise Stanton.

Kasey knew it was time.

"So, Ms. Riteman . . ."

"Please call me Kasey."

"All right, if you wish. So, what do you think of my favorite restaurant, Kasey? Have you eaten here before?"

Kasey knew that only one lie could succeed in any encounter, everything else had to be the absolute truth or that one lie would fail, and along with it, the association itself. At least, that's what she had read during her research at the library. The maxim was from the definitive book on espionage written by a double agent during World War II who had worked for both the Axis and the Allies to his consummate financial advantage; he was never discovered. "Only once," she said, "while I was still married. My husband brought some clients here to try and impress them. I think it took me three months to pay off the American Express bill." The wine came and Kasey took a short sip. "I usually stick to restaurants that are more in my league."

Brandie, who had expected to catch her guest in an early lie, now felt strangely drawn to her; she recalled that it wasn't so long ago that she herself could barely afford to eat at Burger King, let alone an establishment of this caliber. She nodded her sympathetic understanding of Kasey's situation.

Kasey wanted to get on with it. She felt like an athlete who had trained for a race and was now waiting impatiently for the rain to abate. "I guess you're wondering about my call, Ms. Mueller."

"Why not call me Brandie," she smiled, taking a slow sip of her own wine. When she had set the glass back on the table, she leaned forward a bit. "Your call was . . . well . . . quite intriguing. I'll have to admit to you that my first impulse was to treat it as another reward chaser or an outright prank."

"So why didn't you?" Kasey asked, hoping to learn what she had done correctly that had convinced the reporter she was on the level.

"Oh, I don't know. Call it a news nose, woman's intuition, whatever. Something in your voice told me you were more afraid than conniving, that you did have something genuine to say about Donna Stanton. I suppose that's why."

Kasey laughed inside at the irony of Brandie's words. She produced a tight-lipped smile but said nothing.

"Why did you hang up on the police?"

Kasey was not the least surprised Brandie had figured out that it had been she who had made the anonymous call from the Mapco Express. She let out a shallow sigh: "When I heard the detective's voice on the phone, I knew that they would never understand what I had to say." She could tell by Brandie's expression that she had not answered her question. "You remember when you made the comment that I sounded afraid? Well, you're very perceptive, Brandie. To tell you the truth, I'm scared to death."

"Of what?" Brandie leaned closer to the table, resting her arms on its edge.

"Of the images spinning around in my head. Of the dreams I have."

"What kind of images?"

The appetizer arrived. It remained untouched.

"Vivid images, more real than photographs. Images of Donna Stanton being killed." Kasey was starving but decided not to touch one of the mushrooms until Brandie did.

"Then you actually *saw* her die?" Brandie questioned, remembering her pocket recorder. "Hang on a second, Kasey, please. Don't lose your train of thought." She dug around in her purse and then laid the small device on the table between them. Kasey knew Brandie would tape the meeting; the only thing that surprised her was that she had not begun before now. "Do you mind if I use this recorder? I've got the worst handwriting you've ever seen, and my memory is the pits."

"No, I don't mind."

Kasey chuckled at the unnecessary explanation on Brandie's part and took another sip of wine.

"Would you like me to start over, for the tape?"

Brandie pressed the red Record button and the cassette began to roll. "Please, if you don't mind. I asked you if you actually saw Donna Stanton die."

Kasey felt her stomach tense. It was showtime.

She reviewed the two days of rehearsal in her mind. If she wanted to help Donna, see that Joeyboy got what he deserved, and keep out of the fray, it was now or never. There could be no mistakes from this point on. One slip would propel her instantly from psychic to witness, and that would be fatal. She took a breath: "Yes, I watched her die."

Brandie gasped. She actually felt uncomfortable at the relative stranger's bizarre admission. She looked at the tape to be sure it was turning. She also looked over Kasey's shoulder to make sure Robert was not within earshot.

"Oh, my God, Kasey. When did this happen?"

"Monday evening. Last Monday."

"Where?"

"I'm not certain exactly."

"You don't know the exact address, is that what you mean?"

"No. I mean I don't know exactly where, period."

"Now I'm confused. Did you or did you not see her die?" Brandie looked to see if anyone had overheard her words. She lowered her voice a notch. "Were you actually there?"

"Yes and no." This warranted an even more confused stare from the reporter. Kasey continued, undaunted; she had expected the reactions she was receiving. "I saw her die in one of the dreams I have sometimes." She immediately watched for Brandie's reaction to her word "dream." Brandie leaned back in the booth. Kasey smiled impishly, as if to say that she knew a fundamental secret that the other woman had yet to learn. "I see you don't believe in psychics."

Brandie's warm regard for Kasey and her pauper's credibility made an about turn. She had expected an eyewitness, an accomplice, or at the very least someone who had overheard the plot to murder Stanton—not a goddamned *psychic*. She'd gotten a bellyful of them during her years of broadcasting, each promising to lead the police and the media to a missing child or a kidnap victim, always coming up with some cosmic excuse why the celestial tumblers weren't in alignment at the moment, or why the moon was adversely affecting their telepathic powers. In the end, all they ever wanted was their moment in the spotlight, their proverbial fifteen minutes of fame.

Brandie folded her napkin and laid it on the table beside her wine glass. "You're a psychic. Jesus, I should have known." She made no attempt to hide her frustration or her anger.

Kasey had rehearsed for this exact reaction. She'd read repeatedly that the majority of people had little or no belief in psychic powers, and that convincing disbelievers of their existence and authenticity would not be an easy task. She stuck to her game plan. "I'll make a deal with you, Brandie," Kasey challenged, looking directly at the other woman. "Give me just fifteen minutes of your time. If, at the end of that quarter hour, you're not completely satisfied that I'm being straight with you, I'll take a cab home and you can enjoy your expensive wine and your petite filet with crabmeat in the peace and quiet of an empty booth. To you, I'll be just another crank caller, a fake." She lifted her chin a half inch: "You're already here. What have you got to lose?"

Kasey never let her eyes leave Brandie's. To do so would have meant instant defeat. This was the most critical ten seconds of the entire meeting. If she could get past Brandie's initial skepticism, and be allowed a moment to weave her tale, she knew she could be convincing. After all, she had something no psychic in the world could guarantee—she actually knew where Donna Stanton was buried.

Brandie Mueller's mind was processing data as fast as it could, weighing the options that would still allow her to come away with a story, even if it were not the one she had originally intended to file. That was clever journalism, she had often remarked, and she was a clever journalist.

In a heartbeat's span, she decided that exposing a fraudulent and heartless psychic's plan to capitalize on Laurie Latham's sorrow and loss would make a damn good story. Not quite as good as finding Donna Stanton's body, of course. It wouldn't have the same ratings impact or longevity, but it would be interesting enough viewing for a night or two. By then, something else would come along to steal the headlines. It always did.

"Five minutes," she countered, taking up her glass again and silently congratulating herself on her win/win strategy. "I don't want the mushrooms to get cold."

Kasey closed her eyes and touched the fingertips of both hands to her forehead, as if trying to wrench an image from her brain.

Brandie almost laughed out loud, but held it back. *At least she's got the act down pat. This might be amusing.*

Kasey's eyes watered as she began: "On the night of April twenty-second, a clear, moon-filled night, I was awakened from a deep sleep by the image of a woman kneeling in a field. There was a man standing over her, something threatening in his hands, something deadly. He was nude, as was she, though I couldn't see his face, or tell anything specific about him. The woman was Donna Louise Stanton. I later recognized her from your first news story."

Kasey had decided, during her rehearsing, that she would leave catching Joeyboy to the police. With the information she would provide, she figured that would be easy enough for them to do without her having to identify him. She wanted to distance herself from him as much as possible. Whether her thinking was sound, or based entirely upon fear, the decision had been made.

She noticed that Brandie appeared to have lost some of her blatant skepticism, or maybe she just hoped that was the case.

She continued, staring blankly at the wall behind Brandie: "I could hear the two of them arguing about something she had hidden, something he wanted back. She was crying and begging to be set free. He was cursing and pacing back and forth. Finally, after she had told the man what he wanted to know, she agreed to have sex with him in exchange for her freedom. When they had finished, he killed her. Shot her down in cold blood." Kasey was shaking visibly in her seat, but this was no act. The memory, spoken of out loud for the first time to another human being, was unnerving.

Brandie was genuinely impressed with the color and detail of the story. And the part about the unidentified item being hidden—the missing diary pages and tapes, she imagined—was tantalizing. She no longer knew what to think about Kasey. She was unlike any other psychic she had encountered.

The reporter in her needed to press for more specifics before she would allow herself to be convinced. "What happened to her body?"

Again, Kasey rubbed her forehead, probing for an answer. She took a long time responding.

Brandie did not laugh this time.

"After he killed her, he buried her body in a shallow grave and then vanished."

"Where?" Brandie asked. "Where is she buried?"

"She's lying between two trees, in a large field with an old barbed-wire fence running around it. She's south of here, outside Davidson County." Kasey was still staring into the nothingness of the space behind Brandie.

"That's it!? South of here! I'm afraid that's not very damn helpful, Kasey," Brandie announced in frustration.

Kasey turned her gaze directly at the other woman again. "I'll know it when I see it, Brandie. But you're correct about what you're thinking at the moment, I can't tell you the exact spot right now. It's not that specific. It will take time to develop."

Kasey fell back in the booth, as exhausted as after a workout, and sipped on the last of her wine.

"How much time?"

"Time."

"Just time. That's your answer?"

"That is the answer. I'm not making a batch of cookies. This isn't science we're talking about."

Brandie knew it was useless to attempt to pursue more detail at the moment. She found herself troubled by the graphic account Kasey had related, and while feeling an intense pull to believe it, she wanted— needed—something more concrete than the colorful tale to convince her it might be true.

She leaned back once more, to lessen the appearance of being con-frontational, and decided to probe Kasey about any previous psychic revelations.

There was a long moment of silence before she spoke again.

"How often have you had dreams like this?"

Kasey smiled inside. A wave of relief warmed over her. That question was the first one on her list of possibilities.

"Not often, but at least three times in the last ten or twelve years." She intentionally fed out information a morsel at a time; gabby and glib could too quickly lead her down a passage with no easy exit.

"Like what? What else have you dreamed that proved true?"

"The first time I can remember I was in high school. It was at the close of the school term of my senior year. The varsity band was scheduled to perform at another high school in a small neighboring town—Lafayette, Louisiana—a few miles east of New Orleans."

"You're from New Orleans?"

Kasey nodded. "The night before the band was to play, I woke up with the image of a sports car colliding with an eighteen-wheeler in my mind. Two of the senior boys were killed—decapitated."

Brandie moved her hand to her throat.

"It wasn't like any bad dream I'd ever had before, but more like I had just finished watching a news story about the accident, as if it had already happened and was already in the past. When I went to school the next day and told my best friend, she just laughed at me and told me not to be getting into my dad's liquor cabinet unless she was invited."

Brandie smiled.

Kasey easily and accurately related the story she remembered from high school, with the minor exception of it having been her friend—a friend who had died shortly after graduation—who'd actually had the dream, and Kasey who had told her to lay off the booze. It was a lie that could never be disproved—a perfect lie. The lie on which to base her credibility, the lie with which she could do right by Donna while sending Joeyboy to hell.

"What happened?" Brandie asked, anxious for the story to continue.

"That afternoon, while the rest of the band took the bus to Lafayette, the senior band leader, David Linley, and his best friend, Donnie Beard, went in David's car. I think it was an MG or one of those little sports cars." Kasey took a sip from the glass that Robert had just refilled. "As they rounded a turn, less than a mile from the other high school, they collided with a stalled transfer truck. The little convertible went right under the trailer and . . . well . . . the police said that they died instantly. They never had a chance. It was exactly as I had dreamed it the night before."

Kasey shuddered at the thoughts running through her mind. She hadn't talked about David and Donnie's accident since graduation. All of a sudden, it felt completely wrong to have used their deaths as a tool for her credibility.

She could feel her father's disapproval.

"Are you okay?" Brandie asked, seeing Kasey's color turn from rosy to ashen, as if someone had just drained her body of all its blood. She touched her hands across the table; they were clammy. "My God, Kasey, that must have been horrible for you at that age."

Kasey patted her forehead with her napkin and leaned against the booth for support. Her head was spinning. "At first, I thought it was just a fluke, one of those cosmic moments when weird things just happen. You know what I mean?" She was pleased to see Brandie's eyes signal her agreement. "Even my best friend wouldn't talk with me about it afterward, as if it had never occurred. I guess it freaked her out. I know it did me." She inhaled deeply. "Then, a year or so later, when I was a freshman at UT Knoxville, it happened to me again. Only this time, it was about a guy in my American history class drowning during spring break. When he died, I was saddened, but I wasn't as surprised as I had been the first time. The dream had been the same kind: real, too real. This time, I told no one. I figured they'd all start calling me a witch or worse, a pathological liar. I wasn't up for either." Brandie nodded gently. "During the next ten years, it happened only one other time, that is, until Monday of last week."

"Why do you think you had a vision . . . is that what you call it?"

"That's about as good a name as any, I guess."

"Why a vision about Donna Stanton? Did you know her?"

"No, I don't think so."

"But you knew the others you had dreams about. Why a stranger, then?"

"I must have met her once, or at least saw her on television. If I did, I don't remember it clearly. But you're right, though, all of the other visions were about people I knew personally. That's why this one is so strange. That, and the fact that the images are more vivid and frightening this time. There's a real three dimensional feel to this one, Brandie, and it scares the hell out of me."

Brandie was now truly baffled. For the first time in her life, she felt as though she had finally met the real thing, a psychic who could actually see into the future, or the past, or sideways. She didn't know how to word what she was thinking, but she did know that Kasey's story was involving and frightening, and that it would sell papers as the old-timers would say. She had to force her business side to take over; she knew detachment was the only way to objectively and professionally report a story.

And *this* was a story.

She took a large swallow of her wine and stuck a hand in the air for Robert. She stared for a long moment at Kasey and then asked: "How would you like your filet?"

❖

The two women hardly spoke during dinner. The mood wasn't tense or unpleasant, more like the peaceful silence shared by two friends who had known each other for many years.

Yet, it was far more than that.

All through the meal, Brandie had not been able to set aside the possibility—the probability, it now seemed—that the woman across from her could actually lead her to the missing woman's murdered corpse. The mere thought of such an exclusive forced the hair on her arms and the back of her neck to stand at full attention; it almost made her jump from her seat and order Kasey to take her to the spot at once, the hell with dinner.

She knew, of course, that such an impromptu and ill-prepared venture was not possible, even if everything else was in place, which it wasn't. Brandie wanted to be the only reporter at the grave site when Donna Stanton's body was uncovered, and that meant striking a deal with the only person—other than her killer—who could assure that. Something told her the story wouldn't come as cheaply as she had first thought. She sensed that Kasey knew the value of what she, alone, possessed. And, in a paradoxical twist of fate, the very money being offered by Laurie Latham through Brandie's station—money that was assured if Stanton's body was located, regardless of which station covered the event—would provide the previously impoverished Kasey René Riteman bargaining power with Channel 9.

Screw it, Brandie resolved cold heartedly, the polished brass candle holder in front of her having been transformed into the radiant form of an Emmy, the words "To Brandie Jean Mueller, for Excellence in Journalism" engraved in its base. *Clarion Group can afford any amount I agree to pay this woman. This is the story of a lifetime and I'm going to have it. It's the kind of story that will propel Kasey to immediate stardom, and with her, the reporter who brought the story to light. Nothing is going to stand in the way of my being that reporter, least of all someone else's money.*

"How much?" Brandie asked out of the blue, her impatience winning out over reason.

"What?" Kasey asked, almost spitting out her last bite of steak, caught off guard by the first words from Brandie Mueller in twenty minutes.

"For the story. The exclusive. How much?"

"I don't know what you're talking about, Brandie." Kasey didn't have a clue what the woman was driving at.

Brandie leaned across the table. "The reward money is yours, if you can lead the police to the body, but that's strictly between you and Laurie Latham. I'm asking how much you want to give the exclusive story to me, to Channel 9. We're willing to pay for such an unusual story, assuming, of course, that you can actually lead us to Donna Stanton. Now, let's cut to the chase, how much is it gonna take?"

Kasey nearly choked on the woman's brusque words. She folded her napkin on the table. "I'm not here for the money, Brandie. If you had in your head the horrid images that I have in mine, you'd pay your last cent to get rid of them. I only want to see that poor woman removed from that despicable place and taken somewhere where she can sleep in peace. She didn't deserve to die that way, and she doesn't deserve to remain in that place one second longer." Kasey's eyes watered.

"I'm sorry, Kasey," Brandie offered sympathetically, not losing sight of the fact that she intended to have the exclusive, at any cost. If the woman opposite her was faking her compassion and anxiety and playing Channel 9 for more money, she was doing it so skillfully that Brandie couldn't remember having ever seen a more convincing act. Either way, real or fake, the stakes had risen considerably. Of that fact, she was positive.

Brandie tried a different approach as Kasey wiped her eyes with her napkin. "Listen, Kasey, whether you take money for leading us to Donna Stanton or you do it for free, you'll be helping her find peace just the same. Why not take care of yourself in the process? With sixty-five bucks in the bank, you're not exactly in a position to be turning down good money."

Kasey's eyes opened widely. "How do you know how much money I've got in the bank?"

Brandie saw no point in playing games. "You're the only Kasey Riteman in Nashville, and I've got contacts at every bank in town. Don't get angry, Kasey. It's all part of being a reporter, and it's one of the ways I do my job. That is why you called *me*, isn't it?" She sipped the coffee she had ordered with dinner.

Robert took their plates and Kasey folded her arms on the table in the space that had just been made. "I suppose, but I'm not sure I like the idea of you snooping through my personal life like that."

"Really? Well, I'll let you in on a little secret, Kasey. When you go to the cops with your story, which you will have to do eventually—unless you get up from this table right now, say the hell with the twenty-five grand from Latham, and forget you ever tried to help Donna Stanton gain some measure of justice. They're going to snoop through your life worse than a little brother going through your room while you're out on a date. If you've got any secrets at all, no matter how cleverly hidden, they'll shove it in your face like tomorrow's headlines. And, after you've been to see them, if we don't strike a deal first, you're story won't be worth squat; every station in the tri-state area will have equal access to it, and you'll have nothing whatsoever to show for your trouble. It's your choice. Do whatever you want, but I sure as hell know what I'd do." Brandie folded her arms across her chest and leaned back resolutely.

Kasey's mine reeled. She could no longer think clearly. All of her possible scenarios, all of her well-rehearsed words and carefully planned strategy for getting in and getting out with the least amount of hassle and risk had just flown out the window. She found herself asking the next question involuntarily: "How much are you talking about, Brandie?"

Brandie knew she had pushed the right button when she'd appealed to Kasey's need to help Donna. *Damn, I'm good,* she smiled without smiling. "That depends on a number of things."

"Such as?" Kasey fumbled for the cream, adding less than she'd wanted to her coffee because her hand was shaking and she didn't want Brandie to notice.

Brandie missed nothing.

"Can you actually lead us to the place where Donna Stanton's body is buried? Not the general vicinity, but the grave itself."

Kasey had always known in her heart that she would have to go back to the orchard sooner or later; she had unfinished business there; she had not yet provided the help that had been asked of her. Her heart pounded at the thought, but there was no escaping what she knew she must do.

Brandie grew anxious. "Kasey?"

"Yes, but not alone. I won't go there alone, not to that place."

"Fine. There will be at least two other people from Channel 9 besides myself. You'll have plenty of company."

"What about the police?" Kasey asked, surprised that Brandie had left them out of the picture.

"They'll only get in the way of a great story. We'll call them when we locate the body."

"Isn't that against the law?" Kasey wanted no part of a plan that would get her thrown in jail.

"Hell, no. Your dreams aren't gospel. They're not testimony. We'll simply be on a quest, a quest for truth. If we find her, we'll share the news with the cops then. If not, you'll be grateful they weren't in your face the whole time. They don't have my patience or pleasant disposition." She wrinkled her nose at her dinner guest, hoping to elevate the mood of the moment.

Kasey was sure Brandie was right about the police. She remembered how pushy Vanover had been when he'd had nothing but a nameless, faceless voice to go after. She wanted no cops around, not yet. "I'll need someone who knows the area south of Nashville well."

"You got it. You can have anything you need if it will help you lead me and my cameraman to Donna Stanton. Can you do it?"

Kasey trembled. "Yes," she whispered, the images flooding her mind.

"In that case, Clarion will match Laurie Latham's reward offer. That's fifty grand to you when we find Donna Stanton's body. I'll even throw in dinner tonight." Brandie tried to appear professional now, to infer by her demeanor that she had just presented the absolute best offer Kasey would see from any local station. She didn't mind spending more of Clarion's money, of course, she just wanted a deal to be struck so they could move ahead. She was ready to get on with the hunt.

Kasey grew faint. She had not been prepared for such things. Questions, yes. Even probing into her past, that, too. But the reward offered by Donna's sister had seemed unreal: people simply didn't throw such sums around like Monopoly money. Now, without having done a thing, she had an equal sum thrust at her. *Fifty thousand dollars*—she ran Brandie's words over and over in her mind. She couldn't help thinking about the annoying little Mr. Polson from Consolidated Collection. She tried to picture what he might look like. *Just have your lawyer call me now, you little weasel. I'll rain all over his fresh-cut hay.* "How can you do that?" she asked.

"You mean spend other people's money? Hell, I'm a pro at it. It drives them crazy. They'll approve it, though. Trust me." Brandie signaled for Robert. She was secretly relieved that Kasey had not held out for more money, though she would have given it to her. She was going to have a hard enough time getting twenty-five thousand approved by morning, but it would simply have to be done. She had no intention of letting another day go by without beginning the search for Donna Stanton, a search that she only knew at this point would take them south, somewhere outside Davidson County.

When the check had been paid, Brandie leaned back comfortably against the booth. Her mind was busy making plans and coordinating the resources she would need to compile such a story, in the manner she wanted it to be presented. "I want to get started first thing in the morning. Will that work okay for you, you know, is this . . . well . . . the kind of thing you can pretty much do at any time?"

"I don't follow you."

"I mean, can you have a vision anytime you want one?" She wasn't sure how to word the question.

"I've already had the dream, Brandie. All I have to do now is remember enough detail about it to make finding the actual spot possible."

"And you can do that in the morning?"

"I don't think there should be any problem, though I'm never sure about these things. I'm not exactly an expert on the psychic world, you know." Flashes of that horrible night replaced her pleasant daydream about Polson's lawyer.

Brandie squirmed a bit. "But you do think you can find her with our help?" She wanted a definitive answer, dammit.

Kasey paused and then nodded.

Brandie let out a sigh. She had been worried for a moment. "What exactly do you need from me to begin in the morning? Just name it."

"I don't know," Kasey answered. "Someone who can drive while I watch the road and the study the land. Someone who knows the area south of Nashville."

"But we're still talking Tennessee, right?"

"I'm sure it is. It felt close by in my dream, maybe forty or fifty miles away at most. I don't think it should be any farther than that." She began to remember her research and her hours of rehearsing. She knew it was best to remain vague. The tables had turned so quickly that it was disorienting.

"Forty or fifty miles. You're talking about a massive area, Kasey. It could take weeks, months—hell, it could take years." The sense of frustration flushed her cheeks.

"Trust me, Brandie, I'll know it when I see it," she repeated reassuringly.

Brandie watched her eyes and could tell that Kasey's words had been spoken with absolute confidence. It still made her nervous. She had to have this story.

Brandie patted her hands lightly on the edge of the table. "Well, it sounds like a huge undertaking, Kasey, but I'll tell you what . . . if you're sure you can do it, I'm with you a hundred percent. I can have a news truck, a cameraman, a driver who knows the area south of here, and yours truly ready to go by eight in the morning. We'll take all day if necessary searching the area. If we don't find her Monday, we'll try again on Tuesday. If we're still not successful, we'll regroup and rethink the whole thing. All we have at risk are a couple of days time and a lot of Clarion's gas." Her words sounded supportive and yet realistic, but the mere thought of failure was enough to make the Béarnaise sauce begin to curdle.

"And if we do find Donna Stanton?"

The image of her co-hosting *The Today Show* was as vivid in Brandie's mind as Kasey's face before her; it was her destiny, she was sure of it. "Then, my friend, you'll be famous and have one hell of a big check to stick in the bank."

Kasey smiled slightly, but she would not have been able to stand at the moment if the building had been on fire; her legs would have wobbled and folded like a cheap card table. Famous. Her heart almost jumped through her chest at the thought of everything that was about to happen.

She knew she had passed her first real test with honors, though things had gotten out of hand before she had known what was happening. Fortunately, everything seemed to have happened for the best.

Now she would have to face an even tougher test: the cameras, the world—the police.

But at least now I won't have to face Joeyboy, she thought with immense relief. *The rest I can handle.*

❖

Steve Dacus was putting the finishing touches on a story he had just written about the Davidson County Election Commission, scheduled to be read on the air in less than an hour, when Brandie Mueller burst into his office. "You're not going to believe where I've been for the last hour and a half!" she blurted out, panting from having run all the way from her parking space where she had just said good-bye to Kasey. "Is Stewart still in?"

Stewart Parker had been the general manager of Clarion Broadcasting Group's flagship station for nearly a decade. During that time, he had been through one double bypass heart surgery, an operation to remove a bleeding ulcer, two wives, and three news directors.

Dacus—in his fourth year in the role—currently held the longevity record under Parker. The two were workaholic bookends, addicted to their jobs, and so the question from Brandie about Stewart Parker still being at the station after only fourteen hours was ludicrous.

"Of course," Dacus stated, though he had neither looked at a clock to determine the current time, nor had he actually seen his boss since before six P.M. "What's up?"

❖

Stewart Parker and Steve Dacus listened for nearly half an hour as Brandie set the stage for her dinner meeting with Kasey, beginning with the two P.M. call. Then, she set a tiny gold Olympus Pearlcorder on the table between the three of them and ran the tape she had made at the Stock-Yard. While it played, the two sat silently, taking in every word that had been recorded.

When it had finished playing, Parker looked at the clock: news in ten minutes. "Let's make a living, boys and girls," he snapped, rising to his feet, the only one of the three who had thought to check the time. "Let's meet in my office immediately after the news." He took a slow and deliberate breath. "Brandie, if this Riteman woman of yours is not a hoax . . ." He pointed a long, bony finger dramatically at the station's only Emmy, won nearly a decade ago.

Dacus and Mueller followed his slender arm to the glass display case resting proudly on a black marble pedestal by the office door. In it sat the benchmark of broadcasting excellence, the ultimate reward for a news job well done.

When she had driven to the restaurant three hours earlier, Brandie had not even entertained the outrageous fantasy that now seemed to consume her.

FOURTEEN

The phone rang in the newsroom of Channel 2, New Orleans, one of the sister stations of Channel 9, Nashville. The powerful and influential NBC affiliate, serving all of southern Louisiana and much of the Mississippi Gulf Coast, had been the most recent major acquisition by the Clarion Broadcasting Group, bringing to eight their total of stations wholly owned. They had significant, though not controlling-interests in four others, and so the FCC carefully monitored Clarion's business in an effort to prevent the creation of a regional news monopoly.

It was all just bureaucratic government nonsense to Brandie who longed for the days when the Big Three—ABC, CBS, and NBC—controlled the airwaves, the news itself, and network journalists were as respected and feared as federal marshals.

She had never known such power herself, but the stories told by the old-timers at Channel 9 sent shivers down her spine. The thought of power made her horny, in the way no man ever had. Or could.

"Newsroom" came the bored response from a cameraman, not entirely thrilled at the idea of having to be at work at six in the morning.

"Who's speaking, please?" Brandie asked quickly.

"This is Eddie Bryan. Who's asking?" The strange woman's voice on the other end of his line sounded like it was in a hurry, something he wasn't greatly interested in accommodating at the moment.

"This is Brandie Mueller from Channel 9, Nashville. I need some information on a story you might have run around twelve years ago. Who would be the best person to help me with that, Eddie?"

"Well, to tell you the truth, Ms. Mueller, I guess I'd be about as good as anyone, especially at the moment. The place is still kinda quiet. We don't get hoppin' for another hour yet. You got something more for me to go on than ' we might have run it twelve years ago?' " he asked with a touch of sarcasm.

"Sure, sorry. It was an auto/truck accident with multiple fatalities that occurred in the Lafayette, Louisiana, area in either April or May of '85. Does that ring a bell at all?"

Eddie Bryan had been with Channel 2 for twenty years, first as a grip for the veteran cameramen, and then later as a field cameraman in his own right. Due to a lower back injury, he was currently assigned to operate a studio camera, where no lifting and little movement was required. In addition, he had to answer the newsroom phone on Monday mornings. He was ready for his back to be better.

"Hey, I've heard of you." He remembered the name. "You're that good-looking anchor woman they hired a couple of years back in Nashville."

"Anchor person," she teased. "We must be politically correct."

"Yeah, anchor person." He hated that shit.

"And thank you for the compliment, Eddie. Do you think you can help me?"

"You say this accident happened in the Lafayette area?"

"That's what I was told. It was supposed to have involved two high-school band members and a semi-truck." Brandie remembered the awful story and needed no notes to refresh her memory. She looked at her watch: Kasey should be arriving in less than an hour.

"Oh, fuckin'-A!" Bryan unexpectedly bellowed when the memory struck him, startling Brandie who had just begun a wide, overdue yawn on the other end. She had not slept at all. "Pardon my French, Ms. Mueller."

"That's okay," she chuckled. "I take it you remember it then."

"I'll say I do, Ms. Mueller. It was the first fatal I'd been sent out on as a new cameraman. Jeeze-O-Pete! What a friggin' nightmare!" The grisly pictures poured from his subconscious, released from the dark recesses of his memory after nearly a dozen years.

"Tell me what you can about it, Eddie." She pressed Record on the Pearlcorder, the microphone already gripping the phone.

"As I recall, these two young boys were killed when they hit a stalled truck. I believe they were seniors from Central High in New Orleans." His rich native accident with its colorful bayou influence slurred the words "New Orleans" into a thick-sounding "Nawlins." He continued, interrupted for a moment by the violent scene that flashed before his eyes. "It was awful. They were . . . well . . . they had their heads cut off." Drove that little red convertible of theirs right under an eighteen-wheeler that was stopped sideways in the road, and *BAM!*" His words made Brandie jump. "Not a prayer in hell. Didn't even slow down. I swear, I ain't never seen anything like it before or since, thank the good Lord." Being a good Catholic, he made the Sign of the Cross with his right hand, and then after a quick breath, announced: "I remember getting some great shots of it, if I do say so myself. They should still be in the vault. Want me to make a copy and send it to you up there?"

Brandie's skin immediately became alive with goose bumps and she shivered as if a blast of Arctic air had blown down her blouse. "That's okay," she said weakly. "I don't think that'll be necessary after what you've told me. Do you happen to remember the date?"

"Yeah, like I said, it was my first fatal. You don't ever forget a date like that. It's kinda like a birthday or anniversary. It was a Friday afternoon, the twenty-first of May, 1985."

"Thanks, Eddie. You've been more helpful than you could know."

"It was nothing, Ms. Mueller. Nice talking to you."

Brandie lowered the phone and made a quick effort to regain her detachment and composure before Kasey arrived. She looked at her palms: they were both sweating. "This is creepy," she muttered, wiping them on her pants. "Yes!"

❖

"What's up?" Tim Arnold asked, sticking his head into Brandie's office. The welcomed intrusion snapped her out of her daze.

Arnold was Channel 9's best shooter, possessing both a sense of the dramatic as well as flawless technical skills. Brandie had specifically requested that Steve Dacus assign him to her Monday morning outing, without telling him or their driver what they had in mind. Dacus had concurred; they knew how easily a head start on a story could be lost, even with the best planning, so it was Brandie's intention to keep the small group together—and silent—until Stanton was found, even if it meant all of them sharing the same motel room at the end of the day.

Normally, Brandie only worked the weekday shift, the A shift as it was known, leaving weekend news to the less-seasoned reporters. She had agreed to work yesterday, Sunday, because of a vacation schedule overlap that had left Dacus scrambling for a news anchor. In truth, Brandie had been glad to help out; she never minded being on camera. She was doubly glad now because it had put her at the station when Kasey first called. She was certain it had been fate that put her by the phone at two o'clock.

"Hey, Tim," she smiled warmly, and then rose to greet him more formally. "Glad you could make it on such short notice. Sorry about the early hour."

He didn't mind as much as he wanted them to believe. "Got something big going down, huh?" He and Brandie walked toward the lobby.

"Very big, Tim, and I'm counting on the best you've got. Real Hollywood stuff . . . you know, the thrill of victory—"

"And the agony of defeat," he grinned.

"Make sure we've got enough SP tape and batteries for two days' shooting. We're not coming home again until this baby's in the bag."

"Gimme a break, Brandie," he moaned. "I had a date tonight."

"Had—that's the key word here, my friend. I'm glad to see you've got a realistic grasp of the situation." She flashed a sarcastic look at her cameraman and pointed toward the equipment room.

Tim knew it was useless to argue. Brandie must smell a story, and that meant seeing it through to the end, whenever that was. "Son of a bitch," he mumbled under his breath.

No sooner had she sent him off with an affectionate pat on the back than Kasey entered the front door of the station.

"Mornin', Brandie," she offered in a monotone voice. She had slept fitfully last night. The thought of returning to that loathsome orchard had proven to be a powerful stimulant.

Kasey was also having difficulty resolving the moral issue of making money because of someone else's misfortune. She kept telling herself that she wasn't doing anything wrong. On the contrary, she was providing a means by which the police could now solve a murder which would likely have gone unsolved, and she was doing it without endangering her own life in the process. There couldn't be anything wrong with that, could there?

Through the night, the question had been asked time and time again. The words made perfect sense but the torment remained.

"Hey, Kasey," Brandie waved. "Ready to go?" The two met in the center of the lobby and Brandie squeezed both of Kasey's shoulders, sensing her distress. "Rough night, huh?"

"Really rough," Kasey sighed. "Any coffee around here this morning? I sure could use a cup of double-caf."

"That's all we brew. How else do you think reporters start at five in the morning and still do the sign-off every night?"

Kasey followed Brandie to the breakroom near the back door where they each filled a large Styrofoam cup with a foul-smelling liquid as black as ink and snapped on a travel lid.

With coffee in hand, they joined Tim Arnold at the Jeep he was in the process of loading. Jerry Richards—JR to all who knew him—serving as both driver and grip, was there as well, lending a hand.

Tim spoke as soon as he spotted Brandie again. "Brandie, you know JR. Dacus told me to grab someone to grip for us who knew middle Tennessee pretty well. JR grew up in Columbia and should be able to help us find wherever it is we're looking for, such as . . . ?" He cocked his head and smiled exaggeratedly, waiting for her to fill in the blank.

"You'll know where we're going as soon as we're on the road, my boy, not before." She opened the back door of the white Jeep and motioned for Kasey to take the seat behind the driver. Brandie then took the other rear seat and, once the door had been pulled shut, leaned back against the door panel and window glass, facing Kasey.

They sipped their coffee without talking, both feeling anxious, but for very different reasons.

The men finished loading the balance of the gear and then took their places in front. JR drove, with Arnold—camera on his lap—riding shotgun, a position that would permit him to shoot Kasey, seated diagonally behind him, with ease.

JR started the engine and pulled the gear shift into Drive. Channel 9 had spared no expense in obtaining the best all-weather vehicles the station could find. Each news team had its own V-8 four-wheel-drive Jeep Grand Cherokee, with automatic transmission, air, cruise, police scanner, cellular phone, and big, fat, all-terrain tires. "It would help if I had a basic idea which way to head." He alternated his eyes between Tim and Brandie.

Brandie looked at the woman sitting silently on her left, and then at the two men. "Tim, JR, I'd like you both to meet Ms. Kasey René Riteman. Today, *she's* the star. Wherever she says drive, you drive. Whenever she says stop, you stop. Whatever she wants, you get it for her." She then looked only at Tim: "I don't want to miss a single frame of anything that's germane to the story. I want it all on tape—the scenery, the weather, her expressions, her words—everything. Clear?"

"Perfectly."

"All right, then, we're off." She looked at Kasey. "How about it, Kasey, which way?"

Kasey started to answer Brandie. It was then she noticed the ominous-looking Sony Betacam camera pointing at her from the front seat, its digital chips painting a nearly film-quality image in even the lowest of light, its highly sensitive shotgun microphone ready to pick up her every utterance. The massive glass lens—a 22:1 Fujinon servo zoom—with its oversize black sun hood only three feet from her face, made her go mute.

Brandie chuckled.

She had seen it a hundred times: point a camera at a jabbering child and it will immediately stop talking. The same held doubly true for adults.

"Try to relax, Kasey. I know it won't be easy at first, but the more you can forget about the camera, the more natural and believable your story will appear, and appearance is everything in this crazy business."

Kasey found herself vaguely excited by Brandie's last words. It hadn't been the fear of the camera that had caused her to pause, but the reality of it. Where had the old childhood dream of being a star gone? How many side roads had she taken along the way?

None of that mattered now.

She could scarcely believe she was actually here, at this moment, with the camera focused on her. It was time to help Donna, but it was also time to rekindle her own life. She took a breath and blew it out dramatically. "I think we should try the area just east of Columbia first." She flashed a smile at JR. "I studied a map of the state last night, trying to get some sign, and it felt like the right place to start. It may feel wrong when we get there, but let's give it a shot."

"Head for home, JR," Brandie ordered. "You should know the way."

The Jeep surged forward and sped quickly down Knob Road. JR made a left on White Bridge, a right on I-40, and headed south on I-65, taking the most direct route to the city of Columbia, and the farms and hills that lay around her.

When the Jeep had made the last hard turn it would make for quite a while, Brandie grabbed her wireless hand-held mike from Tim's grip bag (it had been configured to record Brandie's voice on a different audio track of the videotape than the one he had selected for Kasey) and tapped him on the shoulder. Tim responded by directing his camera at her, keeping it as steady as he could while riding backward, supported by his body against the dash, his knees against the seat. She touched up her hair a bit and then gave him a nod, indicating that he should roll tape. He knew her habits and signals well and had already begun recording as soon as she moved the last out-of-place hair into its rightful position.

In the ten-minute taped narrative that followed, Brandie set the stage for their unusual quest, and introduced Kasey's character, referring to her at one point as a psychic with a heart as well as gifted insight, a woman tortured by a frightening vision that haunted her mind and her soul. Brandie had no idea how accurate her colorful words had been.

She never referred to Donna Stanton as possibly being dead, saying only that she was missing. When she lowered the mike and nodded again to signify the end of taping, Tim and JR had even more questions than they'd had before Brandie began to talk.

JR knew it wasn't his place to speak, and sat silently behind the wheel, hoping Tim would ask the same questions he wanted answered.

"You're putting us on with this psychic shit." Tim stated incredulously. JR grinned in concurrence. "This is a gag, right?"

Tim noticed that Kasey winced at his rather harsh choice of words. "I'm sorry, Ms. Riteman, but I just don't believe in any of that stuff. I've seen psychics on shows like *Unsolved Mysteries* and they always seem to just send everybody off on wild-goose chases while they think up lame excuses for why they can't find what they set out to find. I think its all just a crock, no offense." JR nodded silently, but the other three had no difficulty determining that he was in total agreement.

Tim was annoyed at the thought of missing a date it took him nearly a month to set up because some dizzy broad hoping to collect a fat reward was hunting for the body of a woman everyone knew was probably down in Key West soaking up the sun.

"Christ, Tim! Have you forgotten what I said before we left?" Brandie barked, surprised by her cameraman's candid outburst; it was not like him. Tim, though possessing strong opinions, normally kept them to himself.

Kasey touched Brandie's arm. "It's okay."

"The hell it is," Brandie snarled. "I'm terribly sorry for Tim's—"

"It's okay, really. I'm not upset by the way he feels." She cut her eyes to Tim. "I'd have been surprised if you'd accepted Brandie's words without challenge."

"Brandie's right. It was not my place to say anything. I apologize." Tim was embarrassed and knew Brandie would mention his indiscretion to Steve Dacus.

Kasey nodded, but continued: "You're not alone in your feelings, Tim. Most people have difficulty believing in things unseen. I guess I'll just have to make a believer of you, too, won't I? Brandie felt the same way when we met yesterday."

Brandie signaled her agreement, which made Tim feel even worse.

JR continued to drive silently, grateful now that he hadn't said a word.

Kasey wasn't surprised to find a detractor, someone who had trouble believing in psychic revelation on any level. She knew there would be many others, and that she was going to have to get proficient at handling their objections if she wanted to succeed in her deception. She wished for a moment that she'd just gone to the police with the truth.

The thought of Joeyboy snapped her back to reality.

❖

As they drove steadily south, Brandie glanced silently at the attractive redhead in the jeans and western shirt sitting beside her and tried to read her mind. Kasey felt Brandie's eyes on her, but never acknowledged them as she watched the rolling hills of Davidson County pass quickly outside her window.

"Do you think you can do it?" Brandie asked quietly, whispering in Kasey's ear.

"What?" Kasey asked. "Make a believer out of Tim?"

"No . . . can you find her . . . I mean, do you honestly believe

your vision was strong enough to actually locate Donna Stanton's body? Are you even certain that she's dead?"

Kasey looked hard at the woman beside her, the energy coming from somewhere deep within her. "She's dead, all right, make no mistake about that. And yes, I think I can locate her." She took a breath. "It just might take a little while."

Brandie tapped Tim on the shoulder and signaled for him to roll tape. Tim swung his camera into position again and was rolling even before he had focused perfectly.

"But how did you know where to begin, Kasey?" Brandie probed. "The sense you got from the map last night could have been wrong, could it not? She might be anywhere, even outside the country. Why here? It seems to me a most unlikely spot."

They were good questions, but ones Kasey had luckily anticipated. "How do salmon find the way to their birth spot in some tiny, remote river, after spending so much time in the vast Pacific Ocean?"

"Are you saying you possess some sort of homing instinct, a sixth sense, so to speak, that none of the rest of us have?"

"I believe we all have it," Kasey smiled, addressing her answer to the camera. "It's just that some people are more in touch with that instinct, as you put it, than others."

"So, I could have it?"

"You do have it, Brandie."

Brandie snapped her head back, surprised by the unexpected words.

"Sure, think of how many times in your own life when you've had a funny feeling about something that made you pull off the road, or stop doing whatever it was you were doing, and then, moments later, found out that funny feeling had kept you from being injured or hurt in some way. We've all experienced it, to some degree or another, but most of the time, we just pass it off as a fluke, a lucky break. We never give that sort of insight the credibility it rightly deserves."

Brandie recalled several things in her life which were just as Kasey had described. It made her lean back in her seat, and put her hand to her heart. She loved the dramatic. "Doesn't it scare you to have such a gift . . . to see the things you've seen in your dreams."

Kasey's face lost all expression. "You have no idea."

Brandie nodded silently, and allowed the segment to end on those heartfelt words.

Kasey returned to her window. She remembered the last time she had traveled this same road. The black thoughts began to fill her mind and she prayed that she would be able to keep them in check long enough to get through the day. She could picture Donna Stanton lying there, beneath the cold, ebony earth, waiting silently for Kasey to come back for her—to help her at last. The image sent a shock wave of guilt down her spine and back up again; the hairs on her arm stood erect and her mouth went dry.

Brandie shook her head silently and Tim Arnold turned his camera away from Kasey. He busied himself with footage of the hills and meadows of the lush Tennessee landscape.

As JR drove steadily south, Brandie began to put the story together in her mind; Tim captured lovely scenes of spring flowers lining the highway; and Kasey struggled with the sight of frightened blue eyes rimmed with tears that hung in the air only inches beyond her window.

❖

For nearly a half hour, the Jeep effortlessly consumed the interstate south of Nashville. JR and Tim chatted quietly in the front seat and Brandie typed notes and ideas in the Sharp Wizard she kept in her purse.

"Pull off here," Kasey announced, startling the other passengers.

"Right here?" JR asked immediately, not sure if the boss meant here exactly, or at the upcoming exit.

"No, the exit coming up, Sharp Road," Kasey responded. "She was on this road, I'm sure of it." Her eyes seemed focused on a spot somewhere in the distance. Tim had not been ready with his camera, and Brandie shot him the evil eye. Kasey was the only one surprised when Brandie asked her to restage the short scene for the camera, but, despite taking a moment to remember exactly what she had said, managed to make it appear just as convincing and unrehearsed the second time.

Brandie, initially afraid of interrupting Kasey's train of thought, but knowing the importance of such seemingly trivial scenes to the cohesiveness of an effective story, was pleased with Kasey's easy willingness to repeat her words on tape, and recognized in her a woman naturally at home in front of a camera.

Brandie spoke off-camera into her own mike in response to Kasey's observation, having instructed Tim to keep his lens trained on Kasey. "What makes you think she took this exit?"

"Just a feeling I had when we got to this point. I see a woman in a car, a large, white car. She's afraid, running from something." She looked directly into Brandie's eyes. "It's Donna."

On the news, Kasey had heard Stanton's neighbor mention that Donna had "driven off in that big white Cadillac of hers," and knew the detail would be safe to use.

It occurred to Kasey that she had no idea how Donna had ended up in Joeyboy's truck. *When had he grabbed her—if he had grabbed her—and where was her own car now?* she wondered.

She fought to keep her mind on the moment, on the work at hand. It was becoming easier to drift away, harder to concentrate.

Brandie had not remembered any mention of Stanton's car—least of all its color—in Deb Jensen's interview with the neighbor, Maggie Ketchum, or with Detective Vanover in front of Latham's home. That Kasey knew Stanton's exact vehicle color excited her. "What is she afraid of, Kasey?" she asked, intentionally referring to Donna Stanton in the present tense for the camera's sake.

"It's not clear to me, but it has to do with something she has, something that belongs to another person, a person she fears greatly."

Kasey remembered from her reading that feelings, not thoughts, were a distinguishing characteristic of psychic imagery. Psychics *feel* as though something or other has occurred, they do not think that it has. She was careful to keep this in mind as she spoke; there were so many things to remember.

Although, on the evening of the twenty-second, she had not noted the exit name that had taken her off I-65—the one that ultimately led her to the orchard—Kasey felt certain this was the same one. She had spent most of last night and early this morning trying to retrace her route and locate the orchard on the only map she could find, a map of Tennessee, Alabama, and Mississippi she had bought for a buck-fifty at an Exxon station after she left Channel 9. For hours she studied every possible combination of roads she might have taken that night, but one made no more sense than the other, and none seemed familiar to her by name. At six o'clock in the morning, she finally realized she was going to have to rely on her visual memories from the night, and hope that JR actually knew the area as well as Brandie had indicated. She knew she wouldn't get a second shot at finding Donna. Her credibility would be destroyed and she would be lumped in the same stew pot with the rest of the fake psychics Brandie had met.

And then, with only the police left as a resource, there would be no helping Donna without the very real risk of becoming a target of Joeyboy—whoever the hell he was—in the process, a thought that was becoming less and less palatable with each passing hour.

Brandie had been left speechless by Kasey's description, while Tim, true to form, mumbled "bullshit" under his breath. He forced his left knee against the door to brace himself and the camera for the Jeep's expected turn at the foot of the ramp.

JR took the designated exit and slowed as he reached the bottom of the small grade, careful not to shake Tim any more than could be helped.

"Which way?" JR asked when the Jeep came to a full stop, with I-65 now on the left and Sharp Road in front of them, its two lanes of better than average pavement going east-west. They were still several miles northeast of Columbia.

"That way," Kasey pointed, indicating east. "I'm sure she turned here."

Tim was getting everything now.

Brandie was puzzled why Donna Stanton would have taken such an unlikely route: it led nowhere. But, then, that might have been exactly what she'd had in mind, especially if she were being pursued.

When they had only gone a mile or so, and the noise and bustle of the interstate was a memory hidden behind a series of rolling hills, Kasey called for JR to stop. They were beside a large field, recently cut and bundled into huge hay rolls scattered across the field.

Kasey opened her door, stepped onto the empty highway, and moved deliberately to the front of the Jeep, her eyes sweeping the landscape. Tim shot each move through the side glass and windshield, and then, after Brandie opened his door from the outside, joined the two women at the edge of the field. JR remained at the wheel.

Brandie remembered Kasey saying that Stanton had been buried between two trees, in a field with an old wire fence around it. She looked quickly for a fence, any kind of fence—there was not even a millimeter of one in sight—and then tried to decide which two trees Kasey could have meant. Her muscles quivered. There were trees all around. *The damned country's filled with trees, for Christ's sake!* she screamed in silent frustration. "Is this it? Is this where she's buried?" Brandie spouted unprofessionally, only then realizing that she had not switched on her wireless mike. She was surprised at how caught up she'd become in the whole thing.

Tim took his eye away from his viewfinder long enough to give her a "you're not serious about this are you?" look. Though she caught his disparaging stare, Brandie's attention was firmly fixed on Kasey's every move.

Tim decided that trying to bring the normally rational reporter to her senses was probably, at least for the immediate future, futile. He zoomed in a little tighter on the star.

Brandie slowly raised the Sennheiser microphone to her lips and flipped the switch. Her usual calm professionalism had returned; she was determined to hold on to it for the rest of the hunt. "For reasons known only to Kasey René Riteman, we are stopped by this vacant field in rural Maury County, a few miles east of the town of Columbia, Tennessee. Perhaps Donna Stanton stopped here as well as she fled Nashville, and whatever demons she believed were in pursuit of her." Tim gave her an approving wink; no matter how implausible the story, he admired the way in which she added drama and audience appeal to it.

Brandie killed the mike and watched anxiously as Kasey wandered quietly and slowly in the short grass, eighty or ninety feet from the road. She remained with Tim by the Jeep. Tim was able to use the powerful zoom lens to keep Kasey tightly framed in the scene, hoping the added distance might allow whatever she was searching for to come more freely. He doubted it would help, but knew he had voiced his skepticism as fully as he dared. Besides, the angle and reduced depth of field made for a better shot—an attractive woman sharply focused, framed against a softly focused backdrop of rolling hills and endless stacks of spring hay.

Kasey dropped to one knee on the ground and picked at the dry splinters of hard, yellow grass left after cutting. She brought a handful to her nose and inhaled their distinctive aroma, a smell she had loved as a child. A hundred feet away, Tim laughed out loud as his mind painted an image of Kasey the bloodhound and the camera shook for a second. The minor technical error was adequate caution to him that he must remain detached from any personal involvement in the story, and shoot the footage as he had a thousand other pieces. He reminded himself that he didn't have to be a believer to be a professional.

Brandie could barely contain herself waiting for Kasey to announce that this was the spot. She cursed silently for not having thought to wire her star for sound, rather than relying solely on the camera's mike to pick her up. At this distance, anything she said would have become a useless hodgepodge of muffled words and wind noise.

"She needs a Tram," Tim whispered out the corner of his mouth to Brandie, referring to a high-quality wireless microphone that clips almost invisibly to the collar of a shirt, its miniature transmitter usually worn on the belt in back; he'd read Brandie's mind when he saw her look of frustration grow with each step Kasey took away from them.

"You bring one?" she asked softly, and then realized he'd probably brought several, as well as everything else they would likely need while they were out. "Thank you," she mouthed when he nodded. When Kasey stood again and strolled casually back toward the Jeep, a look of defeat on her face, Brandie's spirits sank. "What is it, Kasey?" she asked as she reached the road again.

Kasey looked back to the field for a moment, and then turned again to Brandie and Tim. "She came by here, though I can't get a clear sense of why she did. I don't think she was alone by this time. I keep seeing her in a field, between two trees, but not trees like these." She swept an open hand across a mixed stand of oaks and pines that framed the side of the highway at their backs.

Tim swung his camera around to get the shot.

"We need to go farther," she said, looking to the east.

❖

The next three hours became a frustrating series of confused memories and wrong turns. Kasey knew she had stayed east of the interstate that night—the lights of Columbia had disappeared in her rearview mirror as she drove—but the harder she tried to retrace the route she had taken, the more elusive it seemed to become. JR might have known some areas of Maury County well, but by noon, it had become painfully obvious to Kasey—if not to everyone else—that this was not one of the areas.

At one point, she felt like screaming: "What do I have to say to get you to drive to the spot I've been describing all day!" It was equally frustrating for Brandie and Tim. Their enthusiasm at following her from the Jeep, when she thought that she'd felt something that might lead them to Donna Stanton, had diminished significantly. Tim now simply rolled down his window and shot from the front seat, while Brandie usually remained in the back, her door open or her window down.

Kasey could feel her plan slipping through her fingers. The money, which was also becoming less likely with each failed attempt, seemed of no consequence; she'd had no money before that horrible night, she would survive if she still had none tomorrow. But she would not allow herself to be stalked by that creature, Joeyboy, and she couldn't bear the thought of leaving Donna in a field that now seemed impossible to find.

She began to fear that her strategy had backfired: she had initially planned to give JR only as many clues as necessary to find the orchard, afraid that overwhelming them with detailed information about the crime scene would seem implausible, especially to the camera and the unseen audience she knew would eventually be watching; she didn't know how many genuine psychics might see her and easily spot every mistake she made.

Now, her plan in shambles, she had exhausted every memory of that night, from the collapsing old farmhouse and rusting, bullet-riddled car, to the exact number of strands of barbed wire on the fence that surrounded the orchard. Even the curve in the road near the old dirt drive hadn't seemed to help. JR simply didn't know of any field or orchard that met the description she had so painstakingly laid out for him, and, after a half day of wandering down every two-bit road in the county, Kasey was more lost than ever.

How long had she driven that Monday night? she screamed in silence. *Had she driven due east, or was it more southeast?* She knew her frustration was shared by the other members of the party.

It was becoming obvious to all that no body would be found this day.

"Kasey," Brandie said, taking the woman's hand as she stood by the car, a look of anger, pain, and defeat painted across Kasey's face. "Are you all right? You don't look so good."

"It's so frustrating," she cried. "I can see it so clearly in my mind, as if I'd been there myself, but I just can't find it."

"Is this the first time you've tried to locate an actual place you saw in one of your visions?" Brandie asked.

Kasey knew she had to come up with a plausible answer quickly or lose Brandie altogether, and she needed her help if she were to avoid having to go to the police. "It's the first time I've ever had a dream like this. The other times I just saw something happening before it actually occurred, and then, a day or two later, it happened in real life just like I had dreamed. The location didn't matter then, the images were about *what* occurred, not *where*. This isn't like that, this time it matters. I'm trying to find a place, a place which looks like a thousand other places to me. I thought it would be easier than this. It was so clear in my mind when I began."

"It's okay, Kasey. You did your best, we all know that," she said sympathetically, despite her bitter disappointment at not getting the story she had been determined to file. Even Tim nodded his agreement; though he didn't believe in psychics any more now than he had at the start of the day, he believed in Kasey's commitment to finding the missing woman. Her dedication to that cause, however misguided in his mind, had earned his respect. Tim prided himself on being, above all else, a man of principle.

"Maybe this just isn't the right area," Brandie continued, determined not to let the story go without a fight. "It's a big state, and lots of places look just alike. If you're too tired to continue, we'll call it a day and head for a motel. We can start out fresh in the morning, what do you say?" Brandie had allocated two days to finding the body, and by God, she'd take the full two days before she'd quit.

Though she was severely disappointed, Brandie felt sympathy for the other woman. It was clear to her that Kasey had a restlessness in her heart that she simply could not set free; it was tearing it apart.

As she saw the tears well up in Kasey's eyes, she wished she could help, in some way, any way, but knew it was not in her power to do so. Kasey would have to live with her pain, just as she would have to live without her Emmy.

JR, virtually silent until now, spoke up: "Hank Tanner might know," he said in a casual sort of way the others only half heard, directing his words to the steering wheel. "Yep, I bet he'd know if anybody would."

Tim turned his head slowly toward the other man and asked in a flat tone, "JR, who the hell is Hank Tanner?"

JR smiled broadly. "He's been the superintendent of county roads for this area since I was a boy. He knows every square inch of asphalt and gravel in the county. He'll know, you can bet on that."

Kasey looked through the opened back door at JR. He was nodding his head up and down, mumbling something to himself about why he hadn't thought of it earlier. She turned to Brandie, who in turn, turned to JR.

"Where can we find this Hank Tanner?" Brandie asked in such a way that none of the other three took it to mean anything less than: "if this Hank Tanner character can help us find the goddamn spot, then why the hell are we all still sitting here?"

❖

Hank Tanner lived in a modest white frame house at the corner of Terrace Drive and Hillcrest, a quarter mile north of West 7th Street. It took JR only fifteen minutes—once he had gotten them back to 412—to reach the neat, but older, Columbia neighborhood.

JR knew this area well.

Hank Tanner was just finishing a late lunch when the Jeep pulled up in front. His lawnmower, recently used, still tinkled and crackled as it cooled beneath a tree next to the walkway. Spring flowers bloomed in his flower beds, rich yellows, reds, and lilacs all the more striking in contrast to the green lawn and white porch.

Hank looked out from the kitchen window and saw two men and two women he was sure he had never seen before walking briskly up his front porch steps. He laid his bologna-and-cheese sandwich down on a paper plate and brushed off his work shirt in the hall mirror before answering the doorbell.

He didn't often receive visitors, strangers at least, and four at once must mean something important was in the works.

"Yes," he said meekly after opening the door just enough to stick his head out. Hank looked to be a man of perhaps sixty-five, with short gray hair—what little was left of it—who weighed not a pound more than he had at fifteen. He possessed a bit of a slump to his narrow shoulders making his slight five feet six inches seem even shorter. He had been with the county for four decades, far longer than even JR might have guessed, but had decided against taking the retirement he and his wife had planned for thirty years when she died unexpectedly three years ago.

With the house now more quiet than it had been for most of the years he'd spent within its walls, Hank didn't mind the company, even if they were strangers.

"Hey, Mr. Tanner," JR called out from the back of the group. "It's me, JR Davenport."

"JR Davenport? Roy and Martha's boy?"

"Yes, sir, that's me. I've got some important friends here that need your help. Can we come in for a spell?"

With that small town, neighborly introduction to the rest of the group, Tanner threw the door open wide and welcomed them as family. Why any friend of JR Davenport's—son of fellow Church of Christ members, Martha and Roy Davenport—was a friend of his. "You folks care for a bologna-and-cheese sandwich? I'm just having one myself."

The four grinned in unison at his offer, but each remembered not having eaten in nearly six hours. "Sounds great, if it's not too much trouble," JR answered for them all, realizing that the rest of the group might not be all that familiar with rural hospitality, and therefore not realize that "no" to an offer to eat was an unacceptable response.

In the country, if a man's eating and asks you to join him—you eat.

❖

It took only twenty minutes for the six sandwiches to be devoured (Tim and JR had two each) and the need for Tanner's help to be explained in full. He was more than willing to assist on such an important and adventurous undertaking, considering it involved Roy and Martha's boy, of course. And besides, the five hundred dollars Brandie had promised to pay if they were successful more than made up for having to finish the lawn on Tuesday. By two-fifteen, the Jeep pulled away from his home, its passenger count now increased by one.

The hunt for Donna Stanton was on once again.

"Describe that orchard for me again," he said as they reached the last point Kasey thought she had recognized. "You sure the trees where she's buried are apple trees?"

Kasey had been certain on that point, but now, with JR having had such difficulty finding the spot, began to doubt her own memory. "I believe so. At least, they appeared to be apple trees. I could be mistaken, though."

"Make a right here, JR, and drive until I tell you," Tanner directed, heading the Jeep down a well-kept two-lane road that ran between huge fields of corn.

After five minutes, there was a clearing on the right where row after row of carefully planted and well-kept fruit trees stood.

He leaned across Brandie to address Kasey: "Them's apple trees, ma'am. Is that the place?"

Brandie gasped at the thought of Tanner having led them to the spot on the first try. She instantly looked to Kasey for verification.

It wasn't the spot and Kasey knew it at once. She shook her head silently.

Brandie's shoulders dropped.

Then suddenly, while staring out the window at the columns of apple trees, Kasey had a flash of memory which nearly made her gasp. She knew if she could wrench it from its hiding place in her mind, it would be the missing piece of the puzzle, the last key element needed to get them to Donna Stanton; it was a tiny fragment, and it had lain undetected and silent since that horrible night.

"Wait!" she shouted. She squeezed Brandie's arm and both women stopped breathing for a moment.

All eyes were on Kasey.

"I need to get out for a moment," she announced in a claustrophobic voice. She threw open her door and practically fell from the vehicle.

The lens saw it all, and the lapel mike she had been wearing since ten A.M. captured every syllable.

As Tim taped and the other three watched intently from the Jeep, Kasey walked slowly toward the first two trees in the orchard. She could not make out a name she was trying desperately to reconstruct; pieces of words spun before her mind's eye like so many jumbled letters flying through space. She fought to remember, now clearly seeing an old wooden sign with peeling white paint.

What was it called? she kept asking herself. *What was that name?*

Just as Donna had done the night she died, Kasey knelt in the grass between the trees and silently begged for God to intervene; it was time to help Donna in the only way she was able, to free her from the grave she had not deserved, to bring the hammer of the law down on the head of the bastard who had put her there.

The tears streamed down her cheeks, but the hidden words refused to reveal themselves. "Oh, God," she sobbed, "please show me the name."

At the road, only twenty feet away, Brandie was torn between her ambitions and the pain she heard in Kasey's voice. This was too much to ask of anyone, it couldn't be done, it just wasn't possible. She narrated those desperate feelings into her own mike, surprising even Tim with her sincerity.

And yet, had it been within her power to put an end to Kasey's torment, to allow her to be free of this torturous clairvoyance, she would have changed nothing; the story had become too good—with or without a body.

Tim kept Kasey locked in his lens as tears began to fall to the grass at her knees; he heard the painful petition of her words reaching the tape. *Whether she finds the Stanton woman or not*, he thought, *this is incredible stuff.*

Then, from a remote recess of her brain, Kasey began to see a piece of something that looked familiar. The words erupted involuntarily as the puzzle formed itself before her: "Water!" she shouted triumphantly. "It's Water something . . . no . . . something Water Farms!"

"Sweet Water Farms?" Tanner asked quickly, filling in the blank.

"Yes, oh God, yes!" she shouted again as she stood and ran to the Jeep. "She's at Sweet Water Farms, between the first two trees in the row at the bottom of the hill, closest to the old barbed-wire fence."

Kasey smiled the first smile she had worn all day, perhaps the first real smile she had worn in a week. Then sadness quickly took its place, sweeping away the joy in a flood of satanic memories. *At last now we'll get you out of that horrible place, Donna,* she thought, though it seemed so little consolation for having done nothing that night. *At least we'll take you home.*

FIFTEEN

At 4:45 in the afternoon, the Jeep rolled to a slow stop at the top of a hill, just in front of an old fence and gate that had seen better days. Above them, a decaying white sign announced pathetically that SWEET WATER FARMS—or what had once been the farm—lay just beyond its dull black letters.

Though each of the small group had sought this spot for his or her own reasons, much as Arthur's knights had sought the grail and the pilgrims religious freedom, each now stood before this unholy shrine and contemplated the righteousness of their quest.

They stood shoulder to shoulder in silence at the orchard's entrance, like children outside a ball park wall, and looked in unison at the spot Kasey had seen in her dream; it was exactly as she had described, and it took their breath away.

Brandie was the first to break the prayerlike silence. "Is this the spot, Kasey?" she asked respectfully, her own eyes unable to leave the patch of ground that lay between the first pair of trees in the row at the bottom of the hill.

Though each was certain of the answer, all watched as she confirmed their hopes and their fears with a slow, painful nod.

"Get your camera, Tim," Brandie ordered, forcing her feelings to take a backseat to the story—her story. "JR, see if you can get that gate open. If you can't get it open, then drive through the son-of-a-bitch. I'll be damned if I'm coming this far and be stopped by some stupid gate."

"This is private property," Tanner protested at once. "You can't just go traipsing in there without permission."

"Who owns it?" Brandie snapped. "I'll have 'em on the phone in fifteen seconds."

"It . . . uh . . . it belongs to the county now. The original owner died without an heir and the county took it over for taxes a few years back. They pay someone to keep the grass cut, and the locals just kinda pick any fruit they find on the trees. No one works the farm anymore, you see—"

"Who gave the locals permission to pick the fruit?" she asked.

178

"Permission? Uh . . . nobody . . . I guess. They just kinda do it, that's all."

"Great. Wonderful." A grin fell across her lips. "I figure we'll just go help ourselves to some of those free-for-the-picking apples, and if we happen to stumble across Donna Stanton's body in the process, well, hell, that's our good fortune." She looked straight into Hank Tanner's eyes and watched as his diminutive frame appeared to shrink by several inches. "You have any problem with us gathering a little 'community fruit,' Mister County Road Superintendent?"

"No, not really, I guess. And, it's . . . um . . . Assistant County Road . . ."

Brandie was no longer listening. Her mind had already moved on to the next obstacle standing between her and her Emmy.

The commands Brandie barked brought a flurry of activity from Tim and JR. Kasey, however, stood in silence, unable to control the feelings that raced in all directions within her, like summer gnats around a porch lamp.

The night of horror was back, and it was worse than she had feared. She no longer wanted justice or rewards—any part of them.

She just wanted to leave.

"Hop in, Kasey," Brandie said, hoping it would snap her out of the peculiar daze in which she seemed to be lost. "We need you to show us exactly where she is." She could immediately tell that her words had fallen on deaf ears.

Brandie moved closer. "What's wrong, Kasey?"

Tim—with fresh batteries and a new tape in the Betacam—was filming the pair.

"I can't go in there," Kasey said softly, but in a way which left little room for discussion.

Brandie had to try. "Why not, Kasey? We need you to. You've got to finish what you started."

"You don't need me. She's there, all right, exactly where I said she'd be. I just can't go in there."

"You've got to, Kasey."

"You don't understand . . ."

"Kasey, listen—"

"Don't you hear me?" she snapped. "I can't do it! I won't do it. She has no face!"

Brandie and Tim were shocked by the unexpected words. The reporter tried to think of a response: the camera was still rolling. "No face? I don't understand, Kasey. What does that mean, she has no face?"

Kasey just stared mutely at the trees, oblivious to the words of the other woman.

Brandie had no idea why Kasey was so reluctant—after wanting so badly to find the missing woman all day—but she could see that she was not going to change her mind. Brandie thought quickly, rewriting her approach to the story's conclusion as quickly as she could. *Yeah, that will work*, she decided after a moment. *It might even turn out better this way.* She swiped her finger under her throat and the taping stopped. "Tim, can I see you a minute?" Brandie met the cameraman at the rear of the Jeep, while JR and Hank Tanner wrestled with the old gate. "I guess you figured out that she isn't going down with us," Brandie said.

"Yeah, I kinda got that impression." He looked over his shoulder and saw Kasey's face as she stood silently staring at the orchard. Though he had no idea what was going on in her mind, her anguished look spoke volumes about the torment boiling within her. "Something sure has her bent out of shape all of a sudden. What did she mean about that 'no face' thing?"

"Haven't a clue."

"If she's gonna stay up here, how do you want to shoot this then?"

"I thought we'd shoot it from two angles, one inside the Jeep as we make our way down the hill to the spot Kasey indicated, and the other from a spot between the trees, maybe a low angle, even at ground level if you can frame it to suit you. Be sure to keep Kasey in your shot at all times as we make our approach the second time. She won't go down, but I think I can get her to stand by the gate, right here." Brandie pointed to a spot to the left of the gate. "We'll piece the two halves together in post. It might work out well this way: the troubled psychic with a heart too tormented to go near the grave site she alone was able to locate."

"Sounds like Hollywood to me." Tim took a deep breath and blew it out noisily, an obvious release of tension. He turned his eyes toward the closest two apple trees at the bottom of the hill, and then back to Brandie. "Think we'll actually find her . . . you know . . . buried down there?"

The same question had been in Brandie's mind since the hunt began, but she hadn't had to answer it before reaching the orchard. She also inhaled and exhaled noisily, the anticipation in her voice causing it to shake. "Jesus, Tim, I don't know. Part of me hopes so, you know, the reporter in me; but I gotta tell you, there's a larger part, the feminine part, that hopes she's sunning her pretty, rich ass in Florida, and this is all a lot of wasted time and energy."

"You think there's a possibility it has been a waste of time?"

She looked past Tim to the same pair of trees that had held his gaze a moment before. "I think she's down there, right where Kasey said."

Tim shivered as though a cold wind had reached his soul. He repeated his earlier question: "She said that Stanton had no face. What the hell does that mean?"

Brandie shrugged her shoulders and shook her head. "I have no idea, Tim, but it gave me the willies. Let's do this thing before I change my mind."

❖

With the video footage from the first pass already on tape, Tim Arnold looked for an angle between the trees that would allow him to keep Kasey in the shot while the Jeep repeated its slow descent to the corner of the orchard. The two angles would provide greater artistic opportunity in the editing suite later.

As he knelt in the ankle-high grass, the thirty pound Sony Betacam held low to the ground, he lost his balance; his left hand (which was not locked in the handstrap that girdled the lens), reached instinctively in front of him, groping for solid ground. What it found instead was a soft depression that gave way easily under his weight.

He fell to his left side, the camera crashing down upon him.

The sudden fall startled him and he lay in the grass for a moment before moving. It was then that he noticed that his face—his full body, for that matter—which should have been at ground level, was several inches lower than the surrounding area.

Oh, my God! I'm laying in the grave! He jumped to his feet as if he'd been bitten, and backed away from the site as fast as his balance would allow, his eyes riveted to the depression.

Brandie—waiting for Tim's cue to begin their descent—had seen the entire incident. She ordered JR to drive back to the base of the hill at once, practically leaping from the Jeep as they neared the bottom. "What the hell's going on, Tim?" She ran up to him. "Are you all right?"

Tim Arnold was at the brink of panic, his face ashen, his breathing erratic. "It's her," he announced, staring at the ground, the full depression now clearly visible to him from where he stood.

Brandie followed his eyes to their focal point. It took her a few seconds to make out the subtle lines of the two- by six-foot grave. "I can't believe it," she mumbled, unprepared for what she saw. Then, she, too, backed away from it, as if Donna Stanton might actually reach up and grab her by the ankle.

JR and Hank Tanner joined them at the edge of the depression, their words a tangled maze of awe and disbelief.

"What are we going to do?" Tim asked, his camera still on the ground, lying halfway in the depression.

Brandie fought to control herself. "For starters, I'd suggest you grab that fifty-thousand-dollar camera and see if it still works. And you'd better pray it does, because I've got a hunch we're going to need it again."

"No . . . I mean, it's her . . . she's here . . . dead and buried. I didn't believe it, but it's really her. We've got to call the cops."

Brandie the Reporter had taken over the reins from Brandie the sympathetic woman, the adrenaline coursing through her veins. "Cops?" she sputtered incredulously. "We can't call the cops yet. First, we've got to make sure she's actually here—"

"How?" Tanner interrupted quickly. This thing had gone far beyond his expectations of the afternoon's events.

"By digging, of course, unless *you* can see through dirt." Tanner wasn't at all sure he was pleased with this part of the plan but said nothing further for the moment.

Brandie would have ignored him anyway.

"Then," she continued, "assuming we find her body, we can phone the police. Whatever happens from this point on, Tim, I want everything on tape."

JR was still stammering. "But, aren't we disturbing a crime scene? Can't you get in a lot of trouble for that?" he asked, looking to Brandie for assurance that she knew what she was doing.

"Do you see a crime scene?" she asked.

He looked at the ground at her feet as if to say: "Yeah, right there."

"What? That? I don't see anything except a dip in the grass. I have no personal knowledge of what's contained beneath it and neither do any of the rest of us."

"But, Kasey's dream . . ."

"Dreams hardly constitute fact, my friend. Now, *if* we find anything that is of interest to the cops, such as a body, I'll be the first to let them know. We won't touch a thing from that point on—no foul, no penalty. It's as simple as that. Now, we're wasting valuable time. Grab the shovel, JR, the damned camera that's still lying on the ground, Tim, and let's make some news." She clapped her hands together twice loudly and headed for the Jeep.

Tim collected his camera carefully, as if it were a huge bone lying under the nose of a sleeping pit bull, and checked it out thoroughly. It appeared to still work fine—the manufacturer had built it to survive more than a little tumble in the grass. Brandie grabbed her notes and began to go over her script in her head, working on emphasis and presentation. JR—reluctantly—pulled the shovel from the back compartment where he had laid it before they left. He wasn't too crazy about this part of the assignment; he would have preferred to stay behind the wheel.

"Set up over there, Tim, so you can get JR, the Jeep, and Kasey in the shot at the same time. It ought to look strong, dramatic. I'll stand a few feet to the right of JR and narrate while he digs. What do you think?"

It was an easy matter framing the depression, Brandie, JR, and the Jeep in the same shot, but Kasey was over three hundred feet away, and at the top of a hill. It took Tim several minutes to find the right spot from which to shoot, and the right lens setting. When he had all the elements, including Kasey, in his viewfinder, he seemed pleased. "I can get it all from right here, but Kasey will be out of focus."

"Perfect. It'll seem appropriate, us here, her isolated." The reporter took a deep breath and patted her anxious and reluctant grave digger on the back. "Ready, JR?" she asked.

Despite nodding yes, he definitely was not ready.

Tim began rolling tape.

JR set his boot on the blade of the shovel and forced it into the ground, at the end of the depression farthest from Tim. It sank more easily than he had expected, turning up a large bite of sod and soil, but nothing else.

He let out a sigh of relief and looked at Brandie; she nodded for him to continue. Tim had made a slow, sweeping zoom-in from the large scene to the grave and was now concentrating exclusively on the blade of the shovel.

JR sank another blade, and again it rewarded his efforts with nothing but soil and grass. Brandie frowned, knowing her expression would not be seen by the camera.

Twice more the shovel returned only dark, rich earth.

On the fifth try, the blade hesitated upon entry and so did JR. Brandie felt her breathing stop again. "Continue, please," she whispered. JR took a labored breath.

When he jammed his heavy work boot against the shovel and over-turned the blade, the broken halves of a root poked through the surface, startling the three of them as it cracked noisily.

Tanner, still in the Jeep, jumped when they jumped, though he could see nothing of the digging from his position. That suited him fine.

JR, wanting it to be over, moved his blade a few inches toward the center of the depression—still at the end opposite Tim—and put his full weight on a fresh bite. The shovel resisted his initial attempt to extract the earth, he assumed because he had taken such a full blade. He leaned the handle backward, toward the ground, requiring Brandie to move slightly to her right in order for him to have the added room he needed.

Her commentary never stopped, her voice low and reverent, always playing to the unseen audience.

JR leaned on the long wooden handle, trying to lift the full scoop of dirt. Without warning, it gave way, sending him hard to the ground.

Brandie extended a hand to help him to his feet when she noticed the shriveled, rotting remains of a woman's foot sticking through the ground, its lifeless muscles partially consumed by maggots that writhed beneath the pallid skin; the denuded bones of the toes showing clearly, stripped of the flesh which had only recently been vibrant and alive, able to feel the soft texture of rich wool carpet or the cold tingle of ceramic tile.

Her scream came from deep within her gut, the reality far greater than her mind had imagined or would have believed possible. Tim almost vomited, and had to keep his eye glued to the black-and-white viewfinder in order to remain in the world of make-believe—to remove himself from the actuality of death and decay. JR, who had started to get up, dropped back to the ground, his legs too wobbly to support him. Tanner, having not moved, covered his ears with cupped hands, and squeezed his eyes as tightly shut as they would close, like a child at his first horror movie, trying to keep the monsters on the screen from finding him in his seat.

On the hill, Kasey began to weep. She had heard Brandie's scream and knew the search for Donna Stanton was at last over.

"You're next, goddammit!" she cursed silently, the tears beginning to flow like streams down a face that seemed older now than it had at eight A.M. She clenched her fist, striking it angrily and repeatedly on the top of the wooden post supporting the gate. "It won't be long now, Joeyboy, you rotten bastard. Soon, they'll be coming for you!"

SIXTEEN

Buddy Williams agreed to take Taylor's call, despite being in a meeting with Warren Slade and his campaign manager, Fred Martin. Though his mind was focused on his reelection campaign, his secretary indicated that it was most urgent, and that the chief intended to hold until the governor could take the call. Williams wondered why Taylor never bothered with the usual chain of command—going through Slade first—instead of always insisting on speaking with him directly. He decided to speak to Chief Harvey about his detective's lack of respect.

Williams punched the flashing light blinking above line four: "Yes, Taylor, what the hell's so urgent that it requires my personal attention?"

"They've found her, sir."

"Found whom, for Christ's sake?" Williams hated guessing games.

"Donna Stanton. At least it appears to be Donna Stanton. We won't know until the autopsy is completed in a day or two. I'm heading there now. I just thought you'd like to know."

Williams waved his free hand at Warren Slade, indicating that he should pick up on the other line. Slade pointed silently to the door before picking up the phone near his chair, signifying that Fred Martin should hasten to the outer office until he was sent for again. Martin disappeared, the door easing closed behind him.

"Heading where? Do you think you could be a bit more specific, Chief Taylor?"

"It seems that Brandie Mueller and a news crew have found the remains of a woman, presumably that of Donna Stanton, in a field or orchard or something in Maury County, a couple of miles east of Columbia. I got the call from Stewart Parker over at Channel 9 just after he got off the phone with Mueller. Seems she was following a tip she had gotten earlier and struck paydirt, if you'll pardon my pun."

"How sure are you that it's Stanton's body?" Williams asked, his stomach slowly knotting.

"I can't say with any certainty, sir, except to say that Brandie Mueller is convinced, according to Parker, anyway. I didn't speak with her personally."

"Did he say they found anything besides her body? How about the missing pages and tapes."

What a dick, Taylor thought. *He doesn't give a damn about the woman who recorded the tapes.* "Nothing was mentioned. Why the interest, sir?" Jordan Taylor put his feet casually on his desk.

Williams ignored the question. "You said Mueller was acting on a tip. What kind of tip? Who did it come from?" he pressed impatiently.

"You've got all I've got at the moment, Governor. I won't know any more until later tonight. I'm taking my forensics team to the crime scene now. Hopefully, the local sheriff—I believe his name is Smith—won't have any problem with us handling the case."

"You won't have any problem out of Sheriff Smith. I'm sending Slade to accompany you and your team." Slade grinned at Williams' suggestion. He knew how much Taylor hated him.

Taylor grimaced at the thought. "That won't be necessary, sir. I can handle Smith. Besides, this is police business."

"Slade's going and that's that. You can pick him up here on your way out of town. I've got the chance to hang Bill Monroe by the heels for the murder of Donna Stanton, and I'm not having that opportunity blown because of a lack of clear and direct communication with this office. Do I make myself clear, Chief Taylor?"

"You're assuming Monroe had something to do with Stanton's death. Isn't that a pretty bold conjecture, sir? Hell, it may not even be Stanton's body." Taylor was growing less fond of the chief executive he already despised with each passing moment, and loathed the thought of being saddled with his stooge, Slade.

"Who else could possibly have done it?" Williams asked incredulously.

"Oh, I'd say that there are at least a dozen other people who might fit that description nicely, if you don't mind my saying so, sir." His sarcasm was not well concealed.

"But I *do* mind, Taylor. That attitude will only serve to allow a guilty man to go free. That's not what I would have expected from the next Metro chief of police."

It was not the first time *that* carrot had been dangled in front of Taylor's face. "Right, sir. I'll try to have a more open mind."

"When will you be ready to leave?"

"Ten minutes. As soon as Polaski gets here."

"Slade will be ready then, too. He'll be at the rear entrance."

"We'll swing by on our way out."

Taylor then smiled on the other end, a smile he would not have wanted Williams to see. "Oh, and sir, if it does turn out to be Donna Stanton, I'll be sending one of my men to your office to get her tapes and her diary; they'll be evidence in a murder investigation."

Williams and Slade looked sourly at each other across the room. "If it's Stanton, Chief Taylor."

"Tell Slade I won't wait."

"He'll be there."

Williams set the phone in its cradle and opened his desk drawer. He pulled out the large manila envelope containing the diary and sleeve of tapes. "I've got ten minutes before Taylor arrives here plus another forty-five minutes before you can get to Columbia. That gives me nearly an hour to have everything copied before he could have one of his stooges come for them." He laid his hand on the envelope. "I'm not losing the information in here just because some Boy Scout thinks he knows the law. Now, send Dorothy in here on your way out."

The other man didn't move a muscle at the command.

"If you don't mind, Warren," Williams added politely.

Slade didn't bother to close Williams' door as he left.

The governor shook his head in frustration and wondered how in hell he'd ever gotten himself into such a despicable position.

❖

As the small caravan from Davidson County neared the entrance to SWEET WATER FARMS, they were stopped by a pair of uniformed officers who were standing in the middle of the narrow road, a hundred feet from the gate. From his lead car, Taylor could see a flurry of activity at the gate, including several civilians standing around a white Jeep obviously belonging to Channel 9. He could see nothing of the field beyond— a small rise at the road's edge prevented a view of the orchard itself.

As Taylor was opening his door, one of the officers walked over and pushed it shut, catching Taylor's leg in the jamb.

"There's no need to get out, boys, we've got the situation well in hand. You can save yourself a lot of time and trouble and just head on back to the state capital, back to your own jurisdiction. Or hadn't you noticed that you were just a wee bit out of your neighborhood?" L. C. Smith, a tall, stocky man in his early fifties, had been a staff sergeant and a boxer in the Marine Corps for eleven years before coming home to Columbia to be a cop. If there was one thing L. C. Smith hated, it was having his authority questioned.

Taylor knew of Smith but had never met him.

"Sheriff Smith, I'm Chief of Detectives, Jordan Taylor. We're certainly not here to—"

"You're not here to anything, Taylor, except watch from the road if you care to. On second thought, why not go back to the big city and take care of your own problems. God knows, you've got your share up there. We can handle things just fine here." Smith leaned toward Taylor's window, as if to emphasize his words.

His eyes met Warren Slade's, the only man in the state Smith felt anything for that was akin to fear. Smith knew Slade had the power to make or end a career, and had done it often; it was a power he respected. "Oh, hello, Mr. Slade, I didn't see you there. I had no idea you and the governor had an interest in this case. How can I be of help, sir?"

Taylor watched the expression on Smith's face transform from arrogance to humility in less than a second. He turned his gaze slowly to the man seated on his right.

"As you know, Sheriff Smith, Tennessee law states that jurisdiction crosses county lines whenever a crime is thought to have occurred in another county. Since this would appear to be the situation here, the governor wants his own team to handle the case. Just see to it that no TV or newspaper reporters come near the orchard, and tell your men to use utmost discretion when referring to this over the radio. Governor Williams doesn't want this thing becoming a media circus. I'll be sure to mention your cooperation to him."

"Certainly. No problem, Mr. Slade. No one from the press will get within a mile of this place. What do you want me to do about the crew that's already here?"

Taylor found his groveling embarrassing. "Leave them alone," he said curtly, his patience at its end. "We'll want to talk with them ourselves. Now, may we pass?"

"Absolutely. Let them through," Smith hollered up the hill to the rest of his men. He touched the brim of his hat respectfully as Slade passed.

❖

When Brandie Mueller saw Taylor's car entering the orchard, she grabbed Tim and the pair scurried toward it, camera and microphone drawn like a brace of pistols, ready to do battle.

Taylor parked his car to the right of the gate, inside near the fence, while the other car, filled with detectives, took the inside left, also remaining close to the road. The deliberate move allowed the third vehicle, the forensics van, to pull between them and stop just beyond the old wooden sign. Taylor and Slade stepped from his car just as the reporter reached them. Tim was already taping.

"Chief Taylor, any theories on who might be responsible for the murder of Donna Stanton?" Brandie shoved the mike in his face. She hadn't noticed until now that the other man was Warren Slade. She withdrew the mike before Taylor could speak. "Mr. Slade, does the governor's office have an official interest in this case, and if so, what is the nature of that interest?" It was now the other man's turn to stare down the barrel of her gun.

Slade grabbed the protruding end of the microphone and yanked it from her hand, tossing it onto the front seat of Taylor's car as if it were a cheap toy instead of an expensive piece of equipment.

"What the hell do you think you're doing?" she hollered. She was tired of men taking her microphone away from her.

"Shutting you down, Ms. Mueller. Chief Taylor, have one of your men escort these two away from the crime scene until we're through with the investigation."

Tim lowered his camera.

"You can't do that, you son-of-a-bitch," Brandie snapped. "Obviously, you've never heard of the First Amendment. We're not going anywhere!"

"Oh, yes, you are!" Slade shouted, losing control of his emotions. "Obviously, you've never heard of obstruction of justice: you've intentionally withheld information concerning a homicide, disturbed a crime scene, continuously interfered with an official investigation—"

"Hold on a minute, you two," Taylor refereed, though enjoying the heated spat between the pair. "We're all professionals here. I'm sure Ms. Mueller meant nothing by her questions. She's just doing her job, just as we are." He shot her a warning wrapped in a stern look. "I know she's not going to do or say anything which would in any way interfere with our official investigation, including bothering you further, Mr. Slade. Am I correct, Ms. Mueller?" His look told her to agree with him at once or he would leave her to deal with Slade.

Though she was fairly certain she could not actually be prosecuted for the charges Slade had threatened her with, the prospect of losing her exclusive by ending up in jail for twenty-four hours frightened her far worse than the thought of jail itself. "Yes, that's absolutely correct, Chief Taylor. We're only here to support your efforts to get at the truth. We'll try to stay completely out of your way while you do your job." She watched Slade's eyes for some sign of capitulation.

"After all, Warren, we have Ms. Mueller here to thank for locating Donna Stanton. That's worth some consideration, isn't it?"

Slade still wore a sour expression. He looked directly at Brandie. "Just stay out of my face, Mueller. And stay off the goddamn radio. Not one word leaves here until Taylor's team has cleared the site and I tell you it's okay. Do I make myself perfectly clear?"

Yeah, sure, Brandie thought. *Why not just censor the videotapes before we air them as well, you bastard?*

"Perfectly clear, Mr. Slade," she smiled curtly.

Slade headed for the crime scene van, where Barnie Polaski and his forensics team were awaiting orders.

Taylor looked at Brandie. "Just how did you come by the information which led you here, Ms. Mueller?" he asked, though he would have been shocked if she'd revealed the source he was sure was anonymous.

"Please, Chief Taylor, we've known each other for years. Isn't it about time you called me Brandie?"

"I'll swap with you. Call me Jordan. I hear Chief all damned day."

"Deal," she smiled genuinely. It was the first time the two had spoken civilly.

He looked down the hill to where JR and Hank Tanner were still standing. "Is that where you found the body, Brandie?"

She nodded silently.

Taylor waved for Vanover and the rest of his men. "Okay, Pete, let's find out what we've got here. Have Barnie and his men get to work on the grave site right away. You'll find it between the trees there." He pointed toward JR and Tanner. "I want to know as soon as possible whether the body is Donna Stanton. You four comb the area thoroughly, you know the routine. Let's do this one strictly by the book." He looked at the western sky. "We've got an hour, hour and a half of light left before we have to use the floods. Let's use it well."

Vanover and the other three detectives headed for Barnie and the forensics van. After a moment's conversation, they followed the van down the hill. Brandie indicated for Tim to follow, but to give them plenty of room. Tim nodded agreeably and returned his camera to his shoulder.

"Now, Brandie," Taylor said, taking her arm. "You and I need to have a little chat."

❖

Barnie Polaski had been with Nashville Metro Police as a coroner for over twenty years, and now served as the chief medical examiner for Davidson County. Though Polaski had assembled an excellent team of assistant medical examiners and forensic anthropologists, the "professor" was still the best the department had at its disposal. Whenever there was a touchy case that needed his masterful touch, Barnie would be called away from his basement office and asked to head the investigation. It made him grumpy, and he wasn't bashful about expressing it. Though he missed the field, he would never have admitted it to anyone. When Taylor heard from Stewart Parker that the body one of his reporters had uncovered might be that of Donna Stanton, he had sent for Polaski.

"So, which one of you clowns found the body?" Vanover asked when he reached the bottom of the hill.

"I guess that'd be me," JR answered hesitantly. "At least, I was the one who dug her up . . . I mean, her foot. I just dug up her foot, that's all . . . and then I quit." He had always been uncomfortable around the police, though he'd never had so much as a speeding ticket.

"Relax, buddy. You're not in any trouble. For now, what I want to know is how you guys came to be here. You have any problem with that?" Vanover offered JR a smoke which he declined.

"No," he answered quickly. "No problem."

"That'd be Ms. Riteman's doing," Tanner volunteered. "She led us to this exact spot."

"Who's Riteman?" Vanover asked, his note pad in hand.

Polaski had already begun removing his tools from the van, his two assistants operating with practiced professionalism. He indicated for Vanover and the others to carefully step away from the area.

"Let's move over here, you two." Vanover gestured a few yards away from the depression. He took a quick glance at the grisly foot sticking through the scruffy grass and black earth and it made him shudder. He had never gotten used to the infinite variety of faces death could wear. He looked at Tanner again. "Who are you?"

"I'm Henry M. Tanner, assistant superintendent of county roads for Maury County. Been with the county forty-two years."

"Yes, sir, that's fine. Why are you here?"

"They came and got me while I was eating. Needed someone to show them the way to Sweet Water Farms."

Vanover had seen the name over the fence. "*Who* came and got you, sir?"

"JR, here," he pointed a slender thumb at the young man on his right, "and them three from Nashville: Ms. Mueller, Tim—I believe she called him, and the Riteman woman. She's the one who knew about this place."

"I thought you said they needed *you* to find this place." Vanover hated contradiction. It always meant things were not as they were being painted.

"Yeah . . . that's right. What I mean is, she knew what the place looked like, but she didn't know where it was." It all made perfect sense to Tanner.

"Hold on a minute. What do you mean, she knew what the place looked like, but didn't know where it was?" He lowered his pad and looked the man coldly in the eyes.

JR felt the need to lend his assistance: "Ms. Riteman, she's a psychic, and I mean the genuine article, too, buddy. Never thought I'd meet one in person, but she's sure one, all right. She had this dream about where the Stanton woman was buried, and she led us right to the spot. Well, not right to the spot, exactly, but after we picked up Mr. Tanner, we found it in no time." It could not have been simpler for a person to understand, JR was certain. He grinned, proud of his fine explanation.

Vanover looked alternately at the two men. "You two stay right here and don't move an inch. I'll talk to you again in a minute."

Shaking his head, Vanover headed back up the hill, while his partner and the other two detectives began a search of the area directly around the burial site, slowly expanding the circle until Stark had reached the old barbed-wire fence where Kasey had concealed herself the night of the murder.

The detective studied the forbidding weeds which covered the hill to the north of the fence as far as he could see. He leaned over the wire, parting the tall grass with his hands, hoping to see the ground on the other side. Perhaps a clue to Stanton's death lay hidden there.

Without warning, a large red wasp came charging angrily out of the brush and stung him squarely on the cheek, just below his left eye. It felt like a lit cigarette had been jammed in his skin.

"Goddamn-son-of-a-bitch-wasp!" he yelped in a continuous string of profanity, practically tripping as he leaped back from the fence.

The other two cops, Teague and Rinehart, ran to his aid, their hand-guns drawn defensively, but they quickly discovered that the threat to their friend was nothing but a bug.

"God Almighty, Brad, I thought you'd been shot or something," Rinehart roared with laughter.

"Want me to shoot the son-of-a-bitch for you, Brad?" Teague asked jokingly, pretending to follow an imaginary object in the air with his Smith & Wesson 9mm automatic, like an antiaircraft gunner tracking a dive-bomber.

"Oh, kiss my ass, you two. This hurts like shit!" His obvious discomfort didn't lessen his friends' laughter in the least. If anything, it only served to heighten it. "Get back to work," he moaned, staring at the tall grass beyond the fence, constantly on the alert for another attack from the brush.

There's nothing in there I need to see, he decided defensively, touching the large red knot which was forming quickly beneath his eye.

For the rest of the evening, he intended to restrict his search to the mowed side of the fence.

❖

"Are you Ms. Riteman?" Vanover asked as he walked up on Kasey's blind side. She had been watching the forensics team at work from her spot near the gate and had not noticed him approaching. His voice startled her, causing her to jump. "Sorry, miss. I didn't mean to frighten you." It was more rhetoric than sincere.

"That's okay. I'm just a little nervous. I'm Kasey Riteman."

"How do you do, I'm Lieutenant Vanover. I understand you found the body. Is that correct?"

"That's only partially true. I had a vision about Donna Stanton being killed, and this is the place I saw in my dream, but it was actually JR who dug her up, I believe."

"Yeah, that's what he said. You don't mind if I ask you a few questions, do you?"

She did, but knew it was futile to say so. She braced herself for her first encounter with the police. The thought wasn't pleasant, but it was at least a change from the intense feelings she had been experiencing for the last two hours standing by the gate. "No, I don't mind."

"That's good. What I'd like to hear more about, Ms. Riteman, is this vision of yours. You don't actually intend to stick to that fantastic story about dreaming this place up, do you?" He didn't wait for her to answer. "Come on, how'd you really know Stanton was dead? How'd you know she was buried here? You a witness?"

Kasey had not been prepared for the detective's abrupt assault. It snapped her rudely out of her daze and she remembered the name. She knew now—just as she had known when she'd heard his voice on the phone last Wednesday—that the two of them were not going to be friends.

She quickly scanned the area, hoping Brandie might come to her rescue. She was nowhere to be seen.

"How about it, Ms. Riteman, what's your connection to Donna Stanton?" Vanover moved a step closer. It gave Kasey an instant feeling of intense claustrophobia.

Kasey took a deep, silent breath. Her heart had begun to pound like a drum. She was sure the detective could hear it. "I don't know what you mean, Detective Vanover. I had a dream—"

"Say, didn't you and I talk last week," he interrupted, putting the unlikely pieces together in his mind for the first time. He rested his right arm on the post and leaned toward her. "I don't believe we had the opportunity to finish our first conversation, *Mary Jones*," he added with a sinister snarl, "now did we?"

Kasey cursed herself for having ever made the damnable call to the police. Her mind raced, trying to decide what to do, how to respond. She tried to appear calm, and remembered the cardinal rule: for every lie told, the likelihood of being caught increased exponentially. The big lie had been told—she was a psychic who'd merely had a dream about this place. Now, everything else she said had to be the truth, or the whole story would crumble under the weight of statements and misstatements that could never be remembered. She prayed that the double agent had been correct. "No, we didn't, Detective. I called last Wednesday, though after I thought about it, Mary Jones was a rather poor choice of aliases. Sorry I hung up on you." She forced an agreeable smile while the sweat trickled invisibly down the sides of her chest.

The casual and candid admission caught Vanover off guard. "So, it was you who called."

"Yes, it was the day after I'd had the dream, the dream in which I saw Donna Stanton murdered and buried here." Some of Kasey's confidence had returned, though her knees felt too weak to hold up much longer. She knew she was past the point of no return. She had now lied in person to the police, and could no longer hide behind a faceless, nameless voice on a pay phone.

"Oh, and you were doing so well, Ms. Riteman. We're not back on the dream again, are we? You don't actually plan to stick with that ludicrous story, do you?" He began to chuckle, then grew extremely serious and thrust his face less than six inches from hers. "Listen, Ms. Riteman, or Ms. Jones, or whatever you want to go by, I don't believe a word of this shit you're trying to sell me, so unless you want to be booked as an accessory in the murder of Donna Stanton, you'd better come up with something a hell of a lot better than I've heard so far. You did say Stanton was *murdered*, didn't you, Ms. Riteman?"

Kasey tried to maintain her composure, but Vanover was making her feel like a caged animal with a sharp stick being poked into its ribs. She didn't like angry men so close and she instinctively backed away from him. "What?" she mumbled weakly.

"You said, 'murdered,' Ms. Riteman. You knew that before you got here this afternoon, am I not correct?"

Kasey ran what she had said to the detective back through her mind. *I'm still okay,* she decided after a painfully long moment, *but I've got to be more careful—this bastard's after my head!*

"In my dream, Lieutenant. I saw her murdered in my dream," she repeated.

"Oh, my God!" he barked angrily. "Let's get off this dream crap and down to a little simple, run-of-the-mill truth, okay!?"

She jumped again at his words.

"What have you got here, Pete?" Taylor asked pleasantly, joining them at the gate. Neither had noticed him approach.

Vanover turned to his boss. "Chief, I'd like you to meet Ms. Kasey

Riteman, psychic to the stars and seer of dead bodies, far and near. Ms. Riteman, Chief of Detectives, Taylor."

Kasey nervously extended her right hand, but before the two could shake hands, Vanover took his boss's arm and pulled him a couple of steps away. He spoke in a voice she was not able to hear.

"I think we've got a possible suspect here, Chief, or at the very least a material witness. The dizzy broad wants us to believe she had a dream about seeing the Stanton woman buried here. Says she knew she'd been murdered even before they started digging. What's more, this is the same dame who called me last week and hung up; said her name was Mary Jones then. I think she's completely full of shit. If you ask me, I put her pretty ass right here the night Stanton got planted." He considered his theory flawless—or at least close enough to reality to continue hammering at Kasey until he uncovered the whole truth.

Taylor looked over Vanover's shoulder at the attractive, frightened woman with the prettiest red hair he had ever seen. He loved redheads. He had an idea.

"Let me talk to her for a minute, Pete, will you? You go see what Barnie's come up with."

"I'm not done with her, Chief."

"She's not going anywhere. Let me do a little yin and yang on her for a while (referring to their well-rehearsed good cop/bad cop routine). It can't hurt, can it?" Vanover looked back toward Kasey and then nodded his agreement. Taylor patted the man on the shoulder and waited for him to head back down the hill.

He moved back to Kasey's position. "I apologize for his abruptness," he said, extending his hand a second time. "He's a good cop, despite his occasional tendency to oversimplify." He waited for a slight smile to grace her lips. "Hi, I'm Jordan Taylor."

She shook hands with him, grateful that the most immediate threat had passed. At least she would have some time to think before encountering Vanover again. She also hoped that Taylor would not prove to be worse than his buddy, but then, at the moment, she couldn't imagine anyone being worse than Vanover.

"I'm Kasey Riteman, but he already told you that, didn't he."

Taylor relaxed against the fence post. "I'd love to hear your story, if you don't mind repeating it," he said warmly.

"I didn't get a chance to tell it in the first place. He just started attacking me, like I'd done something wrong. I haven't done a thing—"

"I know you haven't, Kasey, that's just the way he is. Try not to let it bother you. He doesn't mean anything by it, really."

She liked Taylor's easy manner, and found him to be rather attractive, not at all like Vanover. "He said he didn't believe in psychics. How about you, Chief Taylor?"

"Oh, Lord, please don't call me that. My name is Jordan." She nodded with a smile. "And I do believe in psychics. I know a number of departments that have used them from time to time, often with surprising success, though I admit I've never met one in person. You feel like telling me about it?"

He held out his arm, gesturing her toward his car.

❖

Brandie joined Tim and the others near the grave site, where Barnie's team had just finished photographing the immediate area and picking through the grass for anything that could be of use in determining the time and cause of death. There had been two heavy rains since Donna Stanton had been entombed on the twenty-second, assuming Kasey was correct about the date. Though at this point he had no way of knowing how long she'd been here, other than a cursory guess based on her partially exposed left foot, Barnie assumed little physical evidence remained on the surface. Even his heavy van had not left noticeable tracks in the grass-covered field. He wasn't surprised that there were no other tracks or footprints worth collecting.

"Anything yet, Doc?" Slade asked impatiently.

"Not much, I'm afraid. There's been a lot of rain here recently. We'll have to learn what we can from the body itself."

"Can you tell if it's Donna Stanton?"

The medical examiner stopped what he was doing and stared disbelievingly over his trifocals at the governor's top man and then at the five bare toes sticking through the ground. He didn't have to respond.

"When will you be able to identify her, Doc?" Slade didn't give a damn about Polaski's condescending look, he wanted an answer.

Barnie wished he could just snap his fingers and make the annoying little man disappear. He took a labored and exaggerated breath. "Tomorrow if I'm lucky. More likely Wednesday. Now please, go away and let me work in peace." He would pay no more attention to Mr. Slade.

Slade walked off toward Brad Stark, hoping he had turned up something of interest.

Tim shot what he could, staying at a comfortable distance while Brandie narrated the events. JR and Hank were still standing where Vanover had left them, awaiting his return.

Neither had moved an inch.

❖

Jordan Taylor shut Kasey's door and walked around to the driver's side. He had already heard a sketchy outline from Brandie about the events leading up to the discovery of the body, including her dinner with Kasey last night.

Now, it was Kasey's turn to tell it.

He shut his door and started the engine, putting the air-conditioning at a comfortable setting. "How does a person get to be a psychic?" he asked as a way to begin without intimidating her; he wanted her to trust him. Despite needing her to talk candidly with him for official reasons, he found Kasey attractive; he had a special place in his memory for redheads.

"You don't get to be one," she smiled, "like becoming a policeman or a nurse. It's something you're born with, I guess, like having a natural singing voice."

"That leaves me out," he joked. "I can't even sing in the shower."

She continued to smile politely but did not respond.

Jordan settled into his seat. "Have you always been able to do it, I mean, see things other people can't?" He leaned back against his door, facing her. Their legs touched briefly; both hesitated for a heartbeat.

Kasey readjusted her position to give him more room. "I guess I have. It wasn't aware of it, though, until I was a senior in high school."

"What happened then?"

Kasey related the story of the two boys who had been killed in Lafayette. He seemed to accept the story, though she was having a difficult time reading him. She found herself guarding her words with Taylor as much as she would have with Vanover, distrusting him for no particular reason that she could put her finger on.

"That's a lot for a young woman to have to deal with."

Kasey nodded slightly.

"When did you first have a vision . . . do you refer to them as 'visions?' "

Again, she nodded silently.

"When was your first vision of Donna Stanton? Do you remember the day?" He switched off the police radio that was crackling distractingly in the background.

"It was Tuesday night, the night before I called Detective Vanover. I'd had a bad dream about Donna Stanton disappearing and I knew she was buried here."

"That's pretty incredible, Kasey, wouldn't you agree?"

She shrugged her shoulders and stared straight in his eyes.

"I couldn't sleep if I thought I was going to have a dream like that," he said amicably, trying to keep the mood light.

"It gets a little frightening at times."

He put a finger to his lips for a second: "Why did you think she'd been murdered, Kasey?"

Kasey stared out the windshield for a moment, to the activity between the two apple trees, and then back to Taylor. "I saw an image of her buried here, nude, with her face missing, like it had been cut away or something." The words stuck painfully in her throat and the emotion showed immediately in her eyes.

"It's okay, Kasey, just take your time." He reached for her hand. His kind touch felt good after the day she'd had.

"I don't know what happened to her, but I knew she died violently here. I could see that clearly."

"Why did you hang up on Pete after you'd gone to the trouble of calling the police in the first place?"

"As soon as I heard his voice, I knew he was never going to believe my story."

"You reached that conclusion pretty quickly, don't you think?"

Kasey narrowed her eyes defiantly: "You heard him questioning me. Would *you* say he believes me, Chief Taylor?"

As he shook his head "no," he began to see the intensity of the day echoed in her sad brown eyes. "Let's not talk about it anymore this evening. Perhaps tomorrow, after you've had a good night's sleep." He wore a look of uncertainty. "You will be able to sleep, won't you? I can get Barnie to prescribe something for you."

Kasey wiped the trace of a tear from the corner of each eye. "I hope that won't be necessary."

❖

Barnie Polaski and his men, wearing heavy rubber gloves, and masks to filter the putrid air, finished removing the earth that covered the front of the body. They knelt beside it, trying to read its hidden secrets. What now remained of Donna Louise Stanton's once-beautiful form was enough to make even the most hardened veteran queasy.

Barnie's attention was immediately drawn to the face—or where the face should have been. Instead of the expected features, there was a ragged hole from the upper jawline, where the teeth should have been, to mid-forehead; not attributable to decomposition, he concluded at once. The extensive damage was probably a gunshot wound—most likely an exit wound, his years told him—and its origin would be found on the other side. They would get to that later. He was pleased that most of the lower teeth appeared intact.

One of the anthropologists busily snapped photograph after photograph, using a sophisticated Nikon camera and flash unit with slow-speed color transparency film. This combination would allow for high-quality printing as well as projection on a slide screen. The camera's on-board data-back imprinted the frame sequence number, the time of day and date of each exposure, and an eight-digit number which could be used to identify any shot from this particular case.

To the extent that Tim could zoom in tight without becoming queasy, he, too, was getting it all, though he knew that none of what he was shooting at this point could be shown to Channel 9's sensitive viewing audience. Brandie did her voice-over from the most distant spot she could stand and still observe the excavation. Not being too close suited her fine.

❖

It took three hours before Barnie and his team declared the crime scene clean and free of additional clues. Donna Stanton's body—what remained of it—had been zipped inside a black rubber bag containing a powerful insecticide. There was still much she was going to tell the seasoned scientist, but in a language a layman could never have understood.

Vanover and the other detectives had recovered a half-dozen items between them, each now residing in its own Ziploc baggie, and tagged and identified as to its position relative to the corpse.

There was nothing further to do at SWEET WATER FARMS.

While the forensics van maneuvered its way slowly up the hill, three of the detectives walked toward the car that had brought them. Vanover trailed behind the van, making his way directly toward Kasey who was sitting on the hood of Taylor's car, talking with Brandie and Jordan.

She saw him coming and braced herself for another frontal attack.

Tim packed his gear. At eleven-fifteen, he was ready to get back to Nashville. JR half slept in the Jeep, barely listening to the local country station. Hank Tanner had hitched a ride back to town with Sheriff Smith when he and most of his men had left around eight. Warren Slade had fallen asleep in the backseat of Taylor's car an hour earlier, bored at not being able to find out tonight what he wanted to know, and angry at not having found the missing tapes and diary pages; he had called the governor at nine-thirty, and had given him a detailed report. Williams had been equally unhappy, and openly blamed everyone but Slade.

It had been a hell of a day for all concerned, one none would willingly choose to repeat. But, as bad as the day had been, none who had spent the day at SWEET WATER FARMS could have predicted the chain of events it had set in motion.

Vanover reached Jordan's car; his tie was in his pocket, his suit dusty, his shoes covered with grass; he looked exhausted. "Done, Chief. Area's clean."

"Good job, Pete, thanks. Come up with anything useful?" Jordan pointed a finger at Brandie. "Off the record, you hear me?"

Brandie rolled her eyes but nodded her agreement. She would listen, though, and remember everything.

Vanover didn't trust the reporter. Jordan's eyes told him to answer the question.

"We found a 12 gauge slug buried in the ground, about ten or twelve feet west of the body. Barnie says he figures it's the one that killed her. Probably fired as she knelt with her back to the gunman. Looks like they might have had sex first. She was nude, clothes piled in on top of her. No identification found."

Kasey was unable to listen to Vanover's recap. The images flooded her mind, spilling out from every hiding place she had stuffed them. She was amazed at how accurate his assumptions had been. She locked in a breath and tried to appear in control.

"Barnie able to I.D. her?" Taylor asked hopefully.

"Not tonight. The slug blew her whole face away. Real fuckin' mess. Sorry, ladies," Vanover offered insincerely. He lit a cigarette, sucking in deeply.

Brandie remembered Kasey's words just before they entered the orchard and the hairs stood straight out from her neck. Her respect for Kasey's abilities took on another dimension.

"Jesus Christ!" Jordan exclaimed. "Sounds like an assassination."

"Yeah, that's what I thought, too." Vanover stared hard at Kasey, who tried to maintain eye contact. "How about it, Ms. Riteman? Was it an assassination?"

"Now wait just a second, Lieutenant," Brandie complained.

"No one's talking to you, reporter, so just keep shut. You're damned lucky you've been allowed to hang around this long, so don't push it. I'm addressing the psychic here." Vanover's eyes grew hard and narrow.

Kasey sat up straight and threw her shoulders back. "How the hell should I know, Lieutenant. It's not like I was here when it happened."

"I wouldn't bet my pension on that. Why don't you and I go back to Headquarters and finish our little chat, Ms. Riteman. I'm sure you can eventually come up with a story I can live with—given time."

Kasey had the horrid feeling Vanover could see straight through her. She cut her eyes to Jordan, hoping for intervention.

"Hey, now, Pete, there'll be plenty of time for that. This investigation is just beginning. We've all had a rough day and everybody's spent. I think it can wait until tomorrow." He gave his subordinate a look that carried a command with it.

"Sure, it can wait, but we're gonna talk eventually, Ms. Riteman." He flipped his cigarette toward the pavement and strolled quietly toward his waiting car.

"Thanks," Kasey said gratefully. "That's the second time you've rescued me." She touched his arm softly.

"You've got to talk to him sometime," he warned. "It's his case." He could tell by her expression that the thought of meeting Vanover again did not please her.

"I know, but the notion would be a little more palatable if I didn't feel like he was trying to blame me for Donna's death."

"No one blames you for her death," Brandie interjected supportively, now that Vanover had gone. "You're the one who made it possible for us to find her. Without your help, I doubt she'd ever been found. You deserve the credit, not blame from some anal-retentive flatfoot."

Jordan chuckled at Brandie's words.

Kasey squeezed her hand as they watched Vanover drive away, his eyes fixed on Kasey until he had disappeared from view. "Tell him that," she mumbled.

SEVENTEEN

Michael Filippo slowly ascended the wide spiral staircase that led to Mario Giacano's bedroom. The news he carried to his old friend would not make him happy, he knew, but it must be delivered, and at once. Decisions had to be made, tracks covered, perhaps even lives ended, but so be it. The opportunity must be preserved—there were tens of millions at stake. He knocked gently on the massive ornate door.

Mario Giacano was sitting upright in his oversize four-poster bed, his back supported by a wall of satin-covered pillows. He knew the standing order not to disturb him while he was "entertaining" would only be violated by one man, Michael Filippo, and that it would never be for anything trivial. He watched with a jaded eye as his most recent distraction donned her silk robe and slipped off toward the kitchen to get them more wine and cheese. She would wait there until she was called.

"Come in, Michael," Giacano said.

"Sorry to bother you, Mario. I have some disturbing news." Filippo watched until the slender bronze form with huge breasts disappeared behind him. She was stunning, and though not yet twenty, more woman than a girl her age had the right to be.

Giacano grinned at his oldest friend. "You need more relaxation in your life, Michael. You're far too serious. Why don't I loan you Sissy for a few nights. She'll take ten years off that worried face of yours."

"Maybe when all this is behind us, my friend," he said somberly, though an intense erotic thought had taken hold and would remain in his mind for the rest of the night.

"Okay, Michael, we'll do business." He put on his glasses.

"Our cop in Nashville just phoned. They've removed a woman's body from a field near Columbia, in the middle of the state. It's her, Mario." He braced himself for the storm.

"Mother of God!" Giacano shouted, hammering his giant fists into the mattress. "What kind of idiot did that fool get to do the job, huh, can you tell me that, Michael? It's so goddamned easy to get rid of a body so it's never seen again. What the hell's wrong with those goddamn rednecks down there? Can't they even kill somebody right!?" His face was blood-red.

Filippo did not respond.

Giacano took another aggravated breath. "It hasn't been two full weeks, goddammit, and already they've found her. Make my nightmare complete, Michael, tell me they have the fucking tapes she made of me and butthead." The veins in his temples bulged.

"I think we're okay there, Mario. Nothing at all was found on or near the body. Our cop says he doesn't feel that Nashville Metro has a prayer of solving the murder based upon the evidence collected at the scene."

That bit of news appeared to have an immediate calming effect on the old Sicilian. "What about a ballistics match?"

"Shotgun. Not a chance."

"Witnesses?"

"None has surfaced. The area was quite remote."

"Well, who found the body then, Michael, if it was so fucking remote?"

"I'm told a psychic phoned one of the local television stations to report she'd had a vision." Filippo produced a disbelieving look in anticipation of his boss's response.

"You're putting me on, a fucking psychic!?"

Filippo shook his head.

Giacano pulled his glasses off slowly. "That's beautiful. We bury a body in a field a hundred miles from nowhere, and some cunt with a sleep disorder dreams about it. What's this world coming to?" He smiled at his own question, but only briefly; there was much to do. "Get back with our Nashville cop, Michael. Remind him that those tapes must never surface. Never."

Giacano took a sip from the glass of red wine on his bedside table. He pressed a button beside the bed that sounded a buzzer in the kitchen.

Filippo turned to leave, pulling the door shut respectfully behind him. Before it had fully closed, Giacano spoke again. "Michael . . . tell our cop to get rid of the loose ends. This thing could get out of hand."

"Consider it done," Filippo said with no consideration whatsoever for the people whose lives were about to end. "And the psychic?"

"Leave her alone for now. She'll be too public to touch for a while. Just have him watch her—closely." He motioned for the young woman standing patiently behind Michael.

"And then?" Filippo asked, making room in the doorway for her to pass.

"Have him give her something to help her sleep. Those dreams must keep her up nights."

The young girl dropped her robe by the side of the bed and glanced at Filippo before climbing into it. Giacano smiled at his friend's blank expression.

Filippo pulled the door shut and went to deliver the instructions.

❖

Kasey sat in the old wooden swing, swaying back and forth slowly on the porch of the restaurant. She knew if she were free of the burden of conversation for a few more minutes, she would be asleep. It wasn't merely that she was physically tired, but more that her mind was full. She felt like her head would split if she had to think again, and she wanted to be in her bed.

Home was still an hour away.

"Ms. Riteman," Tim said in a low and respectful tone.

"Hi, Tim," Kasey smiled, making room for him on the swing. She had no heart to tell him that her headache was an 8.6 on the Richter Scale.

"Oh, no thanks. I just wanted to say something to you I've been meaning to say all night." Kasey could tell that he was somewhat uncomfortable with the thought on his mind. Though the three others had talked nonstop since leaving the orchard, she had barely spoken a word since before dinner.

She stopped the swing and looked up at him. "What is it, Tim?"

He hesitated. "I'm sorry for what I said this morning, I mean, Monday morning, you know, when we first headed out."

Kasey reached up and took his hand. "It's all right. You were just expressing what you honestly felt at the time. Saying how you feel is never wrong—sometimes painful, but never wrong."

"I didn't believe in psychics before today. I'm not sure I would still trust everyone I saw on television, but I sure as hell believe in you, Ms. Riteman. You're the genuine article. You have the gift."

Kasey had been caught off guard by Tim's words. All of her rehearsing had not prepared her for adulation. "Thank you, Tim," she said tenuously. "But I don't know about having any kind of gift. I just see things sometimes, that's all." It was a dumb response and she knew it. She didn't care; her head hurt too much to do better.

"Nope, you've got it, all right. You've got the gift. I never thought I'd see it, but you've got it." He was still shaking his head in amazement as he joined JR in the parking lot.

Don't admire me, Tim, it was all just a trick! Kasey shouted in her mind. *A cheap, deceitful, cowardly trick to keep that bastard from coming after me!* The tearing had not diminished. If anything, the flattery had only served to heighten the pain it caused.

She stood and strolled toward the Jeep, eager to have this day behind her.

Brandie finished paying the bill and joined her three traveling companions. JR took the return ramp and was back on I-65 North in a few seconds.

"Wake up, Steve," Brandie called from the cellular phone. Dacus fumbled with the light switch on the lamp near the bed. It clicked on, filling the room with a yellow glow, temporarily blinding him; he had only been asleep for an hour, but it had been the sleep of the dead.

"Jesus, Brandie," he groaned, trying to adjust his eyes to the light. "What the hell's going on?"

His wife pulled the pillow over her head and cursed the news business.

"You awake?" Brandie asked. Tim and JR chuckled in the front seat; they knew how much Steve Dacus hated being called at home.

"I'm awake, dammit." Brandie was dangerously close to being assigned the weekend traffic report as her boss's brain slowly began to make out recognizable shapes in the room. "Where are you calling from?"

"We're on our way back from Columbia. We stopped at a restaurant at the Franklin Exit and grabbed a bite to eat. We needed to wind down." She took a breath. "You're not going to believe the day we've had."

"Stewart told me. He said you might have found Donna Stanton's body. That true?"

"You bet your overworked ass we did, and there's more: she was murdered. And not just murdered—assassinated! Everything was exactly as Kasey said it would be." She patted Kasey's knee briefly as she talked.

Kasey grimaced at Brandie's words. She tried to keep her mind occupied by watching the headlights on the interstate. She was too tired to listen, and she was ready to see Sam.

Dacus was fully awake now, sitting on the edge of the bed. "Don't go for headlines, Brandie, give it to me straight," he ordered soberly, knowing her penchant for the dramatic. Her silence told him that she could not have been more serious. He stood. "How do you want to play it?" he asked after a moment, grabbing his pen.

"First, I want a crew at Monroe's house in"—she looked at the clock in the dash—"exactly five hours, at six-thirty, standing smack dab in his front door. Wake his arrogant ass up with the news of his mistress's death. Let's see how cocky he is then."

Tim and JR exchanged wide grins. They liked Brandie's style, and neither of them had much use for Bill Monroe.

Dacus was reminded how good a journalist Brandie was. When she sank her teeth into something, it always meant ratings. "My pleasure, Brandie. What else?"

"I'll need at least two investigative reporters to help me assemble the necessary background on Kasey and Stanton. Give me Dusky and Mel. I have a lot already, but I need more if we're going to run a special after the news tonight."

"Tonight!" he gasped. His wife gave him a withering look and headed for the bathroom.

"You're damned right, tonight! You don't think Channel 2 and Channel 4 are gonna sit still on this one, do you? The moment they learn of her murder, they'll grab everything they can lay their slimy little second-rate hands on and put together the definitive 'Donna Stanton Story.' If I have to stay at it all morning and all day, we're running a half-hour special this evening."

Tim was glad he didn't do studio work; he could sleep until Wednesday. The thought brought a smile to his tired face.

"You have enough field footage to pull it off?" Dacus asked.

"More than enough," she answered with pride. "And it's dynamite."

"We should be able to pull together five or ten minutes of good file footage. We've got several pieces on her and Rocky McCall when they were still together. One with Governor Williams, too. If you can get three or four minutes of the sister or some other filler, that should just about do it." He could already see the story coming together.

"Don't need it," Brandie said in a smug tone.

"Why not?"

"We've got something better."

"What?"

"We've got Kasey." Kasey turned from the window.

"Is she good enough to put on camera?"

"She's a natural. The audience will love her. We'll sweep the night. Probably sell it to the network." She saw the Emmy sitting on her desk. It made her nipples hard.

Kasey shot a disbelieving look at her tireless and driven companion. "Me?" she mouthed silently.

Brandie grinned broadly, covering the phone. "Yes, you. It is what you wanted, isn't it, to be famous?"

The old dream rumbled deep within Kasey's soul.

❖

Pete Vanover turned right off White Bridge Pike and slowed to a quiet stop in front of Brad Stark's neat suburban home on Canebrake. It was two-twenty, Tuesday morning, and both men were ready to call it a day. From here, Vanover had only a four-and-a-half-minute drive before he would reach his own home at Whitland and Leonard, three miles to the east. He had made the trip over a hundred times since being promoted to lieutenant last November and had been allowed to take a city vehicle home when his shift ended. He didn't mind picking up his partner; Stark was generally good company, even at seven in the morning.

"You don't believe the Riteman chick, do you?" Stark asked as he reached for the door handle. Since dropping off Teague and Rinehart at Headquarters, they were the first words either had spoken; fatigue leaves its trademark in many ways.

"Not a word," Vanover said coldly, still staring straight ahead.

Stark stepped out and eased the door shut. He squatted by the car and stuck his face in through the open window. "Then let's haul her butt in this afternoon and scare the bejeezus out of her. We'll crack her if she's a fake."

Vanover took a tired breath. "Screw it, man, I'm beat. And besides, we've got to have our happy asses in court at ten on that liquor store shooting last month." His expression was not one of welcome anticipation.

"Oh, yeah, I was trying to forget," Stark said with an equally sour look. The detectives hated the time wasted in courtrooms waiting for the scales of justice to undo all their hard work.

"We'll cook the psychic on Wednesday," Vanover said, lighting a cigarette. "She ain't going anywhere—she hasn't collected her money yet."

"You think that's what this is all about?" Stark asked, not caring at the moment.

Vanover blew out a thick cloud of smoke. He gave Stark a twisted "isn't it always about money" smirk and eased away from the curb.

EIGHTEEN

As the Tuesday evening news ended and Brandie Mueller announced the upcoming Special Report, Kasey sat in front of her television set, a fresh tape rolling in her VCR, her dinner before her, and Sam fed and lounging in his chair by the window. His mistress was on the floor with her back to the couch, feet together, knees apart, her plate on the carpet between her legs—ignoring him.

Kasey was anything but relaxed: her stomach churned like a mixer; a familiar headache was growing in the base of her skull, its origin now over a week old; and her heart galloped to the point of pain. The simple plan to help find Donna Stanton and then get quickly out, without becoming involved with either the police or the bad guys—whoever the bad guys were—had taken a bold and dramatic turn in a direction that scared the hell out of her. She wasn't entirely certain, despite having dreamed of little else as a teenager, that she was ready to be "more famous than the Beatles," as Brandie had put it.

"Heads up, Sam," she called out to her roommate. "It's gonna be on right after this commercial." She knew, of course, that the Burmese could not have cared less, but it made her feel better having someone with whom to share her excitement. Sam looked at Kasey for a moment when his name was spoken, but that was the extent of his interest.

He had been fed and now it was nap time.

Brandie had insisted that Kasey watch the finished piece at the station, joining her and the crew they had worked with all day, taping and retaping segment after segment, polishing copy, rehearsing lines, delivering lines, editing pieces together, and then doing it all again. She declined the offer by telling Brandie she had to feed Sam. Brandie had thought the reason a fabrication, but could tell that her star needed to be by herself. Kasey had always thought of television as impromptu and immediate. She had learned, after only four hours sleep and then ten hours hard work at the Channel 9 studios, that it was anything but spontaneous.

Kasey checked (for the second time) that the tape was recording properly and then dropped back in her spot in front of the couch. She nibbled at a tuna sandwich for a moment but found her appetite gone. She slid the tray away and extended her legs. As the story began, Kasey raised the volume, absorbing every frame, every syllable. She had not seen the final edited version before now, and was amazed at how convincingly the fragments had been pulled together: Donna Stanton was passionately and sympathetically depicted as a tragic product of an unhappy childhood, the likely victim of one of the many secret lovers she'd had during her short and turbulent life, though who had ended that life remained a mystery. Kasey thought it a bit sensational, but was satisfied that Donna had not been portrayed as a woman whose life warranted ending as it had.

Though she had already seen her finished segment at the station, and had approved its content, seeing it within the context of the full half-hour program gave it a different feel, a startling reality. At the end of the special, in a piece not seen by Kasey before now, Brandie referred to her as the most gifted psychic of her day.

Kasey stopped the tape and called Sam. As she rubbed the sides of his face, and his purring filled the now quiet room, she was overwhelmed by emotion, carefully hidden feelings she had not allowed herself to experience since her parents had died.

Sadness at Donna Stanton's loss, opposed by the joy at her own sense of relief, tried to split her mind and her heart. Tears of loss and happiness mixed together in a confused stream that poured from her core. It seemed like an hour had passed before the phone snapped her out of her reverie, though it had been only a minute since the special ended. It was Brenda.

"Kasey?" she shrieked as her friend picked up the receiver.

Kasey wiped the tears away and tried to focus only on the first good feelings since Donna's death—since her parents' death. She was growing weary of the morbid and morose cloud which had been a constant companion for . . . she couldn't remember how long, though she knew it had been there long before last Monday. She held the phone against her chest and forced a smile. "I figured that'd be you. What took you so long?"

"If I hadn't seen it with my own eyes, I would never have believed it. Hell, I did see it, and I still don't believe it! What's going on, Kasey? Did you do all that stuff Mueller said? Is that where you were all day Monday? You're not really a psychic, are you? Why didn't you tell me? I've been trying to call you since Monday morning. You'd think the least you would have done—"

"I take it you saw the special," Kasey interrupted. She chuckled at her friend's barrage of questions.

"Dammit, Kasey," Brenda barked, "don't screw around. I want to know what's going on. I thought I knew you. That stuff about finding dead bodies in your dreams scares the hell out of me."

"Well, how do you think it makes me feel?" Kasey wanted to just drop the whole charade and tell her friend the truth, but knew Brenda's big mouth wouldn't stay shut, no matter how solemnly she swore her to secrecy.

"I don't know. How does it make you feel?"

"It scares me, too, Brenda. It's not like it happens all the time and I'm used to it, you know."

"Why didn't you tell me?" she asked, the hurt at not being trusted evident in her voice.

"I don't know. I didn't tell anyone. It became too much for me to keep inside and I went to Brandie Mueller. It's that simple, really."

"Simple! Seeing dead bodies in your sleep that turn up to be buried where you dreamed they'd be, isn't simple, Kase!" Brenda lit a fresh cigarette and took another swig of her beer.

"Hold on a second, Brenda, someone's trying to beep in." Before Brenda could object, Kasey answered her call-waiting.

"Ms. Kasey René Riteman?" the caller inquired in a formal male voice.

"This is she," Kasey said, not recognizing the man.

"Sorry to disturb you at home, Ms. Riteman, but I felt it was urgent that we speak as soon as possible. My name is Laughton Towns. I'm news director for Channel 4. We'd like to do an interview with you in the morning if you have the time. We'll pay you well for it, of course."

Kasey was astounded. She had not been prepared for another station to call, though she knew what she was supposed to say. "I'm sorry, Mr. Towns, but you'll have to speak with Stewart Parker at Channel 9. I signed some papers this afternoon and I'll have to have his permission before I can talk with you."

"I know Stewart well. I'm not surprised he signed you to an exclusive. I'll give him a call and get back with you. Sorry to have bothered you, Ms. Riteman."

"It was no bother, Mr. Towns. Thanks for calling." She switched back to Brenda to finish her original call. "You still there?" she asked.

"Where would I go? I haven't gotten a single answer yet. Now, you were saying—"

The phone clicked again. "Sorry, Brenda. There's another call. Don't hang up, please."

"May I speak with Kasey René Riteman?" the woman asked.

"This is Kasey Riteman."

"Hi, I'm Debi O'Conner, senior assignment editor for the Nashville *Banner.*" The rest of the conversation was a clone of the one she'd had with Channel 4, except that the paper expected her interview for free.

Over the next twenty minutes, Kasey managed to give Brenda a thumbnail sketch of Monday's events, while answering four more calls from area TV stations and newspapers. Most offered money for her story and each was redirected to Stewart Parker. Brenda, surprisingly, gave up and asked her friend to have lunch with her the following day. Kasey agreed and sat in the welcome silence of the room for a full minute before the phone rang again.

"Hello," Kasey answered cheerfully. She found herself enjoying the spotlight. It filled a painful void in a life that had grown drab and routine.

"Ms. Kasey Riteman?" the man asked.

"Yes."

"I'm Dan Herbert from CNN, Atlanta. Do you have a moment?"

Kasey's heart skipped a beat. She knew her agreement with Channel 9 didn't include stations and newspapers outside its principal viewing area—CNN was hers! "Of course," she answered too quickly.

She took a moment to regain her composure, the receiver held at arm's length.

"I'd like to hear your story, Ms. Riteman. It appears you might be the all-too-rare genuine article, something we see little of these days, I'm afraid. I liked the story Brandie Mueller did on you and the Stanton woman. Good stuff. Do you think you could give me a couple of hours tomorrow?" She hesitated, unable to speak. "I'm prepared to pay you fifty thousand dollars." Dan Herbert was pleasant and professional, but he had no time to play games. "Yes" meant sending a crew to Nashville; "no" meant moving on to the next story on his pad. It was as simple as that.

Kasey fell into the chair, almost landing on top of Sam. His sharp reflexes sent him scurrying to the floor.

She was now unable to even think clearly.

"Ms. Riteman?" Herbert asked.

"Uh . . . sorry," Kasey muttered. "My cat was about to get into some ammonia I had left out. (A quick lie.) When did you want to do this?"

"As soon as possible. I can have a crew at your place tomorrow afternoon, around three. If that would be acceptable, I'll send a certified check with them." The man intended to get the story his network wanted, but saw no need in telling the woman at this point that he had been authorized to go as high as a hundred thousand.

"I'll be here at three," she said with as much composure as she could muster.

"See you at three, then."

When they had hung up, Kasey danced around the room like a schoolgirl who had just been asked to the senior prom by the captain of the football team.

She had never felt such electrifying excitement in her life, and it was intoxicating.

At the height of her giddiness, the phone began to ring. "Yes," she answered breathlessly, certain it was NBC at this point.

There seemed to be no one there.

She repeated the greeting.

Still no response.

She decided it was a wrong number or a prank and put her finger on the Cancel button.

"Ms. Riteman?" came the soft woman's voice. It was barely above a whisper.

"Yes," she answered hesitantly.

"I'm so sorry to call you like this, but I have nowhere else to turn." The woman's voice broke at the admission.

Kasey considered hanging up on the strange caller, but there was something desperately sad in the woman's tone. "Why have you called me?" she asked.

"Because you've been sent by the Lord to find my Denise. She's been missing since a man grabbed her while she was walking home from school. That was three years ago, the day before her seventh birthday. She will be ten this October first. I have a beautiful photo of her I can show you if you think it will help you find her."

Kasey's throat tightened as if a wrestler's hands had wrapped around it; the walls of the room seemed as if they would move in and crush her. As she sank into a heap on the couch—without speaking—the woman continued.

"The police couldn't find her. They assured me they did all they could, but there just weren't enough leads for them to work with. Another child saw a man pick up my little Denise and throw her into his van . . ." Her voice cracked and she began to weep openly. "I'm sorry. I swore to myself that I wouldn't do this."

"It's all right," Kasey whispered. "I understand."

"Thank you. You're such a wonderful person. I could tell that when I watched you trying to find that woman who had been killed. I know my Denise is still alive, though. Mothers know those things. She's alive, she just can't find her way home, that's all. I'm certain of it. You will find her for me, won't you, Ms. Riteman? You're all the hope I have left in the world."

Kasey's mind begged for escape. The woman's words cut her like a razor, bleeding out of her everything that was good and kind and honest. "I don't think I can do that," she stated weakly.

"But, you've got to. Please don't say that. Just take my name and number and call me in a few days when you've had some time to rest. I know you must be exhausted from helping that reporter. It's okay. I can wait a few days longer. I've waited this long for you to come." Despite the polite, controlled words, the voice begged, petitioning for relief from a pain that transcended the physical. It squeezed Kasey's heart as surely as if some giant hand had seized it and was crushing it in its grip.

"I don't think I can help you," Kasey repeated softly. The words left an acidic taste in her mouth as they passed her lips.

The woman refused to hear. "My name is Beth Van Zandt. My daughter's name is Denise, Denise Van Zandt. My phone number is—"

"No!" Kasey screamed into the phone. "I can't do it! I have no control over what I see. It just comes. I'm sorry, but I have to go now." Kasey switched off the phone and held it against her chest. "I can't do it," she wept. "I can't do it, don't you understand," her last words a doleful whimper.

She started to throw the phone; it rang in her hands.

Kasey thought of what more she could say to the pathetic woman. Maybe she could make her understand this time.

"Yes," she answered again.

There was another long silence.

"I'm so sorry, Mrs. Van Zandt, so terribly sorry for your pain—"

"Really?" the man interrupted. "Are you sorry for my pain as well?" She strained to recognize the voice.

"Who is this?"

"Let's just say someone much less excited by your special gift than your showboat friend, Mueller."

A crank call. She had known they would eventually come. "And why's that?" she asked flatly.

The only response was an unexpected dial tone.

She spat a string of profanity as she threw the phone against the wall, silencing it for good.

Kasey forced her hands over her mouth as she lost what little dinner she had eaten. It would be nearly midnight before she would leave the floor of the bathroom, and curl into a fetal ball on the couch with Sam in her arms.

❖

At Sir Robert's—a dark, smoky bar on South Broadway near 8th, in the heart of Nashville's adult book underworld—a quiet, unimpressive man in a worn tweed jacket sat slowly stirring his fourth cheap Scotch of the evening. He was a regular at Sir Robert's, along with the other unemployed and disenfranchised patrons.

The man had only been half watching the television, absorbed in the resentment of dreams that would never be, when a teaser for the upcoming Special Report about Kasey René Riteman leading a Channel 9 news team to the body of Donna Stanton interrupted his self-pity.

He dumped the drink down his throat and ordered the bartender to turn the volume up enough for him to hear over the pinball machine and jukebox. The bartender reluctantly complied, but provided only as much increase as was absolutely necessary: most customers at Sir Robert's had little interest in current events.

"Thanks, dickhead," the man muttered under his breath. "Wanna give me another one of these? Can't you see I'm dying of thirst down here?" he grumbled out loud.

It earned him a short-pour drink and a foul look.

For the next thirty minutes, he watched the story with total concentration until it ended with Brandie's closing comments. "Psychic, my ass," he growled to himself, his initial curiosity having turned to anger, and the anger to hatred. "We'll just have to see about that, won't we?"

The man ordered the bartender to hit him again—a double this time.

The drink, as the others before it, was emptied in a single swallow. As it burned its way down, the man squeezed his eyes shut and shook his head a few times to get past the disagreeable taste of the rot-gut booze. He remembered a time when he had drunk Chivas. He rose from the bar and leaned unsteadily against the chair for a moment, searching for balance. He lit his last Salem and dropped the crumpled pack on the dirty floor.

After digging deep in the front pocket of a pair of wrinkled slacks and tossing two badly faded bills—a ten and a five—on the bar, the man in the tweed jacket disappeared into the street.

❖

Bill Monroe looked ridiculous as he sat alone at a table in the corner of the Cracker Barrel dining room, as far from the other guests as he could get. The attempt to disguise himself by wearing stone-washed jeans, a wrinkled denim shirt, and an Atlanta Braves baseball cap had only called attention to him. It wasn't the second-rate clothing, but the nearly black sunglasses at eight o'clock at night that Fieldman first noticed.

"Jesus, Willie, you look like someone vandalized a mannequin at Wal-Mart." The man dropped in the chair opposite Monroe, his back to the wall, away from the windows. He would not sit any other way, even if it meant not eating in a place where no such accommodation could be readily provided.

"You're late!" Monroe squawked.

The man rocked back in the chair without responding.

Monroe removed his cheap sunglasses, but kept his right hand near his head to partially block his face. He was uncomfortable. "This place is too crowded," he squawked.

"Relax. No one recognized you. They all figure you're just some butthead cheating on his wife. On second thought, they probably think you're gay, now that I've joined you instead of some chick." The man laughed loud enough to earn their table a few new stares.

"Goddammit!" Monroe grumbled.

The man grew silent and his face lost all expression. He pulled a Pall Mall from a half-empty soft pack and tapped it on the table repeatedly. "You've got a much bigger problem than you had on Friday, Willie, my boy." He lit the cigarette and blew smoke just past Monroe's face.

"No shit! What have you heard?" Monroe was obviously stressed.

"Only that your pretty little girlfriend was grabbed, blown away, and then buried in a field somewhere in Maury County, and a part of her diary—the part that points a finger directly at your stupid ass, according to the news media—is still missing. How'm I doing so far, Willie?"

"She wasn't my girlfriend, goddammit! I never laid a hand on her. I was only trying to get some dirt on Buddy Williams, that's all. I knew she had the best stuff on all the big shots in town, including him. But I never touched her, I swear, and I didn't kill her!" He waved an approaching waitress away excitedly when she was still ten feet from the table.

"Hey, Willie, you don't have to convince me. I won't be on your jury." The man chewed on the end of his cigarette and grinned broadly.

"You've got to do something," he pleaded angrily. "Everything I've worked for in this election will go down the crapper if I don't get those pages and tapes to the media."

"How the hell's that going to help you?" the man asked incredulously. He had assumed Monroe wanted the tapes destroyed.

"Whoever she was running from is on those tapes. I know it as sure as I'm sitting here. When she was pulling together what she had on Williams, Stanton mentioned being afraid of someone, but she wouldn't tell me who it was. I got the feeling it wasn't Williams, or his ass-kissing sidekick, Slade. It was somebody else, someone with real power. I've got to find out who it was and hang his ass with the crap they're trying to pin on me."

Fieldman whistled. "That's a pretty tall order, Monroe. If it can be done, and I'm not saying it can, it ain't gonna be cheap."

"I don't care what it costs!" He lowered his voice. "Find me those fucking tapes before whoever else is looking for them gets his hands on them. If they're destroyed, so am I. You're supposed to be good at what you do; it's time you proved it." He looked around to see if his words had attracted unwanted attention. They had not.

The other man remained motionless except for an occasional draw on his cigarette.

"Do you know the cops handling the case?" Monroe asked.

"Yeah," Fieldman said. "I already made a couple of calls to some friends on the force. Don't worry, I can work around Vanover and his worthless partner, Stark. Jordan Taylor may be another problem. He's not as stupid as the rest."

"I don't give a shit if he's a rocket scientist! Just take care of it. There's a hundred grand in the briefcase at your feet, so you know I'm not screwing around. Call me the moment you have anything—anything—understand?"

The man nodded but grinned as Monroe rose to leave. "Hey, Willie, don't forget your shades."

NINETEEN

Barnie Polaski finished the last of his notes and punched in the number for Jordan Taylor's direct line. It was nearly nine o'clock Wednesday morning; the last twenty-four hours had been spent with the remains of Donna Stanton. She had told him a great deal; it was time to share that information, and as directed by Taylor, he was to be the first to hear it. If Slade wanted a copy of the report, as far as Barnie was concerned, he could get it from the chief of detectives. And, if Slade got him fired, he'd welcome the rest.

"Taylor," Jordan answered, fishing for a pencil to stir his coffee. He decided to use a letter opener that resembled a small World War II bayonet.

"I'm through with her," Barnie stated with a yawn. He hadn't slept since Tuesday morning.

"I'll be right down." Jordan forgot about the coffee and grabbed his coat; it was always too damned cold in Barnie's office.

❖

The office of medical examiner of Davidson County was located in the lower basement of the Police Headquarters Building at 200 James Robertson Parkway, two levels beneath Jordan Taylor's office. It took Jordan only minutes to reach the outer door.

"He just called me," Jordan told the old maid Barnie had as a secretary. Taylor decided years ago that no one would have willingly worked around dead bodies as long as she had if they'd possessed the personality to acquire a less gruesome job. And a warmer one. He turned up the collar on his suit coat.

"I know, Chief Taylor, he's waiting in his office. Would you care for some coffee?"

Jordan instinctively said yes before he remembered that the coffee down here always smelled like formaldehyde. He'd made that mistake before. "No thanks, Millie," he corrected. "Just finished a cup upstairs." He shuddered at the thought of the foul-tasting brew.

Barnie was seated behind his desk, mounds of books and stacks of papers piled everywhere. It looked like a garage sale in progress. Jordan watched as the doctor added a second sugar to a fresh cup of black death, the name Jordan had given to the coffee served here. He was certain no amount of sweetener was going to help.

Finally, Barnie looked up. "Sit, Chief, sit. You're making me nervous standing over me like that."

Jordan looked around but saw nowhere to sit. The only other chair in the room was almost hidden beneath manila folders and boxes of file cards.

"Oh, for God's sake, move something. It doesn't matter where it ends up, I'll never sort through all this before I die anyway." The older man made a broad sweeping gesture with his empty hand as he stirred his coffee.

Jordan tried to keep the piles neat as he cleared the chair, but one fell over, and then another, sending papers across the floor. He looked toward the desk.

"Forget it, Chief. Sit. Sit."

"You said you were through with her." The old leather armchair was as hard as a wooden bench. Jordan wished he were standing again, but knew doing so would earn an instant, "sit, sit, sit." He tried to find a comfortable position.

"Finished her about six this morning. It's Donna Stanton, all right. Lower dental records matched perfectly. Also matched her prints to a set lifted by your boys at her home yesterday. I understand her sister took the news real hard."

"That's what they said. Not surprised, though. What have you got, Doc?" Jordan was sorry for Laurie Latham, but he'd seen too many weeping friends and relatives in his career. Life was hard, and death even harder. His job was crime and punishment, not family counseling. Right now, he needed information on a killer.

"Been dead a little more than a week. Didn't the neighbor say she saw Stanton drive off in a hurry on the twenty-second?"

Jordan thought about it for a moment. "Yeah. It was last Monday, the last day everyone we've talked to can remember seeing her alive."

"I'd say that's the day she died." Barnie looked at his desk calendar: "That'd make it nine days today." He scratched his ear with a pencil, considering his timetable in his head. "With the rains we had, the decomposition would be about perfect," he nodded. "I don't think it occurred any later than that, not even Tuesday, the twenty-third."

"How was she killed, Barnie?"

"Twelve gauge slug to the head. Entered at the crown about here"—he picked up a plastic skull from his desk and pointed to the back where the entry wound would have been located in Stanton's head—"and came out here. Took all this with it." The medical examiner indicated the missing area of the face by tracing an imaginary line with his finger.

Jordan was amazed at the huge loss of bone and tissue, but then considered the ballistic energy of a slug the size of half a roll of nickels. "How close was the shooter?" he asked.

"The barrel was no more than a foot away. Muzzle blast badly charred the hair for six inches all around the entry hole. She was kneeling, back to him. I'd put the guy at six foot, maybe six two." He looked over his thick glasses at Taylor. "This is not the first time he's done this kind of thing, and it won't be the last. I'll bet my life on it. He likes it too much."

Jordan respected Barnie's insights into the criminal mind. Though sometimes unscientific in their foundation, they invariably proved to be right on the money. "Talk to me, Doc. Why do you say that?"

"It takes steel nerves and a sick sense of absolute power to put a shotgun to someone's head and quite literally blow their brains out. It's nothing like shooting them at long range, or even with a handgun, for that matter. It's a mess, a real mess. You'd get sprayed with blood and brains." As the image was graphically painted for him, Jordan was thankful he hadn't eaten this morning. "Also, he crushed the chest and abdomen, probably with the shovel, hoping it would cause less of a depression in the ground when the body decayed. That's the kind of thing you either learn from experience, or in the joint from another con who made the mistake of not doing it. If the psychic hadn't picked this place, I doubt she'd ever been found."

"You got any feel for this guy other than being six foot?"

"Caucasian. Blond—very light hair. I found several of his pubic hairs mixed with hers. She died instantly, of course, but not before he'd had intercourse with her."

"How soon before?"

"Two or three minutes. Five at most. Screwed her, then killed her. Real sick son-of-a-bitch." Barnie finished his coffee.

Jordan's years with Polaski had prepared him for thorough, detailed reports, but he never ceased to be amazed by how much the old man could learn from a silent corpse. "What else?"

"There are a couple of other items I found particularly interesting. First, there were two semen samples in the vagina. One from just before she died, the other from ten or twelve hours earlier. Different blood type, different man. Sent both off for DNA profiling in case you get a suspect." Jordan nodded his appreciation. Barnie pulled a huge cigar from a humidor on his desk and stuck it between his lips. It would remain there, without being lit, for most of the day. He had given up smoking them ten

years earlier, but not the habit of carrying one around in his mouth.
"Second, I pulled several small fragments of metal from the soles of the
woman's tennis shoes."

"Metal. What kind of metal?"

"Small bits of bronze and carbon. Welding rod, to be exact. The kind
of particles that flash off during the welding process, like sparklers. They
strike the concrete floor of a shop or garage and cool rapidly. Their edges
are rough, even sharp, and they'll imbed themselves in any sole that's soft,
like a sneaker." He walked to the wall and filled his cup again, turning to
Jordan as he did. "What she can't tell me is: what the hell a classy woman
like her was doing in a welding shop shortly before she died?"

That was a question Jordan Taylor needed to answer.

He thanked Barnie and left. It was time to see just how much this
psychic actually knew.

❖

Sam had been up for two hours, since eight, hunting through the small
apartment for entertainment. He had made two trips back to his mistress's sleeping spot, to see if, by chance, she had arisen since his last visit.
Each time, he found her still beneath the afghan, snoring softly. He
settled for a narrow shaft of light that moved across the bed with the sun,
having found its way through a slit in the bedroom curtains. Despite his
most aggressive attacks, the white snake that moved slowly across the
covers refused to fight back.

When the heavy fist struck the front door three times, Kasey jumped
off the couch.

"Kasey Riteman?" came a voice so deep that it must have originated in
the man's feet. Though disoriented, Kasey was sure she didn't recognize
it. She stood and moved cautiously to where the livingroom curtains
joined in the center of the window. She parted them just enough to see
who owned the voice: the man's face was only two inches from hers,
practically pressed against the glass, the narrow black eyes squinting to see
into the room.

"*AAAHHH!*" Kasey screamed at the sight, backing immediately away
from the window. Her quick movement left the curtains parted several
inches, affording the man a clear view of the room.

And of her.

Kasey realized she was wearing only the tiniest pair of white cotton
panties and a sleeveless undershirt; her other clothes, covered with vomit
from last night, had been tossed into the wash. She had stumbled to the
couch around midnight, too exhausted to concern herself with whether or
not she was dressed to receive callers. Now, it presented a problem.

Kasey grabbed the afghan and pulled it around her, only taking her eyes off the man for a moment. His huge silhouetted form on the drapes gave off an eerie appearance. After a few seconds, he moved out of view.

There was a knock on the door, a little softer this time. "Ms. Riteman, my name is Patrolman King. Chief Taylor sent me to check on you." Though still thunderous, the voice had lost its menacing tone.

She looked through the peephole in the door and saw a black uni-formed policeman standing alone, though at three hundred pounds and seventy-eight inches, it seemed he scarcely required a partner.

Kasey opened the door a few inches, knowing the man could easily get past her if he had a mind to, with or without the chain being in place.

"Ms. Kasey René Riteman?" he asked, checking his pad as he spoke.

"Yes," Kasey answered hesitantly.

"Hi. Like I said, I'm Patrolman King. Chief Taylor tried to call you several times this morning. Apparently your phone is out of order. Is everything all right?"

Kasey looked at the pieces of the shattered Sony portable strewn across the carpet by the front door. She remembered having thrown it, though she hadn't expected it to disintegrate. "Yes . . . fine. I . . . uh . . . dropped the phone last night and now it doesn't seem to be working." She kept the door between them.

"Yeah, they'll do that. Happens at my house all the time. Four teen-agers." He produced a wide smile.

"Why would Chief Taylor be calling me?" Her question suddenly seemed ridiculous to her.

"Didn't say, ma'am. He just sent me to check on you and give you a lift to Headquarters."

"He wants me to come to Headquarters?" she asked, her voice display-ing the concern she was feeling.

King worked his head from side to side a bit, trying to look past Kasey. He sensed that something wasn't quite right. "You sure you're okay, ma'am?"

"Fine. I'm fine. Just a little sleepy still. It's been a rough couple of days." She feigned a yawn and pretended to be waking up, though, in reality, his face in the front window had rocketed her from semi-con-sciousness to fully alert. She was sure he wasn't buying the act. "Do I have time to get a shower?" she asked hopefully.

He looked down at the brightly-patterned afghan covering most, but not all, of her body. He grinned a bit. "Yes, ma'am. I'll wait out here for you. The chief wanted me to have you at Headquarters by eleven, though."

Kasey looked at the clock on the VCR: King had thirty-five minutes if he was going to keep Taylor happy. That left her just twenty to shower and dress. "Great, thanks. I'll hurry."

❖

The Metropolitan Criminal Justice Center—called the CJC, or simply Headquarters by the detectives and officers who worked there—often proved an intimidating sight to anyone encountering it for the first time. Kasey was no exception, her anxiety heightened by the disquieting ride to the building in a patrol car.

As she stepped onto the sea of concrete that formed the front courtyard of the complex and stared ahead to the central three-story red brick cylinder that rose from the white plain like a modern version of the Tower of London, she was sure, beyond any doubt, that they knew she was a fraud.

"He's waiting for you, Ms. Riteman."

Kasey looked back from the curb as her escort spoke. Her knees grew weak.

"Just tell the officer when you go through the glass doors there that Chief Taylor sent a car for you. He'll get him right away."

Kasey realized Officer King meant to be helpful, but his brusque manner was anything but reassuring. "He's waiting for you . . . he sent a car for you." She ran his words through her mind as she slowly crossed the wide courtyard, her leather soles slapping noisily against the smooth surface, echoing menacingly off the angled wings that jutted south and east from the tower. *Why did King have to put it like that,* she wondered contemptuously. *Is he really waiting for me, like a hunter waiting for an animal to cross his sites?*

Her mouth was dry by the time she reached the double glass doors.

As she wrapped her fingers around the cold stainless-steel handle of the right-hand door, the thought came to her that she should just turn around and run. Run for her life! If she went to Brandie and told her why she had lied, certainly she, another woman, would understand the fear that had spawned the crazy scheme. She was sure Brandie could explain it all to the police in such a way that they'd have no choice but to let her go. After all, what had she done? They could keep their money. She was in fear for her life, surely they could see that. Perhaps she could even use Joeyboy as a trump card. Knowing the killer's name should be worth something to them.

Donna Stanton's beleaguered expression, at the moment Joeyboy placed the shotgun casually to her head, burst forth from the miasma, wrapping her thoughts in a shadow of fear. The police might put her in jail, but Joeyboy would take her life, assassinate her with cold, pathological detachment. He would luxuriate in it, as he had when taking the life of Donna Stanton. Kasey wondered how many others there had been. The logical part of her mind fought for some measure of authority over the emotional part that was quickly growing out of control. Her body was frozen, like a statue outside the doors to the tower, her reflection in the bronze glass that of a woman she no longer knew or understood, a woman filled with guilt, fear, and doubt.

"Good morning," Taylor said as he eased the left door open a few inches to greet the attractive redhead in the bright green pants suit.

Kasey reacted like a child surprised by an older brother leaping unexpectedly from a closet.

Jordan saw the effect of his unexpected appearance. "Hey, I'm sorry if I frightened you. I saw you arrive with the officer and came to see you in. I thought you might want to see a familiar face. Your savior . . . remember?" His words were soft and nonthreatening.

Kasey put her hands to her heart. "It's okay," she lied. "You surprised me, that's all." He pushed the door open fully.

She walked beside him as they made their way past the receptionist and down the left hallway. Once they had crossed the floor full of detectives talking loudly on the phone and had entered the relative solitude of Jordan's private office, Kasey began to relax.

"You'll be more comfortable in here," Jordan said as he closed the door to his office behind them. "Want some coffee?"

Kasey would have been more comfortable at home, asleep on the couch with Sam, than in this unfamiliar office tensely awaiting the news that they'd discovered the flaw in her story. She reluctantly took one of the two straight-back chairs in front of the desk. "No thanks," she said with feigned politeness. Though she did want something to drink, the thought of coffee from a pot that probably hadn't been cleaned in a decade wasn't appetizing.

"A Coke, perhaps?" he insisted.

Kasey relented; she figured she'd need something to drink when the questioning began. Her mouth was as dry as sand. "Do you have a Dr Pepper?" she asked.

Jordan sat behind his desk and picked up the phone. He hadn't seen either Pete or Re-Pete since before ten A.M. He punched Feeney's line. "Chuck, have Pete and Brad come in here as soon as they get back. Tell them I have Kasey Riteman in my office. And grab a Dr Pepper for Ms. Riteman, will you?"

"Right away, Chief," Feeney answered.

Kasey mouthed a curt "thank you" and then busied her mind with the plaques and pictures that covered the walls. She didn't want to think about her story at the moment for fear she would begin changing things that didn't need changing—like swapping an answer on a test just before the teacher collects it, only to find out later that you had it right in the first place. She had firmly decided, halfway between the receptionist and Jordan's office, that she would stick defiantly to her original tale. If they could discredit her, so be it—she wasn't going to give them any help. She knew she just had to be careful not to trip over her own feet, and to answer everything truthfully. Everything except the one big lie, of course, and she knew that she couldn't take too long answering their questions. Hers would be a delicate balancing act on a wire stretched over a pit full of alligators waiting to eat her if she fell, but, even that unpleasant situation beat hell out of waiting for Joeyboy to come for her.

"Here's your Dr Pepper, Ms. Riteman," Feeney offered, after Jordan had given him silent permission to enter. He smiled at Kasey; it wasn't often they had such attractive company on the floor.

Kasey thanked him and then fumbled nervously with the tab. Now that she was here, she was ready to get on with it. The longer it took to begin, the worse it became.

"Thanks for coming," Jordan said after a long silence, barging in on her daydream again, just as he had done at the front door. This time she jumped imperceptibly. "It can be pretty intimidating, I mean, coming to the CJC for the first time. I tried to call, but Bell South told me your phone wasn't working." He dropped into the chair next to her, awaiting a reply.

She tried to look confident, but knew her eyes were filled with anxiety. She avoided his last remark. "It's like the first day of high school," she stated weakly.

"I remember that day. I got beat up by a pair of sophomores." Jordan laughed at the image and then remembered that it took until his junior year—after he had gained forty pounds of muscle from two seasons of varsity football—to settle the score with the two bullies who were then seniors.

Their shared laughter faded after a moment. "So, what happened to your phone, Kasey?"

As concerned sounding as it had been put, she knew it was nothing more than polite interrogation. Her look was firm. "It broke."

Jordan grinned, and then told the person knocking at his door to come in.

"Sorry we're late, Chief." As they entered the room, Vanover and his partner purposely positioned themselves in such a way that Kasey, still seated with her back to the door, could not see both of them at once. It had the desired effect of unnerving her and they knew it. The pair had worked together long enough that they could silently communicate volumes by eye or with a nod of the head.

Taylor chuckled inside at the predictable maneuver, but maintained a neutral face. He took his seat behind the desk. "Kasey, I told Pete and Brad that they could ask you a list of questions they've compiled over the last thirty-six hours. Now, try and relax, please. You're not under arrest or anything sinister like that. We just thought you might be able to help us clear up some items that are a little fuzzy at the moment." The three men smiled warmly in unison. She knew it was one of their well-rehearsed and often-performed acts.

Kasey took a long, slow breath and exhaled it dramatically, unconcerned about what they might read into it. "It's not often I have the pleasure of such interested company." She made eye contact with each, turning her head almost fully around to smile at Brad Stark. "How can I help you?" She sat erect and assured, but not defiantly. The curtain was rising—it was now or never.

Vanover slid the unused chair toward the wall and sat on the edge of the desk to Kasey's left. Stark moved to the opposite end of the desk. It was still impossible for Kasey to see both men fully at the same time. Jordan leaned back in his tall swivel chair and folded his arms casually. It was obvious to Kasey that he was going to assume the role of referee, leaving the interrogation to his men.

The show now belonged to the hard-nosed bastard on her left, and the partner who had not yet shown his colors.

Vanover opened a Marlboro flip-top box and tapped a cigarette on Taylor's desktop. "Mind if I smoke, Ms. Riteman?" he asked dryly, though she could tell his question was asked out of some ritualistic adherence to a code of social conduct he clearly didn't subscribe to in spirit. He might not actually light the cigarette if she objected, but she knew he didn't give a damn whether she minded. Kasey had worked in bars and restaurants too long to care whether or not someone smoked around her. She shrugged her shoulders slightly and Vanover wasted no time adding a flame to the cigarette dangling from his lips. "I hope the chief thanked you for coming in, Ms. Riteman. We were concerned when your phone went unanswered." He took a deep drag and made a poor attempt at blowing the smoke toward the ceiling vent.

Kasey nodded slightly, but didn't offer Vanover even the brief explanation she had given Taylor.

He let it pass.

"I got to tell you, Ms. Riteman, we caught your show on Channel 9 last night. It was interesting, don't you think, Brad?"

"Yeah, interesting," Stark echoed.

"Pretty weird, this psychic business you're in. Not like answering the phone at some office, is it?" He moved closer to her. "When did you first figure out that you were a psychic, Ms. Riteman?"

It was the approach Kasey had figured Vanover would employ the next time they met. "I've never actually considered myself a psychic, Detective Vanover, like some men and women do. Sometimes I see things that come true, that's all. Donna Stanton's death was one of those times."

"And the others?" Stark asked.

"Nothing quite like this, I'm afraid, Detective . . ."

"Detective Sergeant Stark, ma'am," Stark answered.

Kasey noted the name.

"So, out of the clear blue one night, you conjured up this little ditty about Donna Stanton, a woman you supposedly never met before, and presto!"—Kasey drew back—"it miraculously occurred exactly as you dreamed." This time, the smoke raced through Vanover's teeth and toward Kasey's face.

She didn't twitch an eye as the thick gray cloud floated past her head. "You're quite a bright fellow, Detective Vanover. Most people don't usually grasp psychic imagery that fast."

Jordan almost laughed out loud at her response.

In contrast to the chief's silent amusement, her sarcasm infuriated the target of her words. "I've spent the last day checking up on your past, Ms. Riteman, and I find nothing whatsoever to support your claim that you're a psychic or that you had a psychic episode. If you know what I think, I think you witnessed the murder, in person, plain and simple. Maybe even participated in it, and now you're trying to pass off this bullshit story to the media for . . . what is it, fifty grand I believe you'll earn for your trouble."

Jordan was surprised by Vanover's revelation. "Is Pete correct about that?"

"Yes. That's the amount the station promised, if you include the sister's reward," she answered calmly. Jordan leaned back again, impressed by the news. He began to reconsider the woman seated across from him.

"That's quite an incentive to lie, don't you agree, Ms. Riteman?" Stark asked. "Lots of people have lied for less."

"What makes you so sure I lied, Detective Stark?"

"Because I don't believe anyone can see the future, Ms. Riteman."

Vanover tried a different approach: "Did you know that her sister told us she had over two hundred grand in jewelry on her when she disappeared, Ms. Riteman, as well as a Caddie worth at least another thirty or so? If you add that up, that's almost a quarter of a million bucks." He leaned even closer. "Someone cashed in big with her out of the way. Any idea who that might have been, Ms. Riteman?"

"I can't say that I do, Detective Vanover, but if I come up with anything, I'll be sure and tell your boss." She was fairly certain the detective wouldn't actually strike her for her continued sarcasm, though the thought crossed her mind.

Vanover was visibly aggravated. "Who was the blond guy at the orchard that night?" he asked, hoping the bit of factual data on the suspected shooter would rattle her.

The memory of Joeyboy's short blond hair as he stood with his back to her between the two trees filled her mind. She wanted to hand him over to them, more than they could possibly know, but she knew to do so would only bring on a reality infinitely worse than the one in which she now found herself. "I don't remember dreaming anything about a blond man," she answered casually, adding a smile. "Is he supposed to have something to do with Donna Stanton's death?"

"You know very well what he has to do with Stanton's death," Stark added sourly.

"I only know what I've already told you gentlemen, nothing more." She remained pleasantly resolute, but her nerve was rapidly failing her. She needed to put an end to this soon, it was too much at one time.

"Really? You gotta admit, Ms. Riteman, even fifty grand pales beside your half of a quarter million bucks."

"Are you telling me that you think I actually had something to do with her murder, Detective Vanover?"

"I'm saying that I don't believe in psychics, and a hundred fifteen grand isn't a bad day's work, especially for a hard-luck waitress with a dog for a car, a couple of dead folks, and fifteen lousy bucks in the bank."

His cruel words burned like fire. Kasey was not surprised that the police had seen her bank account, she'd expected that after Brandie's warning. But knowing it might occur didn't lessen the feeling of violation that overcame her. "If being poor is a crime, then arrest me, Detective Vanover. Otherwise, I'm tired of your accusations and have better things to do than sit here and continue listening to them." She stood, grabbing her small purse from the floor beside her chair.

She knew Vanover didn't have hard evidence that could have linked her to the crime. Somewhere, amid the badgering and broad-based accusations, she had come to that realization. Her eyes went to the man in the middle. "I'd like to thank you, Chief Taylor, for the lovely morning. It's been most entertaining. Now, if you plan to charge me with the murder of Donna Stanton, or with some involvement in her death, tell me now so

I can call my lawyer and Brandie Mueller. I'm sure they'd both love to hear how you came to this conclusion. Be sure and say good-bye to your two buddies for me." She turned and walked to the door. "If you have any questions that are actually worth my time, I'm sure you'll be able to find me."

The three men had not moved from their original positions when the door slammed behind her. Feeney looked up at the sound and watched the shapely visitor stroll casually across the floor toward the front door.

Jordan produced a knowing smile. "I don't think she's very happy with you, Pete, and I can't say that I blame her." He grew more serious. "And what's this about her being a possible suspect? I agree she knows more than she's telling, but she's no killer."

Vanover lit another cigarette and tumbled his lighter between his fingers. Still stinging from her uncooperative spirit and Taylor's chastising reaction, he didn't feel much like explaining.

"Don't tell me you were just trying to rattle her," Jordan said in amusement.

"She knows more than she's telling, Chief, and you know it." Vanover's eyes were glaring.

"I can smell a cover-up, too," Stark added. "She might even know where the missing tapes are, might even have them."

"I don't give a damn what you smell or what you think she knows. For all I know, she's the genuine article. And she's got the public behind her now. They absolutely love her. It's not going to be easy to bring this lady down without something more concrete than your sense of smell, Stark." He looked at Vanover. "Did you come up with anything in her past that would lead you to believe she could be capable of such a crime?"

He hesitated.

"Well . . ."

"No. But I didn't come up with anything that would prove her to be a goddamn psychic, either!" Vanover's tone was adamant.

"How about the two boys in her high school that were killed during her senior year? She predicted that, you know?"

"How do you know she did? Because she told you?" Vanover huffed.

"Why the hell would she lie about it?"

"I can think of fifty thousand reasons," Vanover argued, "even if she wasn't party to the actual crime."

"But she called here first, before there was any money involved at all. You scared her off, remember?"

"If she'd been on the level, she would have stayed on the line with me, not run to that nosy bitch over at Channel 9." Vanover turned to the window, his thoughts lost in how to unmask the woman who had just burned him.

"That's the real deal, isn't it, Pete? I know how you hate Mueller. Now you're doubly pissed because she didn't fall to pieces under your questioning. Sorry, buddy, but it doesn't sound to me like you've got a thing to go on. Let's face it, Pete," Taylor began to laugh, "you just don't believe in fortune tellers."

"She didn't tell us a goddamn thing. I think we should question her further, maybe even get a warrant to search her apartment." Stark stood and assumed his most uncompromising posture.

"It ain't gonna happen, Brad. There's no probable cause, you know that. You're just mad, too. And question her again? Why? So she can tell you the same damn thing. She doesn't know anything other than what she's already told you. I'll bet on it."

"Well, I won't," Vanover grumbled as he stared back at his boss.

"Listen, guys, you struck out being a couple of hardasses this time, and it won't work any better on her in the future. In her own way, she's as tough as a nickel steak. Now, if you can link her to Stanton's death, any concrete evidence at all, I'll let you haul her in and grill her until she tells you things she didn't even know she knew. Until then, let the old pro work on her." He grinned broadly and rocked back in his chair. "God knows, I can't do any worse than you two."

❖

Giacano's man answered the call that had been transferred to his desk by the switchboard; he did not recognize the caller's name, though the man had specifically asked for him.

"Hello," he said in a bored voice, taking his chair. He got calls all the time from people he didn't know, people who had caught his name on television or in the paper.

"Iiiiiiit's Johnny" came the irritating reply.

"What the hell are you doing calling me on this line? You're supposed to use my cell phone," he barked, careful not to be overheard.

"The Bell South Mobility customer you are calling cannot be reached at this time. Please try your call again later." Joeyboy made his voice sound like the operator's.

Giacano's man looked at the Nokia cellular phone lying on the desk; it was switched off. "It doesn't matter. Never call on this phone again."

"Relax, you'll give yourself an ulcer. No one knows my voice. They'll think I'm just another one of your devoted fans."

"Fuck you," the cop spat. He hated Joeyboy and would have gladly put a bullet in his brain if it had been his choice to make. Perhaps someday. The thought made him smile.

"Oooh, now that's more like it. I won't bother asking you if you saw that fucking special last night. I suspect half the goddamn state was watching."

"The psychic?" he said, though it was more a statement than a question.

"No, the fucking Pepsi commercials. You talk to her yet?"

"Just now. She left less than a minute ago."

"And?"

"And what?"

"And, what does the psychic know she hasn't told that Mueller bitch yet?" It was obvious Joeyboy was more than a little upset by the broadcast.

"I'm not sure at this point—"

"You're not sure!?"

"I'm reasonably certain she knows nothing else. I'll be glued to her for the next several days, though. If she knows a thing she hasn't told us yet, I'll find it out soon enough." The cop wanted to end the conversation before he had company. "What's your point?"

"My point? Simple. I don't like it, in fact, it makes me fucking crazy. She leads Mueller to the grave like she was standing beside me when Stanton got planted." Joeyboy pulled the tab on a fresh beer, his third of the morning. "She needs to be burned. Now!"

"That's not your decision to make, and don't forget it. You take your orders from the top, just like I do."

"Yeah, well, I'm not gonna just sit by and let her take me down, with or without the old man's permission, and don't you forget that." He swallowed half his beer.

"You'll do nothing until you're told, or you won't be able to count the number of guns the old man will send for you." The cop was on his feet. "He doesn't want her touched for now; she's too hot." He made sure his voice hadn't carried to other ears. No one was close enough to hear.

The threat—the fact—that had just been put to him was the only thing keeping Joeyboy from blowing Kasey's head off as soon as he could make the short drive to her apartment. He finished the beer and crushed the can angrily. "Yeah, well, if the bitch has one of her fucking dreams about the guy who did Stanton, don't think for a second that she's gonna live to make another television appearance. Fuck the old man."

"Yeah, well, that's then—this is now. And for now, you don't go near her. Understood?"

"Sure, sure, no problem." Joeyboy rolled his eyes. "Hey, listen, man, one more thing before you get back to catching crooks."

"What?" His patience was spent.

"Hey, don't get testy. We both take orders from the top, remember?" Joeyboy smirked.

"What!?" the man repeated hatefully.

"You know that titty dancer that was found in the alley the other day?"

The detective dropped the phone to waist level. He needed a moment's relief from the presence on the other end. He moved the mouthpiece back to his lips. "Don't tell me that was some of your work, you sick son-of-a-bitch."

"Hey, she was gonna be a problem. She overheard something. The old man would've approved." Giacano's approval or disapproval had never entered his mind; the dancer was self-preservation, nothing less, nothing more.

"I suppose now I'm supposed to sit on the investigation?"

"She was a titty dancer, for Christ's sake, not a real person. Just don't get carried away looking for people who knew her, that's all."

"You clean?" he asked dryly, feeling like he was checking the diaper of a spoiled child.

"Of course, man. Spick 'n' span, as always."

The detective was relieved, though not surprised. Practice makes perfect. He knew that, without someone pushing for a solution from the inside, the case would end up like a hundred others before it: nowhere. She was a stripper, after all. Not the head of the PTA or the Rotary Club. "Anything else?" he asked.

"No, that about does it. You've been most helpful, Officer Friendly."

Giacano's man made a tight fist with his free hand. "You know that you and I are going to have to settle our little differences when this is all over, don't you?"

Unlike the earlier threat of Giacano's wrath, the detective's words did not raise Joeyboy's pulse by a single beat, except in pleasant anticipation. "I think I'll enjoy that more than I will fucking your daughter after you're dead."

He hung up before the cop could respond.

❖

Kasey had slipped off her heels and was walking briskly—and barefoot—down James Robertson Parkway when Jordan eased up behind her in his unmarked car. She was still shaking from her outburst in Taylor's office, and was positive they would be coming to arrest her at any moment.

When she looked over her shoulder for the twentieth time in ten minutes, and Taylor waved at her through the windshield of his sedan, she didn't stop. She did, however, reluctantly resign herself to another agonizing bout with Vanover and Stark. She wasn't sure she could do it again this soon without losing it altogether.

"I remembered you didn't have a ride," Jordan said as he rolled down the passenger window and tried to avoid the curb as he drove. Kasey only glared at him, the heels swinging from one hand, the purse from the other. "You planning on walking all the way home?"

When he almost struck a fire hydrant and realized that his efforts were gaining him nothing, he pulled a hundred feet ahead and stopped his car.

He stepped out and stood in her path on the sidewalk.

Kasey walked past without a word or a look.

Amused, he followed her, staying a step behind. "You have every right to be angry, Kasey, but not at me. I had no idea Vanover was going to come up with that insulting line of questioning."

Kasey stopped dead in her tracks, causing Jordan to bump into her slightly. He took a step backward.

"He works for you, doesn't he?" she snapped.

"Sure, but he doesn't run everything he's thinking past me before he opens his mouth." He put his hands in his pants pockets to appear more benign.

"You know he's been trying to blame me for Donna Stanton's death since he saw me the first time. I don't like it and I'm not going to stand for it. I had nothing, do you hear me, nothing, to do with her getting killed!"

"I know you didn't, Kasey" he said softly, hoping to calm the moment.

"Furthermore, I wasn't. . . . What did you say?" she asked in mid-sentence, certain she hadn't heard him correctly.

"I said that I know you didn't have anything to do with Donna Stanton's death."

Kasey was dumbstruck by his words.

He smiled warmly at her. "Listen, I believe you're the real McCoy, and I'd like to express my appreciation for coming forward. Without you, Kasey, we might never have known what happened to Donna Stanton. She'd still be lying in that remote field. As it stands, we've got some solid evidence and can charge the bastard with her murder when we catch him."

Kasey was astounded. And relieved.

Until a moment ago, she'd had it with cops—all cops. Now it seemed this man who had already rescued her twice before was doing it again. She produced a huge smile. "You're welcome," she said.

They laughed together on the sidewalk for a moment, the tension between them escaping like pressure from an open steam valve. "You hungry?" he asked.

"A bit, I guess." Her stomach growled at the thought of food.

"Want to grab some lunch before I run you home? The least I can do after subjecting you to Pete and Re-Pete is buy you a burger." He raised his eyebrows and cocked his head playfully.

"Sure," she grinned back. "You seem harmless enough."

TWENTY

Kasey devoured the hamburger and fries Jordan had gotten for her at the Back Yard Burger on Wayne Avenue, two blocks from Headquarters. His lunch remained virtually untouched while he watched with quiet interest as she satisfied a ravenous hunger.

Her stomach had been complaining loudly since Patrolman King had awakened her two hours before, and with the added anxiety of the morning's events—coupled with losing last night's dinner—even fast food tasted unusually wonderful. It was much like the time she'd tried pot in college, and found herself eating everything in sight the following morning.

"They make a great burger," she said as she finished the last bite. The fan above the patio picnic table gently tossed her hair, and brought a pleasant breeze to a day that was warming up quickly. "I've meant to stop at one of these places before but always seem to end up at Wendy's or McDonald's." She ate her last fry, adding a little pepper before popping it in her mouth. "You come here often?" she asked, reaching for her drink. It was not her best effort at witty and stimulating conversation, but she decided it would have to do under the circumstances. She was too drained to be sexy or clever.

Jordan chuckled at the animated personality of his lunch guest. She seemed so different from the sad, frightened woman he had met at the orchard. "Once a week or so. It's close. I'm glad you liked it."

"You haven't eaten much of yours."

"Not hungry, I guess. All the coffee." He poked at a fry and watched as a couple ordered from the walk-up window.

"What is it?" she asked, sensing something remained unsaid.

He turned his eyes back to her. "I had wanted to ask you a few questions about your vision once we got away from the CJC, but it doesn't seem all that important anymore." His eyes were kind.

Kasey reluctantly tried to put her mind back on the issue she knew had not been fully resolved in his office. She decided if she had to answer more questions, she would rather be questioned by Jordan than by the boorish pair she'd dealt with earlier. She put her elbows on the smooth concrete table, head cradled in her hands. "Go ahead, copper, ask your questions. I'll try not to bite your head off this time."

He took a sip of his iced tea. "You know a lot more about that night than you've told us, don't you?"

Kasey was startled by his question and found herself unable to answer. Her mind groped for the correct response. Was he on to her despite his profession of belief? Her stomach knotted. "What?" It was the best she could do.

"Your vision wasn't restricted to the location of her body after her death, was it? If I remember your words correctly, you saw details in your dream about her being killed and then buried."

Kasey let out a silent sigh of relief. "I'm not sure I know exactly what you're driving at, Jordan. Could you be a little more specific?" She took a sip from her tea, not so much out of thirst as from the need to be doing something with her hands.

"I have to know as much about her murder as you can tell me. If you can give us any lead to go on, no matter how insignificant it might seem to you, it may prove invaluable to our investigation. Right now, I'm afraid you're all we've got."

"I thought you said you had collected evidence that would nail Donna's killer." She was distressed by the detective's admission that his department was at a dead end. Joeyboy simply couldn't be allowed to go free.

"We have several items that can be used to convict the man, or men, once we catch him, but first we've got to catch him. I'm afraid that doesn't look promising." He seemed frustrated to Kasey; his eyes had lost their sparkle.

She wanted to shout out Joeyboy's name, but she couldn't get past the fear of him coming for her. She couldn't escape the image of him placing the shotgun to her head. "You said 'man or men.' Why do you think there might have been more than one man?" she asked. The black Jaguar flashed before her mind's eye like a home movie playing on the wall behind him.

"You can't tell anyone what I'm about to share with you, do you understand?" He was not kidding and his expression showed it.

"Of course," she vowed.

"There were two semen samples collected from her body, one fresh and the other several hours older, probably from that Monday morning. Without a man to match to each of them, we've got nothing more than a few cells in a glass slide and a DNA signature with no name attached."

Kasey was moved by the news that two different men had had sex with Donna on the last day of her life, men who had used her and then thrown her away like yesterday's garbage. She knew who the last man had been, his name, if not his face. *Had the first man been Bill Monroe?* she wondered. *Was he the man in the black Jaguar?* "You can't just let the bastards get away with it!" she blurted.

"Who?" Jordan asked quickly.

"What?" Her angry words had come involuntarily.

"You said, 'I can't just let them get away with it.' Let who get away with it? Did you see more than one man?" He leaned forward and took her hands.

Kasey wanted to put aside the fears that had haunted her for nine days, the images that had stolen her sleep and her peace. At times, she felt as though they would rob her of her sanity. She jerked her hands away and put them to her face, as a child does when frightened. "Give me a minute, please." She put her face against her palms and rested her elbows on the table. For almost a minute she didn't speak a word.

Jordan sat quietly, waiting.

Kasey moved her hands away and looked at him. She couldn't bring herself to speak the name, even if it meant Joeyboy would go free; the fear was overwhelming, all-consuming. "I can't see anything about the man. It's all just a blur. I can only see Donna Stanton kneeling on the ground, crying out for us to find the men who killed her." Kasey blew out a long breath and reached nervously for her tea.

"But, you're still talking about more than one man, Kasey. Was more than one man involved in her death?" He could easily picture Monroe, with all he stood to lose, behind the brutal crime.

Kasey knew, because she had accidentally mentioned a second man, that she had to give Jordan something to placate him. "I see the faint outline of someone standing behind her when she died. He's holding a short rifle of some kind."

"That would be the shotgun that was used to kill her," Jordan interjected. He leaned closer to her. "What else?" His impatience began to show.

"I see the shape of a car near the field, a car that drives off right after she dies. There's someone else in it, but I can't tell anything about the driver." She folded her arms around her as if a cold wind had just blown across her chest. The feeling was genuine. "That's all there is, really. I'm afraid I can't help you further."

Jordan was obviously intrigued by the mention of a second vehicle at the orchard. He could not let it pass. "What kind of car was the other man driving, Kasey?" he pressed.

"I can't make it out," she answered, her voice now low and monotone.

"Try, Kasey," he said louder, as if raising his voice might help her see more clearly.

"I can't see it," she mumbled.

"You must be able to see it," he snapped, shaking her from her daze.

"I said that's all there is, goddammit!" Her eyes, fixed on him, grew narrow, their warm brown tone now dark and foreboding. "Don't push me, Jordan. I can't see something that isn't there just because you want me to. It doesn't work that way." She cut her eyes away, obviously angered by his insistence. "I don't know when, or if, I'll ever have another vision."

Jordan could tell that he had pushed too hard. "I'm sorry, Kasey, really. Please understand that I'm just trying to find the answers, and you're the only source I have at the moment. I want the men responsible for this punished, and I want to know why it happened." He took her hands and held them firmly but gently.

"No more than I," she whispered.

❖

As Jordan weaved his way skillfully through the moderately heavy afternoon traffic of downtown Nashville, Kasey sat silently observing the cars on her right. She was still upset from his insistent questioning at lunch and wanted nothing more from him than a lift back to her own apartment.

Jordan had other plans.

When he passed Murphy Street at Charlotte Avenue, Jordan took a quick left turn and made his way down 25th Avenue to Leslie. A hundred yards to the west sat the Parthenon—a full-scale reproduction of the famous Greek structure—set comfortably amid eighty acres of beautifully manicured park land.

He took a space between two cars parked at the north end of the small, man-made lake and switched off the engine. "It's such a beautiful day, I just can't pass up the opportunity to start over with you. Will you walk by the lake with me for a moment?"

"What for?" she responded coolly. "So you can question me again?"

"I am the guy who saved you from the mean old cop at the orchard. Isn't that worth something."

"You're also the guy who sicked him on me again this morning," she reminded him, folding her arms and sulking.

Jordan offered no response. He tapped on the steering wheel rhythmically with his thumbs, waiting. He knew she'd weaken.

Kasey silently studied his profile. She saw in it the same boyish look of innocence that she had found so hard to resist since she had begun dating.

She jabbed an index finger into the side of his shoulder with emphasis. "If you mention one word about the case, I'll take your car and leave you stranded in the middle of this park. Do I make myself clear?" She sounded serious and Jordan half believed she would do it. As he nodded agreeably, he caught a slight smile forming in the corners of her mouth. She erased it as soon as she realized it was there. "I mean it," she added emphatically.

"Would you like my gun for insurance?"

"No thanks, I don't like guns. Your keys will do just fine," she said, and held out her hand.

He dropped them obediently in the outstretched palm.

❖

"May I help you?" the resident manager asked as she greeted the well-dressed man who had just entered the leasing office.

"Good day, Angie," the man said pleasantly, closing the door quietly behind him. A small placard bearing her name and title sat at the edge of her modest desk. "I wonder if you could show me an apartment."

"I'm afraid at the moment we only have two units available, Mr. . . . "

"Stanley," he smiled, shaking her outstretched hand. It was not his true name.

"Well, Mr. Stanley, we certainly appreciate you considering Bradbury Arms for your next residence." She gave him one of her best corporate smiles and held it long enough for him to smile back. "I have a lovely three-bedroom on the ground floor just behind the office, with dual covered parking spaces. It's a steal at $675 a month."

The man's expression didn't change. "And the other?" he asked.

"The other unit is just a one-bedroom, toward the back of the complex. It's on the third floor, near the pool. I'm afraid it gets rather noisy there at times. We have a lot of college students here, and they like to party around the pool on weekends. Would you like to see the three-bedroom?" She stood and went to a cabinet which contained floor plans and other literature on the complex.

"I sleep like a rock. Noise doesn't bother me at all, and since I have no family, the three-bedroom might be a bit large. If you don't mind, Angie, I think I'd like to see the unit near the pool."

She didn't mind, though she was surprised. As a matter of fact, she thought she'd have the less desirable third-floor unit vacant for months, at least until the start of the next school term. She shot him another broad smile and introduced him to her assistant, Lisa.

❖

As Lisa fumbled with the deadbolt key, the man leaned on the balcony and looked across the pool and common area toward the apartment building to the south. In a livingroom window, directly opposite where he now stood, a black Burmese cat lay soaking up the afternoon sun. He grinned at his good fortune, and watched as an attractive young woman, lying on a chaise longue by the pool, unhooked her bikini top.

"There," Lisa said as the door opened. "This apartment has just been cleaned and detailed, and it appears the painters got a little paint on the jamb. I'll have it taken care of as soon as I get back to the office." They stepped inside.

The man made a cursory inspection of the interior, though he would not have cared if the floors had been bare dirt. "It's perfect," he smiled. "I'll take it, but only if I can move in right away."

"Wonderful, Mr. Stanley. I'll have Angie draw up the papers at once. I don't see why we can't let you have a key as soon as you sign. The rent is $425 a month. We'll need the first month in advance plus a $100 damage deposit as well. The damage deposit will be refunded if—"

"I'm sure it's all perfectly standard and acceptable. I'm having my account changed at the bank at the moment, though, and I haven't received my new checks yet. You won't have any problem accepting cash, will you?"

The woman grinned broadly as she pulled the front door shut and locked both locks. "Cash? No, we have no problem whatsoever with cash, Mr. Stanley."

❖

The early May warmth, without the torturous humidity the later months of summer would bring, was just enough to make their slow walk among the trees relaxing.

For ten minutes, neither of them spoke. Just walking beside each other without talk of murders or suspects or psychic dreams brought a needed measure of release for Kasey. As she stole brief glances at Jordan, she realized that he was the first male company she'd had in a week and a half. There had not been so much as a phone call from an interested man during that time. She chuckled to herself; it had not mattered with all that had been occurring in her life.

There had been a time not long ago when things were different, but that time—and the woman who lived within its days and nights—seemed to have been transformed, to have vanished.

"Want to sit for a while?" Jordan asked as they neared a small, curved bench. The broken rays of the sun poured through the tapestry of leaves above them, scattering countless pools of flickering light across the deep green grass, like a giant living canvas.

"All right," she agreed, taking a place at one end.

Jordan sat at the opposite end and looked for a long moment into the face of his companion. The ribbon that had held her hair tightly bound had been removed, allowing the long auburn tresses to flow across her shoulders and down her back. "Tell me about Kasey Riteman," he began pleasantly.

She brushed the hair back from her eyes and looked directly at him for a moment. "What's there to tell that you don't already know?" she asked, not at all surprised by his first question. It was one of three basic male approaches she had categorized over the years. It had been used before—many times. She could not, however, remember it having been employed by anyone quite as attractive as the man across from her now.

She decided not to hold the lack of originality against him.

"Actually, I don't know anything more about you than you told me at the orchard Monday. Pete may have the lowdown on you, but he hasn't shared a word of it with me. Besides, the kind of information available to us never reveals the real person, just a jumbled assortment of fragments from a person's past." He loosened his tie and unbuttoned his collar. "I want to know who you are, not whether you've had a speeding ticket in the last three years."

"Why?" she asked without emotion.

Jordan grinned. "Why not?"

"Let's just say that the only man I've ever bared my soul to turned out to have been a poor choice." She looked at his left hand and then straight into his eyes. "You married?" There was no ring.

Jordan had thought of a dozen different ways to answer the question he knew would inevitably be among the first asked by this woman, and each time his planned approach had ended up sounding contrived. He knew that getting involved with another woman, especially this woman, at this time in his life, could cost him everything he had worked for since becoming a cop. "Yes," he answered simply.

"Thought so," she said flatly. She knew the minor disappointment could be seen on her face despite her effort to remain aloof.

"How'd you know?" he asked, pulling a long blade of grass from beside the bench leg and sticking it between his teeth.

Kasey sighed and then smiled. "It doesn't matter." She settled back fully in the curve of the bench, draping her right arm across the wooden back and allowing her left arm to hang loosely at her side. "Why do you want to know about my life? If it's part of some elaborate plan to get me into the sack, just say so. I'm not a kid."

Jordan was surprised by her casual frankness. He knew playing games with her would be a mistake, though he wished she hadn't seen through him with such ease. "Are you always so direct?" he asked.

"Oh, I can play games with the best of 'em," she smiled. "Though I prefer simple honesty any day of the week. It's probably because you so seldom encounter anyone who is honest in a relationship, especially a man."

"A bit cynical, aren't you?"

"A bit experienced, I'd prefer to say. For example, if I hadn't asked you about being married, how long would you have gone without bringing it up?"

"I didn't try to hide the fact from you," he rebutted.

"Then, you don't own a wedding band, is that correct?" She folded her hands across her lap.

"I'm separated from my wife," he answered honestly.

Kasey was surprised by his response, figuring him to be a solid family man with a house full of kids who mowed his grass every Saturday morning. Like her father had. She offered an insincere, "Sorry," glad she wasn't toying with another woman's man.

"It's okay, just one of those things that happens. Now, seriously, I'd like to know about you," he repeated. "I didn't say I wanted to sleep with you."

"Then you don't?"

"What?" he said, confused.

"Want to sleep with me."

"I didn't say that either. I'd be lying if I said the thought hadn't crossed my mind."

Kasey grew silent and looked off to the right, toward the ornate columned structure that seemed so out of place in the center of Nashville. "Why me?"

"Because I think you're good, genuine, and I don't meet many people I can say that about. It doesn't matter what you think of my motives because I know what I feel, even if I'm doing a poor job of explaining myself."

Kasey looked back at him. His eyes seemed soft and warm, his words felt gentle and sincere. She didn't know where to begin; it had been five years since she'd trusted any man enough to tell him about her past, her life, her feelings. Why she was about to share these things with this relative stranger was unclear to her, yet she found herself speaking before she knew it. "I was born in New Orleans on June first, 1967. So now you know my age," she grinned. He grinned back, but said nothing. "My parents were both killed when I was a freshman at UT Knoxville. I have no living relatives closer than third or fourth cousins, if I remember my mother correctly—none that I can recall in any case—so I guess I'm technically an orphan." The words came hard. "I'm a waitress at Leonard's Steak House and I have a cat named Sam. Actually, his name is Sam-I-Am, like in the children's book. He's my roommate and my best buddy." For a moment, Kasey lost her nerve and turned away again.

Jordan placed his hand softly on her right arm but elected not to say anything.

"My dad was a commercial real estate developer. You know the Rivergate Mall in New Orleans?" she asked.

Jordan nodded that he knew of it.

"My dad built that. Designed the whole thing himself. It was the first mall of its kind in the state of Louisiana," she stated proudly.

"Your mom?" he asked.

"She didn't work professionally. Sometimes she would help out in his office when bids were due and things got really hectic, but mostly she raised me and kept the house. She was a special woman." A tear made its way hurriedly down her right cheek. She quickly wiped it away and took a short, exaggerated breath, as if to defy any more tears to attempt such a treasonous act.

Jordan squeezed gently on her forearm, and could feel her muscles quivering beneath his fingers. "How'd they die?"

Kasey was poker-faced now, though she still looked off to the east. "They had this huge motor home, an Airstream LTD, I think it was called. It was great. My dad didn't like to fly, but he was building stuff all over Louisiana, Mississippi, and Alabama. He even had a high-rise office building going up way out in Phoenix. It was his first time building anything that far from home. The long hauls got too much for him—my mother never did learn to drive the thing—because they said he fell asleep at the wheel on the interstate outside Amarillo, Texas. That was Wednesday, the ninth of October, 1987. He'd been up for nearly forty-eight hours. He did that sort of thing when he was in the middle of an important project." She tried to find the next words. "Anyway, when he fell asleep, the motor home crossed the median and hit another car head-on. It killed my mom and dad instantly they said, and paralyzed the other driver. There was this huge lawsuit with lawyers from both sides running around everywhere pointing fingers and placing blame, and when it was all over, the only thing left of my father's life's work was the car he had given me when I went off to college. I had to beg the other guy's attorneys to let me keep even that. I don't think they would have agreed then if it hadn't been for the bad publicity it would probably have generated. They wanted to prove that lawyers actually have hearts." Jordan saw Kasey's jaws tighten beneath the soft skin of her cheeks. The eyes were again narrow and hard. "Don't you find that hysterical: lawyers with hearts?"

He nodded sympathetically. "Did you have to quit college?" he asked, unable to think of anything more profound to ask.

"Yeah. With the funeral and the lawsuit going on, I wasn't able to attend class much the first semester of my sophomore year. By the time the spring semester rolled around, it was obvious there wasn't going to be any money left for my tuition and books. I didn't mind, though. I wasn't interested in school anymore. I guess my life had lost a lot of its focus and direction by that point."

"That's understandable," he offered reassuringly. "I can't imagine going through an ordeal like that at any age, especially just out of high school."

Kasey looked at him, trying to determine if he was being sincere, or just trying to be kind.

He seemed to sense her uncertainty. "I mean it, Kasey. That's quite a load for anybody to carry. I admire you for not blowing your brains out."

A smile chiseled some of the hard edge off her expression. "It's not that I didn't consider it," she assured him. "More than once."

Jordan wasn't about to comment. He knew anything he said would be wrong. "So what then?"

"I didn't want to go home to an empty house that was being gobbled up by the lawyers, so I stayed in Knoxville and worked at a bar near the UT campus for a while, you know, waiting on the other kids who had enough money not to have to work. It didn't take long for the friends I had made my freshman year to realize that I wasn't going to be returning to college. They all went their own ways, leaving me to wash their dishes and bus their tables. I handled it for a few months, but then I had to get the hell out of there." Kasey stood and stretched fully. "You mind if we walk?"

Jordan responded by standing quickly. They strolled slowly toward the museum.

"You sure you want to hear this crap?" she asked.

"Sure, and it's not crap. Please don't stop now," he insisted.

She smiled at him. "After I left Knoxville, I headed for Music City, looking for fame and fortune as a country singer." She stopped in the small, paved path and faced Jordan squarely. "I've got a pretty good voice, you know. It wasn't like I didn't have a prayer of making it big."

"I'm sure you do," he said.

Kasey again considered his words but refrained from commenting. She chose instead to continue. "Anyway, I went to this club on Printer's Alley one night and won the amateur contest. I sang, 'Don't It Make Your Brown Eyes Blue,' the song Crystal Gayle made popular. Two hundred bucks! I can still remember how good that extra money felt."

Jordan watched as the pleasant memory temporarily swept the sadness from her face. He was glad to see that recalling the loss of her parents had not ruined their afternoon; he had no way of knowing their deaths were only the first in a long string of misfortunes. "Did you sing any more after that?" he asked.

They reached the steps of the Parthenon.

"A guy in the audience came up to me afterward and told me he had a band that was looking for a female singer. He went to all the clubs on amateur night searching for a fresh, undiscovered voice. He told me that I had the best voice he'd heard in a year and asked me to join his band." Kasey and Jordan reached the front door of the museum. "Do you want to go in?" she asked.

"Not really. You?"

Kasey shook her head. She'd already been a number of times. They walked to the edge of the stone steps and sat on the top two, Kasey one step above Jordan.

"What happened?"

"Well, I didn't get rich and famous as you've probably already guessed."

His look said, "Then what?"

"We played every Moose Lodge and Elks Club within two hundred miles of here; half the fraternity parties and even a Klan rally, if you can believe that, but we never got asked to perform in the big time. We were pretty good, worked steady, even made a little money, but it always seemed to have to go for tires for the van or a new guitar or amp for one of the guys. After three years of it, living out of one suitcase and eating Taco Bell or McDonald's seven days a week, I'd had enough of fame and fortune. I might have stuck it out if the guys hadn't started taking turns seeing who could get me into bed first. In the beginning, it was comical. It didn't take long for it to turn into something else."

"What happened?"

"One guy at a time has always been pretty easy for me to handle," Kasey said with despair returning to her voice as she recalled the feelings that went with the memories. She could still feel the glowing cigarette being ground into the quivering flesh of her left breast as one band member held her while another exacted his revenge for her kneeing him between the legs. She looked defiantly at Jordan. "Why do you bastards always gang up when you can't get what you want by yourself?"

She didn't need to paint a picture for him, his mind quickly finished the scene. "Jesus, Kasey, I'm sorry," he said as gently as he could. "Guys can be real jerks sometimes—"

"Most of the time," she snapped, flashing a fiery eye at him. She took a long breath and turned her head to the sky for a moment. "Sorry," she said as she looked kindly at him again. "I didn't mean to lump you in with those bastards."

"It's okay," he said. "We can all be bastards at times."

❖

Kasey thanked Jordan for the ride to her apartment and closed the car door behind her. She had an uneasy feeling that she needed to be somewhere, or that she'd forgotten to do something.

As she crossed the small patch of grass near the pool and began her ascent of the seemingly endless steps that led to her unit, a man's voice from above asked: "Are you Kasey Riteman?"

Kasey stopped and looked quickly around her for the face belonging to the unfamiliar voice. A man she had never seen before stood at the top of the landing, ten steps away, staring down at her. Kasey looked to her right, through the spindles of the metal railing that bordered the landing, and saw two other men standing near her door. At their feet lay three large equipment cases covered with airline baggage stickers and ragged pieces of gray-and-black gaffer tape. "Yes," she said with uncertainty, ready to bolt down the stairs if necessary.

"My name is Terry Leigh. Dan Herbert with CNN sent us to do a story on you. I was afraid you'd forgotten us."

Kasey looked at her watch. She was nearly twenty minutes late for the three o'clock appointment. She thought of the fifty thousand dollars that had almost gone up in smoke and nearly cursed out loud. "Oh, God, I'm late, aren't I?" she said at once. "I've been helping the police with the case. There was no chance to get away, really. I'm so sorry you had to wait."

She unlocked the door and the three men filed in behind her.

❖

Across the yard, in the unit directly opposite hers, a video camera captured every movement. Unlike the one she would be performing for in a few minutes, the tape in this camera would be seen by an audience of only two.

TWENTY-ONE

Sam sniffed the odd-looking piece of paper in Kasey's hand and found it inedible and unworthy of his continued interest. Why his mistress had played with it all night, falling asleep with it still clutched in her grasp, was beyond his feline comprehension. He was just glad the three strangers had left, and that they had taken their boxes of lights and cameras with them. It wasn't until after nine that his home had been back to normal, but then his mistress had been preoccupied with the stupid piece of paper, and had found it more fascinating than petting him.

He gave it another sniff, just in case he was mistaken, and then left to find something more entertaining. Perhaps the warm, dancing lights had returned to the livingroom floor.

Kasey stretched beneath the covers, knocking one of the pillows to the floor. She was dreaming of beautiful dresses, yellow sports cars, and vacations at the beach. Though she was technically awake, the part of her brain that used to drift away in the middle of high-school English class refused to acknowledge the morning, or the hunger that had begun to twitch in her stomach.

She giggled within her cocoon of covers when she realized that the check was still in her grip, and that it was real. She decided, after ten years with her faithful old blue Honda, it was time to think about a new car. A sports car. A yellow one. Perhaps even a convertible with a CD player. "Later," she moaned softly, folding her arms around the pillow which still covered her head. "I'll go later."

❖

The phone at the Mapco Express was still in use when Kasey came out of the convenience store with her large cherry freeze. She mumbled something creative under her breath and dropped to the curb, her back against the gleaming white stand which housed a fresh stack of *USA Today* newspapers. After another ten minutes, the woman on the phone put her appointment book back in her purse and climbed back into a white Taurus with a Hertz sticker on its bumper.

Kasey sucked in the last bit of melting red slush and stood. "Story of my life," she muttered. "I've got more money than I've ever seen, and I have to use a damned pay phone." She shook her head in amused amazement as she dialed the number scribbled on the back of the plain business card.

"Taylor."

"Good morning," Kasey said, intentionally sounding indifferent.

He recognized the voice at once and pushed aside the paperwork that had previously held his attention. "I hear traffic in the background. Is your phone still out?"

Kasey thought about the box of phone fragments she had dumped in the trash after CNN left. "Yeah," she grinned, "I think it may be time to get a new one."

"So, we still on for lunch?" Taylor leaned back in his tall chair and put his feet on the desk.

"I didn't say I would have lunch with you. I only said that I'd think about it."

"So, have you thought about it?" he asked playfully.

"I have. You're still married, remember? I don't go out with married men."

"I didn't realize we were going out, I just thought we were having a casual lunch."

Kasey hesitated, frustrated by her strong attraction to the cop and unable to rationalize the chain of events she knew had already been set in motion. Part of her wanted to hang up and get on with her life. Her little protective voice kept warning her that an affair with this man would bear a heavy price in the end.

Before she could make a rational choice, the portion of her brain that was in charge of want and desire shoved aside the part responsible for right and reason. "Why do you want to have lunch with me? I've already told you everything there is to know about me."

"I find that hard to believe. You can't convince me you told me your whole life's story in the time we spent at the park yesterday. I'll bet you haven't scratched the surface." Jordan waved away the detective who had started to enter his office.

Kasey was intrigued by his tenacity. She liked being pursued. "All the interesting stuff."

Jordan sighed loudly in the receiver. "All right, if there's nothing interesting left to tell of your life, then I'll tell you my story. That can consume at least one entire lunch, perhaps two. How about it, Kasey? Market Street Brewery on second, noon, my treat."

"Isn't that near the Wild Horse?" she asked, having never eaten there but having seen the sign.

"Right beside it."

Kasey weakened and produced a coltish smile. "Make it twelve-thirty," she said. "I'm not even close to being ready."

"Twelve-thirty it is."

She darted back across the street to her apartment, oblivious to the man in the tweed jacket who crossed the street a few seconds behind her.

❖

Kasey pushed the door shut behind her and yanked off her T-shirt, pitching it skillfully toward the open hamper as she passed the bathroom on her way to the bedroom. "Two points," she mocked as it dropped squarely into the wicker basket. She slipped each sneaker off with the opposite foot and slid her sweat pants down, kicking them away as soon as they dropped to her ankles. She grabbed a towel from a pile of clean laundry sitting on the dresser and headed for the shower. She wanted to look her best at lunch.

❖

The man in the tweed jacket stepped out from the shadows of the ground-floor landing overhang and carefully watched as Kasey dashed up the three flights of stairs. With great interest, he made note of the door Kasey entered: end apartment, third floor. He lit a fresh Salem and stepped back into his hiding place in the recess of the stairwell. He checked his watch—she would be leaving soon.

❖

Across the pool deck and narrow strips of yard, Fieldman trained his powerful binoculars on the odd figure who had followed Kasey to her apartment building. He watched intently as the man skillfully avoided being seen by her, and wondered about his motives. The man had a face Fieldman didn't recognize, but a face he quickly decided he would get to know better.

He slid his chair beneath him and sat, locking the binoculars on the dark recess into which the strange man had once again slipped.

Waiting wasn't his favorite part of the job, but it was something he did extremely well.

❖

At twelve-fifteen, Kasey skipped down the steps, zipped around the corner of the ground-floor stairwell, and headed for her car.

Her mind was on lunch, not on shapes hidden in the shadows.

The man in the worn tweed jacket watched as her CRX left the parking lot and disappeared from view. When he was certain she was gone, he climbed the steps to her floor. As he reached the top, he stood quietly for a moment. He noticed that all the units in view had individual front door lamps, though he noted that both Kasey's unit and the unit to the left of it contained no bulb. This made him smile.

He looked toward the stairs and spied a single light with a solar sensor designed to illuminate the stairwell and nearby landing at dusk. He checked to the far end of the third floor, and then studied the building across from him; he decided that he was alone for the moment.

He stepped to the lamp and lifted the small brass latch that secured the front glass. With the lamp door swung open, he loosened the bulb enough to prevent it from working, but not enough to remove it completely. He closed the small door and moved quickly to the end of the landing, to the window in Kasey's livingroom which was located on the narrow end of the building, at a right angle to the front door. Of the four apartments on each floor, only the end units had the luxury of an additional window in both the livingroom and kitchen. That hers had a side window made him smile. In his crouched position beneath the side window, he was hidden from view of anyone on the main landing, and free to pursue his work without detection.

As he knelt before the open window, a wide gap formed between the curtains and the mischievous fat Burmese filled the void it had just created. The cat balanced precariously on the narrow window ledge, his body pressed against the screen, and stared with intense interest at the man crouched before him.

"Hello, Sam," the man whispered. "Remember me?"

❖

By twelve-forty on the clear, warm May afternoon, every seat in the Market Street Brewery was filled with men and women from the surrounding office buildings trying to grab a quick lunch, as well as curious vacationers who had come to peruse nearby old Fort Nashborough on the Cumberland River. With the wait for a vacant table having grown to twenty-five minutes, Jordan leaned impatiently against the brick wall near the entrance, simultaneously waiting for his name to be called, and for his lunch guest to arrive. He studied the entrance that faced Broadway and then studied his watch. Though it didn't surprise him that she was late, it nonetheless irritated him. He smiled politely as a couple squeezed past him.

"Your table is ready, Chief Taylor," the soft voice announced. He turned to thank the hostess and saw Kasey standing in the doorway, grinning broadly.

"Hey, where'd you come from?" he asked, surprised by her sudden appearance.

"I knew there'd be no place to park in front, so I found a spot around the side. I came in through the back." Kasey stood pressed against the open door as a large group of patrons left, making their exit clumsily between Jordan and her.

"I guess our table isn't ready then," Jordan managed to say between the bodies. "It's only been ten minutes."

"Are you kidding?" Kasey leaned close to Jordan when the group had passed, and whispered proudly, "We're at the top of the list. Come on." She indicated with a wiggle of her index finger for him to follow.

The hostess grabbed two menus and led Kasey and Jordan to a booth in the corner, to the left of the bar. "Thanks for seating us so quickly," Kasey smiled.

"There's a table for you anytime, Ms. Riteman. My name is Ashley. Let me know if you need anything." She smiled warmly at the pair and then disappeared once again into the crowd at the front.

"This place is always packed," Kasey said, turning her menu right side up.

"Sorry," Jordan apologized. "I usually eat here around two or three— whenever I can steal a lunch break—and it's never like this." He unwrapped his silverware and spread his napkin across his knees.

"It's like this between noon and one-thirty where I work, too. I'm glad I don't have to do lunches anymore." Kasey realized she didn't have to do dinners anymore, either. For a brief, solitary moment, though still technically employed by Leonard's, she missed the restaurant and her friends. The thought of Cal quickly ended the melancholy.

Puzzled by the young woman's comment, Jordan felt compelled to question it. "Do you know the hostess?"

"Nope, never met her before." Kasey played with her silverware, arranging it to suit her.

"Then how did she know your name and why did we get a table so quickly?" It was not in his nature to leave any question unanswered.

Kasey leaned against the padded booth. "She saw me on TV Tuesday night." The words made her blush, though the unexpected notoriety had brought a sweet rush with it.

Jordan put his elbows on the table. "I guess I'm having lunch with a star then." He pulled his pen from his suit coat. "Can I have your autograph, Ms. Riteman?"

"Not right now. I only do autographs between ten and ten-fifteen," she joked, pushing his hands away playfully.

"By the way, you look great," he said, having admired the way her jeans fit. Kasey was wearing a pair of tight teal Rocky Mountain denims, with two diamond-shaped panels of tan suede originating at the beltline in back and running six inches down where pockets would normally have been. The western design, combined with the medium heel of her boots, accented her shape. It had not been overlooked by him.

"Thanks," she smiled. The jeans had worked.

The next half hour was spent consuming a shared entree and listening to Kasey tell of her first Mardi Gras experience. Jordan, normally quiet and reserved, was surprised to find himself laughing out loud as she recalled the trouble she had gotten into. He felt like a different person around her; she was so fresh and vibrant—so unlike his wife.

He wadded his napkin and laid it on the end of the table. "I can't eat another bite."

"I guess not. You ate the whole thing yourself." She moved the vermicelli and peppers around with her fork looking for any remaining trace of the grilled chicken or mushrooms. "That'll cost you a dessert," she said, giving up on the entree.

"I'll split something with you."

"Not on your life, Taylor. I've seen how you split things. I'll eat what I want, and you can have what's left."

"Deal," he grinned.

As the waiter cleared the table, Jordan settled comfortably against the booth. Kasey was watching the other patrons come and go but sensed his eyes on her. She brought her attention back to the table. "So, tell me about Jordan Taylor," she said, nestling herself into the corner where the booth back met the wall. "You said it was worth a lunch or two."

"What do you want to know?"

"Don't give me that routine, Jordan," she kidded. "Now you sound like me."

They laughed. "To begin with, I was born in Seattle, Washington, on July twenty-first. My father—"

"What year?"

Jordan tilted his chin down and stared at her. "Nineteen forty-seven," he said, watching her response. "And don't tell me I'm almost as old as your father." He remembered that her father was dead as soon as the words passed his lips. "Sorry," he mouthed.

Kasey touched his hand, but did not speak.

The dessert arrived and Kasey quickly downed three quarters of it. "There, we're even," she smiled, pushing the remaining bite and a half toward him. She was surprised to learn that he would soon be fifty, though not disappointed. She often found older men more attractive than the men her own age, and nothing about Jordan had led her to believe he had even reached forty. "Continue," she said when he had put a spoonful of dessert in his mouth.

"What?" he asked, swallowing quickly.

"You had just finished telling me that you weren't quite as old as my father."

Jordan grinned at her pluck. "My father started with Boeing during the war and my mother worked for the City of Seattle. They're both retired now and still live in the house I grew up in on Mercer Island.

"When I graduated from high school, I got a partial scholarship here to Vanderbilt. Luckily, my folks could afford to pay the difference, so I headed off to college in Nashville. Never looked back." He ate the last bite of brownie. "Did you know that it rains two hundred days a year in Seattle? I didn't, until I left there. I always thought we had normal weather when I was a kid."

"What made you want to become a cop?"

"The standard reasons you hear about in the movies: honor, duty, adventure—all that *Dragnet* stuff. It's not like that, though. No one's gotten it right in Hollywood yet. I guess there's just no way to do it without either shocking the public or boring them to death."

The check came and Jordan placed a Mastercard on top of it. By one-thirty, the lunch crowd had thinned. With two or three vacant tables in view, Jordan was in no hurry to give up their seats.

Kasey sipped on the coffee she had ordered with dessert. "You have any kids?"

Jordan knew this part of the conversation was inevitable and tried to display no difference in expression. "A daughter. Amber."

"How old is she?"

"Ten—going on eighteen. She's in the fifth grade and the goalie of her soccer team," he said with a father's pride.

"I'll bet you and her mother . . ." Kasey waited for the name.

"Gloria."

"I'll bet you and Gloria are proud of little Amber," she said as evenly as she could.

"I guess at this point you'd like to know something about my wife, huh?" Jordan rested his arms on the table.

"I didn't say that. If you want to tell me about her, go ahead." Kasey hadn't moved.

"She and I are different, that's all, and not just in years. You've heard that one, I guess." Kasey didn't blink. "I loved her once, but I can't even remember who I was back then. A lot has happened in the last twelve years."

"You've been married for only twelve years?"

Jordan was more uncomfortable than he had imagined. Despite his unhappy marriage, and his separation three months ago, he'd never had an affair. This was uncharted territory. "Yes, since 1984. I was a bachelor for fifteen years after college, getting my career going, saving money, dating a couple of people, you know. Almost got married once or twice along the way, but I stayed buried in my work. I was determined to be the youngest chief of police in the department's history.

"One night, at a fancy party for newly appointed captains given by Senator Stafford, I met his youngest daughter. Gloria was rich, well placed, beautiful. All the things I needed to take me to the top. The senator had plans for his baby girl to marry a surgeon or a fat corporate lawyer—not a cop twenty years older than her. He didn't know his daughter as well as he thought. She had plans of her own—anything that was contrary to his wishes and would annoy the family. To her, I must have seemed the perfect guy to do the job. It worked all right, but not exactly the way she planned. The day we got married, he canceled her trust fund and cut her out of his will. The old bastard died two years later without having spoken another word to her."

"Did he ever see his granddaughter?" Kasey asked, saddened by the thought of a father who would willingly turn his back on his child.

"Once. We saw him standing in the back of the church when she was baptized. He left before Gloria could speak to him. In his will he provided a large trust for Amber when she turns twenty-one, but Gloria got zip.

"I didn't care. I didn't want a penny of the old goat's dough, but Gloria has never gotten over it." Jordan finished his coffee, despite it having grown as cold as tap water. "You can't exactly live in Belle Meade on a cop's salary. The adjustment was a real shock for her."

It was not at all the tale Kasey had expected; she felt sorry for Jordan. She put her hands on top of his and whispered, "I can tell it hasn't worked out the way you wanted, either." She needed one more answer: "How long have you two been separated?"

"It's been about three months now."

"What brought it on?"

"Everything. Nothing. What can I say? It's okay, though. In a way, living without her is easier than living with her."

Kasey squeezed his hands.

The couple left the restaurant and walked toward her car. She dropped into the seat and cranked down her side glass, pulling the door shut as she did. "Thanks for lunch, Jordan. I had a nice time."

"Maybe we'll do it again, then."

"I'd like that," she said.

He watched until the car became lost in the 2nd Street traffic.

❖

Kasey arrived at her apartment shortly before seven-thirty, having spent the balance of the afternoon telling Brandie about the CNN interview, as well as discussing the list of other interview offers Stewart Parker had compiled over the last two days.

After she left Channel 9, she spent an hour at her bank, opening a savings account and filling out the paperwork necessary to acquire a Gold Mastercard.

It's amazing, she thought, *how quickly they ignore your past credit problems when you slide a hundred grand across their desks.*

A trip to Nashville's largest Ford dealer and dinner with Brenda had completed the long and tiring day.

With a brochure on the new Mustangs rolled tightly in her hand, she opened the door and laid her purse and sales literature in the chair by the window. "Sam" she called out. Nothing. She shrugged her shoulders and decided to get out of the tight jeans and into something more comfortable.

Kasey stopped at the edge of the bathroom and peered into the darkened room. The hamper lid was standing open. *So that's where you're hiding,* she thought to herself.

She finished unbuttoning her blouse and wadded it into a tight ball. In a perfect free-throw shot, the blouse entered the basket.

Still no response.

Kasey cocked her head and moved toward the bedroom. "Sam" she called out louder, surprised that he had not greeted her yet. "Independent little shit," she grumbled, certain he was at his food bowl in the kitchen.

She unzipped the jeans and sat on the end of the bed.

As she worked to remove one of her boots, she heard a sound in her closet, like something had just moved behind its closed door. "So I left you locked in there," she whispered. She chuckled at the thought of having accidentally shut him up all day. "Serves you right," she grinned, considering his penchant for always searching out undiscovered spots in which to hide or sleep.

Kasey moved slowly to the closet door and gently gripped the knob. With a rapid jerking motion, she yanked the door open and shouted toward the floor: *"Boo!"* Sam bolted between her legs, across the bedroom carpet and disappeared down the hall.

Kasey immediately followed him as far as the bedroom door and leaned out into the hallway, supporting herself with a hand on each side of the doorjamb. "Oh, sweetheart, I didn't mean to scare you so bad, you big sissy," she giggled, careful not to let him hear.

She knew he'd pout for a while and then get over it. She wanted a hot bath more than she wanted to make up with him at the moment.

She turned back into the room.

The man's right hand was over her mouth at once, his left behind her head completing the vise. He forced her backward, onto the bed, and straddled her body with his own. Kasey's heart almost burst through her chest, her breathing locked, made impossible by the hand which fully blocked her nostrils as it gagged her mouth. Her eyes searched frantically for anything recognizable. Joeyboy's blank face flashed before her and her fear soared.

The man moved his left hand to her throat, squeezing painfully. He leaned toward her face, his stinking whisky breath choking her. "If you promise not to scream, I'll let go."

He sat up but did not move to relieve her pain as he awaited an answer.

Kasey remembered the voice even before she recognized the face that had come into focus. Though the man in the tweed jacket was now twenty pounds lighter and wore a scruffy beard, the eyes were unmistakable.

She nodded.

The man moved his hand away slowly, watching her closely as he did.

"That's better," he whispered.

"Jesus Christ, Fred, you lousy son-of-a-bitch!" she shouted at the top of her lungs. "What the fuck are you doing in my apartment? How did you—"

"Quiet, goddammit!" he barked, covering her mouth again. "I don't want to hurt you." His gaze fell to her upper body, clad in only a black lace bra. Her left breast had nearly come out of its cup, exposing the nipple. Her anxious breathing raised and lowered her chest in rapid movements, sending small waves across the soft mounds of flesh. "God, I had forgotten how good you look in black lace, Kasey. You through with your tantrum?"

She nodded, her eyes as hard as he'd ever seen them.

He moved the hand from her mouth and leaned back from her, though he kept his full weight on her hips.

"What are you doing in my home?" she repeated, her voice lower but retaining all of its initial hate.

"That's actually quite a long story and one I'm sure we'll cover in great detail a bit later. Right now, I could use a drink. You got a bottle hidden somewhere? I didn't see one when I looked earlier." He produced that old smug grin she had originally been attracted to, but had eventually come to despise.

"I've got some cheap white wine in the fridge . . ."—his expression grew sour and he pretended to gag—". . . and a little tequila in the kitchen cabinet," she added, supporting her upper body with her elbows. She yanked at her left bra cup and filled it with her breast again. "Get off me, you bastard. I've got half a mind to call the cops and have you arrested for breaking and entering. I might even throw in attempted rape for good measure." She tilted her jaw at him defiantly and locked her teeth behind tight, angry lips.

"You gonna make that call from a neighbor's," he grinned, "or from the Mapco Express again."

Kasey remembered that she still had no phone. Her eyes went cold. "I won't tell you again to get your ass off me, Fred." She took both hands and pushed against his chest.

The man stood and stepped away from the bed. Kasey sat up and swept her tangled hair behind her head and out of her face. She stood and looked at the closet. "Excuse me!" she snapped impatiently.

The man stepped away from the closet and Kasey yanked a pullover from a hanger on the rack. She zipped her jeans but left the shirttail hanging out.

"How 'bout that tequila," he said.

Kasey slammed her closet door and walked past her ex-husband, giving him a kiss-my-ass look as she did.

❖

Doug Fieldman lit a Pall Mall and closed the lid on his lighter. Other than the brief yellow glow of its flame, and the small monitor which cast a pale emerald wash across the handmade panel holding remote controls for the bank of audio and video recorders, his rented apartment was dark. The curtains through which his camera was aimed were parted no more than a foot to accommodate the powerful zoom lens. He stood nearly motionless behind the camera, bored and hungry.

He turned his attention to the small Sony monitor that served as the eyes of the low-light camera, its image intensifier tube producing not a full-color display, or even a picture in shades of black and white, but painting the darkened scene in eerie hues of unearthly green. His ears were covered by the stereo headphones that heard every word spoken within Kasey's walls.

Fieldman now had a name—Fred something—to accompany his video of the man he had taped entering the same window in Kasey's apartment he'd used three hours earlier.

"You're getting to be quite a popular little lady," he reflected. He reached for his cellular phone: he needed to know who this Fred character was.

❖

The unmarked police car rolled to a quiet stop at the end of the parking lot, a hundred feet or more from Kasey's Honda. Its lights had been off since it entered the apartment complex. The cop behind the wheel flipped the switch in the overhead light, preventing it from illuminating when he opened his door.

As he crept quietly along the back of Kasey's building, he noted everything around him. He had been there three times already, and nothing appeared to have changed, beyond the tenant in the middle ground floor unit having planted some Silver Dust and Azaleas by her back door. He made note of this meaningless item, continued silently to the end of the building, turned right and stopped beside the first-floor livingroom window—the one on the side of the building. Kasey's matching window was two floors above him.

The man pressed himself tightly against the wall, against the two feet of brick that lay between the window's edge and the corner that defined the front of the building. His view of the twelve units across the pool was now unobstructed, and he was careful not to reveal more of his own body than was absolutely necessary to get the job done.

He knelt in the short grass and opened a black Gore-Tex bag, withdrawing a strangely shaped device that looked like futuristic binoculars. He slipped the retaining harness over his head, positioned the soft rubber eye cups so that all external light would be blocked, and flipped the switch on the top of the unit. The device immediately emitted a soft whirring sound and the lenses snapped into sharp focus, the image they produced little more than a collage of meaningless shapes. The magnification was too great.

The detective quickly zoomed out, giving both lenses a wider field of view. Suddenly, a bush across the pool deck was recognizable, though to the unaided eye, it had been as black as the surrounding area for more than an hour. He raised his head, training the night vision goggles on the bedroom window at the end of the unit, three floors up. With his body steadied against the building, he framed an area two by three feet, encompassing the windowsill and the slit between the drapes. The image was still not as clear as he wanted. He pressed the multiplier on the side of the unit, raising the light response another 200 lux. The picture became instantly brighter, as though a desk light had been turned on in the bedroom.

The image he had been after lay before him.

"Fieldman, you worthless motherfucker. I should have known he'd hire you."

He switched off the unit and disappeared the way he had come.

❖

Kasey resentfully poured Fred a second tequila and took a short shot for herself, though she had refrained from drinking one on the first round. Her ex-husband had not spoken since he had dropped onto the living-room couch a few minutes earlier; he just sat quietly, thumbing through the brochure on the new Ford Mustangs, and grinning like he alone was privy to some elaborate joke.

Her patience had worn thin.

She took the chair opposite the couch and folded her legs beneath her. Sam filled her lap, though he kept the man on the couch locked in his feline stare.

"Dammit, Fred, I may not be able to call the police from here, but unless you tell me why the hell you broke into my apartment—and right now—I *will* call them from some other damned phone!"

Fred Daniels looked up from the brochure but continued his smirking. Finally, he tossed the literature onto the carpet and stretched his arms out along the back of the couch. "Pretty smart, Kasey, this psychic bullshit. I, for one, freely admit that I'd never have thought you capable of such a clever scheme." He leaned toward her. "How much you collected so far—thirty, forty grand? Hell, Kasey, that's a shitload of money for one person to keep all to herself." He shook an outstretched index finger at her several times, as if admonishing a bad child.

"What the hell are you driving at, Fred? You never could just come out and say a goddamn thing. Why do you always have to play games?"

"I'm just saying that I could do wonders with just half of that money. In no time, I'd be living on easy street." He waved his empty glass at her.

"If you want another drink, get it yourself." Kasey pulled Sam to her and kissed him on the side of the head.

Fred's agreeable expression turned ominously quiet. He rose and disappeared into the kitchen, returning with the nearly empty bottle. "You're a hell of a host, no more booze than this in the house." He sniggered as he dropped back onto the couch.

"Listen, Fred, I don't know what you've got in mind, but you're crazy if you think I'm going to give you another dime. I supported your drinking and gambling for thirty-nine and a half months, and that's enough hell for two lifetimes. Now leave!" Sam decided he wanted to be in the hamper. He'd seen them fight.

Fred lifted the bottle to his lips and poured down the last of the Cuervo

Gold. He wiped his mouth with the back of his hand. "I wonder how much that Brandie Mueller dame would pay me for exposing you as a fake? I bet I could get as much as you got for lying to her and the police."

Kasey had thought she'd seen Fred at his worst, living with him during the lean, financially embarrassing years, but she had never thought him capable of extortion. She was annoyed with herself for having underestimated his greed, and enraged at finding him in her home. She wasn't about to share her money with her worthless ex-husband. If she'd been able to fool the police, and the media—and God knows they were a hell of a lot smarter than Fred—she should be able to do it again. She took in a deep breath and settled back in her chair. "Let me ask you one thing, mister know-it-all. What makes you so certain I'm a fraud?"

"Oh, give it a rest, Kasey. This is ole Freddie you're talking to, remember? Don't you think I'd have known it if I'd been married to a damned psychic?"

"Not necessarily. Just because I didn't have any visions in the three years we were together, you're convinced I'm a fake." She grinned broadly. "How do you account for my locating Donna Stanton then?"

Fred started to speak, but his initial response seemed pointless. "I don't know. Maybe someone told you where she was buried."

"And miss out on the reward themselves?"

"Okay, maybe you were there."

"There?" Kasey laughed incredulously. "Don't you think the police would have thought of that—or Brandie Mueller? Do you think Clarion paid me money because they're stupid? You're such a complete loser, Fred. But then, you always were."

"So you have been paid!" His eyes grew larger.

Kasey sat pokerfaced for what seemed a full minute, and then produced a catbird grin.

"You're such a bitch, Kasey," he snapped, "but then, you always were."

"I think it's time for you to leave." She stood and moved to the door, taking the knob in hand. "Or I'm going to the cops. They hate extortionists even more than frauds."

"Hang on, goddammit. We're not through talking about this. If you were a psychic while we were married, why the hell didn't you ever tell me? Do you realize how much we could have made at the track, for Christ's sake?" he growled, standing and moving unsteadily toward her. "I could have known every winner even before the fucking races began."

"You're such a dumb shit, you know it, Fred? Do you think that's how it works? Do you think that I have visions about stupid race horses or football pools? I'm afraid that's your fantasy world, not mine. Now get out!" Kasey pulled the door fully open and leaned against it.

"We're not through with this, Kasey."

"Oh, yes we are." She jabbed her index finger into his sternum, causing him to grimace. "And if you ever again enter my home uninvited, I'll call the cops so fast, it'll make your head spin like a top."

Fred Daniels started to respond to her threat but Kasey shoved him out onto the balcony and slammed the door behind him before his brain could form a suitable retort. He made his way noisily down the stairs, mumbling profanity with each shaky step.

When she was certain he was gone, Kasey went to the small livingroom window, yanking the curtains apart. "Goddammit!" she swore, finding the screen ajar and the lower aluminum window track bent slightly. She slammed the window shut.

Within ten minutes, she had fashioned a jamming bar from a section of her only broom and had wedged it firmly in the window channel.

She decided it was time to move.

❖

As Fred sulked angrily across the common area between the buildings, contemplating a new plan of attack, Fieldman stopped the tape in the video recorder. He searched for his cigarettes and decided to call it a day. With her apartment now empty except for her cat and herself, and no phone, he expected to record nothing further of value from Kasey's unit before morning. He stretched out on his sleeping bag and twisted the top off a lukewarm Miller bottle.

Giacano's man also watched as Fred Daniels left Kasey's apartment. He withdrew the cellular phone from his jacket pocket and pressed a sequence of ten numbers from memory. It was answered on the second ring.

"Yes." It was all the response needed on this number.

"A man came to visit our little dreamer. I believe she knows him."

"Is he someone important?"

"Not likely, judging from the car he drives."

As Fred pulled out of the parking lot, the cop followed closely behind. He would not be noticed.

Filippo covered the mouthpiece and repeated the cop's words. Giacano took the phone. "Who is the son-of-a-bitch?" the old man asked. "What did he want?"

"I don't know, but I can find out if you want."

"Then find out! If he knows anything about my tapes, get it out of him, do you hear me!?"

"Yes, sir. What if he's a nobody and doesn't know a thing?"

"Either way, there are too damned many people at this party. If some of them aren't turned away quickly, I'll be the one who gets stuck with the fucking check."

"I understand. You can count on me."

"I am counting on you," Giacano said threateningly.

Silence. Dial tone.

The cop pressed End and stuck the phone back in his jacket.

In less than fifteen minutes, his man had come to a stop behind Sir Robert's; he needed a drink.

As Fred Daniels sat in the front seat of his aging Plymouth sedan, digging through a squashed pack of Salems for one of the few remaining cigarettes, the butt of a Smith & Wesson automatic crashed into the side of his skull.

❖

The knock on the door was soft and short, just loud enough for Doug Fieldman to hear it in his state of half-sleep. As he lay on the cotton sleeping bag, he scratched his bare stomach for a second, and then his crotch, trying to decide if the sound had been real or imaginary. When he heard it a second time, he sat straight up, grabbing his Browning .380 as he did. It was seldom far from his reach. He flipped the hall switch, its yellow light spilled into the livingroom. With weapon in hand, he opened the front door.

"Hello, Fieldman," the cop said with a warm smile. "Long time, no see."

"No shit, man. I ain't seen you since I left the department in ninety-two. Say, how did you know I was here anyway?"

"I'll tell you all that later. Right now, there's a little matter we need to discuss. It has to do with your boss, Monroe."

"I guess we need to talk inside then."

"That'd be best, I think."

Fieldman lowered the small automatic and gave the door a gentle shove, turning away from the opening. The cop closed the door behind him, the thin, almost invisible surgical glove on his left hand leaving no trace of prints.

Fieldman laid his weapon on the card table which served as the only piece of furniture in the room, and grabbed the pack of cigarettes that were lying there. "No kiddin', man, how'd you know—"

The six-inch stiletto entered Fieldman's back between a pair of ribs at the point where they joined the spine. He let out a pathetic, pain-filled groan and groped behind him with both hands, as if trying to find the cause of the intense burning in his back. His cigarettes fell to the carpet.

In a powerful upward thrust, followed by a practiced clockwise twist of the blade, the sharp tip lacerated his heart.

Fieldman died where he stood.

The cop stuck his heel into the back of the man's knees, dropping the body to the floor. He allowed it to fall gracelessly on its face.

Within three minutes, all of the audio and video tapes had been collected, and a machine on which to play each had been crammed into a black canvas bag the cop had found near the window. As he was about to leave the bedroom, he noticed a briefcase standing in a corner that he had previously overlooked in the dim light. He knelt before it, laid it flat against the carpet and popped its twin latches. When he lifted the top, he leaned back. "Sweet Mary," he stammered. It was more money than he had ever seen at one time. He closed it quickly and grabbed the handle with his empty hand.

In an effort to put off the body's discovery for at least a few days, the cop turned the air conditioner to its coldest setting and checked all blinds and curtains to be certain they were tightly shut.

Satisfied, he headed for the door. "Sorry, Doug," he said, lifting the briefcase slightly in mock salute. "Dying sucks, doesn't it?"

TWENTY-TWO

The Mustang GT responded effortlessly to Kasey's touch, its powerful 5.0 liter V-8 and five-speed close-syncromesh transmission acting in perfect harmony to convey her commands to the aggressive sixteen-inch radials. Kasey played with the radio as she entered the passing lane on Interstate-40 at the Charlotte Street Exit heading west, wishing she had a familiar CD to stick in its slot. The salesman's eyes remained on the traffic in front of him that was being quickly overtaken by the woman driver at his left, and pressed more than once on a brake pedal that didn't exist on the passenger side of the car.

Kasey didn't notice the gesture and jammed the accelerator to the floor. Every horse under the hood jumped as if a whip had just cracked across its back. When the needle reached the century mark, the salesman could no longer remain silent. "I'd like you to—"

"I'll buy it," Kasey interrupted, returning to the speed limit with a generous application of the ABS brakes. "Can I take it with me?"

"What? Yes . . . well . . . of course. I mean, once your loan has been approved—"

"I'll be paying cash," she cut in again. "You said twenty-six thousand, didn't you?" She winked at him as she took the exit which would lead back to the dealership.

The salesman started to speak but thought better of it again. He could still remember the sale he had lost by ignoring the old farmer in dirty coveralls, an unseen roll of hundreds stuffed in his pocket. He smiled at the attractive young woman in the pressed jeans and starched white blouse. "Will you be trading in your CRX?" he asked ingratiatingly.

Kasey thought of the faded blue Honda sitting humbly in the space back at the dealership and a lump formed in her throat. "Yes, and I want a good price for her. She's been a real friend."

The salesman considered his commission at full retail and smiled broadly. Hell, she could call the old wreck a member of the family for all he cared.

They reached the parking lot. Kasey looked at her old car and sighed.

263

"Would you like some coffee while we take care of the paperwork, Ms. Riteman?" the salesman offered before she could change her mind.

❖

Kasey leaned against the rail of the third-floor balcony, at the end opposite her apartment, and gazed down at the nearly incandescent yellow convertible. For several minutes she stood quietly, immensely proud of her purchase. It was the first car she had ever bought. *What do you think of her, Daddy?* she asked silently, her face lifted to the heavens.

Kasey knelt on the livingroom floor, the box that had held a new 900 MHz cordless answer phone (because the salesman had assured her it would have the best reception) beside her right knee. She looked at both ends of the phone cable and decided that they were identical. She plugged one end into the wall jack and then turned the base unit toward her, hoping to be able to make out the small words above a pair of matching sockets in its back. "Why do they always make the letters so small?" she grumbled, unable to identify which of the sockets to use. She squinted her eyes, and tilted the base toward the window until she could just make out the word "Line" above the socket closest to the edge of the unit. She snapped in the other end of the cord.

She squealed as the unit erupted in a flurry of ringing. She dropped it to the carpet as if it had just scalded her hands, but began to laugh when she soon realized that it was just an incoming call. She searched through the pile at her knees for the hand unit. "Hello," she blurted out on the fifth ring.

"Kasey?" Jordan asked, surprised he had finally reached her and equally surprised by her excited tone.

"Yes," she gasped, "this is she."

"It's Jordan."

"Oh, hi. I was afraid I'd missed you."

"I thought you might get your phone working today. I've called a couple of times."

"Yeah, I just got in a minute ago. I had just plugged it in when it started to ring. I thought I'd been shocked." Kasey slid across the carpet and leaned against the couch.

Jordan chuckled at the image her words created. Though nearly seven P.M., he was still at Headquarters. Since he would not be able to pick up his daughter until nine—when the last rehearsal for the end-of-the-school-year talent show let out—he had seen little reason to hurry home. Even the stressful grind of work beat the isolation he felt in his empty house. "What kind of day did you have?" he asked.

"It was great," she said excitedly. "I bought a new car! You've got to see it." Kasey proceeded to tell Jordan about her day. As she spoke, her line beeped an incoming call. "Can you hold for a second, Jordan? I've got another call."

"Sure." He pressed the speaker button, set the phone back in its base, and grabbed the report he'd been reading before he called. "Take your time. I'm just catching up on some paperwork."

"I'll hurry." Kasey switched calls. "Hello," she said.

"My God, Kasey. I thought I was going to have to send a driver to get you. Why has your phone been out so long?" It was Brandie.

"It's a long story, Brandie, but it's taken care of now. What's up?"

"Sit down, if you're not already."

"Tell me, Brandie."

"I'm not kidding. You'll want to be sitting down when you hear what I've got to say."

Kasey drew her knees up to her chest. Her eyes grew larger and she felt her pulse quicken. "What is it, Brandie? Did I do something wrong? Am I in trouble?" She had no doubt that Fred had been to see her today. *I'll kill that no good son-of-a-bitch!* she swore silently.

"I got a very interesting call today. Want to guess who from?" Her tone revealed nothing.

Kasey took a breath, closed her eyes, and blew it out slowly. "Fred."

Brandie laughed. "Who the hell's Fred? I got a call from *20/20.* They want you in New York City tomorrow afternoon to tape a feature segment. Barbara Walters is going to interview you." Now Brandie took a deep breath. "The producer said he loved the special we ran, and thought you had incredible audience appeal. It's the big time, Kasey, and its big bucks."

Kasey had barely heard a word after *20/20* was spoken. She was so relieved and grateful that the call had not been from her ex-husband, her mind went blank. "Say that again."

"Be in my office at eight in the morning and I'll give you all the details. Any problem making a one o'clock flight?" She didn't wait for Kasey to answer. "I sure hope not, because that's what they've booked for you—first-class."

"Uh . . . one o'clock . . . fine, I guess." Kasey's mouth stayed open. "What's going on, Brandie? I don't understand."

Brandie laughed robustly. "Just be in my office at eight sharp. Good night, Kasey. Pleasant dreams." She was still laughing as she hung up.

Kasey had forgotten about Jordan being on hold. As she was about to set the phone on the floor, it rang back. "Hello," she answered lamely.

"Hello?" he echoed.

"Oh, God, Jordan, I'm sorry. I forgot about you." Though he was on the line again, Kasey's mind was miles away—in New York City. "Can I call you in the morning?"

"What's wrong, Kasey? Are you all right?" he asked, surprised by her tone.

"All right? Yeah, I'm fine . . . fine. I'm sorry, Jordan. Can we just talk in the morning?"

"Sure. Call me when you get time. I'll be here, as usual." He switched off and rocked back in his desk chair.

Jordan Taylor tapped a pencil against his chin and stared at the manila folder on his desk, its corner flap hand-labeled: RITEMAN, KASEY RENÉ.

❖

Brenda filled her palm with Hawaiian Tropic Dark Tanning Lotion and dropped the squeeze bottle back into her deep canvas tote bag, adding it to the Gatorade, cups, chips, snack crackers, hair brush, makeup, watch, towels, and Anne Rice's latest novel in paperback. Despite Kasey's repeated warnings, Brenda refused to use or even acknowledge the existence of sunscreens. It wasn't her fault that Kasey was a redhead, and subject to sunburn unless she covered every inch of exposed skin in SPF-15. Brenda lived for the sun. She didn't worry about wrinkles—that's why they made Oil of Olay.

As she smoothed the clear, coconut-scented oil over her shoulders and across her breasts, she wondered where Kasey's plane was at the moment. Probably over Washington or Baltimore by now, she imagined. She was sorry Kasey wasn't there to spend the afternoon with her, they had such fun by the pool in the summertime. Brenda rubbed the last of the lotion that remained on her hands across the lower part of her back.

She didn't see the man approaching from her left.

"Need some help with your back?" he asked pleasantly, kneeling beside her chaise longue. "Hi, I'm Ray." He extended his hand. "I've been watching you from the other side of the pool. You don't live here, do you . . . I mean, in these apartments?"

The man's manner was unusually friendly; his teeth white and perfect within a generous smile; his body lean and hard. Brenda was captivated. Men with his looks didn't usually come on to her. Kasey, yes, but seldom her. "I'm Brenda." She took his hand, realizing then that hers was still covered with oil. "Oh, I'm so sorry," she apologized at once, grabbing the smaller of two towels from her bag and handing it to him. "I forgot about . . ." She didn't finish the sentence but instead made a silly face, knowing he understood what she meant.

"That's okay. I'll get it all over both hands when I do your back." He pulled the lotion from her bag, squirting a generous amount into his palm. Brenda remained frozen, lost in the haunting stare of his dark eyes. "Your back . . ." he reminded her in a whisper, rubbing his hands together to distribute the oil.

"You don't have to bother with that," she said.

"It's no bother. Roll over."

Brenda turned onto her stomach, and then reached behind her to loosen the clasp of her bikini top. She was careful to keep her upper arms close to her side, though she tried to make the modest act seem automatic, and not directed at him. She remembered his unanswered question. "You were right . . . I mean, about me not living here. My best friend lives up there"—she made a head gesture toward the building to her right—"and she lets me use the pool as her guest. There's not one where I live."

"Me, either. I bum off one of my buddies here as well. I haven't seen you out here since they opened the pool for the summer. I would have remembered." He slowly spread the cool lotion across her shoulders and down her back, careful not to touch her in any way that would cause her to feel uneasy.

Brenda blushed. She'd heard every line used, and thought herself incapable of being affected by mere words. She was pleased to find a chink remained in the armor that surrounded her heart.

When Ray had finished with her back, he carefully fastened the hook on her bikini. "All done," he said, sitting on the towel he had brought.

Brenda rolled onto her back, straightening her top to prevent the accidental display of something she'd rather keep private for the moment. "Thank you. You want some Gatorade? I've got plenty, plus another cup." She produced a thirty-two ounce plastic bottle from her tote bag, its contents still partially frozen. "I stuck the whole thing in the freezer last night. While it melts, it stays nice and cold."

"Sure. That sounds good."

She grabbed the spare tumbler and filled it three quarters full.

"Your friend's not joining you?" he asked.

"No. She left for New York a little while ago. She's gonna be on *20/20*. Her name's Kasey Riteman." Brenda was proud to know a celebrity.

"Is she that psychic I saw on Channel 9 Tuesday night?"

"That's her."

"Really? Man, that stuff's way over my head. Have you two been friends long? I mean, has she always been able to do things like that? I gotta tell you, it really impressed me, her finding that murdered woman's body when everyone else thought she'd skipped town."

Brenda saw the opportunity to share a little of her friend's limelight. She knew Kasey wouldn't mind. "Oh, yeah, I've known her for years.

She's been able to see things, you know—visions, since she was a kid. She and I talk about it all the time. As a matter of fact, I don't think she would have even gone to Brandie Mueller if it hadn't been for me telling her it was the right thing to do. We're really close. She tells me everything." She opened the box of Wheat Thins and offered some to Ray.

"No thanks. I just ate." He looked toward Kasey's apartment for a second and then back to Brenda. "By chance, Brenda, was that the famous psychic herself I saw leaving here around noon or so? I think she was driving some kind of little Honda."

"A couple of hours ago?"

"Yeah, just as I was arriving?"

"Nope. She drives a new yellow Mustang convertible. If you saw someone in a Honda, it wasn't her. Not today."

The man's face showed his disappointment.

"Is something wrong, Ray?"

"No, nothing. So you've got a genuine celebrity for a best friend, huh?"

"Kasey's one all right," Brenda said with a touch of jealousy.

"How is that?" he asked, watching her face for the truth that would lie beneath her words.

"It's okay, I suppose, but we hardly have time to talk anymore. Her phone rings all the time. They're throwing cash at her like it was Monopoly money. I've seen a change in her in the last week and I guess it's only going to get worse—or better, depending upon your point of view—after this *20/20* thing."

Ray nodded.

"I'm glad I'm her friend, though, even if her mind's elsewhere at the moment," Brenda said dolefully. "She's someone you can depend on in a pinch, but she's also the kind of person who needs a shoulder to cry on now and then."

"And that's your job, right?"

"Always has been. Probably always will be. At least I hope so."

"Sounds like you two are pretty close."

"No friends are closer," Brenda said proudly, crunching on one of the crackers to keep from getting too pensive.

Ray stood and grabbed his towel. "Well, I guess I'd better be going. I've got to help a friend move a car we've been working on for a while. It was nice meeting you, Brenda." He turned to leave. Brenda's heart sank. "Say, you want to grab a beer and a burger sometime?" he asked suddenly.

She couldn't resist playing at least a little hard to get, even if she wasn't. "I might, but I don't even know your name."

"It's Ray. You haven't forgotten already?"

"I know it's Ray, silly. You have a last name though, don't you?"

"Last time I checked my driver's license. It's Griffin. Ray Griffin. My buddies call me Joeyboy, though."

"What would you like me to call you?" Brenda asked.

"I like it when a woman calls me Ray, like my momma did."

"Ray it is," she smiled. "You want my number so you can call me, Ray?"

"I was hoping you'd ask," he smiled, making certain his perfect white teeth showed fully.

❖

From her fifteenth floor suite, Kasey had a commanding view of Central Park. The massive expanse of greenery bordered by walls of stone and iron seemed like a giant stockade trapping what remained of God's original handiwork in an elaborate prison fashioned by man. She had never before thought of trees as things that were permitted to live, or grass allowed to grow. The sight both fascinated and haunted her, as did the ocean of skyscrapers that seemed to run from horizon to horizon.

The nonstop flight from Nashville had been uneventful with the notable exception that Kasey now understood why people would elect to pay the extra cost for flying first-class.

The phone rang in her room.

"Yes," Kasey answered, falling back into the plush king-size bed.

"Good afternoon, Ms. Riteman. My name is Ann Lennon-Masters. I'm Ms. Walter's assistant. The driver phoned to say you had arrived on time, and that you had indicated your flight from Nashville was fine."

"Yes. I like first-class." Kasey realized that she must have just sounded like Ma Kettle. She vowed to act more cosmopolitan.

"I trust you've found your room to your satisfaction. The Plaza has a wonderful staff who know exactly how we wish our guests to be treated, so if there's anything you need, please let them know, will you?"

"Everything has been perfect," Kasey said as evenly as she could.

"Wonderful. A driver will call for you at six forty-five. Will that give you enough time?"

"More than enough."

"We'll have dinner after the taping. There are many great places to eat in the city." She hesitated. "You like northern Italian?"

"That'll be fine," Kasey agreed easily. She would have said yes to pizza.

"Excellent. I'm looking forward to meeting you in person, Ms. Riteman. Your story fascinates me."

Kasey cradled the phone and languished in the thick down comforter, running the assistant's last words over in her mind. She closed her eyes and prayed that Brandie had been right—that she was a natural. "You'll do fine, Kasey," she mumbled halfheartedly, echoing Brandie's parting words. It was time to get her mind on other things; the lines would come to her when she stepped under the lights. "You'll do just fine," she repeated confidently, hoping to convince her heart.

Kasey looked at the clock by the bed: just over ninety minutes before the driver arrived. She returned to the bathroom she'd only glanced at earlier and was pleased to find the large tub was also a Jacuzzi. She ran the water as hot as she could stand—knowing it would cool in the hour she intended to soak—and began to undress.

"Room service," the voice answered crisply when Kasey pressed the button on the phone that bore its name. She lay on her stomach on the comforter; its plush satin covering felt heavenly against her bare skin. "What can I get for you this afternoon, Ms. Riteman?"

Kasey was initially caught off guard, but then found a wide grin on her face. "Could you send up a plate of fresh fruit and a cup of coffee, please?" she asked, not bothering to consult the menu on the table in the sitting area. "I'm afraid I'm in a hurry and it just dawned on me that I haven't eaten a bite today."

"Right away, Ms. Riteman."

"I'll be in the bath. Can you just leave it on the table?"

"Of course, Ms. Riteman."

"Don't I need to sign something?"

"Everything's been taken care of. Will there be anything else, Ms. Riteman?"

"I think that's all for now. Thanks."

"Thank *you*, Ms. Riteman."

Kasey hung up the phone. *Thank you, Ms. Riteman. Right away, Ms. Riteman. Everything's been taken care of, Ms. Riteman.* She echoed the words happily in her head as she strolled naked across the large suite, stopping again at the window overlooking Central Park.

"I believe I could get used to this," she said as she scrunched her toes in the thick wool carpet.

Her little voice began to grumble its displeasure.

"Oh, shut up, you," she admonished as she skipped toward the waiting bath.

TWENTY-THREE

Kasey had left Manhattan with mixed emotions, a bittersweet amalgam of sadness and anticipation, of leaving the magic world of Oz for the routine of Kansas. As she breathed the crisp, clean air of Tennessee for the first time since Thursday afternoon—twenty-four hours earlier—she felt a blanket of sadness overcome her. Though she was in Nashville again, the thought didn't carry with it the rich sensory images of Hollywood home-comings, where weary travelers were met by loved ones and friends, eager to hear of their adventures, and welcome them back into the bosom of security and love. Even Brenda's incessant questioning about the trip would be preferable to walking the long concourse alone. It had been, unfortunately, necessary for her friend to be in court in her ongoing custody battle, and even Kasey's globetrotting wouldn't take precedence to an appeal to get her son back.

Kasey watched as a man she recognized from the plane kissed his wife and knelt to hug his two young children, the smallest bearing a brightly painted helium balloon with the inscription, I LOVE YOU DADDY, splashed across it. All at once, the pain of having no brother, sister, mother, or father there to greet her, became too much to bear, forcing her to pause briefly as her eyes began to water.

Stubbornly, she fought back the tears—as she had done for nearly a decade—and continued down the crowded, lonely walkway.

With each new step, her spirits began to lift. She grew anxious to see Sam and eager to tell Brandie all about her adventures in New York. She twirled the keys to her new convertible in her fingers and added it to the list of reasons for being glad she was home.

As the escalator slowly lowered her toward the crosswalk that led to long-term parking, she thought, for one fleeting second, that she had seen a familiar face in the crowd at the bottom of the steel steps. She moved her head side to side, straining for a better look, but all eyes she met belonged to strangers. She smiled briefly at the man next to her and then stared straight ahead again, ready to be on her way.

At the bottom, she twisted and turned her way through an army of motionless bodies until she was at the doors to the crosswalk. She stepped through them as they opened with a noisy hiss, and stopped at the edge of the curb, bag in hand.

"Welcome home" came a deep male voice from behind her.

Though it had been only two words, something about them felt familiar. Kasey turned crisply toward the voice. Jordan raised both eyebrows and grinned broadly, pleased with himself for not having missed her. "Hi!" she beamed. "What are you doing here?" She hugged him tightly with her free arm, the involuntary act surprising her. In the brief instant during which the embrace lasted, she decided she liked the way he felt against her.

"I don't know about you, but I always hate getting off a plane and seeing no one around that I recognize. I thought you might appreciate it if I was at the gate when you landed." He shrugged his shoulders like a little boy who was late for school: "Sorry. I didn't count on the plane being twenty minutes early."

"It's all right, really. The pilot said we made good time on the way back, headwind or tailwind—some kind of wind. It's just so great of you to come." She frowned playfully at him. "How'd you know which plane I'd be on?"

Kasey had not been able to reach Jordan before she left on Thursday, and decided it would be better for both of them if she didn't call his office from the Plaza. As much as she had wanted to talk to him—to tell him where she'd gone—she knew the decision had been the right one.

"You keep forgetting that I'm a cop," he grinned, grabbing her bag. "Brandie told me you were at ABC in New York taping an interview for *20/20*, and they told me you were booked on American Flight 1323 due to arrive here at one fifty-nine." He looked at his watch: her plane was still not due to land for another six minutes. Kasey patted him on the arm to reassure him everything was okay. "I told them both that I needed your help with the case as soon as possible."

"You do? What's up, Jordan? Have you found Donna's killer?" She looked concerned—and hopeful. He took her arm and motioned her toward the parking garage.

"Nothing's up. It was just an excuse to find out your itinerary. I hope you don't mind." He stopped in the middle of the crosswalk and looked down at her, his eyes searching for approval.

"What do you think?" she smiled, squeezing his hand.

"Is that suit new?" he asked, able to get a full view of her now that they were out of the crowd. She nodded. "It looks great on you."

"Brandie and I bought it yesterday morning before I left. Do you really like it?" Kasey turned slightly to the side to show him the back. She knew the skirt flattered her figure.

"It's lovely."

She wrinkled her nose. "By the way, you look fine in jeans. I knew living in Nashville this long, you had to have some country in you somewhere."

"Thanks."

"You're not working today?" she asked hopefully.

"Said the hell with it and took the whole day off. It seems like I've been glued to my desk lately."

"Good for you. A little R&R never hurt anyone. Like my mama always used to say, ' sometimes, you've just gotta stop and smell the gumbo.' "

Jordan chuckled.

"Where'd you park?" she asked.

"Next to you." He anticipated her question: "You've got the only yellow '96 Mustang GT convertible in the garage with a drive-out tag. You described it for me in great detail Wednesday night, remember? It was about as hard to spot as a lemon in a bucket of blueberries."

Kasey felt something that had been absent for many years. It warmed her and caused a funny tingle deep inside. She was beginning to fall for the tall, black haired cop with the warm voice and easy smile.

She closed her eyes and told the scolding little voice of her conscience to shut up and take a nap for a while.

"Is there somewhere you have to be this afternoon?" Jordan asked as they reached her car.

Kasey's heart skipped. "Not particularly. Why?" She popped her trunk with the keyless entry and he set her bag to one side.

"Feel like spending the afternoon with me?" Before she could answer, he opened his own trunk and produced a large wooden picnic basket. He set it gently in her trunk and opened one end proudly. "Cheddar cheese, summer sausage, French bread, grapes—seedless, of course—a bottle of Merlot and a bottle of Zinfandel. The Zinfandel's on ice. I didn't know whether you preferred red or white. And for dessert, brownies with bits of walnut." He stuffed the red-and-white checked tablecloth back into place and closed the basket. He stood beside the trunk with a wide smile.

"And, just where are *we* going?" she asked coyly.

"Ever been to the Hermitage?"

Kasey shook her head "no" and smiled back.

"You'll love it." He headed for the passenger door.

"Don't you want to drive?" she asked.

"Nope. It's your new car, you drive. Besides, I get a better view this way."

"Better view?" she asked.

"Of you," he grinned.

❖

Monroe dialed the number he had been given by Fieldman for the sixth time, but still there was no answer. He left another cryptic message on the ex-cop's voice mail and hung up, his impatience obvious not only in his words but also in his tone.

He slammed his phone down and paced in front of his office window, as he had done for much of the morning and afternoon. He was tired of waiting. It was time to hear from Fieldman, time to get on with this damned thing. He grabbed his electronic notebook and entered his PIN. A secret phone directory revealed itself to him.

In a few more seconds, he had the new number he was after. He punched in the digits and waited. He didn't have to wait long. "I can't reach the bastard," he began without the slightest greeting. "You guaranteed me he would be reliable. I've got to reach him, now!"

"Be calm, sir. He is reliable, just as I said. If he's not where he's supposed to be, something's wrong. I'll check it out right away and get back with you." The man withdrew a Beretta 92F from his file cabinet and crammed the 9mm automatic into his shoulder holster as he spoke.

"You do that, and do it quickly. It's only a matter of time until those fucking tapes show up somewhere, and that somewhere had better be in my hands, or I'm going to make a lot of people's lives extremely miserable as I go down the shitter."

"Yes, sir."

Monroe's end became arrogantly mute.

The other man flicked off the portable phone and dropped it unceremoniously on the desk. "You already make everybody's life miserable, you pompous ass, so what's new?" He grabbed a scrap of paper bearing Fieldman's last reported location, his coat and cigarettes, and disappeared into the street.

❖

Kasey had insisted on stopping at an Amoco station on Lebanon Pike to change into something more practical for their outing. Though the new suit had been perfect for her *20/20* interview, she didn't relish the thought of sitting in the lush spring grass wearing six hundred bucks worth of silk and wool. The change into her most comfortable denim shorts and cut-off T-shirt had only taken a few minutes, and had brought with it not only comfort and practicality, but a new round of compliments from her companion as well.

Another ten minutes northeast put Kasey and Jordan on Rachel's Lane, and the home of the nation's seventh president.

The Hermitage, Andrew Jackson's residence, sat nestled in a picturesque setting of stately cedar trees—many planted by Jackson himself—and manicured grounds that more resembled a country club than a private home.

Kasey parked near the visitor center. "This place is spectacular!" she shouted as she ran to the fence which bordered the west side of the property. "Jordan, come look! The old carriage drive is shaped like a guitar!" Her words were giddy.

Jordan stepped beside her, basket in hand. He returned the keys to her. "I guess the old boy liked music. You hungry?"

"Starved."

"Come with me." Kasey followed Jordan to the small brick building beside the visitor's center where he purchased two tickets permitting access to the mansion and grounds. Side by side, without touching, they strolled up the narrow paved pathway toward the antebellum mansion. Kasey would like to have held Jordan's hand, but decided she'd wait for him to make the first move. At a fork in the path near the kitchen and smokehouse, they took a left leading to a small picnic area by the original fresh-water spring, a hundred yards or so in back of the mansion. The canopy of leaves that covered the wooden table provided a welcome respite from the full afternoon sun; it was already well past eighty without a cloud in the sky. "How's this?" he asked. A bead of sweat coursed slowly down the center of his back.

"Perfect." Kasey helped spread the tablecloth and then sat on the bench seat, facing the rear of the home. "Jordan, do you think the President and his wife ever picnicked here?"

Jordan gave a silent shrug of his shoulders and set about opening the bottle of Merlot.

Kasey rested her head in her hands and stared in respectful awe at the stately home which had withstood one hundred and seventy-five years of chilling winter rains and sweltering summer heat. Though the structure was in pristine condition, and had been admired by countless tourists over the years for its classic architecture, it was the people who had lived and loved there that Kasey could see most clearly in her mind. Without difficulty, she could see herself standing on the upper balcony in a long velvet gown, its rich fabric billowing gracefully over layers and layers of petticoats; at her arm, the most powerful man in the country joining her in welcoming their arriving dinner guests while servants parked the elaborate carriages and watered and fed the horses. She let out a melodramatic sigh. "I wish I had a home like this, with hundreds of trees and acres and acres of flowing meadows so my horses would think they lived in Paradise."

"I didn't know you had horses." He poured her an ounce of wine, in case she didn't care for the Merlot.

"I don't. I just figured, if I could afford a place like this, I could throw in a horse or two."

"At least two," he smiled.

Kasey put her glass to her lips.

"Oh, no you don't," he scolded. "A toast first. To your newfound fame and fortune—may it be all you ever hoped it would be."

"And," she added, "to my new friends, Brandie and Jordan."

Jordan touched his glass to hers.

"This is good," she said, pleased, usually not a fan of red wine.

Jordan sat beside her on the bench and took a small handful of sweet green grapes, holding them just above her head. "It gets better," he said. "Tilt your head back, open your mouth, and close your eyes."

When Kasey sheepishly obeyed, Jordan gently laid a grape on her tongue, and followed it with a short playful kiss to the lips. Kasey's eyes shot open and she pulled away in surprise. She opened her mouth to speak, to challenge, but that part of her, the part that begged for romance and love, for passionate embraces and long, wet kisses, kept her silent. She closed her eyes and tilted her head back again. This time, his kiss was sensuous and full, and it filled her with longings that had been dormant too long, and her thighs with a sensation that spread through her body like a wildfire through dry prairie grass. Her nipples grew hard and her body yearned for him to be inside her.

"I think we better eat," she said as she caught her breath after the second kiss. Her little voice had grabbed the reins and had brought her runaway desires to a reluctant halt.

Jordan poured her a full glass of wine and one for himself. He picked at a piece of French bread for a moment before speaking. "I apologize, Kasey. I should have asked before—"

Kasey put her fingers to his lips. "It's okay," she whispered. "Just give me a little time. My life has been in overdrive for ten days without the slightest letup. Things are happening that I don't understand, and people keep shoving and pulling me in every direction. I want to make sure I'm thinking clearly, that's all." She leaned to him and kissed him on the lips, once gently. "I just don't want to make a mistake with you."

❖

The Mustang took the curves through Hermitage Hills with ease, the wide high-performance tires held the pavement in a grip that defied Kasey's occasional—though unintentional—efforts to free it. As she relaxed for a second during one of the only straight stretches in the last several minutes, she realized that Jordan was at ease, as if he had ridden with her a thousand times. He sat comfortably at her right, one hand tapping rhythmically against the outer door skin, and the other on her right thigh, just above the knee.

In her mind, Kasey went over the list of men she had known in the last year, and then extended it to two, then three and four, and finally all the way back to the first date she could remember.

This man is so different, she decided in silent amazement, *like no other man I've known.*

She looked into his eyes, trying to find that telltale sign of deceit, that one subtle glint that would tell her she was wrong, that he was just like the others. She saw nothing to fear, only the same warmth she had felt at the orchard. She touched him on his cheek with her right hand and ran her fingers around to his lips.

"How was New York?" he asked when she had again taken the wheel with both hands. For the next half hour, Kasey talked in detail about her interview with Barbara Walters, the Plaza Hotel, her tour of ABC, and the incredible Italian restaurant where they'd all eaten. When she took a breather, Jordan seized the opportunity: "Did she ask you about Stanton's killer?"

"Yes. She wanted to know if I thought I could find him."

"What did you say?"

"I told her the same thing I told you, that I wasn't sure, that I could never tell when a vision was going to come." Kasey looked at Jordan to gauge his response. He seemed indifferent all of a sudden.

Jordan turned away for the first time since they had begun the drive back to the airport.

"What's wrong, Jordan?" she asked.

He watched the trees racing by for an interminable moment, at last turning back toward her. "I need to catch this bastard, Kasey," he said solemnly. "My career may be riding on it. I was just hoping . . . you know . . . oh, hell. You've got enough on your mind right now. Forget I said anything." He patted her knee.

Kasey desperately wanted to help and began to speak, but an image of Joeyboy obliterated all rational thought. "I'm sorry, Jordan," she said in frustration. "You know I'd help you if I could, don't you?"

He turned to her. "You would, wouldn't you." He smiled and brushed the hair from her face. He knew there would be no answers to his questions today.

For the next quarter hour, neither of them spoke, allowing the radio to keep the silence from becoming awkward. As the rural curves yielded to the less picturesque thoroughfares of Nashville proper, Kasey merged onto

Briley Parkway and blended into the steady flow of afternoon traffic heading south toward the airport.

In another five minutes, she had pulled alongside Jordan's unmarked car in long-term parking. She turned off the engine and leaned against her door, facing him. "Thanks for the most wonderful afternoon I've had in a long time."

"It was my pleasure."

She leaned across and kissed him passionately on the mouth. "I mean it, Jordan, I had a great time."

Jordan stepped from the car and produced his keys. "I'm glad," he smiled. "That was the idea." He opened his door and slid into the front seat.

"What about your picnic basket?" she asked, remembering that it was still in her trunk.

Jordan produced a coy smile. "Hold on to it. We may need it again someday."

TWENTY-FOUR

Brandie stood in the livingroom, awaiting Kasey's approval. It was not yet eight in the morning; she had been eager to show Kasey the apartment: a one-bedroom, bath-and-a-half in Belmont Place, the same unit in which Brandie had lived for two years before buying her present home in Brentwood. Brandie had elected to keep the apartment and had rented it to a fellow reporter at Channel 9 for the last twenty-three months; it had just become vacant again. After Kasey had mentioned on Thursday morning that she wanted to find someplace safer to live—something with secure parking and without three flights of stairs to climb every day—Brandie had suggested her previous residence.

"I love the view," Kasey remarked with excitement as she stood on the balcony of the twenty-third-floor apartment, staring out at the city which was slowly coming to life beneath her. "It feels like the top of the world."

Brandie stood beside her. "You're going to be happy here, Kasey. The view is never the same two days in a row." Brandie remembered Kasey's current situation. "Will you be able to get out of the lease you're in now?"

Kasey nodded. "I'm on a month to month. I've already paid May's rent; all I'll have to do is give them a check for June and I'm free." Kasey looked sincerely at her new friend. "I don't know if I can afford to rent a place like this, though," she said humbly. "It's got to cost a fortune to live here. I mean, it's already beautifully furnished and everything." Though she still had most of the money in the bank, her conservative upbringing told her it might have to last for quite a while. There would be no Donna Stanton's in the future to help pay the bills. After only two days, she already regretted the money she'd blown on her new car; she missed "old blue."

Brandie grinned. "Relax. I'm only paying fifteen hundred dollars a month. You can have it for that. And no lease to sign."

Kasey was surprised at the amount; though high, it was far less than she had imagined. "Why so little?" she asked.

"The Fortune 500 company that owns the building uses it as a tax shelter. They apparently don't need the revenue, and besides, they keep the two floors above you vacant, but fully decorated, so the big dogs from

279

Europe and Japan can use them whenever they visit Music City. They go crazy over country music.

"The building is immaculately maintained, and you get a great view of the city at half the market rate. That's why there's rarely a vacancy for more than a few hours." Despite the fact that they were alone, Brandie leaned closer to Kasey. "They never advertise when an apartment becomes available. The units just . . . well . . . sort of change hands silently, if you know what I mean. It keeps the undesirables out." She threw Kasey a crooked smirk. "But don't worry, I vouched for you."

"You're a pal!" Kasey quipped.

"So, you want it?" Brandie asked when Kasey went to the balcony again.

Kasey nodded enthusiastically. "How can I ever thank you?" she asked as Brandie joined her at the railing.

"I'm glad to do it, Kasey. Just don't forget who your friends are the next time you have one of your visions."

"Don't worry. If I ever do, you'll be the first to know." Kasey's mind went to the cop with whom she was rapidly falling in love. She knew the time for another dream was closer than the reporter might have imagined.

❖

The balance of Saturday passed quickly for Kasey. After moving her clothes and her few meager possessions worth keeping to the new apartment, she had spent most of the evening rearranging Brandie's furniture, moving pictures and accessories about, and carefully placing the few things she had bought to add a personal touch until the place took on the quaint charm of a home featured in the pages of *Southern Living*.

Kasey stood at the front door, imagining how Jordan would view it when he saw it for the first time. She bit nervously on her bottom lip as she made trip after trip from the doorway to whichever object or piece of furniture needed a millimeter or two of adjustment. After an hour more of this ritual, she finally approved. The work, though not physically demanding, had continued nonstop for nearly twenty hours, until four in the morning. Now all the effort and care seemed justified: the apartment represented far more than a place in which to live in relative comfort and security—it had become the embodiment of a decade-old dream that had all but died, the dream to return to the life she had lived as a child.

She had crashed just before sunrise Sunday morning, and with her phone not due to be activated until after five P.M., intended to sleep most of the morning.

During the hectic and hasty move into the new apartment, Kasey had been too busy to miss Sam during the day, and too tired when she'd stopped. She was grateful to Brenda for offering to baby-sit—she and Sam had always gotten along well. Now, with the stillness and quiet of the new surroundings overwhelmingly loud in her ears, she found herself missing him greatly. She would get Sam first thing tomorrow morning, she vowed, and have Brenda over for dinner tomorrow night. That is, if she could tear her friend away from the new man in her life.

Maybe she'd have them both over. Brenda would like that and the man—whatever his name was—did sound heavenly. She wondered why her friend was being so secretive about him. *Probably just wants to keep him all to herself for a while,* Kasey thought. She considered her relationship with Jordan: *I can understand that.*

❖

Kasey sipped on her glass of Merlot and went to check on dinner. Jordan would be arriving in just over an hour and there was still much to do.

When the salad had been tossed and set in the refrigerator, Kasey tasted the sauce for the last time. "I sure hope you like spaghetti, Chief, 'cause that's what we're havin'," she mumbled into the wooden spoon as she blew on the small bite she held in front of her. It was perfect—thick, meaty, and spicy, filled with peppers, sausage, and mushrooms—just like Desmondo had taught her.

She set the spoon aside and covered the sauce.

Kasey sniffed the small bag of cinnamon-hazelnut coffee she had bought for later; its rich, European aroma would blend sensuously with the thick, crimson sauce for the spaghetti and fill the apartment with the fragrances of romance in bloom.

She smiled as she brushed her hand across the smooth plastic surface of the coffee maker—with the exception of Sam and her clothes, it was one of the few items from her previous life that had been allowed to make the move. The Salvation Army had been more than happy to arrange the removal of the rest of her possessions—those that Brenda had not wanted.

She checked the clock: forty-five minutes left. She turned the sauce to simmer and darted for the shower.

As Kasey stood at the mirror of her new dresser, she was pleased with the image it returned. The difficult days and nights she had just endured had taken their toll: she had lost nearly twelve pounds, and while not bad in concept, not all were in places she would have chosen. Her face was thinner than she liked—as thin as it had been during her divorce—and her legs seemed too skinny to her. She turned to the side and studied her breasts. *At least I still have you,* she grinned, pleased that they hadn't suffered the brunt of the weight loss.

Kasey opened the top drawer in the lingerie chest and selected a new pair of midnight-blue bikini panties, pulling them high on her hips. She found the matching underwire bra and filled it with her soft, round breasts, the tender flesh pressing tightly against the loosely woven lace. She adjusted the straps to create just the right amount of cleavage and took one more look in the mirror. A pleased expression lit her face.

Kasey turned to the bed and opened the small plastic bag containing her most recent purchase. She withdrew a sand-washed midnight-blue silk minidress with spaghetti straps and a wide scoop neck. She slipped it over her head and pulled it across her hips. It fit comfortably—not too loose, not too tight—its hem breaking three inches above her knees. She slipped on the matching suede heels and added a thin gold serpentine chain to her neck; her earrings were simple quarter-carat CZ studs. As she turned to the full-length mirror on the back of the bedroom door, she smiled again: "If you think you wanted me Friday afternoon, Mr. Jordan Lee Taylor, you ain't seen nothing yet, sugar." Her little inner voice immediately formed an imaginary image of Gloria Taylor, standing tearfully at the front door of her home while her husband made love to another woman. "And you stay the hell out of it tonight. They're separated, remember," she admonished instantly. "Tonight is *my* night."

❖

The last orange light of afternoon painted long, gray forms across the floor which crept slowly up the wall opposite the balcony's wide French doors. The walls of the dining room seemed to be alive as the shadows created by the candles danced to the rhythm of a ceiling fan turning slowly in the livingroom. Jordan leaned back in his chair and stared between the candles at his hostess; in the light of the twin yellow flames, she was, while not the most classically beautiful woman he had ever known, certainly the most desirable. "I've never had a better meal. Everything was perfect."

"Never?"

"Well, not for as long as I can remember."

"What would you have said if you'd hated it?" she teased.

"That's easy," he said with a shy smile. "I'd have said I've never had a better meal. You just spent an entire afternoon cooking for me, not to mention looking stunning in your new dress. Do I look like a complete fool?" He drank his wine. "Honestly, it was the best spaghetti I think I've ever eaten."

"I'll tell Mondo," she smiled.

"Mondo?"

"A friend. Someone I used to work with." She leaned back against her chair and surveyed the increasing darkness of the livingroom. "Someone from another life, it seems now." She took a short sip of wine. "It's hard to imagine that only a couple of weeks ago I was waiting tables and trying to figure out how I was going to buy a new pair of Nikes when my running shoes finally died. Now . . ."

"Now?" he asked softly when she had been silent for a long minute.

"Now this," she finished, making a sweeping gesture with her wineglass.

"You deserve it, Kasey. You should be proud."

"I'm also scared, Jordan."

"What are you afraid of, Kasey?" He leaned forward and put his elbows on the heavy glass table.

"Of losing it." She continued to stare into the darkening room on her right.

"Why would you lose it? I don't mean to pry, but you're not talking about money, are you?"

"Oh, there's no problem with money at this point," she said solemnly. "I suppose it's no news to you I've got more cash in the bank than I would have brought home in ten years as a waitress. It's just . . ." Again her words tapered off without completion. How could she tell him, ever tell him, that her life was a lie, that she'd gotten the money because she had been too damned frightened to tell the police that she had witnessed Donna's murder? A grandiose lie had created an equally grandiose world, filled with comforts and conveniences galore, but the price was proving far greater than the currency she had traded for them. Slowly, surely, her soul was paying as well, and no amount of denial or deceit or wine could change that.

There was only one way out, only one thing she could do.

"Kasey?" Jordan said as he placed his hands on her shoulders.

She jumped slightly when he touched her; in her self-imposed moment of isolation she hadn't noticed him leave his chair. "I'm sorry, Jordan. Everything happened so suddenly that it doesn't seem real. I'm afraid someone is going to walk through that door any minute and tell me that it's all been a mistake and it's time to return to the restaurant again." She touched his hand on her bare shoulder.

"Sort of like Cinderella."

"Only I'm not sure this fairy tale will have a happy ending."

Without moving his hands from her shoulders, he caressed her back tenderly with his thumbs. "Tomorrow will take care of itself, Kasey. You're safe tonight." He pulled her chin up toward him and bent to kiss her lips.

"I hope coming here won't put you in any kind of jeopardy with . . . you know what I mean."

He shook his head but didn't speak.

Kasey slid her chair back and stood, turning into his arms. "I told you I could cook."

He pulled her to him, feeling every curve of her body, and kissed her fully on the mouth. They stood in a warm lover's embrace.

Finally, Kasey nestled her face against his neck and chest and wrapped her arms around his waist, feeling safe and secure for the first time in a decade. "Want some coffee?" she whispered, hoping he would decline for now, praying he didn't have to leave.

"I'd rather have you," he whispered in her ear.

❖

Kasey lay on the cool cotton sheets at the edge of the bed, her head on the pillow, her eyes on the man standing above her.

Jordan slid his tie away from the top button, and with a quick, easy gesture, pulled the small end through its knot, dropping the tie to the floor. He removed his suit jacket and shirt, neither hurrying nor hesitating, and stood motionless in the light of the bedroom window, his body painted in alternating stripes of black and white as the lights of the city crept through the half-open blinds. Kasey watched each move, taking in his fit and muscular form. She wanted him, even more than she had imagined.

Jordan stepped out of his loafers as if they were sandals, then slowly removed his pants and black cotton boxers, sliding both down along his thighs and then dropping them to the floor. He sat on the edge of the bed, cradling Kasey in his arms. He lay his chest against her breasts and kissed her, his tongue searching for hers.

He put his arm behind her shoulders and pulled her upward, swinging her legs off the side of the bed and fitting his body between her knees. He took the dress at its hem and gathered it slowly, sliding it upward past her hips. As the delicate fabric slipped over her breasts, she lifted her arms toward the ceiling, allowing the dress to pass over her head with ease.

When he got his first look at her body, his eyes slowly scanned every inch of her form from her head to her knees. She reached between her breasts and released the catch that secured the bra. She slid it slowly to the sides, across her breasts, pausing briefly as the fabric was about to pass her nipples. His gaze was fixed on her fingertips.

When at last she allowed the bra to fall to the sheets behind her, and he had slipped the panties down her thighs, dropping them to the floor, he pulled her to him, feeling the firm, round orbs of her breasts pressing into his chest. Their mouths met violently.

Kasey fell back against the sheets and pulled Jordan with her. She could feel his heart pounding against her breasts. Jordan placed one hand beneath her and lifted her slightly, placing her more squarely on the bed, allowing their full weight to rest against the covers.

With both hands, he raised her arms above her head and began the long-awaited adventure of exploring her body. He placed his lips against her face, kissing the soft, freckled skin; his lips moved to her eyelids and then to her cheeks; they met her waiting mouth again and lingered there.

When he ran his tongue across her chin and down the front of her neck, her head threw back in reflex, her chest rising to meet his touch. He continued down the slope of her right breast until his mouth passed over the nipple, devouring it. He moved to the left breast. Time and again he made the sensuous circles, and each time, her nipples grew more responsive and taut.

He moved to the flat plane of her stomach, easing his tongue backward from between her breasts to the shallow depression at her navel. He circled it several times before kissing the tender flesh of the sides of her abdomen, at the point where a slight depression rose to form each hip. Again Kasey strained upward, this time adding a deep, low cry to her movement.

His mouth moved back to the pink plateau below her navel, then journeyed downward. His chin touched her soft auburn hair, followed by his lips. When he pressed his face to her, she lifted herself against him; her hips rocking involuntarily; the scent of her desire filling his senses.

In her mind, nothing in the universe existed now but this man and his touch.

She rose toward him and then fell back, drawing his body to hers, parting her knees widely for him to easily enter her. She climaxed immediately, her body erupting in a spasm of ecstasy. She dug her fingers into his back and kept her mouth pressed to his, savoring every delight, every wave of pleasure.

As he felt her shudder beneath him, he moved deeply and rhythmically, feeling her around him, against him. He adjusted his movements several times to keep her desire alive. For twenty minutes they met in silent union while she regained the sensitivity to climax again, with him. It had not happened more than a few times in her entire life, and then only by accident. But this man was different, patient, confident. She knew it would be easy with him.

It was better than she had hoped.

Jordan dropped his head, no longer able to support its weight, and then lowered his body against her, easing to one side but maintaining contact.

He laid his right arm across her chest, beneath the breasts, and held her in a secure and gentle grip, his face buried in the nape of her neck.

They would remain there, motionless and exhausted, until Kasey fell into a deep and tranquil sleep.

TWENTY-FIVE

Kasey rolled to her right and pulled one of the pillows to her chest. She had been sleeping soundly beneath the covers for nearly three hours, her dreams animated by the fantasies of her youth. Within the solitude of her emotional cocoon, Kasey became aware that she was alone—that he was no longer beside her. She sat straight up and fought for something recognizable in the dark, unfamiliar room. Only thin horizontal streaks of light crept through the blinds he had closed as he left.

Kasey stood and stumbled to the bathroom. When she stepped into the bedroom again, the light of the bathroom fell across the bed. She saw a small piece of paper, folded twice, lying on the table beside her alarm clock. She sat on the edge of the bed and switched on the small reading lamp. She took the paper and unfolded it. Jordan's words made her smile:

> *You're wonderful.*
> *Can we have lunch tomorrow?*

Kasey refolded the paper and laid it back on the table, in the exact spot she had found it—she wanted to discover it anew when she awoke. She set her alarm for eight and turned out the lamp by the bed, allowing the bathroom light to remain burning through a generous slit in the door. It made her feel less alone, as it had when she was a little girl.

She needed the light now that Jordan was gone.

She closed her eyes and searched her heart for the perfect image of him pressed against her.

Kasey slipped between the rusted strands of the old barbed-wire fence and walked slowly toward Donna Stanton. Joeyboy stood silently, watching everything. The shotgun was just inches from Donna's tangled blond hair. Kasey could still see the blades of grass jutting from the golden strands—the frightened look in her eyes.

"Kasey," Donna called to her.

Kasey stopped a few feet from the couple. Joeyboy lowered the gun and lit the cigarette that he had stuck between his lips.

"Aren't you going to help me?" The tears began to well up in Donna's eyes.

"What can I do? Don't you see, he has a gun?" She glanced at Joeyboy and then back at Donna. "I've already taken them to you."

"That's not enough. You've got to help me, Kasey."

"I'm sorry, but it's all I can do. I'm so afraid."

"You must," she pleaded.

"But I didn't put you here. I'm not responsible." Kasey saw the woman shaking, unbridled terror in her eyes.

"Your money, your fame, your new lover—they're all gifts from me. Won't you help me in return?"

"What more can I do. What do you want from me?" Kasey tried to run, but her body would not respond.

"I want what you would want, Kasey—justice, that's all."

Joeyboy grinned and nodded slowly, sucking in a deep cloud of smoke. He blew it toward Kasey, making her cringe.

"I'm so afraid he'll come for *me*. Don't you understand?"

"I do understand, Kasey, more than anyone else, but you're the only one who can give me what I deserve."

"No, it's the job of the police to do such things. They should be helping you."

"But they're not helping me, Kasey, you can see that. Your lover doesn't even know about Joeyboy." Kasey looked at Joeyboy with contempt, but her disapproval meant nothing to him. Less than nothing. "Only you can help now," Donna petitioned. "Won't you give me justice?"

"Stop saying that. I'm not the only one who can help you. Stop asking me! I can't . . . I just can't."

"Then my life will mean nothing, my death less. They'll never know why I died. They'll never know who was responsible." Donna turned away. She addressed the man behind her: "I'm ready now. There's nothing more I can say to her."

Joeyboy raised the barrel of the gun again.

"No!" Kasey shouted frantically. "Don't do it! You can't do it! I know who you are!"

"Who gives a fuck," Joeyboy laughed. "Now go away, chicken-shit little girl. Spend your blood money and leave me to work in peace."

The explosion rang violently in her ears as Kasey watched the other woman fall to the cold, hard earth.

Kasey let out a scream as she bolted upright in bed, her body shaking violently, the sheets beneath her soaked with sweat.

She ripped the covers from her legs and raced to the bathroom.

❖

"Good morning," Brandie answered cheerfully as the operator put through Kasey's call. "How's the new apartment?"

Kasey squeezed her eyes tightly shut for a moment. Somewhere between the end of the awful dream and the warmth of the new day's sun pouring across the balcony where she'd spent the balance of the night, the decision had been made for her. It had come about because she wanted to help Jordan find the brutal killer the media was hounding him to arrest, and because the nightmares finally had to end. She chose her words carefully. "I've had another vision, Brandie. I need to see you at once."

The reporter killed the radio playing quietly on her desk. "Was it about . . . her?" she asked, crossing her fingers.

"I saw the man who killed her."

Brandie stood between her desk and her chair, having been catapulted to her feet by Kasey's unexpected words. "Yes!" she mouthed excitedly, the phone momentarily away from her mouth.

"I have to tell someone." After nearly a dozen paid interviews, Kasey had become an accomplished liar, and with her proficiency came a self-hatred that was consuming her. She wanted to stop, to be forgiven, but knew it was far too late for such simple penance.

"How soon can you get here?" Brandie asked impatiently.

"I'll be there in twenty minutes," she answered without expression.

"We'll be ready, Kasey." Brandie hung up the phone. "Steve!" she shouted across the newsroom floor.

❖

Brenda Poole rolled over in the twin bed and gave Ray a lingering kiss on the lips. He opened his eyes sluggishly and produced a half-smile. She laid her head against his chest and ran her fingertips through his pubic hair, hoping—now that his brain was awake—she would be able to arouse the rest of his body. They had already made love four times since she got off work at midnight, six hours earlier, and while he looked as though he'd run a marathon, she was ready to go for five. It had been a long spell since a man had paid so much attention to her.

"What's wrong, baby?" she asked teasingly when he failed to respond to her stroking. "Too tired to go again?"

Ray groaned in mock agony. "I've got to eat something first. If I don't, I'm going to waste away. You got anything to fix around here?"

"I can make us some bacon and eggs. Got a little coffee left, I think."

"That'll do. Anything to get my strength back. You're a wild bitch, you know it?" He grabbed her left breast and squeezed it painfully.

"Oowww, careful, baby. They've got to last me a while." She sat up in bed and put her hands against his chest. "Do you enjoy sex with me, Ray?"

"Hell, yes. You're something. I'm glad I got up the nerve to speak to you at the pool."

"Me, too. I'm sorry I had to stuff to do Friday and Saturday and couldn't spend much time with you. Sam was freaked out with Kasey's move and I just couldn't leave him here alone. I hope last night made up for it a little." She felt the muscles of his upper chest and admired his muscular arms. They had felt good against her body.

"You didn't say where your friend was moving."

"It's supposed to be a secret." Sam stuck his head into the bedroom but didn't enter. He didn't care at all for the man with the black eyes.

"A secret?"

"Yeah, she's been getting all these calls from people wanting her to find missing relatives and lost jewelry and stuff. One jerk even wanted her to find his dog. Can you believe it? Her new number's unlisted."

"I can't say that I blame her. You've got it, of course."

"Of course. Got a key, too. In fact, I'm supposed to drop Sam by there this afternoon."

"Why doesn't she just come by here to get him?" Joeyboy thought how perfect that would be. He could do both of them at once. Neat. Easy.

"She's got something important to do today. I don't mind making the trip." Brenda stood and slipped on a new teddy she had bought for their first night together. There hadn't been time to wear it before now. She remembered the parking garage security. "I wish I'd thought to get her gate code before she left, dammit." She modeled the skimpy lingerie for her new man. "You like?"

"Sure, it's great. What gate code?" He sat up in bed, his back to the headboard.

"Oh, there's a security gate on the underground parking garage. You need a special code to open it. I'll just have to go around front, I guess." She moved to the door. "How do you like your eggs?"

"Scrambled. Don't leave the whites runny." He stuffed a second pillow behind his shoulders.

"I'll bet she's glad she doesn't have to park that new Mustang of hers out in the open like she did her old Honda. The paint got screwed sitting in the sun all the time," she explained as she made her way down the hall toward the kitchen.

Joeyboy was at the doorway before she had gone another ten steps. "I thought your friend had had her Mustang for a while."

Brenda stopped at the door to the kitchen. "Only about four or five days, actually. She got it the day before we met at the pool, come to think of it."

"And before that she had a Honda?" he asked, leaning casually against the jamb. He did not want to appear too interested.

Brenda didn't understand Ray's peculiar interest in Kasey's mode of transportation but figured it was some kind of guy thing. "Yeah, a CRX. Had it since high school. About time she got rid of the thing, don't you think? You want cream in your coffee?"

"No," he whispered.

Joeyboy's mind quickly put the pieces together, like a cheap child's puzzle. The talkative best friend had at last served her intended purpose—besides having been pretty good in the sack—and was of no more use. He looked at Sam. The cat, on the other hand, might still be of some value.

He smiled generously at the woman, his perfect teeth gleaming in the dim hallway. "Want some help in the kitchen?"

"Sure. You know how to cook?" She took the carton of eggs from the refrigerator and grabbed an iron skillet from beneath the stove.

He followed Brenda into the cramped room. "You bet. I've created some real masterpieces in kitchens." As Brenda busied herself with breakfast, he pressed his nude body against the lace teddy, running his tongue across the back of her neck to the lobe of her left ear.

A chill hardened her nipples and goose bumps covered her arms. "You're gonna have to wait now," she said, cracking the first of the eggs they would share. "But your ass is mine the minute you finish eating."

"Will you scream for me again?"

Her mind went back to the first time she had climaxed last night. "If you want me to. Some guys hate that."

"I love to hear women scream." He gently massaged her shoulders, his bare hips firmly against her.

She tried to stir the eggs, but his touch was arousing her. "That's one thing good about not having any neighbors in the other half of the duplex at the moment. I can scream as loud as I like and no one is going to hear a thing."

Her words excited him far more than she could have imagined. As he ran the fingertips of his left hand slowly down her back, Joeyboy quietly eased a carving knife from its cheap wooden holder on the counter behind him, lowering its nine-inch serrated edge to his thigh. "That's wonderful, baby, because I want you to scream really loud for me this time."

❖

Brandie Mueller was already standing at the lobby doors of Channel 9 when Kasey arrived. The reporter was impeccably dressed—as always—

her makeup perfect. Kasey looked like she'd been on an all-night drunk. "Kasey, are you all right?" Brandie gave her a firm hug.

Kasey's nod said yes, but her appearance betrayed her.

"Want a cup of coffee before we meet with the others?" Brandie asked.

"I'd love one," she said with a deep sigh. "Make it a double."

The two moved briskly toward the canteen.

"Want something in it?"

"How about some arsenic," Kasey mumbled.

"Sorry. Fresh out. Hey, you sure you're okay?"

"Actually, no, but I'll either be better or worse in a few hours."

"Let's hope it's not worse. I don't think I have enough makeup with me," Brandie teased.

❖

Pete Vanover stuck his head into Jordan Taylor's office and announced that he and Stark were heading to Columbia to check a lead they had just received from a bank teller there.

"Wait a minute, Pete," Taylor said as he set his first cup of coffee of the day on his desk. "Tell me about this lead."

"All I know is that this First Tennessee Bank teller swears the Stanton woman withdrew a bundle from her bank in Columbia on Monday afternoon, the twenty-second of April, but said she used an alias. It took her until now to realize the two women were the same."

"Does the bank have film on her?"

"The teller said there's a camera right above her station. Takes a picture every three seconds. We should be able to get all we need from that."

Taylor nodded. "Call me the second you finish with her. Get the lab to print every frame of film covering the transaction. If it's her, and he grabbed her as she left the bank, we just might get lucky and have a shot of our killer in one of them."

He patted his friend on the back and watched as the detective disappeared toward the rear of the building.

❖

Tim Arnold packed his video camera and stored it carefully in its case in the back of the Jeep. He had gotten what they had come for—more than enough footage for any story Brandie might choose to write. He took a final look at the orchard: how different it felt now—peaceful, serene, inviting. It was hard to imagine that such a sickening crime had been committed within the tranquil setting.

He shook his head and mouthed the name Joeyboy, wondering what made a man become an animal—a killer of women.

Brandie looked through her phone directory, searching for a name she hadn't needed in months. "There you are," she grinned. "Johnny Foster, Detective, Intelligence Division, Nashville Metro." She climbed into the front seat and told JR to head back to Channel 9. She checked on Kasey: the sad, quiet woman in the backseat was obviously shaken by the morning's events. She patted Kasey's knee and then punched Foster's number into the cellular phone. Kasey would be fine, she consoled herself. For now, there were more important things to consider.

"Intelligence Division—Goff speaking."

"Is Detective Foster there?" she asked impatiently.

"Hold on." The phone was dropped noisily onto the old wooden desk.

After nearly five minutes wait, it was picked up again. "Intelligence—Foster." He sounded even more bored than his buddy, if that were possible. She knew Foster well and chuckled: all the dumb ones ended up in Intelligence.

"Hi, Johnny—Brandie Mueller. I need a favor."

"Hello, Brandie. Long time. What can I do for you?" He hoped it would be something big. He remembered the last time she had needed a favor—it had earned him a pair of front row seats at a Reba McEntire concert that had been sold out for weeks.

"I need you to check out a tag for me, who it's registered to, what kind of vehicle, etcetera. You know what I'm looking for, Johnny."

"A Davidson County tag?" he asked.

"I'm not sure. It's a Tennessee tag in any case."

"What's in it for me?" he asked unabashedly.

"What do you want?"

"There's a George Strait concert here on the thirty-first. It sold out in forty minutes and I couldn't get a single damned ticket."

"I don't think the station has any."

"But you can get them, can't you?"

"Maybe. How many are we talking?"

"Six."

"Six!" she cried.

"They're getting strict about this unauthorized shit, Brandie. I could get in a lot of trouble."

"Fine—six. The tag is a vanity plate: J-O-E-Y-B-O-Y." She spelled the name for the detective and covered the mouthpiece. "This usually only takes a minute or two," she informed the other three in the Jeep.

Foster put Brandie on hold and spun his chair around to face his computer. He closed the screen he'd been using earlier and entered D.C.A.T. (Davidson County Automated Tracking). This screen gave him tag registration data. He quickly typed: TMVRI, PL, 00JOEYBOY followed by the Enter key. In ten seconds he had the VIN, lien information, make, model, color, type, owner's name, address, town, and zip on the computer screen in front of him. He punched the Hold button again. "Brandie, that vehicle is a 1996 black Dodge Ram 3500 truck belonging to a Griffin, Joey. His indicated address is 16068 Old Highway 318, Davidson County. There's no lien on the vehicle which was purchased from Music City Dodge in Nashville on April fourth of this year." He rocked back in his swivel chair and put his feet on the desk. "That'll be six, I repeat, six George Strait tickets. And not in the peanut gallery, either."

"Hang on a minute, Johnny, will you? I'm going to put you on hold while I talk with someone."

"Sure, Brandie."

This time Brandie pressed Mute on the cell phone and turned to Kasey with a proud smile. "Bingo! The son-of-a-bitch's real name is Joey Griffin, and he drives a new black pickup, just like you said." She squeezed her friend's knee. Tim and JR nodded their heads respectfully and approvingly, though neither was surprised this time.

After hearing Kasey's emotional depiction of the senseless assassination, both men wanted to see Joeyboy fry.

Brandie wanted more information. "You still there, Johnny?" she asked as she released Mute.

"Still here, Brandie."

"I need more data, Johnny. First, I want a physical description on this Griffin guy."

"What the hell for, Brandie?"

"I can't tell you, but no one will ever know you got it for me, I swear to God."

"*Front-row* tickets, Brandie. Six of them."

"Front row, Johnny." She made a face at the phone.

Again Foster turned to his computer. He typed: Z, RNAM, GRIFFIN, JOEY. In another fifteen seconds, Foster reported that there were three "Griffin, Joey's" in the computer: one, a white female, 23—Brandie instantly ruled the woman out; the second was a white male, 67—again Brandie vetoed the choice; the third and final Griffin, Joey Ray was a white male, 33, blond hair, brown eyes, 6'1", 195 lbs. Brandie covered the mouthpiece and repeated the last description to Kasey, who immediately put her hands to her mouth. She didn't utter a sound, but Brandie and the others saw the confirmation in her eyes.

"That's the guy," Brandie told the detective.

"Is that all?" Foster asked.

"Just one more thing, Johnny. I want to know if this clown has a record."

Foster dropped his feet back to the floor and stood. "Now wait a goddamn second, Brandie. You're asking for some serious shit now, not the Mickey Mouse stuff we've been playing with so far. I could lose my job over this."

"Well, if you're afraid, or it's over your head, Johnny, I'll call one of my buddies at the CJC. Thanks for your help. I'll send over your concert tickets."

"Hold on a minute, dammit." He sat again. "I didn't say I couldn't get the information for you. I just said it was serious shit, that's all. And, it's gonna cost you more than a few lousy concert tickets."

"How much?" she asked.

He thought for a second. "A pair of full-season passes to Opryland and the Grand Ole Opry."

"Those are a fortune!" she complained, playing her part perfectly. She didn't care if they cost five grand—her Emmy was waiting for her. Besides, Clarion was going to have to pay for them, not her.

"How bad do you want the information?" he countered.

Brandie covered the phone only partially and pretended to be annoyed. "Deal," she groaned.

For the third time, Foster turned to the screen. He typed 3333, tabbed to the next field and typed AHIS (Arrest HIStory). In half a minute he was staring at Griffin's complete criminal record. The words he read made his chin drop. "Brandie, this guy Griffin is one bad motherfucker. I don't know why you want to know about him, but if it were me, I'd cross the street if I saw the bastard coming, and I carry a gun."

"Tell me about him, Johnny," she said boldly.

"His rap sheet fills my entire screen, beginning with attempted murder at eighteen . . . uh . . . three, no four counts of aggravated assault— let me see what else—one count of carrying a concealed weapon . . . and no less than a dozen other arrests for various felonies—all of a violent nature. At least there's some good news."

"Yeah, what the hell could that possibly be?"

"He's in Brushy Mountain for the next thirty years, and that's if he's a good boy."

"What do you mean?" Brandie asked immediately.

"I mean, he's serving thirty years to life for murder-one." Foster studied the screen again, scrolling down to reveal more of Griffin's file. "Seems he killed a biker at a topless club in December of '91. Popped him right in the head with a shotgun while he sat with his back to him. As far as I can see, it's the first time he's ever gotten any hard time."

Brandie was puzzled. How could Joey Griffin be in prison for murder, and yet be in the orchard killing Donna Stanton two weeks ago? She was about to change her mind about Kasey's newest vision. "Someone thought she saw him in Maury County on the twenty-second of April, Johnny," she said hopefully.

"Not possible, Brandie. He's not exactly the kind you'd let out on a work release program."

"Check it for me. Please." She looked at Kasey.

"I don't care what your guy says, Brandie, it was him." The look in Kasey's eyes was absolute.

"You could be wrong, couldn't you, Kasey?"

"I'm not."

"Well, son of a bitch! This is pure bullshit," the detective practically yelled into the phone.

"What have you got, Johnny?" Brandie asked, her mind still trying desperately to make sense of the conflicting pieces.

"I can't believe it . . . well, maybe I can at that. The whole system's going to hell in a hand basket."

"What, dammit?" Brandie snapped impatiently.

"They let the bastard out four months ago, after serving just four lousy years of his sentence. Ain't that some shit! We bust our asses trying to catch 'em, and some judge puts 'em back out on the street after a short vacation with three hots and a cot. Probably be back in the joint in a year."

"Or less," Brandie said defiantly. "There's one thing I don't understand, Johnny. I know the system is screwed up, but how the hell could Griffin have made parole?"

Foster studied the screen. "Well, well," he remarked.

"What?"

"The old boy himself signed him out. It must be nice to have friends in high places."

"The old boy?" Brandie asked. "You mean the warden?"

"Not the warden, he doesn't have that kind of power. Williams," Foster smirked. "I'm talking about good ole boy Buddy Williams."

"I'll have your passes on your desk in a couple of days, Johnny," she stated flatly as she searched for the End button. She didn't hear Foster's warning to be careful.

Brandie looked at her silent friend. She put her hand on Kasey's knee again. "I have a funny feeling this thing is about to get way out of hand."

Kasey nodded slowly and silently. She could feel her heart beating harder beneath her blouse.

I was afraid of that, her little voice whispered in her brain.

❖

Joeyboy pulled a new Schlage key from his front pocket: it worked both locks easily. He stepped inside Kasey's apartment and pitched the annoying black cat to the carpet. The only reason he'd let it live was to buy a little time. If Brenda had been right about Kasey expecting the beast home today, he didn't want to spook her any more than necessary, and he definitely didn't want her visiting Brenda's duplex. If the cat was at home just like it was supposed to be, the friend must be okay, whether she came to the phone or not.

Sam landed squarely on all fours and gave the man who smelled like death an evil glare from the center of the livingroom floor before vanishing into the kitchen.

The man already knew Kasey wouldn't be in her apartment. He had tried her unlisted number only moments before from a pay phone across from the Magnolia Towers. It would have been so sweet if she'd been home. He cursed under his breath at his unusual stroke of bad luck as he moved quickly through the rooms.

When he reached her bedroom, he pulled open what he guessed to be her lingerie drawer. Within it, were several pairs of pretty new underpants and matching bras. He pushed his hand deep into the satiny contents and withdrew a pair of black silk panties. As he watched his movements in the mirror, he ran the delicate fabric under his nose and across his lips. "I like these, Kasey Riteman. Black's always been my favorite color." He pushed the drawer carefully shut. "I think I'll let you model them for me before I kill you."

❖

Jordan took the call in his office. Having been unable to reach his intended lunch date all morning, he hoped it might be Kasey. "Jordan Taylor," he answered pleasantly.

"Hi, Jordan, it's Brandie Mueller." She looked at the clock on her office wall— 1:25 P.M. "I wonder if you could come to my office around two. I think you'll find it a most interesting visit."

Jordan had little use for the reporter, but knew something had to be up for her to call. "It's possible. Depends on the reason, Brandie." He dug through some paperwork that had been piled on his desk during the night.

"I just thought you might like to know the name of the man who murdered Donna Stanton."

"And I suppose *you* know it," he said with sarcasm.

"I do now. Kasey Riteman told it to me this morning."

He bolted to his feet. "I'll be there in ten minutes."

❖

The receptionist sent Jordan Taylor right up, without the protocol required to get to the office of the general manager. He had been there
before and knew the way.

When Jordan stepped from the elevator, Stewart Parker's personal secretary was standing by the doors to greet him. "Good afternoon, Chief
Taylor. Mr. Parker is waiting for you. If you'll follow me, please." He
stayed at her heels as she led him across the third floor toward the stately
corner office of her boss.

Parker met him at the twin walnut doors. "Thanks for coming, Chief
Taylor. I think you know everyone." He gestured the detective toward an
empty chair at the leather and cherry conference table. Tim Arnold stood
in a corner, sipping on a Diet Coke.

Jordan gave a quick nod to the group as a whole and took his seat. It
was difficult for him not to ask Kasey about not coming to him first, but
he understood the reason. "Okay, I'm here," he said in his most businesslike voice.

Brandie nodded for Steve Dacus to start the tape. It had only been
rough-edited, but contained all the information the detective would need
to see.

For the next twenty minutes, Jordan Taylor sat quietly in his chair, his
mind and eyes on the monitor screen. When Kasey—kneeling between
the apple trees, her hands touching the depression left by Polaski's forensics team—uttered the name, "Joeyboy," and then collapsed in a tearful
heap, Jordan's bright blue eyes grew hard and narrow.

Dacus stopped the tape.

"Joeyboy?" Jordan asked. "That's it—just Joeyboy?"

"It's not just his name," Brandie said, "it's also his license plate number."

"Let me get this straight, his truck, the black truck Ms. Riteman
mentioned midway through the tape, had the word Joeyboy on its tag?"

Brandie, Kasey, and Tim all nodded silently. If JR had been invited, he
would have nodded, too.

"Give me a phone," he said after he had looked into all three faces. It
took him less than five minutes to get the same information Brandie had
gotten earlier in the day—all the information except the part about
Joeyboy having been released. Taylor hung up before Feeney had read that
far.

He leaned back in his chair and folded his arms. He felt sorry for Kasey
for what he was about to say, but putting the pretentious Brandie Mueller
in her place made up for it. "Sorry, guys," he said, "but this time you've

struck out. I'm afraid your alleged murderer was indisposed at the time of Donna Stanton's death. It seems he was—and still is—a guest of the state. As a matter of fact, I helped put away your Mister Joeyboy in 1990, though he went by a different name back then. If he's damned lucky, he'll be eligible for parole in the year 2011." He glanced briefly into Kasey's eyes.

"Call your office back, Chief Taylor. Have them read you the rest of Griffin's file . . . the part about him being released in January." Brandie now leaned back and folded her arms.

"Impossible," he said resolutely.

"Want to bet?" she smiled.

Jordan wanted to say what he really thought, but took the phone and pressed Redial. "This is Taylor. Put Feeney back on," he ordered. As soon as the ex-Bostonian grabbed the phone, Taylor told him to put Griffin's file back on the screen and read him any information he had not heard earlier. When he got to the part about Griffin's January release, Jordan quietly set the phone back in its cradle. He stared into Kasey's eyes, his respect for her abilities now absolute.

He turned to Brandie. "You already knew."

She nodded.

"How? Oh, never mind. You'd give me some crap about the First Amendment, wouldn't you?"

She continued to nod.

He looked again at Kasey. "Your vision is not admissible in court, you know that, don't you." She barely moved. "I'll never be able to get a search warrant based on your dreams, but"—the detective tapped his fingers on the table and thought for a moment—"there might be another way to get to Griffin." He turned to Stewart Parker. "I'll need that tape."

"Bullshit!" Brandie and Steve Dacus spouted in unison.

"Wait a minute, you two. Let's hear what Chief Taylor has to say." Stewart Parker put his own elbows on the table, ready to do battle if need be to keep his reporter's work—and the-once-in-a-lifetime story—from leaving the building. "Why the tape, Jordan?"

"I can't have that kind of information leaked to the public before we can tie Griffin to the killing, if we can tie him to it. It would probably mean a mistrial—might even prevent a trial from happening at all." He held out his hand for the tape.

Parker thought for a second. "What if I give you my oath that not one word of this will air until you phone personally with a release? Can we hold on to the tape then?"

Jordan knew that, tape or no tape, Channel 9 was going to air a story on Griffin during the next broadcast—anything to stay ahead of the competition. The best he could hope for would be a gag order from a judge—though he knew he'd play hell getting one. After that, second best was Parker's word that the station would sit on the story until Griffin had been linked to the murder. He looked at Brandie for a second and then at Kasey. Their emotional involvement with the story showed in their faces. "Your word, Stewart. Not one frame of video, not one syllable of audio about Griffin until I phone you personally."

"Deal," he agreed. Everyone finally relaxed.

"You've got to call the second you make an arrest," Brandie added. "The story won't do us any good after it's picked up by all the other stations."

"We'll also want an exclusive on what you find linking Griffin to Stanton's death," Dacus chimed in.

"You don't want much, do you?" Jordan said sarcastically.

"That's the deal," Parker said through tight lips, backing his people.

"As soon as we establish a link to Stanton, I'll phone you from my car. You should beat the others by a full day." He turned to Kasey. "But either way, you're still the only ones with Ms. Riteman, here, aren't you?"

Kasey allowed her eyes to smile at Jordan for a moment. "Perhaps you'll make chief of police after this."

Brandie looked at Kasey and then at Jordan again. She sensed something electric between them beneath the facade of polite detachment.

She decided to let it pass for the moment.

❖

At two-fifteen, Jordan tore across the parking lot of the station toward his car. He threw it into gear and darted out onto Knob Road. "This is Taylor," he stated hurriedly when a detective in his department answered. "Have Pete and Re-Pete gotten back yet?"

"Pete's right here, Chief. You want him?"

"Put him on!"

Vanover took the phone from the other detective. "Yeah, Chief."

"Pete, pull the file on a Joey Ray Griffin, RNI number . . ." Jordan tried to recall the number Feeney had mentioned. "Shit! I can't remember it, Pete—get it from Chuck. Have it on my desk in ten minutes. I'm on my way there now. And get hold of Mike Castle. Tell him to have his boys ready for an urban assault in fifteen minutes." He made a hard left onto White Bridge Road and pressed the accelerator.

"Why Griffin, Chief?" Vanover asked. Brad Stark, who had just arrived at the desk, looked over Vanover's shoulder and tried to decipher his notes. He put the coffee his partner had asked for next to the phone and sat down.

"Kasey Riteman—you remember, that cute little psychic you don't believe in? Well, it looks like she just handed us Stanton's killer." He pressed End and threw on his lights and siren when a slower car got in his way as he hit the on-ramp for I-40.

❖

At two-twenty-one P.M., the phone rang in the office of Mario Giacano in Chicago. Michael Filippo answered it with a curt "Yes."

"Griffin has just been fingered by the psychic who found Stanton's body. We've got no choice now but to go after him."

"Can you warn him?" Filippo asked, the acid in his stomach beginning to churn.

"Tried. No answer. It's too risky to try again. He'll just have to take his chances. I'll do what I can, but it can't be much, I'm afraid."

Filippo quickly relayed the information to his boss.

Giacano stood as his face grew red. He tore the phone from Filippo's hand. "If you can't help him, kill him. Griffin never reaches your jail, is that understood?"

"Understood, sir."

"I'm sick and tired of this whole fucking mess. Clean it up, do you hear me? Clean it all up, now!"

"It will only take a day or two. There will be no loose ends, I give you my word."

"You will be rewarded generously if you can take care of this situation without any further jeopardy to my efforts down there. Do I make myself clear, my friend?"

"Perfectly clear. You can count on me."

Giacano laid the receiver down. He looked sternly at his oldest friend. "When our cop who wants to retire early completes his work, Michael, I think he should retire. Take him someplace eternally quiet. And do it yourself, Michael. I'm through with amateurs."

Filippo grinned. "It will be my pleasure, Mario."

TWENTY-SIX

Lieutenant Mike Castle had been with the tactical support group of the Nashville Metro special weapons and tactics (SWAT) team for eight years, its commander for the last two. He was as tough a cop as Jordan had ever known; fearless, relentless, highly skilled. Castle typified the best in law enforcement.

His only failing—though few of his peers would have referred to it in such a disparaging manner—was that he hated the rules. Not the ones that protected citizens from losers and low-lifes (as he chose to call them), but the ones that let these same dregs of society go free after committing heinous crimes, merely because of some ACLU-sanctioned technicality.

His feelings were defiantly strong on the subject, though he rarely spoke out. He and his confederates knew that their private agendas would be served better in silence.

Castle was a man of action—a jackboot Jordan would say—because he would rather put his size-thirteen, steel-toed jungle boot through a door and shoot it out than have to sit idly by while some mealy-mouthed assistant DA negotiated away an opportunity to rid society of its trash.

It was for this reason that Taylor had ordered Mike Castle to take the point when he went after Joey Ray Griffin.

❖

The man Castle had assigned the task of ground reconnaissance came sprinting back toward the mobile communication unit, a heavily modified, mid-size Winnebago filled with Pentium-powered PCs, elaborate radio and phone communications, daylight and low-light cameras, videotape machines and monitors, and a host of other technical support equipment.

"Nothing, sir." The man was barely breathing hard, despite having sprinted two hundred yards in body armor and fatigues while carrying an M-16 rifle with sniper scope. Training was everything. "The perimeter is void of any personnel, including the suspect. The vehicle we were alerted to is parked on the north side of the suspect's trailer. It appears to be empty, skipper."

"In back?" Castle questioned.

"Nothing. Not a sign of the suspect."

"Very good, Conners. Heads up men." Castle knelt in the dirt road at the door of the MCU and pulled a dull-finished combat knife from his boot sheath. His four squads of three men, along with Taylor, Vanover, and Stark formed a tight circle around him.

The SWAT commander scratched a rough sketch of the trailer, truck, incoming road, and surrounding tree cover in the loose soil. He stuck the tip of the knife in the ground, moving it from point to point in the drawing as he spoke. The main entrance to the trailer was—following standard operational procedure—designated as side one; the left end (facing the structure) as side two; the rear, three; and the right end, side four. After a careful study of the target, Castle had decided that he would deploy his men for a High/Low entrance of the main door which was centered on side-one of the suspect's trailer (during a High/Low entrance, one man of the two-man entry team takes the high position to maintain point and cover, while the other man stays low and performs the primary search. This method produces the least likelihood of cross-fire injury, while maintaining a high degree of aggression). "Sorowoski, your team covers side one; Conners—two; Merle—three; Blackstone—four. One man advances, two spot and cover. As soon as the advance men reach the inner perimeter, I want sound readings at two and four. Once the entry team penetrates, no one is to fire his weapon into the structure—is that clear?"

"Clear, skipper." The response was collective.

Castle looked at Taylor for a second before continuing. Jordan gave a brief nod for him to proceed. "We are Code-Yellow, men. If anything, I repeat—anything, presents itself as a threat to any member of the group, neutralize it with extreme prejudice. You've all been briefed on the suspect. You know what he looks like and you know his history. It is our belief that the suspect will not surrender without a fight. I want him alive, boys, if possible, but not at the expense of any member of this group. Be sharp—let's all go home tonight." Castle made eye contact with every squad member before he continued. "Take your positions and wait for my signal."

He and the three detectives took their positions in the MCU. A small video camera with a telephoto lens had previously been set up at the edge of the woods between their position and the trailer, providing a full view of the near perimeter. Castle and Taylor stood at the console, Vanover and Stark behind them.

Castle checked with the SWAT team helicopter for a final report before deploying his men. The McDonnell-Douglas 500E twin-seat chopper held two men: the pilot, Anderson—a lieutenant with Metro, but not a SWAT officer; and Goldman, one of Castle's team serving as spotting officer. Goldman was also a sharpshooter, a bolt and scope man, as they were referred to in SWAT.

The chopper pilot, hovering six hundred feet above Griffin's trailer, answered Castle's call. "Nothing, TACT-1. Not a sign of movement. I'll let you know the second anything changes."

"We'll move in two minutes, chopper, that's two-zero, do you copy?"

"Two-zero minutes, that's affirmative, TACT-1."

"Keep an eye on the highway but stay as low as you can. I don't want that son-of-a-bitch being spooked by you if he shows."

"Roger that, TACT-1."

Castle eyed his quick-list again: though he'd done this same exercise a hundred times, he never assumed anything. The only item not checked off was having the telephone company kill Griffin's phone. He'd once had a well-meaning neighbor alert a suspect to the SWAT team's presence outside the suspect's home, thinking them to be burglars. It resulted in the unnecessary death of one of his men. He now put a check mark by the item—he had personally verified that it had been taken care of just prior to leaving the highway—and silently reprimanded himself for having not marked it off at that time. Fully ready, he looked to Taylor for word to send in his men.

Jordan took an anxious breath. "Let's do it."

Castle grabbed the mike and spoke deliberately into it. He called to each squad leader: "Merle—"

"Ready, skipper."

"Conners—"

"Ready."

"Sorowoski—"

"Ready."

"Blackstone—"

"Ready, skipper."

"Send 'em in" came the command.

From each side of the trailer, one man snaked his way toward his appointed corner of the structure, while the second man in each team kept the scope of his M-16 trained on a previously assigned window or door. The spotters maintained a wider field of view of the structure and near perimeter with binoculars.

Under a Code Yellow, they had been given authority to neutralize any threat that might present itself. All understood. None would hesitate.

It took only forty seconds for the advance men to reach the trailer. Conners' man stood quickly and attached the suction cup of a highly sensitive microphone to one of the glass windowpanes—it was repeated at the opposite end of the structure in unison. He dropped back to a crouched position and placed the earpiece in his left ear. He could clearly hear the sound of a faucet dripping regularly and the steady ticking of a clock, but nothing else. He looked fifteen feet to his right and signaled to Sorowoski's man that the suspect did not appear to be inside. This was then relayed to the rest of the advance team.

When a second man from Blackstone's group reached the trailer, it was time to force an entry. Only two men would enter the front door—Stone and Martini, with Denton smashing the door if it was locked. The remaining men at the near perimeter were to create diversions by breaking windows on sides two and four an instant before the entry team made its move.

Martini crept up the unpainted wooden steps which led to the front door. He stayed low, reached above his head and gently tried the knob. It turned slightly each direction, but did not open. He signaled this silently to the other two men with him. Denton moved carefully up the steps carrying a short-handled sledgehammer. He stood beside the door, his back to the trailer. Adrenaline flowed through each man's veins like a powerful drug, tightening muscles and electrifying nerves.

Martini took a firm grip on his weapon and held up three fingers, holding them until the men at sides two and four nodded their understanding. He counted down silently, using his fingers.

When the last finger dropped, each man moved. In an explosion of fractured glass and battered aluminum—made all the more intense and startling by the screams and shouts of five armed men—the entry team burst through the thin trailer door and onto Griffin's livingroom floor. Their weapons searched skillfully for any sign of a threat.

Nothing!

The trailer was deserted, though from the partially melted cubes of ice still floating in a pale glass of Coke on the kitchen counter, it was apparent that someone had been there as recently as an hour ago.

When each room had been checked and cleared, Martini called the MCU and announced an all-clear. Castle and the three detectives left to join the group.

"Suspect's not here, skipper," Martini stated when Castle arrived. "Looks like he *was* here a little while ago. What next?"

Castle took a piece of gum from his shirt pocket and stuck it between his teeth. The rest of the advance team gathered at the front of the trailer.

Jordan spoke: "Mike, have your men search the perimeter for anything in view that might tie Griffin to Stanton's murder or violate his parole. My men will cover the inside." Vanover and Stark took the cue and headed for the trailer. "Can you have someone open his truck, Mike? I'd like to get a look inside it as well."

"You got a warrant for all this, Chief?" Castle asked casually. "I'm just curious."

"Yeah. It's called exigent circumstances."

Castle grinned. He knew declaring exigent circumstances would allow them a great deal of freedom to search areas that would normally be off limits without a warrant. He liked Taylor's style. "My kind of warrant, Chief."

Castle pointed at one of his men and waved him over. "Turn my van around and put it near the highway, McGowan. Leave the keys in it. Be sure it can't be seen from the highway."

"You got it," McGowan snapped. He ran across the field and disappeared into the woods that lay between the trailer and their vehicles.

"What are you doing, Mike?" Jordan asked.

"Getting ready, sir. If Griffin shows up now, he'll be spooked sure. I want to be ready to move on him immediately if need be."

Jordan nodded. "Have your man put my car behind yours as well, will you?"

"Consider it done."

❖

"Hey, darlin'," Joeyboy said in his most pleasant tone. He could spot a runaway across a crowded bar even when he was too drunk to stand. He knew as soon as he saw her that the pretty, thin, frightened young girl sitting by herself in the corner booth was a virgin—to the road anyway. He sat opposite her.

The girl slid her small bag from the table and put it protectively on the bench beside her. "Hi," she offered meekly. He was not the first man to come on to her, though he was the closest to her age. And the most attractive.

"How long you been gone from home?" Joeyboy asked.

"What do you mean?" she answered defensively. Maybe the biker was actually a cop. She studied him closer.

"Hey, relax, baby, I ain't no five-oh," he assured her, reading her mind. The girl smiled. She liked his dark eyes. "Name's Joey."

"Mine's Bridget. Nice to meet you."

"Yeah, same here."

"Three weeks."

"What?"

"I've been gone for three weeks. How'd you know I'd run away from home?"

"Hey, I'm a sensitive kind of guy, Bridget. I could tell you needed a friend. I hope you don't mind me coming over."

"No, that's okay. It was getting kinda lonely sitting here by myself." She thought about the ninety-three cents she had in her bag as her stomach began to growl again. She hadn't eaten since yesterday morning when an old geezer at the Greyhound bus terminal in Crossville had bought her breakfast in exchange for a hand job.

"You hungry?" Joeyboy asked. Her face spoke volumes about her short life on the road. "They got great bar-b-que here. I was about to eat and I hate to eat alone."

"What about your friend?" she asked, pointing toward Slammer.

"Oh, him? He likes to eat alone. He's harmless, though."

She looked at the horrid tattoo that appeared to be devouring his head and questioned Joeyboy's last statement. She was too hungry to care about his taste in friends. "I don't have any money left."

"Did I say anything about money, Bridget? I told you I was a sensitive guy. I knew you were broke when I asked you if you wanted to eat. You want the jumbo pork plate? It comes with beans, slaw, fries, and a drink. That's what I'm havin'."

"Sure, if it's not too much to ask."

"Hey, that's what friends are for. We road people have got to stick together, know what I mean?"

"You're sweet, Joey. How can I thank you?"

He put his hand on hers. "No need. Just enjoy your meal."

❖

A general search of the area continued for nearly fifteen minutes. Castle had four of his men positioned at the outer perimeter, fifty yards from the sides of the trailer. He knew Griffin could show at any time and did not intend to be surprised by him.

As he and Jordan looked through the Dodge Ram for evidence, one of his men came running toward the truck. "Found this under the trailer, skipper. It was stuffed in a hole in the ground, almost completely buried. Damn near didn't see it." He set a heavy canvas duffel bag at the commander's feet. From the objects jutting against the ends of the material, it appeared to be filled with tools of some kind. The bag was zipped shut.

Jordan came around to Castle's side of the truck. "During the videotape I saw earlier, the psychic mentioned Joeyboy having a long bag with a zipper. She said he put the shotgun and digging tools in it after he killed Stanton and buried her body." He knelt at the bag and examined the zipper. It would be so easy to just open it and look inside, but he knew doing so would surely get any evidence he found within it thrown out of court. Even exigent circumstances didn't permit rummaging through closed drawers or opening sealed bags. He'd have to wait for a full warrant to be issued by a judge. He felt the bag, trying to guess its contents.

"I sure wish I knew what was in that goddamn thing," he said, standing again.

Castle grinned broadly and kicked his boot squarely into the end of the bag, forcing the most prominent object through the material. It was the barrel of a sawed-off shotgun. "Your wish is my command, Chief."

Jordan gave Castle a stern look, followed by a smile he couldn't contain. He pointed a rigid index finger at him. "You and I need to have a talk about ethics one day, Mike."

He knelt again and studied the shotgun. "Would you say this baby is under the legal limit, Lieutenant?"

"Definitely, sir."

"And, as such, does it not constitute a felony for the possessor of same, as well as representing a major parole violation?"

"That it does, sir."

"Then, as I see it, we have the absolute legal right to seize this fully visible and highly illegal weapon, the bag, and all of its contents."

"That we do, sir." Castle was enjoying this immensely.

Jordan unzipped the bag and peered inside. "Hey, Mike, take a look at this."

Castle knelt beside him.

"Does that look like blood to you?"

Castle stared closely at the folding shovel Jordan had indicated. The end was covered in dried dirt and a hardened, nearly black, residue that ran up the blade for several inches. "That'd be my guess, Chief. Barnie'd know for sure."

Jordan zipped it shut. "Mike, have your man put this bag in the trunk of my car, will you. I want nothing inside of it touched until the lab boys get a look at it."

"You got it." Castle gave McGowan a quick thumb gesture and the officer instantly disappeared toward the vehicles again, the duffel bag and its valuable contents tightly in his grip.

Jordan leaned against the truck and folded his arms. "Where do you suppose that son-of-a-bitch is, Mike?"

Mike put his boot on the middle step of the porch and rested his arms on his raised knee. "You got me, Chief. Maybe he's out—"

"TACT-1, TACT-1, we've got company!" It was the chopper. "Two bikers coming down 318 from the north."

"They spot you yet?" Castle called back on his handi-talky. Jordan gave a quick yell for his men in the trailer to exit at once and pull the fractured door behind them. From a distance, at least, it would appear to be intact.

"Don't think so, TACT-1. Those big Harleys are damn noisy. What do you want us to do?"

"Get on their blind side, chopper. Swing wide if you have to. How much time do we have?" He directed his own men back to the outer perimeter with a series of well-rehearsed hand gestures and then darted for the mobile communications unit.

"A minute, maybe ninety seconds—hold on, TACT-1, we may have a problem." Goldman had just spotted through his powerful binoculars the presence of an unexpected passenger on one of the bikes.

"What kind of problem, chopper? Talk to me!" He and the three detectives reached the MCU and leaped through the door.

Jordan anxiously studied the trailer on the video monitor. From their point of view, it appeared undisturbed. It should not spook the bikers until they were practically upon it. By then, Castle's men would be able to spring their trap.

The chopper radioed back: "TACT-1, there's a woman on the back of one of the bikes. I can't tell how old she is, but it's definitely a woman. She's riding with the man fitting the suspect's description."

"Goddammit!" Castle shrieked. "This screws everything!" He addressed his squad leaders. "Merle, Conners, Sorowoski, Blackstone—you guys copy the chopper's last send?"

"Loud and clear, skipper. How do you want to play it?" Blackstone asked.

Castle looked to Jordan. "This is real trouble, sir. We can't do a thing without risking a hostage situation, and knowing Griffin, he'll use the woman for cover the second he spots the first cop."

"Son of a bitch!" Jordan's mind raced, groping for a solution to the unexpected turn of events.

❖

Joeyboy and Slammer negotiated the last lazy curve on Highway 318 before turning onto the dirt road that led to the trailer they shared. They rode side by side, as they had done for countless miles. Their bellies were full of bar-b-que and beer, their Harley-Davidsons thunderously loud, and their minds preoccupied with the thought of sharing the young runaway they had picked up at the roadside diner.

Perhaps it was Joeyboy's natural inclination to paranoia, or a peripheral glimpse of the chopper between the trees lining the highway that first alerted him, but whatever it was, he buried the brakes on his bike just short of the drive and stared wildly in the direction of his trailer.

Slammer stopped sixty feet ahead. "Hey, man, are you crazy? What the fuck are you doing?"

Joeyboy held up a single hand to silence his friend. He continued to stare down the drive but saw nothing. Instinctively, he pressed the kill button on his bike, and swiped his finger under his neck, indicating for his buddy to follow suit. As soon as the deserted highway became silent, the unmistakable beat of the helicopter's thump-thump-thump screamed in their ears. "Get the fuck out of here!" he shouted instantly at Slammer.

They restarted their bikes and roared south on 318, Bridget now frantically clutching Joeyboy's waist with all her strength; her fun-filled afternoon of drugs and sex was about to turn into something she could never have imagined.

"They made us, TACT-1!" the pilot shouted into his mike.

"Stay with him, chopper!" Castle bellowed. "If you lose that son-of-a-bitch, I'll shoot you down myself!" He jumped to his feet and pointed a rigid finger at Jordan. "You coming with me?"

"You bet your ass!"

Castle was already halfway to his van by the time Jordan had yelled for his two detectives to follow in his car.

"Go!" Jordan shouted as he dove into the passenger seat.

Castle threw the Plymouth Voyager into Drive and nailed the throttle. Within ten seconds, he was squealing his tires on the asphalt of 318, barreling south on the trail of the two bikes. "How do you feel about high-speed pursuits, Chief?" Castle asked tensely as his vehicle neared an even 100 mph. He fastened his harness.

"To tell you the truth, Mike, they scare the crap out of me." Jordan grabbed the handle above the door with his right hand and gripped the center console firmly with his left. His own shoulder harness and seat belt had been on since the van first touched pavement.

"Me, too, buddy," Castle replied. "Me, too." He pointed at the radio.

Jordan understood and switched the police radio in the truck to channel nine, the operations channel. "Chopper, this is Taylor. Do you still have our suspect in sight?"

"That's affirmative, TACT-1. We can see your vehicle as well. You're about a half mile behind them at this point. Goldman says there's no way for them to head but south on 318 for the next few minutes."

"Can you see our second car, chopper?"

"Negative, sir. They must be a mile or more back, probably hidden by the tree cover. Be careful, TACT-1, you've got a hard right, followed by a hard left coming up in about twenty seconds."

Castle heard the warning as well, though he kept his foot harder in it than Jordan would have if he'd been driving.

Both men braced for the first turn.

As they raced frantically, only seconds ahead of the law, Joeyboy and Slammer had forgotten all the pleasures of life. Their only thought now was survival: that pure, instinctive need to live one more hour, one more minute, one more second. They would do whatever was necessary to guarantee it.

The young girl who clung to life by two chrome foot pegs and sixty square inches of black seat vinyl, pleaded tearfully in Joeyboy's ear, "Let me off, please. I want to go home!"

"Shut the fuck up, you little whore!" Joeyboy screamed, braking for the turn.

Despite his normally expert ability on any motorcycle, Griffin nearly lost it in the first curve, his rear tire coming dangerously close to the shoulder. Slammer, riding alone, had a much easier time of it, taking the curve with room to spare and gaining a considerable lead on Joeyboy's more heavily loaded bike. Joeyboy saw the blind left rapidly approaching and suddenly had a plan to buy him some badly needed time. As he leaned the bike into the curve, he savagely drove his left elbow into the girl's nose and left eye. She lost her fragile grip and slid backward, striking the pavement at nearly 80 mph, her body a pathetic rag doll, rolling, tumbling, sliding on the abrasive blacktop.

Joeyboy completed the left and grinned triumphantly when he glanced back and saw her come to a stop in the apex of the curve, her form sprawled lifelessly across the center line. "Perfect!" he yelled, his fist raised in celebration.

Highway 318 was a well-kept two-lane farm access road cut into the rolling Tennessee hills. On the east side of the road—in the stretch south of Joeyboy's trailer—the bank was high and rose ten feet vertically from the shoulder. On the west, it rolled steeply down a natural bank for several hundred feet ending at a stream, its slope dotted with trees.

Castle slowed only slightly as he reached the first turn, determined to overtake the bikers.

The van's tires screamed on the pavement as he fought the curve. Jordan dropped the mike he was still holding to regain his grip on the dash. Neither men realized that the mike's Send key had gotten depressed when it lodged itself under the passenger seat, preventing all incoming communication.

Somehow, Castle made it through the curve without losing control, though for a moment, Jordan would have sworn they were going head first into the high bank. The pair took an anxious breath in unison as they entered a brief section of straight road.

Before they could enjoy it, the hard left turn appeared immediately ahead of them.

With the opposite tires now squalling at a high pitch, the van roared into the curve. Castle set an expert line that put the vehicle on as straight a course as possible through the arc.

Jordan spotted the girl's body at the same instant. "Mike!"

Castle jerked the wheel hard to the left, in a desperate attempt to avoid hitting her. A sickening thud nearly lifted the van from the road, sending them into the high bank. With ripping sheet metal and flying glass, the Voyager slammed into the rocky east shoulder. Jordan was thrown painfully against his harness; Castle's head brutally struck the driver's door pillar. The van then shot out of control perpendicularly across the highway—despite the brakes still locked by the weight of Castle's body, and the radial tires leaving four wide bands of black rubber on the pavement.

It left the highway going backward and came to rest against the base of a broad oak tree twenty feet down the west embankment.

Vanover and Stark had been alerted to the girl's body and had slowed immediately, but the chopper had not been able to get the primary pursuit vehicle to respond to its repeated warnings. The detectives approached the second curve with caution, in search of their fellow officers.

The scene that met their eyes was horrifying: in the dirt at the edge of the road lay a mangled snarl of torso and limbs, the bleeding and abraded remains of the innocent young runaway, her slender shape barely recognizable as human; shards of ragged bone jutted out through soft, pink tissue; the pavement was smeared with the familiar color of death.

They negotiated the turn carefully, not wishing to add to the carnage. "Over there, Pete!" Brad Stark pointed, as he spotted the distorted grill and hood of the Voyager, barely visible from the road. Vanover jammed their vehicle into Park and raced down the hill following Stark toward the twisted van.

Just then, Jordan stumbled from the passenger seat and out onto the grassy slope, losing his footing. Vanover grabbed him and braced him against the door. "Christ, Jordan, you all right!?" he asked, studying his friend's eyes.

"Yeah, Pete, I'm okay, I think. Give me your radio and go check on Castle."

Vanover handed Jordan his portable radio and joined Stark.

"Chopper!" Jordan shouted.

Anderson responded: " TACT-1—why didn't you respond to my transmission?"

"Just shut up and listen! The girl's dead. We have a Code Purple here—Castle's down. Does your spotter have his M-16 with him?"

"That's affirmative, TACT-1."

"Get ahead of the bikers! Find an open spot where they have to pass and put the SWAT officer as low as possible. I'm ordering you to take those son-of-a-bitches out! I repeat—you have a Code Green, you read me!"

"We copy loud and clear, sir—we have a Code Green. Will do." Goldman grabbed his rifle and checked his magazine—30 rounds high-velocity, .223 full-metal jacket. He chambered a round.

The pilot, Anderson, had already responded to Taylor's order.

"We'll join you as soon as we can, chopper," Jordan shouted. He tossed the radio back to Vanover. "How's Mike?"

"Hard to tell, Chief. It appears to be a concussion, maybe even a fractured skull. He's breathing okay, but he's out cold," Stark responded.

"Stay with him, Brad. Tell the rest of the SWAT team what happened—they should be here any minute—then call this mess in. Get an ambulance coming and don't use the radio, use your cell phone. I don't want a lot of goddamn reporters running around here until we get this cleaned up and nail this bastard!" Jordan studied the scene; he could feel the anger mounting within him.

"Don't you want me to come with you?" Stark asked quickly.

"Just take care of Mike—Pete, let's move!"

"Right behind you, Chief."

Anderson had managed to keep the two bikers in sight, despite almost losing them twice in the heavy tree cover. Goldman frantically studied the map and reassured himself that there was nowhere for the pair to leave the highway until after Hamilton Creek.

"That's it!" he yelled to the pilot. "We can stop them at the bridge! There'll be room to set down. Head south!"

The two Harleys blistered the pavement, their riders desperately trying to lose their pursuers. Joeyboy cursed violently under his breath. When he looked to the sky during a break in the trees, he was surprised to find the chopper nowhere in sight. He snapped his head to each side, and as far behind him as he could manage at his speed—nothing but blank sky. He grinned, certain the officers had turned back to help their fallen comrades.

He could not have been more wrong.

Goldman was as much a member of the SWAT team as any man on the ground—skilled, hardened, fiercely loyal to every other member of the unit. If Taylor had not sanctioned him to take out the two bikers who had just sacrificed a young girl, and who had tried to kill two of his fellow officers, he would likely have acted on his own and worried about the consequences at the hearing.

Absolution is easier to attain than permission, the unit often said.

Joeyboy and Slammer again hit the brakes on their bikes, coming to a noisy and unexpected stop at the top of the last rise before Hamilton Creek Bridge. Hovering at twenty feet, midway across the four-hundred-foot span of concrete, the helicopter looked like a giant wasp.

For a confused second, Joeyboy lowered his head and shook it slowly side to side. His world was upside-down, and he could do nothing about it.

"Joey!" Slammer shouted. "What the fuck are we gonna do?"

Griffin slowly looked up from his enraged silence and stared into the frightened, frenzied eyes of the only person he had ever called friend. He had just discovered that he was no longer armed—his .45 Colt automatic having fallen from his belt during the frantic attempt by the young girl to regain a hold as she fell from his bike. He said nothing.

"Goddammit, Joey, talk to me! What are we gonna do?"

After an agonizing moment, Griffin spoke—his understanding of the situation evident in his flat tone. "What are we going to do?" he repeated. "I believe we're gonna die, my friend."

They were not the words Slammer wanted to hear.

"I'll be goddamned if I'm going back to the joint—ever! I don't give a shit what you do, Joey, but if I'm gonna die, I'm taking a few of the motherfuckers with me!" Slammer pulled a Browning BDM 14-shot automatic from his belt and waved it in Griffin's face. "You never know, buddy boy—I might just get lucky. See you in hell."

Goldman watched through his open Plexiglas window as the biker kicked the massive Harley into gear and rolled the throttle back. The pair had been too far away for a sure shot from the hovering chopper, but now, with the bike heading full speed toward Goldman's position, it would only be a matter of seconds.

He took careful aim.

Slammer felt it the moment his tires hit the rain-grooved surface of the concrete bridge. He raised his automatic and let out an inhuman scream, firing wildly at the only remaining obstacle to his freedom.

Joeyboy quickly surveyed the terrain: the left shoulder still rose steeply at a right angle to the asphalt; the right shoulder had now become a sharp grade, falling sixty feet to a wide stream below. Densely packed trees lined both sides of the road.

There was only one chance.

He accelerated toward the chopper as soon as Slammer had covered half the distance to it. He was counting on the confusion of their exchange of gunfire to buy him a few precious seconds.

That's all he asked—all he figured he'd need.

He pointed the front wheel at a narrow gap between the bridge railing and the maze of trees at the edge of the road. The opening that existed was no wider than a door, perhaps less. He knew he had to hit it perfectly—or die.

As Slammer began spraying the chopper with bullets, neither officer gave Joeyboy a thought.

Goldman returned fire at once, sending a dozen well-placed rounds in the direction of their crazed assailant. Slammer was struck in the jaw, chest, abdomen and neck (they would later learn that a total of seven bullets had ripped through his body), shattering bones and destroying vital organs. He fell lifeless across his bike as it slammed into the concrete railing, fracturing the engine and fuel tank and showering flaming gas and hot oil across the width of the bridge.

The pilot had instinctively added evasive altitude as soon as the shooting began. Had he not done so, the chopper would have been engulfed in the blaze.

Amid the dense cloud of billowing black smoke, tossed and blown by the wash of the rotors, the officers searched for the remaining threat; their eyes scanned the bridge for any sign of the second biker, but there was nothing to be seen. They could not imagine what had happened to the other man. Anderson took the craft higher and studied the highway beyond the road. He could see for nearly a mile to the south and still there was nothing. Griffin could not have covered that much distance.

Taylor came to a skidding stop at the north end of the bridge, opposite the chopper. He leaped from his car and knelt behind the opened door, his weapon drawn and ready. Vanover assumed an identical stance at the passenger door. It took only a few seconds for them to determine that the shooting had ended—the situation at a standstill for the moment.

Jordan grabbed his radio. "Talk to me, chopper!" he shouted.

"One of the bikers is down, TACT- 1, but we lost the primary suspect during the confrontation! You must have passed him!" Anderson was thoroughly confounded at the disappearance of the second man and his bike.

"What the hell are you talking about, chopper—we didn't pass a damned thing!"

"Sir, we thought he must have turned back when the other biker made a run at us. One second he was there—the next, he was gone!"

"He must have gotten past you!" Jordan shouted.

"Not a chance, TACT-1!"

Jordan looked at Vanover, but the other detective just shrugged his shoulders. "You have enough room to set that thing down on the bridge?" Jordan asked.

"That's affirmative, TACT-1."

"Then set the son-of-a-bitch down and have Goldman start checking from that end of the bridge. We'll take this end. I don't know how he did it, but somehow he made it into the water."

Jordan turned to Vanover, his eyes angry and narrow. "I want this bastard, Pete. I don't care if he's fish bait or trying to swim his way to China, I want him! There's nothing, I mean nothing, more important than finding this scumbag!" His voice lowered. "There's more at stake here than you could possibly know."

Vanover did not understand all of his chief's words, but his intent was unmistakable. He nodded silently.

Jordan stared over the railing into the thick, brown soup flowing beneath them. He spoke to the water: "If he happens to resist arrest when you find him, Pete . . . well . . . that'll just save a lot of courtroom time, won't it?"

TWENTY-SEVEN

Brandie Mueller was touching up her hair in the ladies' restroom near the canteen when Steve Dacus burst through the door. "He's on the phone, Brandie! He wants to speak to you—now!" She threw her brush in her purse, grabbed the jacket to her suit and was less than two steps behind the news director as he sprinted toward her office.

She punched the speaker phone. "This is Brandie," she answered out of breath. Dacus stood by her side at her desk.

"Run your story, Brandie, and get a film crew out to the Hamilton Creek Bridge on old Highway 318. I've already told the men to let one of your Jeeps through." Dacus leaned into the newsroom and shouted for Tim Arnold.

"What's out there?" she asked quickly.

"One hell of a mess. Should be right up your alley."

"And Griffin—you have him in custody?"

Jordan took a short breath and blew it out in angered frustration. "Not exactly."

"What the hell does *that* mean, Taylor?"

"It means we've linked Griffin to the murder of Donna Stanton, just like Kas—Ms. Riteman—said, but for now . . . well . . . let's just say he's still at large. I might add he's presumed dead, though we have no way of confirming that for the moment."

"When will you be able to confirm it, Chief Taylor?" She jotted on her scratch pad.

"Soon, Brandie, I hope. That's all I can say at this time. Is Ms. Riteman still with you?"

"No. She left here more than an hour ago. I believe she was heading back to her apartment. Why?" Brandie could sense the connection between Kasey and him.

"I think she deserves to be warned about Griffin's escape, that's all."

"I thought he was presumed dead!"

"He *is*, dammit! But I'd rather be safe than sorry, wouldn't you? If he is still out there somewhere, he's going to be less than thrilled when he learns it was Kasey who pointed a finger at him."

For once, the reporter agreed with the cop. "Do you have her new phone number?"

"I've already tried it several times."

"But you left a message, right?"

"Would you want that kind of message on *your* goddamn answering machine?" he asked sarcastically.

"I see what you mean. Do you want me to try to reach her?" she asked.

"I'll take care of it, Brandie. I'm the one who let him get away. I suggest you get a crew out to 318—we won't be able to keep the lid on this mess for long. I'll drop by Ms. Riteman's apartment on my way back in. She'll be safe enough for a while yet."

Brandie punched off the speaker phone and ran Taylor's words back through her mind. She grinned at the lewd thoughts that formed, and then tempered them with the sobering image of Joeyboy coming for Kasey. She dismissed both for the moment and grabbed her note pad. "Tim," she shouted across the newsroom, "don't even think of leaving without me!"

❖

Kasey stepped from the elevator and turned down the hall, toward her apartment. She had been by Brenda's to pick up Sam, as agreed, but had received no answer to her repeated knocking, despite finding Brenda's car in the driveway of the duplex. She was annoyed at not being able to get Sam after having not seen him for two days, but also sorry she had not been able to fill Brenda in on the events of the morning.

Like a catchy tune, she kept running Brenda's words about her new boyfriend over in her mind. *Did she mention that his name was Ray?* Her heart stopped at the thought. *Quit it, Kasey. You've just got that bastard's name stuck in your brain, that's all.* She tried to dismiss the unsettling feeling before it could get a grip on her frayed emotions.

Kasey placed her key in the deadbolt; as soon as she stepped through the door, she knew something was different. She instinctively left the door ajar—an escape route—and moved cautiously to the center of the living room, trying to determine the cause of her uneasiness. There: a sound, something that hadn't been there before she left for Channel 9. She moved reluctantly toward its origin.

When she rounded the corner of the dining room leading into the kitchen, she froze, startled by the sight. "Sam!" she shouted as the cat jumped into her arms. "How did you get here?"

As soon as she set her keys on the counter and began to stroke Sam's head, the phone rang. "Hello," she said, cradling the phone between her shoulder and ear so she could cuddle Sam with both hands.

"Kasey, where the hell have you been!?"

"I'm sorry, Jordan, I just walked in. I went by Brenda's, but she wasn't there. I filled my tank and then came straight home. What's going on?" His tone concerned her. She knew Joeyboy was at the root of it.

Jordan lowered his voice. "No, I'm the one who should be sorry, Kasey. I've been trying to reach you for the last hour, and I got a little frustrated. I apologize for my tone."

"Don't be silly." There was more in his voice than mere frustration at not finding her home. "What is it, Jordan?"

"How would you like to go out of town with me for a couple of days?" he asked in his most up-tempo voice.

Kasey dropped into one of the dining-room chairs. "Jordan, tell me what's wrong."

"Nothing's wrong. I just thought you might like to spend a couple of days alone with me. You know, get away somewhere secluded, someplace where no one can find us. We'll make love all night, sleep all day. How about it?"

"It would sound heavenly except for two things: you're hiding something from me . . . and . . . you've got a wife, remember?"

"Let's get this straight once and for all: Gloria has been staying with one of her old friends across town for the last three months, and Amber, who normally spends half the time with me, is spending this week with her mother. That leaves me on my own for at least four days."

"What if your wife calls and you're not there?" Kasey asked quickly, thinking like a woman.

"Gloria never calls. She didn't call when we lived in the same house, why the hell would she start now?"

Kasey felt sorry for the man she knew deserved better. There was something else, though, something more pressing. Her hand went to her heart. "But you've got bad news about Joeyboy, don't you? That's why you want me out of town."

Jordan cussed under his breath. He should have known it wouldn't be that easy. "Listen, Kasey—"

"Oh, my God! That's it, isn't it!? I knew this would happen!" The horrid picture of Donna Stanton's face at the moment it exploded was painted on every wall, turning the rooms into an abattoir in hell. She raced to the door and slammed it noisily. She spun the deadbolt.

"Kasey! Listen to me! Griffin is not going to hurt you!"

"What . . . ?" She barely heard his words as she backed away from the door. The walls dripped blood, her blood, and the carpet seemed to be soaked with it.

"I said, Griffin is never going to hurt you. He's not going to hurt anyone again. I'll be there in a little while and explain everything to you."

"Is he dead, Jordan? Just, please, tell me he's dead." She sank into the couch, her legs tucked beneath her body, her eyes locked on the door.

"I'll be there soon, I promise. I'll tell you all about it. You're safe, I swear."

"Can't you come now?" she pleaded softly.

"Not yet. There is something I have to take care of first. Trust me, I'll be there before you know it. We'll get away for a couple of days. Everything will be fine."

"Hurry, Jordan, please."

❖

The unmarked car rolled to a slow stop near the old tin building, its tires growling against the gravel of the drive.

After the driver switched off the ignition, he reached into his left coat pocket and felt the silencer that matched the .32 automatic in his right pocket. The pair had once been the property of a slain drug pusher—property that he had made sure never appeared on the victim's crime-scene inventory report.

For a moment as he sat there, he considered the one annoying loose end that would remain after he had finished here, and the best way to go about eliminating it. Unlike Joeyboy, Kasey Riteman was not an unwanted piece of human debris that could simply be discarded without fear of reprisal.

The cop knew that while few in authority would notice or care about a biker ex-con's violent death—beyond the onerous obligatory paperwork—he couldn't just walk up to the current sweetheart of the celebrity interview and put a bullet in her brain without someone, like Brandie Mueller, wanting to know who and why.

Those were two questions he didn't want answered.

Nor did Mario Giacano.

The best way to ensure that was to guarantee they never got asked in the first place. The solution hit him with childish simplicity, producing a grin of appreciation for his personal stroke of genius. He returned his mind to the moment. There was still plenty of work to be done before he could take some long-overdue time off.

The cop stepped from the driver's seat and closed the door deliberately. He straightened his tie in the side window reflection and stuck his hands casually in his jacket pockets. He had nothing to fear at this place.

Wet, hurting, and furious to the point of insanity, Joeyboy watched as the man walked toward the door. He stepped back into the shadow of the old air compressor and clutched a short-barreled .357 Magnum in his left hand. His right arm was injured and of little use. Over his right eye, a nasty gash refused to stop bleeding. He spat a half-spent cigarette to the floor and crushed it out with his boot, still oozing muddy water from its sole. In less than two hours, he was into the second pack of cigarettes he had left in the welding shop the day he finished stripping Donna Stanton's Caddy. He rolled back the hammer of the revolver with his thumb and waited silently for the man to enter the darkened building.

"Griffin!" the cop called out as his eyes fought to adjust to the sudden absence of light. He stepped in and scanned the splinters of sunlight that carved irregular shapes across the floor and work benches. He spotted the half-covered remains of the Seville, though it would not have been recognizable even to its owner had she been there to see it.

Again he called out.

The answer came in a form he had not expected.

Joeyboy stuck the barrel of the old pistol to the cop's head and pulled the trigger. The hammer dropped with an unmistakable slap as the officer simultaneously clenched his eyes tightly shut.

There was no explosion, no bullet scrambling his brain at eighteen hundred feet per second. The cop almost pissed himself.

"The next one ain't empty," Joeyboy said hatefully. "What the fuck is going on? You gave me your word none of your guys would come near me. I got half a mind to waste your lying ass right here, right now. Give me one reason why I don't."

The officer turned slowly, his hands still in his jacket pockets. "I didn't have shit to do with this thing, so just relax. You need me, now more than ever."

"Yeah, well, somebody's gonna pay in blood for this shit, man."

He was surprised at how bad Griffin looked. "That was some vanishing act you pulled, Joeyboy. Half the force is out looking for you, dragging the river. Hell, they even got the dogs out."

"I got lucky, man, but then I always get lucky when it counts. I'm charmed, don't you know that by now?" He tucked the pistol under his injured arm and grabbed a fresh cigarette. He took a wooden match from behind his ear and snapped a flame with his thumbnail. His eyes were narrow slits in the flickering orange glow. "Who the fuck burned me, man? It was that Riteman bitch, wasn't it?"

"Yep, the psychic," he confirmed.

"Psychic, my ass, you dumb bastards. She was there that night. Must have been hiding in the bushes or something."

"Bullshit."

"No shit. I found a piece of her car near the scene. Had me fucked up for a while with that new yellow Mustang of hers, but her girlfriend put the pieces together for me."

"Her girlfriend?"

"Late girlfriend, I should say."

The cop was glad he didn't have to take care of that loose end as well.

"That lousy fucking bitch!" Joeyboy erupted, remembering his lost money and possessions now in the hands of the police. "I'll rip her heart out and show it to her before she dies!" He took a long drag and blew it out angrily. "That no good bitch!" he repeated.

"Don't worry about Riteman," the cop stated flatly. "She'll be taken care of shortly. Right now, you need to get a thousand miles away from here. The big man sent you some traveling money."

Joeyboy put his hand on his pistol as the cop reached for his inside coat pocket. He held his jacket open so the other man could see that he was not armed.

"Easy, now, my gun's out in the car. Don't be so jumpy. Like I said, I'm the only friend you've got." He withdrew a manila envelope, folded twice.

Griffin continued to grip the butt of the pistol under his arm for a moment, but relaxed his hold and left it where he had tucked it. He reached out his hand.

As Joeyboy took the envelope, the cop stuck his hand into his right outside pocket and withdrew the palm-size .32 automatic, instantly firing twice in the biker's direction.

Joeyboy had predicted the traitorous move and turned to his side as the shots echoed ominously within the tin building. He managed to send one round of his own toward his assailant before crashing backward into the old compressor.

As his body dropped hard against the filthy concrete floor, he could see Giacano's man staggering toward the door.

TWENTY-EIGHT

It was dark by the time Jordan reached Kasey's floor. As he put his hand on the doorknob, he took a deep breath. It produced a wave of pain in his chest and he instinctively placed his hand against his left side, grimacing as he did. The pain had been growing steadily worse since the adrenaline rush of the high-speed pursuit had subsided a couple of hours earlier. He took several more short breaths, trying not to expand his chest too much, and knocked softly on the door. He saw the peep-hole go dark and then light again.

"Oh, Jordan, I'm so glad you're here!" Kasey threw her arms around his waist and hugged him tightly. He let out a faint groan of pain and attempted to hug her back. Kasey noticed nothing but his welcome presence. "What's going on, Jordan?" she asked fearfully.

Jordan put his arm around her shoulder and closed the door behind them. He threw the deadbolt latch and kissed her softly on the lips. "It's okay, Kasey. Everything's fine. Do you have any of that Merlot left from last night?"

"Sure. I'll get us a glass." He followed her to the kitchen.

As Kasey poured each of them a glass of wine, she tried to read his face. There was something going on beneath the reassuring exterior, though she couldn't tell what it was. "You went after Joeyboy, didn't you?"

"Yes." He leaned against the countertop and tried to appear relaxed. "We got his current address from his parole officer and went in with the SWAT team."

"And you caught him, right? Tell me you caught him." She stood in front of him, erect and anxious.

Jordan took a long, ragged breath. His eyes betrayed the growing pain in his chest.

"What's wrong? Are you hurt?" Kasey lovingly put her hand to his chest in a gesture of affection and support, not expecting the anguished expression it brought. She jerked her hand away. "My God, Jordan, what is it!?"

"You're gonna see it all on the news in an hour anyway, so I might as well tell you. We didn't exactly catch Joeyboy. There was—"

"What the hell do you mean, 'not exactly,' Jordan? Did you, or did you not get the son-of-a-bitch?"

"Calm down, Kasey, and listen to me for a minute—please."

She backed against the counter opposite him, her hands shaking. "I'm sorry."

"It's okay. We surrounded his trailer, but he spotted our helicopter before we could grab him. He was riding with another biker and a . . ." He hesitated when the images of what had happened flooded his mind.

"And a what?" she asked quickly.

He knew it would be on the news in living color whether he said anything or not. He chose his words carefully. "Griffin had a young woman on the back of his bike."

Kasey's hand went to her mouth. "Don't tell me the girl is . . ."

Jordan nodded solemnly.

"Oh, God. How?" she asked in a whisper.

"The bikers ran when they saw us. We only intended to block their exit so we could arrest Griffin. We never meant for her to get hurt."

Kasey's eyes commanded him to continue.

Jordan recounted the events of the afternoon, being as nonspecific about the young girl's death as possible. His chest hurt terribly as he spoke. "After our van crashed, I had to wait until Pete and Brad caught up with us. By the time we got to the bridge at Hamilton Creek, Griffin's running buddy was dead and Griffin and his bike were in the water."

"Did you find his body?" Kasey asked without hesitation.

Jordan understood her fear, but knew he had no good answers for her. "No . . . we didn't."

It was her turn to take a deep breath. "Then you don't know for sure that he's dead, do you?"

"He's dead, Kasey. He has to be. He hit the water at a hundred and fifty feet a second. No human being can live through that."

Kasey's eyes became cold, uncompromising. "He's not a human being! Never include that bastard with the rest of us who care about love and feelings, do you hear me!? He has no understanding of any of those things, and I hope it took him an hour to drown! I hope he was pinned only an inch beneath the surface, able to see the sun, to almost feel the air against his skin, and not be able to do a goddamn thing about it but suffer and drown!" Jordan held his arms apart for her to come to him. She allowed him to hold her gently. "Are you sure he's gone for good? Don't tell me what you think I want to hear, tell me the absolute truth. Are you sure, Jordan?"

"As sure as I am that I'm here with you now. Do you think I'd let anything happen to you?"

Kasey felt his warmth against her body—felt his strength, heard his loving words. She shuddered at the thought of the most evil man she had ever known at last being gone from her life, gone from the world. She knew he would remain in her mind for years, as would Donna Stanton, but at least the threat to her life was over.

If the horror and torment of the last two weeks had left anything good in their wake, it was that she remembered that her life had once meant something to her. When her parents died, a part of her had died with them. The years alone had brought on growing cynicism and emotional isolation—the grief medicated with a volatile mélange of hard liquor and worthless men. Perhaps, with Joeyboy gone, that forgotten piece of her could be reborn.

She wrapped her arms around his waist again and returned his hug, only to receive the same agonizing reaction. "Were you hurt when your van wrecked?" she asked sympathetically.

"It would appear so," he said with a crooked smile. "The shoulder harness."

"Have you seen a doctor yet?"

"I was busy. I had too many things to do before I came here."

"Men! You're so damned macho that you'd all be dead if it weren't for women." He didn't argue with her. "Take off your jacket and shirt."

After leaving Hamilton Creek, Jordan had stopped by his home and had changed into jeans, a polo shirt, and a light windbreaker. He unzipped the jacket and tried to slip it off his shoulders. A bolt of pain shot through his chest doubling him over. Kasey helped him stand.

"Oh, Jesus, that hurts," he grimaced.

"Come with me. I'm going to have a look at that chest of yours." They moved toward the bedroom.

"No . . . I mean I'll be fine in a little while, Kasey. I've been hurt worse than this and still put in a full shift." Jordan sat on the edge of the bed. Kasey sat beside him.

"That's a bunch of bull! You need a doctor. You could have broken ribs."

"I do have some broken ribs. Four, I imagine. I poked around on them when I changed clothes at home."

"I'm driving you to the hospital. Get up." She stood and placed her hands defiantly on her hips.

Jordan fell back on her bed instead of doing as he was told. He held up his left hand and wiggled his index finger at her. When she moved to his side and knelt by the bed, he touched her face. "I'll be okay without a doctor. All he'll do is verify what I already know and wrap my chest with tape. I've done that so there's nothing left but to heal. Wouldn't you rather be lying beside me in this bed than sitting beside me in some crowded emergency room?"

"Let me see the tape."

"It's just tape. There's nothing to see."

"I'll decide that. Off with your shirt."

Jordan eased the shirttail from his jeans and pulled it high on his chest. "See—just tape."

Kasey saw something she hadn't expected from a shoulder harness injury. "You're bleeding," she said, instinctively touching the spot of bright red that tried to escape past the three layers of adhesive tape. "Why is it bleeding?"

"Bleeding?" He bent his head to check for himself. "Oh, that. I guess that's where my pen jabbed me when we hit the bank. I thought I had gotten that under control."

"You're going to the hospital, now."

"No, I'm not, Kasey. I'm staying right here with you. Got any surgical tape and gauze by any chance?"

"Yeah. I fell jogging a couple of weeks ago. Bought a first aid kit from the pharmacy. There's tape and gauze in it. I'll do it for you," she offered.

"I'll do it myself," he rebutted.

"Men," she huffed.

❖

When Jordan finished in the bathroom—refusing to allow Kasey to even watch—she tucked him lovingly in her bed and ordered him, under threat of further bodily injury, not to move an inch. He decided not to argue with her.

Kasey fixed a couple of grilled cheese sandwiches and some chicken soup for dinner, and then spoon-fed Jordan like an infant. His protesting had no apparent effect on her. He leaned back against the thick stack of pillows and allowed himself to be pampered.

"Full?" she asked as he finished the last spoonful of soup.

"Stuffed, thanks. I believe that was the best grilled cheese sandwich I've ever had."

Kasey playfully smacked him, remembering his comment at dinner last night. She set the dishes in the kitchen sink and strolled back to the bedroom, switching out lights as she went. When she reached the bedroom again, she had Sam in her arms. He had been hiding under the dining-room table, not at all pleased with the new furniture or surroundings.

"So, that's the infamous Sam-I-Am. Where's he been?"

"At my friend, Brenda's. I figured the move and all the stuff going on around here this weekend would be too traumatic for him. She must have dropped him off earlier this afternoon. He's still a little weirded out." She stroked his head softly and held him against her chest. "Funny she didn't leave me a note."

"I always wondered how you could tell that, I mean with a cat—how you could tell when they were acting weird."

"If you tell me you don't like cats, we're going to have a serious sleeping problem." She raised one eyebrow and stared defiantly at her bed guest as she kissed Sam softly on the top of his head.

"Oh, hell, yes, I like them. I absolutely love 'em! I've often thought about getting a couple of them myself." A sudden look of pain swept away his playful smile.

Kasey put Sam on the floor and quickly went to Jordan's side. "Is there anything I can do?"

He pulled her to him and kissed her warmly on the mouth. "There's only one thing that will get my mind off the pain." He gave her another full kiss and then began to play with the top button of her blouse. His face took on that little boy lost look that never failed to melt her heart.

"You up to it?" she asked.

"You'll have to be on top," he grinned.

"The top's my specialty." She stood and began to undress.

❖

"Good morning, good-looking," Kasey said, placing the bed tray across Jordan's body. She bent over him and gave him a warm kiss. She had risen at seven and made breakfast, anxious for them to be on their way out of town. She had dreamed about their two full days and nights together. It was the first time since the twenty-second of April that she had not had her night shattered by one of the nightmares from the orchard.

Jordan had been partially awake since she'd slipped from the bed a half hour earlier, though he was in less of a hurry than she to begin the new day. While making love to Kasey had taken his mind off his injury for nearly an hour, the rest of the night had been a mix of restless sleep and painful awakenings. Each time he would drift off to sleep, he would invariably roll to one side or the other and awaken in pain.

"Take these first," she said, handing him four Advil. He took the small brown tablets with a large gulp of orange juice. "Need me to feed you again?"

Jordan smiled. He raised himself slowly against the headboard and studied the feast: buttered toast, jelly, scrambled eggs with mushrooms and cheese, bacon strips, orange juice, and coffee. He took a small piece of bacon and crunched it. "This is some breakfast. You always cook like this when you have company?"

"I'll tell you a secret. I've never allowed a man spend the night in my home until you, not counting my ex-husband, of course. And, I never cook breakfast. I always wanted to . . . for a man, you know . . . but I never had a good enough reason until now." She took a sip of her coffee.

"Does that mean that I'm a good enough reason?"

"Does that look like Corn Flakes to you?"

"No it doesn't. Thanks."

"Eat," she scolded. "You're going to need your strength these next two days." Kasey dug into her own share of the breakfast. "You haven't told me where we're going, Jordan," she said excitedly.

"Where do you want to go?"

"Can I choose?"

"Anyplace we can get to and from in two days. With that caveat, it's your choice."

"I've never been to St. Louis. Do we have the time to go there?" She sat cross-legged on the bed, her short silk gown gathered between her thighs.

Jordan couldn't help admiring her body, her full breasts moving animatedly against the soft material. "St. Louis. Sure. We can be there in a couple of hours, in time to eat lunch on one of the river boats at the foot of the arch." He smiled warmly. "St. Louis is a great choice. You'll love it."

"Oh, I'm so excited, Jordan! Let's go now!" She jumped up and dropped her gown to the floor. With a wrinkle of her nose, she disappeared toward the bathroom.

❖

While Kasey showered, Jordan made a quick trip to his car in the underground parking lot of Belmont Place, returning promptly with the light travel bag he'd packed.

He shaved and brushed his teeth in the half-bath while Kasey fussed with her makeup and hair at her vanity. He had elected not to remove the bandage, which seemed at last to be providing some measure of relief. The bleeding had stopped.

When he had finished, he checked on Kasey's progress.

"Go like that," he insisted as she leaned naked across the vanity applying the last of her makeup. He kissed her on the back of the neck. "How much longer?"

"Five minutes," she smiled. "All I have to do is toss the rest of my stuff in the bag on my bed and throw on my clothes."

"What are you going to do with Sam?" The cat was curled in a tight ball in the middle of her pillow.

She looked around the edge of the door and grinned at her cat. "He'll be fine for forty-eight hours. Food, water, climate control, a king-size bed to sleep in. It's a rough life." She went back to her makeup.

"You need any help with your bag?" he asked.

"Nope. It's light."

"I'm going down then," he said. "I've got to check with Headquarters."

"You can call them from here if you like," she offered.

"They can tell where a call originates. I'd rather not give them anything to talk about if it's all the same." He kissed her neck again and patted her on the butt. "See you downstairs in five minutes?"

"Five minutes. Hey, Jordan," she called quickly as he headed down the hall, "we going in your car or mine?"

"We'll go in mine. It's new. My turn to show off. I'm parked on the top level, right next to you."

"I'll be right there," she smiled, grabbing her brush.

TWENTY-NINE

The elevator stopped at parking level B-1 and the brushed stainless steel doors parted obediently with a quiet metallic hiss. Kasey grabbed the bag she had set at her feet and scooted through the opening, stopping just outside the doors to remember where she'd parked her car last night. Her mind was filled with images of St. Louis, and it took her a moment to get her bearings. In the dozen occasions she'd had to park in her new surroundings, she had only been able to get the same space twice.

She studied the brightly lit but crowded concrete catacomb, with its low ceiling and block walls, and finally spotted the distinctive yellow bumper of her Mustang. It was almost obscured by a Toyota van. Jordan appeared at the rear of her car. It had been ten minutes.

"Come on, sweetheart. I thought you were in a hurry to leave," he called to her across the floor. He popped the trunk on his car and walked to her aid as quickly as he could without wincing. "Let me help you with that," he said as he reached her.

"Thanks," she smiled, wrapping her arm carefully around his waist. He put his free arm across her shoulders. As they walked, she studied his strong face and steel-blue eyes, and thought about what a handsome man he was, and how lucky she was to have met him. She had decided she would worry about any future they might have together some other time. For now, she was just going to enjoy her good fortune.

They reached the back of his car, parked between the van and her Mustang. He set her bag in the trunk next to his, wincing as it pulled on the sore muscles of his chest.

"You all right?" she asked as he stood.

"Couldn't be better. Ready?" He closed the trunk and led her toward her door.

It was then that she noticed it—a hellish shape from some recess of her memory. Her brain refused to believe what her eyes were showing it and yet there it was: the black Jaguar with the gleaming gold wheels. Her knees tried to collapse beneath her body. Her mind fought to clear away the fear and panic that had begun to rob her of the reason she so desperately needed at this moment.

330

Jordan grabbed the handle and opened her door. "How do you like it?" he asked proudly.

"What?" Kasey said in a garbled whisper.

"My new Jag. She's a beauty, isn't she?"

Kasey's eyes scouted the area quickly, hoping to spot someone—any-one—in the garage who might help her. At eight o'clock on Tuesday morning, when the rest of the world was at work, it was not to be.

They were alone. Frighteningly alone.

She felt her body involuntarily resisting Jordan's gesture to take her seat.

"What's wrong, Kasey? I thought you were all fired up to leave. Are you okay?"

Kasey turned toward Jordan, who was standing with his right hand on the top of her door and his left at his side. She shot him a false smile and tried to think of anything that might buy her a little time. "I'm fine. I just thought about something I forgot upstairs."

"What?" he asked.

Her mind went blank.

"What'd you forget?"

"I . . . uh . . . didn't set any food out for Sam."

"His bowl is that little blue thing by the fridge, right?"

Kasey nodded.

"I saw it before I left. It was practically overflowing with dry cat food only twenty minutes ago. I doubt if he's polished it off this quickly." Jordan raised his left hand to the roof pillar and leaned forward to kiss her. Kasey then noticed, when his jacket moved away from his side, that he had stuck his gun in his belt. She kissed him back and dropped into the passenger seat.

She decided that even if she had to jump from the car in traffic, an opportunity to escape would present itself.

If it didn't—she'd have to make one.

❖

The Jaguar moved through the streets of downtown Nashville with the effortless grace of the cat for which it was named. The traffic on Commerce Street was light, especially for a workday, and the sleek sedan made the I-24W-St. Louis on-ramp without having to come to a complete stop once along the short route. Kasey watched in muted horror as the ground passed her window at a hundred feet per second.

Her memory played back the night when she had first seen the vile car. There was no doubt in her mind about her own fate if she didn't make a move before he got her away from the city.

"You like country music, right?" he asked, touching her leg. Without waiting for a response more affirmative than her forced smile, he tuned in WSM-FM and turned up the volume. Martina McBride sang soulfully about being safe in the arms of love.

Kasey found the words ironic for a moment, but her thoughts soon returned to the highway flying past her window.

"Are you sure you're all right?" Jordan asked for the second time. "You've been so distant since we left. Is it something I said?" He patted her thigh affectionately.

Kasey hesitated. "Why do you have your gun with you today? You've never worn it around me before." She prayed that her question would not alarm him.

"I always carry a gun. It's part of my job, remember?"

"You didn't have it Sunday night, or last night."

"I left it in my car when I came up to see you, that's all. I always keep it with me when I'm out. You know the old saying, it's better to have a gun and not need it . . ."

Kasey nodded silently, not giving a damn about old sayings.

"Hey, look, if it makes you nervous, I won't wear it while we're in the car." He reached to his side and quickly withdrew the blue steel Smith & Wesson automatic from his belt, handing it to her butt first. "Here, just stick it in the glove box."

Kasey deliberately took the pistol in her right hand, wrapping her thumb and fingers around the grip. It was much heavier than she had expected. It felt menacing, its power intoxicating. She touched her index finger to the trigger and her mind flooded with possibilities that had not been available to her only seconds before. For a long moment she sat holding it, staring at it as if it were alive.

Jordan noticed her hesitation and pushed the barrel away from his body, toward the dash. "That thing's loaded, you know. I'd hate for it to go off accidentally, it makes a hell of a hole." Kasey still held it tightly. "I thought you didn't like guns."

"I don't," she said, allowing it to go limp against her leg. She could not fathom his reason for having handed her a loaded weapon.

He doesn't know that I know, she realized. *That's it—the stupid bastard hasn't figured out that I'm on to him yet.*

She let out a deep sigh and shut the weapon inside the glove box.

Perhaps I have a chance after all.

❖

Small stalactites of early-morning light seemed to cling to the walls and ceiling as the May sun forced its way through the rusting roof panels. For almost an hour, Joeyboy had lain there, certain he was dying, or that he had died. His head hurt even more than his right arm, though it didn't feel like any other pain he could remember. The room continued to spin, as it had since he reopened his eyes. It didn't seem to matter.

The room went dark again.

When he regained consciousness, the shafts of light had moved down the wall. The room was spinning less and the pain had subsided to a tolerable level. He tried to sit up, but a wave of nausea forced him back to the greasy concrete floor. He lay there, motionless, watching the formations grow longer on the wall.

After several more minutes, a fresh round of throbbing shattered the emptiness in his brain, reminding him that he was still on the earth, a member of the living, and there were scores to settle. He struggled to his feet and into the filthy bathroom at the rear of the shed. With his good hand he wiped the mirror glass clear. He was amazed to find that the bullet which struck his head, which he had thought must have surely removed most of the right side of his skull, left nothing more than a grazing wound running along the right temple. He had been hurt worse in barroom fights and gotten laid the same night. He grinned at his filthy reflection, wondering if the man who had shot him had fared as well.

He set about the annoying task of getting himself into a condition that would allow him to leave, to begin the hunt for those responsible for his current state without attracting unwanted attention. He tossed his wet clothing into the corner and grabbed the jeans and denim shirt he'd left in the shop a few days before. He had dry socks, as well, but the damp, muddy boots would have to be worn.

When he emerged from the building, he was both amazed and pleased at the good fortune that lay, literally, at his feet.

❖

For nearly half an hour the Jaguar cruised the interstate at a steady 70 mph, while Kasey sat quietly, plotting her escape, pretending to be listening to the music that surrounded her without registering.

Without warning, Jordan jammed his foot on the brake. The heavy sedan screamed to a sudden stop. Kasey's heart leaped into her throat. An eighteen-wheeler, a quarter mile ahead of them, was throwing off chunks of steel reinforced rubber as one of its massive tires began to disintegrate after a blowout. The pieces, some as large as a football, flew into the grills and windshields of the vehicles immediately behind the truck.

The Jaguar, the four cars ahead of it, and the semitruck came to smoky, screeching stops. Jordan's car was blocked by a station wagon that had turned perpendicular to both west-bound lanes. A woman, dazed and shaken, sat speechless behind the wheel.

Jordan opened his door and stood with one foot on the pavement, the other on the sill, trying to determine whether the driver of the station wagon had been injured.

It was all the opportunity Kasey needed.

She grabbed the pistol from the glove box, threw open her door, and bolted across the right lane, jumping the shoulder railing and sliding—tumbling—down the grassy slope beyond. In only a few seconds, she had disappeared into the pine thicket to the north.

Jordan screamed for her. He couldn't believe it. He pulled the Jaguar off the road and into the wide, grassy median. The man behind him honked repeatedly at Jordan's unexpected move. "Fuck you!" Jordan yelled as he darted across the twin lanes of white concrete and sprinted over the railing. He struck the slippery grass surface faster than anticipated and began an uncontrolled slide down the face of the grade. At the bottom, his right shoulder and chest burned painfully, leaving him on all fours like a wounded animal. "Goddammit!" he howled.

Kasey ran for her life, darting among the trees and dodging branches and fallen limbs like a creature of the forest. She wanted to look back but wouldn't stop long enough, afraid of what she might see, afraid that he was right behind her. She could hear him calling her name, and his voice chilled her bones. She never caught a glimpse of the limb that struck her forehead, just above the left brow, sending her to the ground in dazed agony.

She lay there in shock, the thick, warm blood covering her left eye. As she sluggishly began to regain her senses, she rubbed the bloody eye with the palm of her hand. A nauseating wave pounded her pain center the instant she made contact with the laceration. She wanted to lie there and cry but she heard her name again—closer this time—and knew that she had already lost precious time. She rolled to her side and then to her knees, forcing herself to stand. Dizziness whirled around her. "Oh, God! Which way!?" she wept. Nearly frantic, she chose a direction that seemed to be opposite his voice, and stumbled away as fast as she could move. In her mind, she could picture herself lying in a shallow grave, her chest and abdomen being crushed by the maniac closing in behind her.

She drove herself onward as the blood poured across her left eye and down her face. It ran into the corner of her mouth and dripped from her jaw. Three or four times she had to stop and wipe it away with her shirtsleeve to be able to see ahead. Her legs became mush, her lungs burned. She became clumsier with each step, and twice ran into limbs when her vision was too blurred to see.

Then, without warning, the ground before her simply vanished. As far as she could see, ahead or to either side, the flat earth within the forest gave way to a sheer drop-off, falling three hundred feet to the valley floor. The sides of the cliff were too steep to allow a safe descent—any descent. She dropped to her knees and leaned over the edge, praying for a route to the bottom. "Help me!" she cried, again wiping the blood from her face. "Please help me!"

It was then she realized she no longer had his gun.

Jordan yelled out when he spotted her kneeling at the edge of the woods.

Kasey spun around at the sound of his voice, her feet dangling precariously over the edge of the cliff. The soft earth gave way slightly beneath her knees, sending small clods of reddish-brown dirt falling into nothingness. "Don't come near me or I'll jump, I swear to God! I'm not going to let you bury me like you did Donna Stanton!"

Jordan stopped several yards short of her position, frozen by her crazed words. He put his palms flat out in front of him, fingers up, arms extended. "I'm not going to take another step toward you, I promise. I'll just stand right here and we'll talk, okay? Just talk." He studied her dangerous position and realized any sudden move would send her over the side. "Why don't you come away from the edge a bit, Kasey. I'll back up and give you some more room."

"I'm not moving! If I fall . . . then . . . that's the way it will be. I'd rather be found at the bottom of this cliff than put in the ground by you." Her eyes never moved from his. Even when she wiped the oozing blood from her cheek, she kept her gaze locked on his face.

"Goddammit, Kasey, what's going on?" He lowered his arms and tried to stand relaxed. His chest was on fire, his broken ribs digging into his lungs.

"Oh, that's good, Jordan! Keep up the lies as long as possible, right? Why don't we just have sex again so you can kill me afterward like your sick little friend, Joeyboy!?"

Jordan took a long breath and exhaled painfully. "Kasey, I don't know what the hell you're talking about. How can you think I would try to hurt you?"

"Stop it, Jordan! Just stop it," she wept. "I saw you! I saw you that night. You were driving the other car!"

Jordan knelt slowly, careful not to move toward her. Still, his movement made her draw back. He tried to assure her with his open hands that he would not come any closer. When he reached a kneeling position, he sat back on his heels. He had done his share of negotiating with criminals and knew this had to be his best performance. He put his hands on top of his thighs, in plain view. "Kasey, try and pretend for a moment that I don't know what you're talking about. Tell me your side of things. You may not believe it, but it is possible that you're wrong. It's not going to hurt you to tell me how you came to believe these things. Will you at least do that much?"

Kasey still hadn't moved from her position on all fours at the edge of the cliff. Every muscle in her body screamed for relief, and her eye and forehead burned like a hot coal was being pressed against them. She was too tired to continue trying to save her own life. She was weary, ready for it all to be finished. She wiped the clouded eye and pushed herself into a kneeling position. Again, more of the earth beneath her broke free from the wall of the cliff.

Kasey didn't understand the game: appeasing the man across from her while he pretended he didn't know a thing. She looked at him and tried to see the man she had made love to last night. It was no use. There was too much fear.

"Please, Kasey," he repeated. "Talk to me."

"You know your little buddies, Pete and Re-Pete?" she began. "They're not as dumb as they look. They don't believe I'm a psychic, do they?"

Jordan shrugged. "They weren't convinced at first. I think they are now."

"Then they are as dumb as they look," she laughed hysterically.

Jordan's look was one of thorough confusion.

"Want to know how good a psychic I am, Jordan? I'm the goddamn best there is! I can describe every second of Donna Stanton's last moments on earth. I know every syllable Joeyboy spoke to her. I can tell you what a pig he was when he forced her to have sex with him before he killed her. I can tell you what her eyes looked like when they met mine, as I hid like a goddamn coward in the grass thirty feet away. I can tell you everything—because I was there that night!"

She grew angry and drew her shoulders back defiantly. "And, I can also tell you about seeing you drive away from the orchard, only a few feet behind Joeyboy's truck—drive away in your black Jaguar with its gold wire wheels!"

Jordan stared at the sky for a moment shaking his head before he spoke. "So that's how you knew so much," he whispered with an admiring grin. "Son of a bitch." He laughed out loud before he grew serious again. "If you were actually there, Kasey, then you couldn't have seen me."

"I did, you lying bastard!"

"You couldn't have, Kasey. The murder occurred on a Monday night, right? The twenty-second of April."

Kasey agreed.

"What time?" he asked.

"Seven-fifteen . . . maybe seven-thirty."

"On Monday night, the twenty-second of April, I was in Washington, D.C., at a conference on DNA typing. There are at least a dozen FBI agents that will be happy to verify that for you if you'd care to call them. But the part about the car has me puzzled. If you're sure about the gold wheels, then someone else was in my car that night."

"I'm sure about them," she said sternly. "I'll never forget anything from that night." Kasey adjusted her position, moving slightly away from the edge. She was astonished that Jordan had simply given his alibi and expected it to be believed, as if the last twenty minutes had never occurred. "Jordan!" she snapped angrily.

He looked up.

"Do you expect me to believe you were in Washington simply because you told me you were there?" Kasey was still shaking, her head pounding, her emotions at their limit.

"Of course," he said simply. "Why would I lie to you about that?"

Her jaw dropped. "Because you were involved in Donna Stanton's murder, that's why! And now, you want to kill me."

"Is that what you think, that I want to kill you?"

"I saw your car. You own it. You were there that night. That's all I know."

Jordan stood again, holding his chest as he did. "If I wanted you dead, Kasey, all I'd have to do right now is take a single step toward you. It'd be that easy. No witnesses. Nothing to tie me to your death. I could just walk away."

She watched his eyes closely, her mind confused, dazed.

"I'm going back to Nashville now. I've got to solve this puzzle once and for all before any more people die. You can come with me or you can stay here. Either way, I'm no threat to you. Whatever you decide, you need to see about that eye." He reached behind his back and pulled his gun from his jeans belt, tossing it at her knees as he turned to leave. "You dropped this. That's twice I've given you my gun."

Kasey watched as he started back through the trees. She grabbed the gun and pulled the slide back. She had seen her ex-husband do it with the automatic he owned before he had to pawn it. A 9mm hollow-point ejected from the breech and another took its place. It had been loaded. "Jordan!" she called after him.

Jordan stopped a few yards away and turned toward her. She ran to him and threw her arms around his waist. Though it still hurt to be hugged, he was too grateful for her touch to be concerned. "I'm such a fool," she cried. "I should have known you couldn't hurt me."

Jordan tilted her chin up and looked at the injured brow. He took a folded cotton handkerchief from his back pocket and pressed it directly on the laceration. It was her turn to grimace. "Sorry," he said sympathetically. "You need to keep this pressed tightly against the cut. It'll help it clot."

Kasey nodded and handed him back his weapon. "I told you I don't like guns."

❖

It took much longer to get back to the car than it had taken to get to the cliff, though the return trip was far less strenuous and painful. By the time they were on the interstate headed back to Nashville it was almost ten o'clock.

"How's the eye?" he asked as he pushed the speedometer past eighty.

Kasey looked in the visor mirror for the first time. The right side of her face was streaked with dried blood. Small dark red crusts of blood had dried in her hair near her ear. She looked closely at the gash that ran parallel to her left eye, just above the eyebrow. It was about an inch long and would probably benefit from several stitches. For the moment, it was a dry, wide black line, in the same spot as the cut she had gotten the night Donna had died. "Seems to have stopped bleeding," she answered. She wet the handkerchief with her saliva and wiped some of the streaks from her cheek and forehead.

"Care to tell me why you were in the orchard that night?" he asked.

"I had car trouble."

"Why were you way the hell out in rural Maury County?"

"I was just driving, trying to run from my problems. Instead, I ran smack into the worst of them." She leaned back in the soft leather seat and tried to relax.

"So, you actually witnessed everything?"

Kasey nodded.

"Does Mueller know?"

"You're the only one who knows."

"It happened exactly like you said?"

"Yes, exactly! I wouldn't lie about something like that."

Jordan took his eyes off the road for a second. "Where were you when all this was going on, Kasey? Why didn't Griffin see you?"

"I was hiding in the tall grass by the fence. He never knew I was there."

Kasey could picture the scene and her voice cracked. "She saw me, though."

"What do you mean?"

"We made eye contact before he killed her."

"Why didn't she yell out, call to you for help?"

"I guess she knew he'd just kill both of us then. At first, I thought she was trying to get me to go for help, but . . . now . . . I don't know."

"Do you think she knew she was going to die?" Jordan asked.

"He wasn't going to let her live after she told him what he wanted to know. She knew that."

"Told him? Told him what, Kasey?"

Kasey closed her eyes and tried to remember the exact words. "When I could first make out their conversation, they were shouting about something she had hidden, something he was sent to get."

"The tapes," Jordan said. "Are you sure he said he was 'sent?' "

She thought carefully. "Yes. He said he was told not to come back without it."

"That means he was working for someone else. What did she tell him?"

"She said that she had hidden what he was after under the sink in the bathroom of her apartment."

"You mean her home, don't you?"

"No. I remember her saying apartment because I thought at the time that it seemed odd that someone like her would live in an apartment instead of a home. She looked like the type who would have a husband and a large home with—"

"Goddammit!" he shouted, causing her to jump. "We found the rest of the tapes she had made, and her handwritten diary, hidden in her bedroom in Belle Meade, not in her apartment downtown. If the others were there, that must mean she took them with her!"

"Maybe she hid them after she left her home."

"Not a chance. They were too valuable. She'd have kept them with her at all times."

"That's not possible. He went through her purse. He had her strip. She couldn't have hidden a match."

"But you said you got there after they had started arguing, right? She could have gotten rid of them before he searched her."

"How?"

"I don't know how. That's what I'm trying to figure out. I believe she would have found some way of keeping Griffin from getting his hands on them."

Kasey tried to put the actions and words into their proper sequence. It required bringing back details that she had fought so hard to banish and forget. "I suppose she could have. I know he didn't leave with them."

"Think, Kasey. You said she made eye contact with you. Did she do anything else?" He watched her expression.

"She tried to send me for help, I told you that. I mean, it seemed like that at the time."

"How! What did she do—exactly!"

Kasey shut her eyes and moved to that moment in time: "When Joeyboy turned his back on her, while she was kneeling in the grass, she motioned to me with her head. I thought she was—oh, God! Jordan, that's it, isn't it!? She wasn't trying to send me for help. She was telling me where she had hidden the tapes. She knew she was going to die and she wanted someone to know why." Kasey was now fully erect in the seat, facing Jordan. She grabbed his arm. "We've got to go back to the orchard, Jordan!"

Jordan nodded. "You did great, Kasey. I don't know who they are, but there are a lot of people looking for those tapes." He touched her left cheek and rubbed her lips tenderly with his thumb. "We'll go to the orchard, all right, but first, we've got to make a stop."

"A stop?" she asked. "Why?"

"I need to know who was with Griffin that night—who was driving my car."

"How are you going to find that out?" she asked.

He grinned. "I'm a detective, remember."

THIRTY

Jordan pulled into the police impound lot at 11 Russell Street. He stopped the car to the left of the front door of the double-wide trailer that served as an office without turning off the engine. "Wait here," he said, reaching for the door handle. "This'll only take a minute." The officer he had asked to meet him was already in the office.

"What are we doing here, Jordan?" Kasey asked, puzzled by the odd surroundings. On all sides of them and as far as she could see were vehicles of every description and in every conceivable condition.

He pulled the door shut. "I bought this car from Metro last week. It was a drug confiscation—"

"What's that?"

"It used to belong to a pusher we busted. Under Federal seizure laws, it becomes property of the arresting agency, to dispose of as it chooses. I've always wanted one of these, so I bought it at a mock auction on Saturday, the twentieth. It's not fair, I suppose, but being chief has its advantages." She smiled at his little confession. She was in no position to lecture anyone about ethics. "Anyway, I didn't take physical possession of it until Wednesday, the twenty-fourth of April, the day I got back from D.C. Someone else had to be driving it when you saw it at the orchard. When we get his name from the log, we'll have the bastard."

❖

The plain white Chevy covered the miles toward Nashville without complaint, its new radial tires singing rhythmically against the pavement. Behind the wheel, Joeyboy—dirty and unshaven—looked like death incarnate. On the other hand, the passenger, if not for the wide band of gray duct tape pulled tightly across his mouth, and the tormented, frightened look on his face, would have looked right at home. After all, it was his car, or at least the one normally assigned him during his shift.

Brad Stark fought with the shackles that held his wrists painfully behind his back but knew his efforts were hopeless. Even if he had not lost so much blood—and strength—from Joeyboy's bullet that was still

341

lodged in his right shoulder, he would have been unable to free himself from the stainless handcuffs.

Joeyboy noticed the futile struggle. He cut the wheel sharply, throwing the detective painfully against the door. "Hey, Brad, buddy—relax. You'll start bleeding again, and I don't want you dying just yet. We're gonna visit ourselves a famous celebrity, Ms. Kasey Riteman. Then, after I blow your brains out in front of her—I've already done it once and I think she really digs it—I'm gonna drag her to the spot where I did Donna Stanton and shoot her in the liver. It'll take her fifteen minutes to die and I'm going to fuck her the whole time. If I'm lucky, I can come just as she's going. Now, why would you want to miss out on an afternoon like that?"

Stark thought of kicking his way to freedom, but the seat belt and shoulder harness that had been tightened across his hips and chest kept him securely in place. He cursed himself for not killing Joeyboy as soon as he entered the old shack. If he managed to get free, he would not make that mistake again.

The police radio's chatter grabbed Joeyboy's attention: Jordan Taylor had just ordered dispatch to send an officer to the police impound lot on Russell Street with keys to the office, since the lot was normally closed on Tuesdays.

"Did you hear that Brad, ole boy? He just told us where he'll be and it's only a block from here. That was considerate of him, don't you think?" Joeyboy made a hard left turn onto Union Street. In three minutes, he parked Stark's car behind a tractor trailer in a storage lot across from the police impound, concealed from sight but with a clear view of the parking spaces in front of the small office. "All we have to do now is wait." He slipped the silencer on the end of the small automatic. "See how easy it is to kill someone, Brad? If you'd learned in prison, instead of that pussy cop school, I'd be dead now and you'd be driving your own car." He looked amusingly at Stark. "You want a pencil? You should really be taking notes."

❖

Kasey was studying the cut above her eye in the visor mirror when Jordan came out the door he had entered only two minutes earlier. He dropped into his seat without a word, threw the Jaguar into gear, and tore from the impound lot. They were soon speeding west down Union Street, toward the I-40 loop to 65 South. Their destination was less than forty-five-minutes away.

"Son of a bitch!" he shouted in a mix of anger and excitement.

"Who is it?" she asked quickly. "Who had your car?"

Jordan made a hard sweeping turn onto the on-ramp and powered around a truck that showed no interest in hurrying. He switched off the radio. "Warren Slade."

Kasey recognized the name as the man the media usually portrayed as actually running the state. His reputation left little room to debate his ruthless nature—or the extent of his connections. "We're screwed, aren't we, Jordan?"

Jordan looked straight ahead. "No, my love. If you're right about the tapes, it's Slade who's about to be screwed."

As they formulated their plans for the rest of the afternoon, neither noticed the unmarked car that slipped in behind them, a distance back. There was no need to crowd the Jaguar, Joeyboy knew where it was heading.

He smiled at the good fortune that was about to deliver Stark, Jordan, Kasey, and the tapes into his waiting hands. Giacano would reward him well. It might even make up for all he'd lost.

❖

Since Kasey last saw it on Monday morning, the faded wooden sign over the orchard had fallen at one end. Partially delivered from its man-made shackles, it was now free to sway and twist gently to the silent chant of a light breeze, its softly creaking chain lending a haunting quality to the orchard, the sound now more like a warning than an invitation.

Jordan stopped the Jaguar at the gate beneath the sign and opened the trunk, withdrawing the gas-powered trimmer that had been rented from Ken's Lawn and Garden in Columbia before Kasey and he drove the remaining miles to the orchard.

The couple walked to a point along the fence where Kasey had concealed herself that night. As she stood near the fence, Kasey studied the alignment of the last two apple trees for a moment. She then looked behind her, to the tall grass across the barbed-wire fence. The bush nearest to her looked different in the light of day, but she was certain it had to be the right one. "Here, I think," she said. "I was beside that bush when it happened."

Jordan considered the short distance between the trees and the fence. "You're a lucky girl. It's a good thing you didn't try to be a hero. The slightest sound from you and Griffin would have buried two women that night instead of one and we'd have never had a clue what happened to either of you."

In an effort to justify her cowardice and fear, Kasey had repeated those exact words to herself for fourteen days. Her only redemption: there was nothing she could have done. She nodded her understanding and her thanks.

"Can you tell where Stanton was pointing?" he asked.

"She didn't point exactly. She nodded with her head. I think she meant over there." Kasey pointed her finger at the thick brush to their left.

"Let's get started there, then," he said resolutely. He tossed his windbreaker across the fence and put on the heavy cotton work gloves the man from the garden center had loaned him. The gas trimmer started on the second pull, springing to life with an angry buzz.

Jordan ran the trimmer near the fence for a minute, clearing away the grass that concealed the barbed wire strands. He put his foot on the second strand and held the top one high with his gloved hand. Kasey slipped through the opening and then returned the gesture for him. It was now past noon, and the summer sun was mercilessly hot. In a few minutes, both were soaked with perspiration.

As Jordan trimmed the tall grass, Kasey gathered the fallen weeds and tossed them over the fence. Every few minutes, both would get on all fours and comb the newly cleared area. They cleared an area ten by fifteen feet, but found nothing.

"Are you sure this is the right place?" he asked in frustration.

Kasey studied their position relative to where Donna had knelt that night. "I'm sure this is where I was that night, but she could have been indicating anything along the fence here." Kasey was equally frustrated.

"Hold on to this, will you?" Jordan asked, handing Kasey his gun again. He pulled off his sweat-soaked shirt and wiped his face. With the only remaining section of relatively dry cloth, he wiped Kasey's face, carefully avoiding the area around her injured eyebrow. He kissed her gently on the lips. "You taste like salt."

"So do you. I like it, though. Do it again." She took the shirt from him.

Jordan kissed her passionately this time, pulling her against his battered body. When he looked into her lovely face, he smiled broadly. "You're the only woman I've ever known who could make me completely happy."

Kasey lowered her head. She thought about the morning. "I'm sorry I didn't trust you," she whispered. "I'm sorry I lied to you about being here. I was so scared—"

He put his finger to her lips. "I would have done the same thing. You've been through hell and you're still trying to do the right thing. That takes guts, Kasey, more than most people have." He winked at her. "Don't worry, your secret is safe with me. I'll never tell a soul you're not the world's greatest psychic. Now, let's find these damned things and put an end to this once and for all."

Kasey started to lay the gun in the grass but decided that the top of one of the fence posts would be a better place. She covered it with his polo shirt and returned to her task.

The cut, clear, and search continued until they had doubled the size of the original area. A dozen times in the dense grass Jordan had to clear the cutting blades when they became too entangled to operate. It was slow, exhausting work. After an hour of sweat, their efforts had yielded only blisters and grasshoppers.

"This is crazy!" Kasey blurted out. "It's not here! She wasn't trying to tell me anything, dammit!" She sank to the ground in despair.

"Maybe we haven't looked far enough back from the fence," Jordan said, always the last to quit anything. "Let's go a few more feet in that direction." He pointed to the area that led north away from the fence.

"Why?" she groaned. "What's the point?"

"Because it's the only lead we've got. You asked me if we were screwed a while back. If we don't find the tapes, we will be screwed. The only way to put those bastards away, and guarantee your safety, is to find what they're looking for before they do. Now, let's get back to work so we can get a shower and fool around."

"You can think about making love at a time like this?"

"I can't be around you and not think about making love." He bent over and kissed her again.

"I still think we're wasting our time," she grumbled as he cranked the trimmer again. Its buzzing was driving her crazy.

While Jordan began cutting a new section, farther from the fence line, Kasey stood slowly and repeated the boring process of tossing the cut grass over the fence and then searching through the stubble. As she crawled on all fours, the sweat dripping from her brow, her knees and palms raw from the sharp stubs, her left hand came down on something smooth and firm. She dug at it, sweeping away the coarse dust and leafy residue that blanketed the ground. Here, more than forty feet from her hiding place, she uncovered a small silver box. "Jordan!" she shouted excitedly.

Jordan stopped the trimmer and moved quickly to her, dropping to his knees in front of her. He spotted the gleaming shape she had exposed. It was a silver cigarette case bearing the initials DLS.

"Donna Louise Stanton," he said reverently as she lifted it from the stubble. He looked into Kasey's face. She was staring into his.

"I'm afraid to open it," she said.

"Go ahead," he said. "Open it."

Kasey pulled gently at the two ends of the case. It resisted. She added a little force and the halves separated, spilling out a small bundle of paper with a single rubber band wrapped around it. Again, they looked at each other. She laid the halves of the case at her knees and took the small package. Carefully, she removed the rubber band and unfolded the paper. Inside were four pages of a diary and an equal number of microcassettes, each labeled with a date. Kasey laid the tapes in Jordan's hands and began to read the pages, starting with the oldest date. He moved beside her and stared over her shoulder. They read without speaking.

When the last line had been reached, Jordan took the tapes and secured them in the paper. He wrapped the band around them, like before, and put the package back in the case, pressing the halves together. They remained kneeling, their backs to the fence.

"It's unbelievable," she said weakly.

"I always thought Slade was dirty, but I thought Williams was only stupid and pompous. I never expected him to be working for the mob. But I can't figure out why. What does the mob want with the governor of Tennessee?"

"It's simple." The man's voice came from the orchard side of the fence. Jordan and Kasey spun around and froze at the sight. Looking like the living dead, there stood Joeyboy, his face scruffy from two days' growth of beard; his blond hair stained a mottled tan from the muddy river water; his right jaw lined in dried blood. In his left hand was a small automatic, pressed tightly against Brad Stark's right temple. The detective's wrists were bound by his own handcuffs, a wide strip of duct tape covered his mouth. He looked worse than his captor, the loss of blood leaving his skin sickly pale. "It's all about greed," Joeyboy continued. "Buddy Williams and the mob are buying off or blackmailing every legislator who has previously opposed riverboat gambling in Tennessee. Once they get a few more votes, Music City's gonna become the Vegas of the South. I love it."

It now all made sense to Jordan. He looked at his detective. "Are you okay, Brad?"

"This scumbag?" Joeyboy answered for him, jabbing the point of the barrel forcefully into the side of Stark's head. The man's frightened eyes immediately reflected the pain.

"Leave him alone," Kasey snapped.

"I haven't started with him, darlin'," Joeyboy threatened. He looked coldly at Jordan. "You know what this little bastard tried to do, Taylor? He tried to kill me. Came on like he was there to help me and then fired a couple of shots at me. With this gun! Can you believe that?" Taylor could—easily. "And after all we've been through together. I thought we were buddies, me and Giacano's little stooge here."

His words had not been expected. "What are you talking about, Griffin?" Taylor asked angrily. He saw his shirt lying on the fence post twenty feet to his left and knew his gun was beneath it. It was too far away to make a try for it.

"You are a dumb shit considering the job you've got, you know it, Taylor? Your boy here works for Chicago, too. They sent him to cap my ass after you sicked the SWAT team on me and missed. Well, guess what?" Joeyboy fired the small automatic, sending a bullet into the right ear of Brad Stark. He was dead before his head finished recoiling from the blast. His limp body fell grotesquely across the barbed-wire fence, sagging the top strand until it touched the middle wire—"He didn't know about the charmed life I lead. Nobody kills me. Nobody!"

Despite the toy gun pop of the silenced .32 automatic, Kasey jumped as the slug entered Brad Stark's head. His body seemed to fall in slow motion toward the rusting wire, just as Donna's had fallen to the ground that terrible evening.

Jordan made a move toward Joeyboy, but the gun was turned back in their direction before he could take two steps.

"Don't be a hero, cop," Joeyboy warned, the weapon now squarely in Kasey's face, "Or your fuck-bitch gets it right between the eyes while you watch."

Jordan pushed Kasey partially behind him, hoping to protect her. "Leave her out of this, Griffin. This is between you and me."

"On the contrary, asshole, this is definitely between the psychic—or should I say eyewitness—and me."

Kasey grew unnaturally calm. She thought how ironic it was that she was going to die in the exact spot where the horrid sequence of events had begun. She wondered if she had actually died that Monday night, and the weeks since had been just one long nightmare. She took Jordan's right arm for support, gripping it with both hands; her eyes riveted to Joeyboy's gun.

Joeyboy opened his right hand, turning the palm upward. "I'll take those tapes now."

"No!" Kasey shouted, gripping Jordan's arm tighter. "If you give them to him, he'll kill us."

"I'm going to kill you both anyway," he laughed. "Taylor knows that. He and I have an old score to settle, and you, little lady . . . well . . . let's just say you and I have some unfinished business, too. You can either hand the tapes to me or I'll get them myself after I've killed you. It's simply a matter of whether you want to live another five minutes or another five seconds." He alternated the barrel between their faces.

"Answer something for me before you kill us," Jordan said, stalling for time. "Why was the hit on Donna Stanton ordered?"

"Hey, I don't mind granting you a last request. I'm a generous guy. The good-lookin' bitch should have stuck to giving blow jobs to the rich and famous instead of trying to steal business secrets. She made the mistake of taping the old man and Williams doing their gambling thing. The old man found out. Simple as that."

"Giacano."

"Yep."

"So Monroe had nothing to do with Stanton's death?"

"That dickwad couldn't order a hit on a lame dog. He just wants to be governor. Guess he's fucked now." Joeyboy was tired of talking. "The tapes, Taylor."

Jordan started toward Joeyboy with the cigarette case.

"Oh, no, not you, cop," Joeyboy warned. "Give them to your bitch."

Kasey moved alongside Jordan and took the small package. She knew there was only one chance. She rolled the silver case in her fingers and took a few slow steps forward, pretending to offer it obediently to Joeyboy. When she was within five feet of Joeyboy and halfway to Jordan's weapon, she tossed the hard metal case like a Frisbee at Griffin's face, running for the fence post at the same time.

Griffin bobbed to miss being hit by the cigarette case and fired at Kasey at the same time, striking her in the left forearm and sending her in a spiral to the ground. Jordan had made a move toward him simultaneously, hoping to draw Griffin's attention from Kasey. Joeyboy snapped the gun toward the man who had sent him to prison for life. He fired twice, striking Jordan in the chest with both rounds. Jordan staggered for a moment, a disbelieving look in his deep blue eyes. He drooped heavily to the ground, coming to rest squarely on his back, his legs folded beneath him.

Joeyboy turned his attention again to the woman he wanted to kill more than any other in his twisted life—only not yet. "Going somewhere?" he asked flatly, lowering the gun. Kasey struggled to get to her feet, her arm on fire like a white-hot poker had been shoved into the muscle and left there to burn.

She then realized that Jordan was no longer on his feet. "Jordan!" she cried as she stumbled to his side, the tears filling her eyes. He didn't respond to her touch.

"Get up, bitch. We've got work to do." Joeyboy retrieved the cigarette case and stuck it in his back pocket.

Kasey turned her head slowly toward the vile man. "I swear to God, I'm going to kill you for this." Her voice was surprisingly calm and even.

"I don't think so, not in this life anyway. Maybe you'll get a second chance in hell. I know I'm going there, and I'm pretty certain that lying to God and everyone to save your pretty ass is gonna put you right beside me." He winked at her as he motioned her toward him with the gun.

Kasey looked back at Jordan and stood slowly, her mind now consumed with one thought: killing the man who had brought such misery to so many. She prayed for God to give her the strength and the opportunity. She hoped God would understand and forgive her.

Joeyboy backed away from the fence and allowed Kasey to slip clumsily through the strands of barbed wire. He was surprised at how cooperative she'd become. He reached into his pocket and withdrew the stiletto Stark had in his coat pocket. He clicked the blade into position. "Still with me, I see. I was afraid you were going to miss the final act. Stress can do that to some people. Me, I've never experienced stress. Must feel pretty bad, huh?" He poked Kasey's bleeding forearm with the point of the knife as they walked slowly toward the depression between the two apple trees. Her brain fought to force the pain aside so it could remain focused; it was only partially successful. "That hurt?" he mocked.

She didn't give him the pleasure of an answer.

When she was standing at the edge of the grave where she had watched Donna Stanton buried, she turned to face her executioner.

"Recognize these?" Joeyboy asked, pulling the black silk panties from his shirt pocket. He moved them slowly under his nose.

Though they looked like any other piece of lingerie, Kasey knew that they had come from her apartment—that he had been in her home. The feeling of complete violation overcame her. "Fuck you!" was the only response she could imagine.

"I had that in mind, to tell you the truth, darlin'. Just like with the rich bitch. Only I'm gonna put another bullet in you first, right about here"— he touched the knife point just below her sternum—"and see if I can get off before you die on me. Been thinking about it ever since I found out it was you who watched me kill Stanton. Now, put these on like a good little girl."

Kasey repeated her last words to him.

"That's not very cooperative of you, psychic. I thought you wanted this. If not, why the hell didn't you just keep your sweet little mouth shut? I think you're sorry you didn't join the rich bitch that night." He poked her in the injured arm again with the tip of the blade. "Am I right?"

"I wanted to die at times for what I didn't do, but there was nothing I could have done to help Donna that night, not with a worthless piece of shit like you standing over her." Kasey threw her shoulders back defiantly. "You've had all of me you're ever going to have. I'm through being afraid, of feeling guilty. You can kill me, you sick bastard, but you'll never have my body while I'm alive."

Joeyboy scratched his chin with the knife blade and considered her words. He pitched it at the apple tree on his right, sticking it expertly in the trunk at shoulder height. "That presents a little problem, Riteman." He swapped the gun to his now-empty right hand and let his left arm fall to his side. Then without warning, he drove his left fist into her solar plexus, dropping her like a stone to her knees.

Kasey fought for a breath, her eyes blurred, her mouth filled with bile.

"That's better. I like women on their knees." He aimed the gun directly at her liver. Kasey rocked back and forth trying to catch her breath. "If you don't stop all that swaying shit, I'm liable to shoot you in the heart. Then where'd we be?" Kasey closed her eyes as his finger wrapped around the trigger; she thought of her parents and prayed.

The explosion echoed in her ears like a thunderclap. She waited for the pain, but none came. The explosion echoed again and she opened her eyes. At the fence, Jordan was leaning against an old wooden post, his weapon in hand, trying desperately to get off an accurate shot before Joeyboy could do the same. His arm quivered and the barrel moved about like a leaf in the wind.

"You're gonna have to do a lot better than that if you're gonna take me out, Chief," Joeyboy laughed as a third bullet struck the ground several feet to his right. "You seem to forget I'm charmed." Without raising his own weapon in defense, Joeyboy moved boldly toward the fence.

Jordan tried desperately to bring the barrel into alignment, but could not get his battered body to cooperate. Twice more he fired wildly, almost striking Kasey with the last round.

Joeyboy stopped halfway between the trees and the fence—a distance that would not allow his own shot to miss. Jordan fought to raise the heavy automatic one more time as Joeyboy aimed his own weapon at an imaginary spot between Jordan's eyes. The pain that bore through his neck was not like any the biker had ever experienced. He dropped his gun and groped with both hands, trying to eliminate the agony. Buried to the hilt in the left side of his neck was the stiletto. The ebony handle was still in Kasey's grip, and she twisted it savagely as they made eye contact. For the first time in his brutal life the man experienced fear. Pure, unbridled terror.

"This is for Donna," Kasey spat as she gave the knife a final push. She waited to release her grip until the light behind the nearly black eyes had extinguished.

Joeyboy dropped to his side and then rolled onto his face; there would be no reprieve. There was but one final judge to face now.

Kasey bolted for the fence, making her way between the strands as Jordan slumped to the ground. "Oh, Jesus!" she cried as she knelt beside his motionless body. "Don't leave me. Tell me what I can do?" The faintest sign of life still raised his chest in shallow breaths. She pressed her hands against the two oozing wounds, trying to keep the life from pouring out; the tears streamed down her face. Kasey lifted his head to her lap. She begged God not to take this man from her life. "Hold on, my love, please," she wept.

When he still did not respond, Kasey pounded her fists against his chest, trying to keep him from that endless sleep. Her tears fell on his skin. "Wake up, goddammit!" she yelled.

"Oh, shit, that hurts," he groaned when she struck him again. Jordan looked up at her and forced a weak smile. "Trying to kill me?"

Kasey brushed the hair from his forehead and kissed his face repeatedly. "You're alive!"

"Seems so. You don't think I was going to let that son-of-a-bitch Griffin kill me, do you?"

Even in her joy, she knew he needed immediate medical attention. "What should I do, sweetheart?"

"My car. Use the radio in my glove box to call for help. Tell them Code Purple—"

"Code Purple," she repeated, having never heard the term. She ran her fingers through his hair.

"Give them our location. That should bring the closest help." He coughed painfully. "I'll be okay while you're gone."

Kasey nodded tearfully. She kissed him on the forehead and then again on the lips. "Don't you die on me, goddammit, you hear me! I'll be right back." She lowered his head gently to the ground and knelt beside him, watching him carefully for a second before she left. "You sure you're okay for the moment?"

He smiled his best smile. "Okay for someone almost old enough to be your father." It hurt both of them to laugh, but it felt good against the backdrop of numbing pain.

"Can you still make it with that arm?" It was all he could do to hold his head up as he spoke.

"I'll make it," Kasey said defiantly as she clamped her right hand around her left forearm to stem the flow. "You just hold on until help comes, you hear!"

He nodded with a wan smile.

She stood as quickly as she could. She was afraid to leave him but knew she had to make the call—now.

"Kasey," he said softly. She looked down at him. "I've never loved anyone the way I love you. Whatever happens, whatever we go through, never forget that."

The tears returned. "I won't, sweetheart. You hang on now. I'll be back in no time, I swear."

His blue eyes had never seemed brighter to her. "I'm not going anywhere."

THIRTY-ONE

Brandie Mueller watched the videotape monitor in the general manager's office, mesmerized. Though she had written and reported the story, she could barely believe her own words. At the conference table with her, Steve Dacus and Stewart Parker also watched in awed silence as the report neared its end. U.S. Attorney General Janet Reno addressed the media:

> *"I would like to read a prepared statement from my office: Within the last hour, a task force of United States marshals, acting on my orders, has effected the arrest of Wayne "Buddy" Williams, Governor of Tennessee, at the governor's mansion in Nashville. This is in response to information provided to my office by Detective Peter Vanover of Nashville Metropolitan Police, following a week-long investigation into the Governor Williams' link to organized crime, specifically, the Giacano crime syndicate based in Chicago, Illinois.*
>
> *"My office has charged Governor Williams with a number of crimes, chief among them: racketeering, conspiracy to commit murder, accessory to murder, extortion, bribery, and income tax evasion.*
>
> *"In a simultaneous action conducted by marshals in Chicago, Mario Antonio Giacano has been arrested and similarly charged.*
>
> *"My office also attempted to take into custody Williams' chief administrative assistant, Warren Allen Slade. When marshals arrived at Slade's home early this morning, he was found dead from an apparent gunshot wound. Suicide has been ruled out as the cause. Governor Williams has offered to cooperate with my office in exchange for Federal protection. No agreement has been reached at this time.*
>
> *"Thank you. That's all I have for you at the moment."*
>
> Brandie Mueller to camera: *"You have just heard Attorney General, Janet Reno. To recap: Tennessee governor, Buddy Williams, has been indicted and charged with numerous crimes, including accessory to homicide for his part in the murder of Donna Louise Stanton, the woman whose death began one of the most bizarre sequences of events in our state's history.*
>
> *"This is Brandie Mueller, Channel 9 News, reporting to you from the steps of the Federal Courthouse in Washington, D.C."*

"Son of a bitch!" Stewart Parker blurted excitedly, as he slapped his hand noisily on the wide table. "Kasey got 'em all, from Griffin to Giacano—everyone connected with Donna Stanton's death." He looked at Brandie. "Outstanding, Brandie! Thank Tim for me. It's going to be a hell of a news week. I hope you didn't plan on sleeping for a while. I want the special ready to air by Wednesday."

Parker and Dacus joked with their associate for another moment about the week she was facing, and then left the office, each stopping respectfully to shake Kasey's hand and to offer their heartfelt sympathy at the loss of her best friend.

Kasey could only nod in response.

She would miss Brenda.

Brandie looked at Kasey, still seated quietly in the corner of the office. They had talked at length over the last several days about Brenda and about Kasey's involvement with Jordan. For once, Brandie had meant it when she'd said their conversation would remain off the record.

The reporter stood and pulled a chair next to her friend. "You sure you're doing okay?" she asked. "It's only been a week. Your doctor told me your arm would take a couple of months to heal completely."

Kasey took a long, slow breath, her eyes tired and sad. It had been the longest week of her life since she and Jordan had left the orchard in the ambulance. "I'm fine, Brandie. It only hurts if I try to use it too much."

"You need to take it easy, dammit."

"I've got a lot of things to do. I can't just lie around."

"Listen, we've finished all the taping we're going to do with you. We've got enough footage to put together the whole story for that special Stewart mentioned. You've done enough. Tell the vultures that want to interview you they can just wait."

Kasey nodded. "I've put several of them off already, but I can't just hide forever. I wanted to be famous, remember?"

Brandie pulled the envelope marked HBO Pictures, Hollywood, from Kasey's open purse. She waved it playfully in front of Kasey's nose. "Technical consultant on a made-for-TV-movie doesn't sound like someone planning on hiding for the rest of her life."

"Can you see me as a technical consultant?"

"Sure. I can see you doing anything you set your mind to, Kasey."

Kasey only smiled, her mind too full to respond to Brandie's words. Her heart kept painting images of her childhood in New Orleans; she missed the world she had once known and loved so much. Perhaps it was time to close the book on the things she had lost and open a new one on the things she had found.

Brandie reached to the conference table behind her and grabbed the two white envelopes Parker had left. "This is for Griffin," she smiled. "We never had the opportunity to give it to you with all the crazy things that happened." She dropped the first envelope into Kasey's purse. "And this—this is a bonus for handing Buddy Williams to us on a silver platter. You'll be getting another check—a big fat one, I suspect—from Clarion if they sell your special to the network." Brandie added enviously, "All things considered, your new-found wealth should allow you to sit on the beach for quite a few years."

Kasey seemed indifferent, lost in a void beyond Brandie's shoulder.

Brandie slid the second envelope beside the other two in Kasey's purse and let out a melancholy sigh: "So—it's off to the land of sushi bars and movie stars, huh?"

Kasey returned from her daydream and shook her head gently. "Thinking about going back to New Orleans when we're finished shooting."

Brandie was surprised, but then understood. "Good for you, Kasey. The town will be brighter with you around again."

Kasey took Brandie's hand and squeezed it affectionately. "And you?" she asked. "How are you going to make it through a whole news day without me?"

Brandie looked at the office door to make sure it was still closed, and then turned back to Kasey. "New York!" she mouthed excitedly.

"You're kidding?" Kasey whispered, truly happy for her friend.

"As soon as I can wrap things up around here. The big time in the Big Apple—can you believe it?" Brandie's eyes widened.

Kasey nodded her approval.

As they stood, Kasey slipped her purse strap over her shoulder and hugged Brandie. "I'm glad your dream finally came true," she said warmly.

"I'd say both our dreams came true."

Kasey thought about her success, her new appreciation for all that life had to offer, and the love in her heart for the blue-eyed cop with the little boy lost smile.

"I suppose they did," she said without a trace of emotion.

THIRTY-TWO

The warm June sun felt good against Kasey's back as she knelt in the soft, green grass at Jordan's side. She rocked casually back on her bare heels. Her thoughts were filled with images of the first time they touched; the way his skin felt against her body; the way he smiled; the way his eyes sparkled whenever he saw her.

She played with the bright yellow flowers in her hand, putting them to her nose to inhale their fresh, natural scent. "I remember you told me once that you thought wildflowers were the prettiest. I found these along the road on my way here, and I thought you'd like them."

Her hands trembled nervously and she stared at the bright azure sky for a long moment, unable to speak.

Finally, she found the strength to continue. "Sam and I are heading for California for a few weeks, sweetheart, so I won't be able to see you for a while. You and I know that I can't stay here with all the memories haunting me.

"Want to hear something to laugh about? They're going to make a TV movie about Donna Stanton's death and all the things you and I went through trying to put the pieces of the puzzle together. They've asked me to help with it—technical consultant, if you can believe it. That's kind of funny, don't you think?"

She grinned wickedly. "Of course, I'll never tell them the truth about . . . well, you know . . . about us. That will always be our secret, okay? No one would understand anyway.

"I wish you could have seen me with the Feds. You'd have been proud of me, sweetheart. I was at my best when I told them about us figuring out where the tapes were hidden, and about Joeyboy trying to take them from us. Vanover even believes me now. He's a good guy, you know. He found our bags in your trunk and hid them from the media and the other detectives. He said what you did with your life was your business, not the rest of the world's. I know you would never be able to thank him properly, so I gave him a big hug from both of us."

The tears filled her eyes.

"They said they were going to give you a medal for bravery when I told them how you saved my life. Amber was impressed by her daddy's hero-ism. Did I tell you that I had a chance to talk with her? She's beautiful, and getting to be quite a young lady. She's got your smile—and I think maybe a little of your strength."

Kasey's voice cracked as the tears began to stream down her cheeks. "I told Amber that you wanted her to know that you loved her more than anything in the world, and that her name was the last word you spoke before . . ."

For a second time she stared silently at the sky.

"I have to go now, sweetheart. Do you remember telling me that you loved me like no one you had ever known? Well, I didn't get the chance to tell you that I feel the same way. I don't think I'll ever meet another man who makes me feel like I did when I was with you. We may have only had a few days, but what we shared will last a lifetime."

Kasey laid the wildflowers on the ground by her knees and kissed the fingertips of her right hand. She reached down and traced his name, etched deeply in the simple granite marker. "Sleep well, Jordan, my darling. I'll see you whenever I can.

"Remember . . . always . . . that I love you."

❖

The Mustang convertible eased down the on-ramp at Commerce Street and rapidly overtook what little traffic was on the road on the storybook summer morning. The wind dancing through her long auburn tresses felt like a breath from heaven, and the clear, cloudless sky seemed to promise that today was not the end, but the beginning of her life. She silenced its soothing voice.

Sometimes, sadness is the best company of all.

Kasey reached her fingers through the slotted door in the pet carrier and lovingly brushed Sam's soft fur with her fingers. He was resting well and she knew he would adjust in time. She was grateful for his quiet companionship. Somehow, just having another soul beside her at the moment was enough.

She would ask nothing else of this day.

She peeled the wrapper from the new CD of Chris Isaak's *Forever Blue* she had bought a few weeks earlier but had not had time to play. He would be a familiar and pleasant passenger on the road—soothing medi-cine for her battered spirit.

She shoved the disc in its slot and turned "Graduation Day" up loud enough to drown out the wind and the highway and the angry inner voice that was trying to be heard. She was in no mood to hear all the things she should have done.

Perhaps some other day . . . when his sparkling eyes were not so blue . . . and the vivid images had faded a bit, like the photographs of her childhood.

Perhaps not.

She added more volume.

Kasey always listened to Chris Isaak loud when she wanted to forget.